WHEN DAVID
LOST HiS VOICE

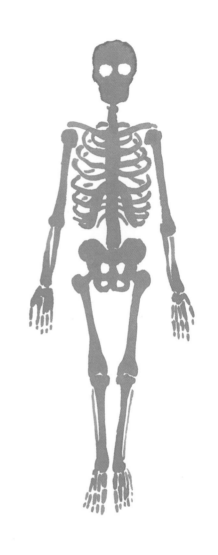

WHEN DAVID
LOST HIS VOICE

Judith Vanistendael

Published in English in 2012
by SelfMadeHero
5 Upper Wimpole Street
London WIG 6BP
www.selfmadehero.com

English translation © 2012 SelfMadeHero

Written and Illustrated by: Judith Vanistendael
Translated from the French edition by: Nora Mahony

Editorial Assistant: Lizzie Kaye
Publishing Director: Emma Hayley
With thanks to: Doug Wallace and Nick de Somogyi

Published in French as *David les femmes et la mort*
© Éditions du Lombard (Dargaud-Lombard S.A.)
2012, by Vanistendael (Judith)
www.lelombard.com

A CIP record for this book is available from the British Library

ISBN: 978-1-906838-54-6

10 9 8 7 6 5 4 3 2

Printed and bound in China

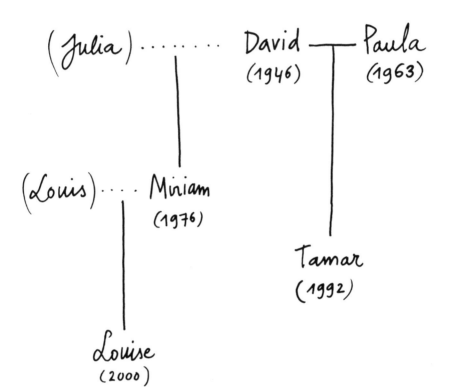

(Julia) · · · · · · · · David ——— Paula
(1946)   (1963)

(Louis) · · · · Miriam
(1976)

Tamar
(1992)

Louise
(2000)

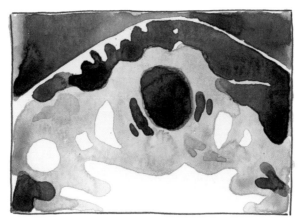

PROLOGUE

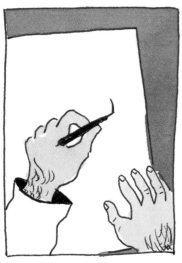

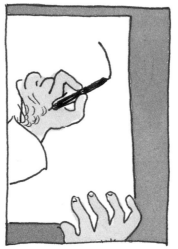

Here is the nasal cavity.

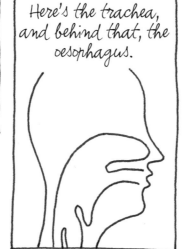

Here's the trachea, and behind that, the oesophagus.

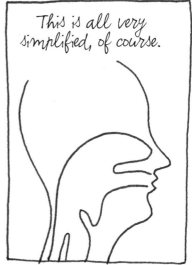

This is all very simplified, of course.

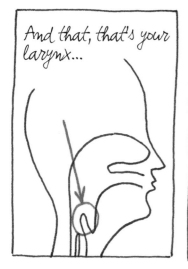

And that, that's your larynx...

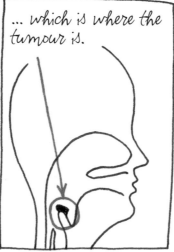

... which is where the tumour is.

8

Tumour??

Supraglottic cancer of the larynx.

Type $T_3 N_{26} M_0$.

That means you can make it.

It's a stage-three tumour that has spread to more than one lymph node, with no metastases...

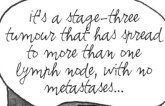

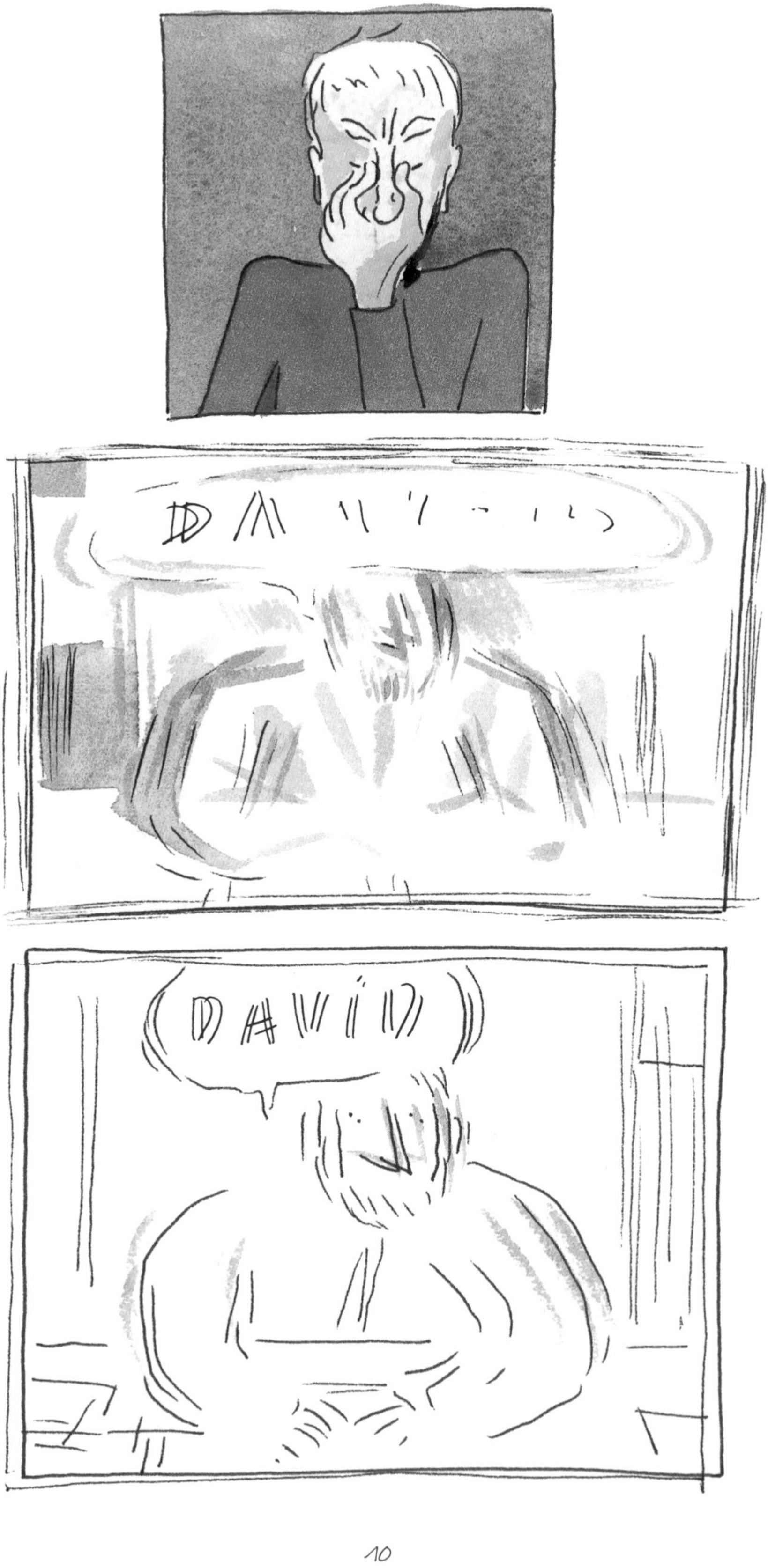
DAVID

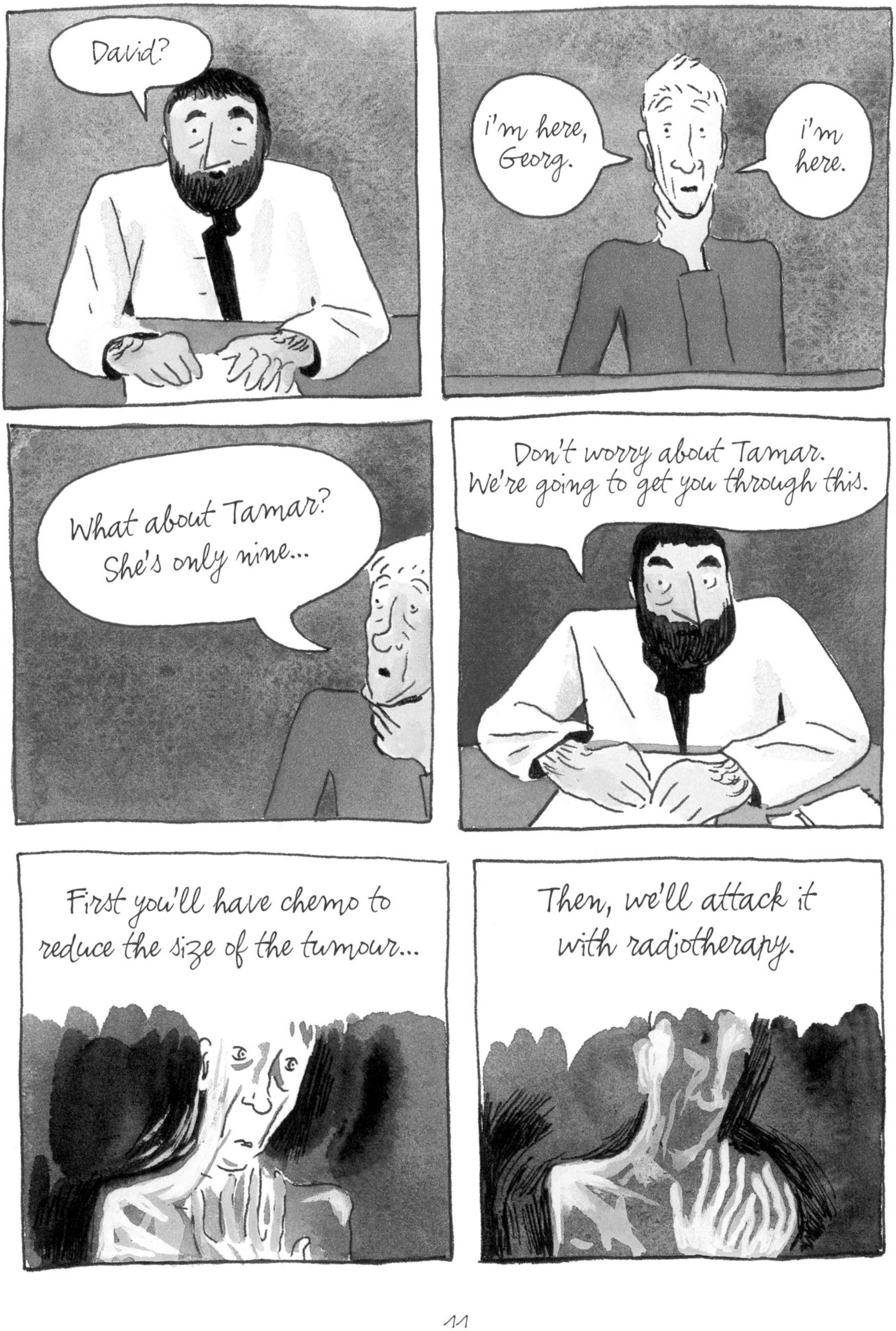
David?
I'm here, Georg.
I'm here.
What about Tamar? She's only nine...
Don't worry about Tamar. We're going to get you through this.
First you'll have chemo to reduce the size of the tumour...
Then, we'll attack it with radiotherapy.

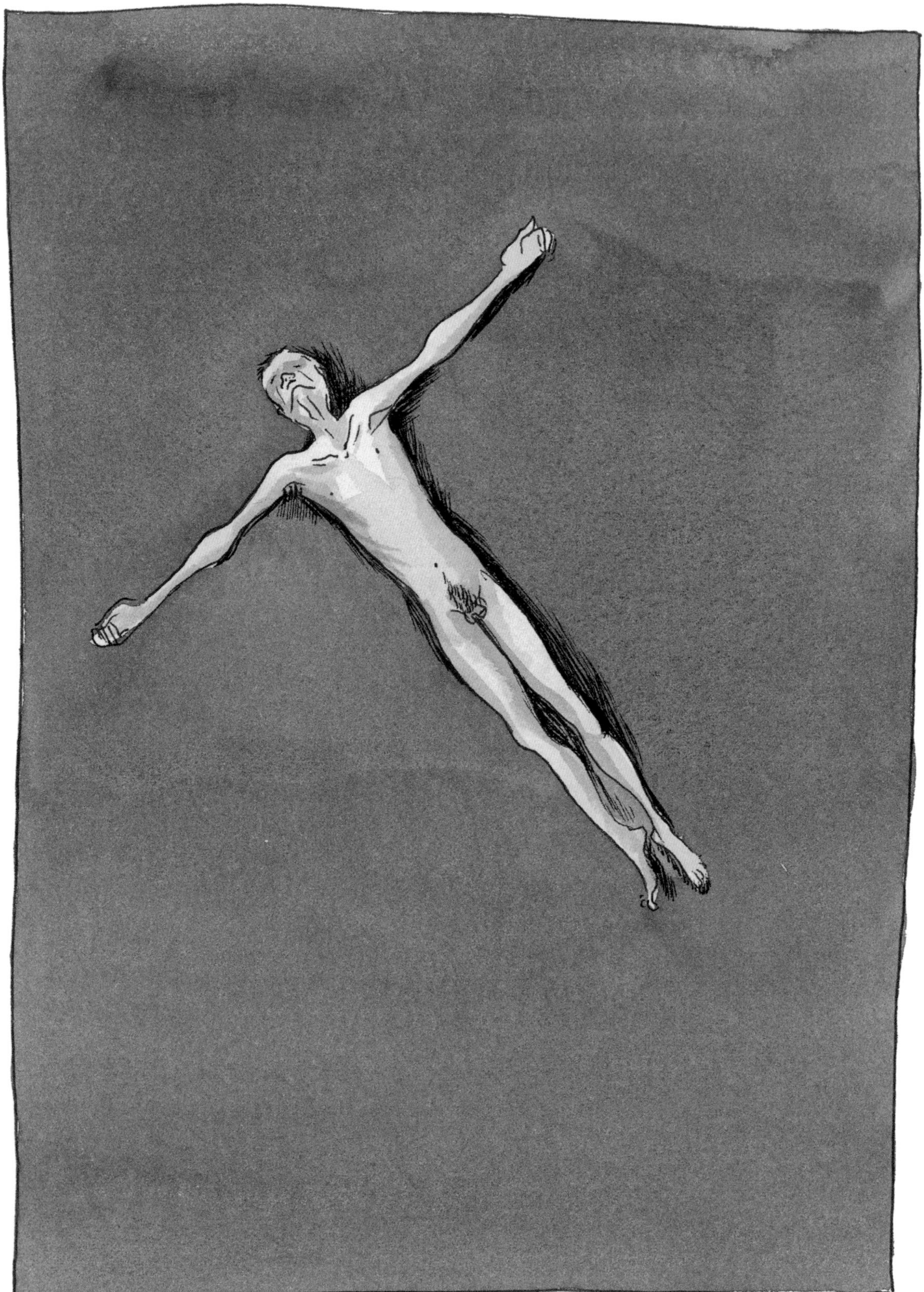

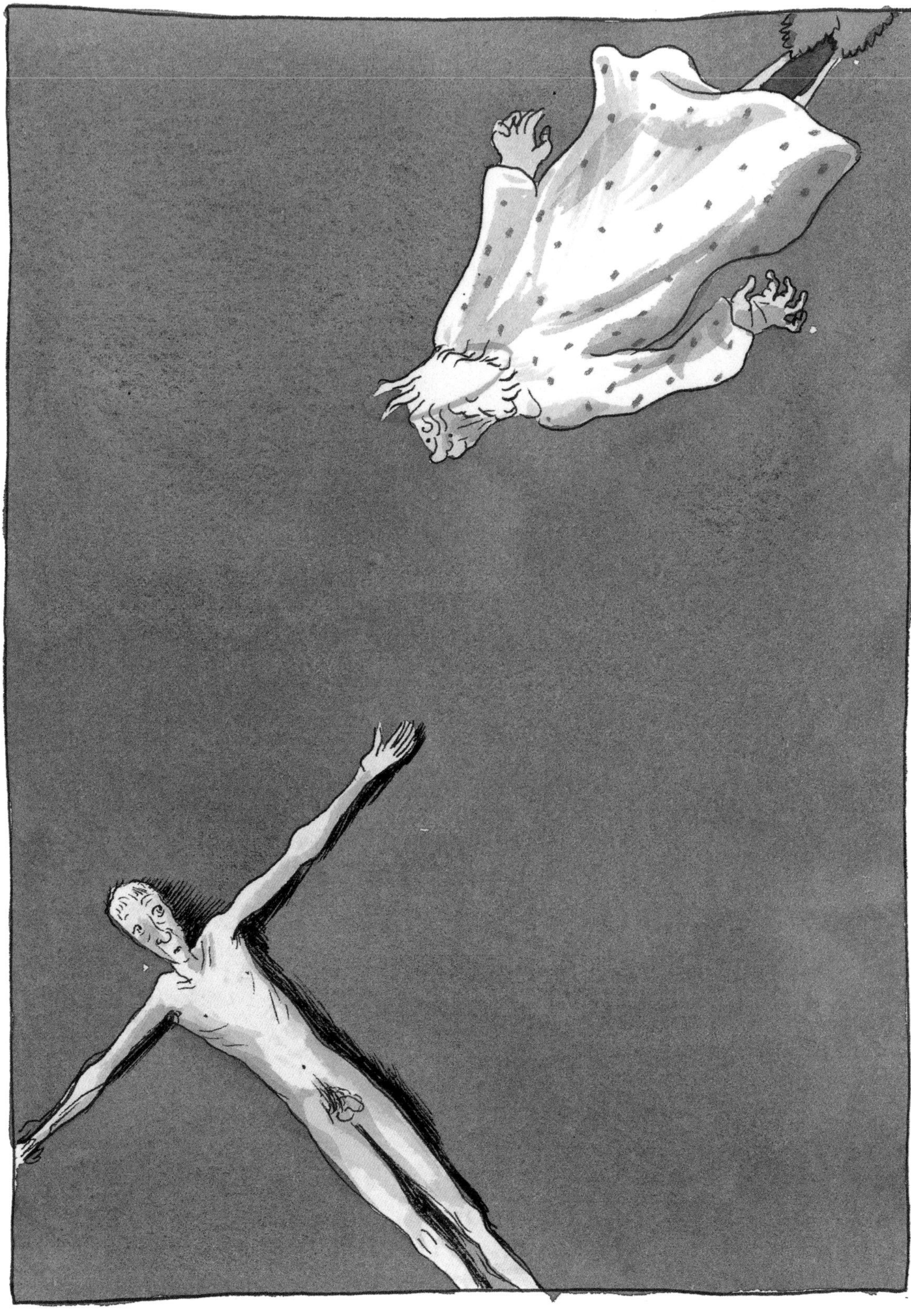

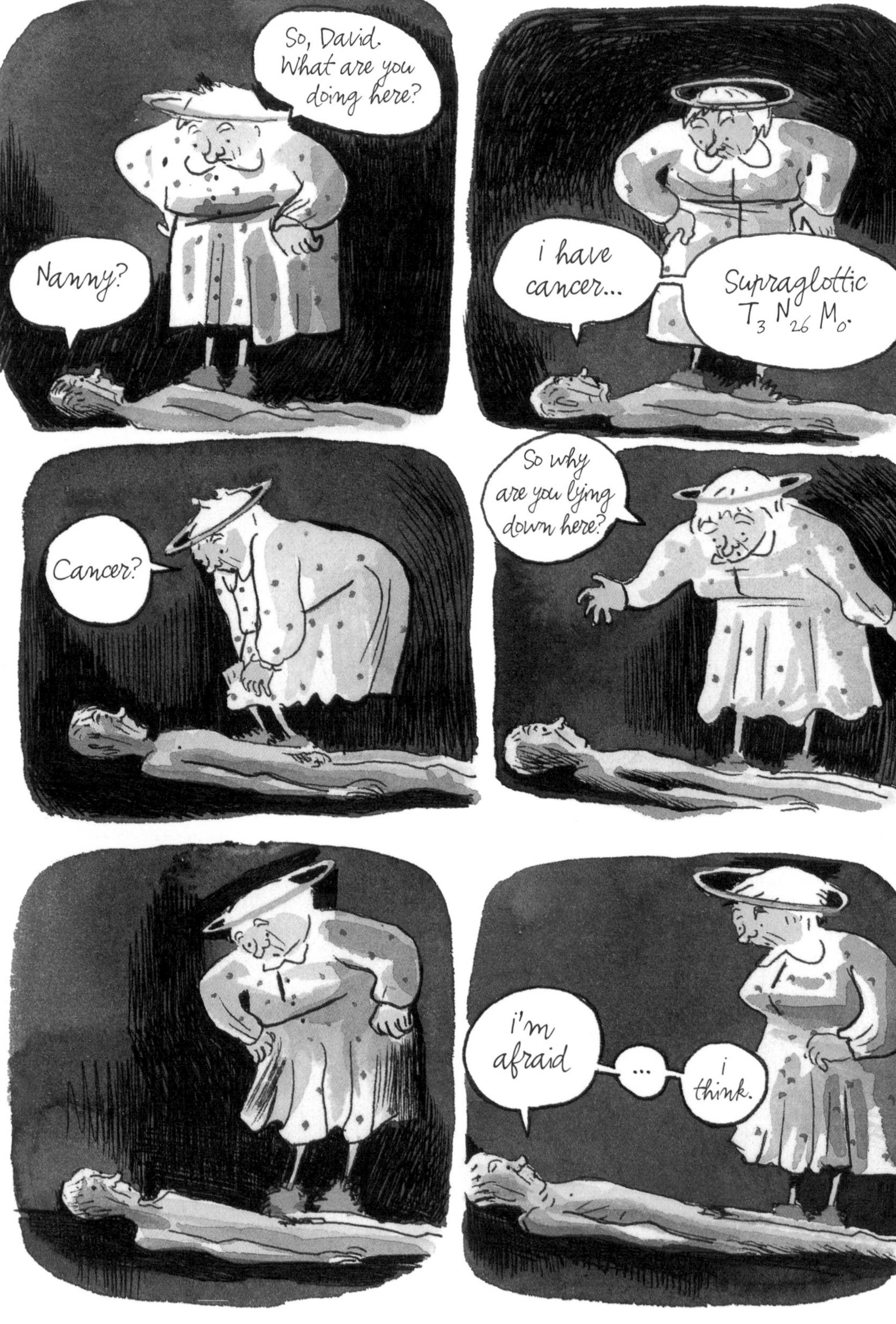
So, David. What are you doing here?
Nanny?
i have cancer...
Supraglottic $T_3 N_{26} M_0$.
Cancer?
So why are you lying down here?
i'm afraid
...
i think.

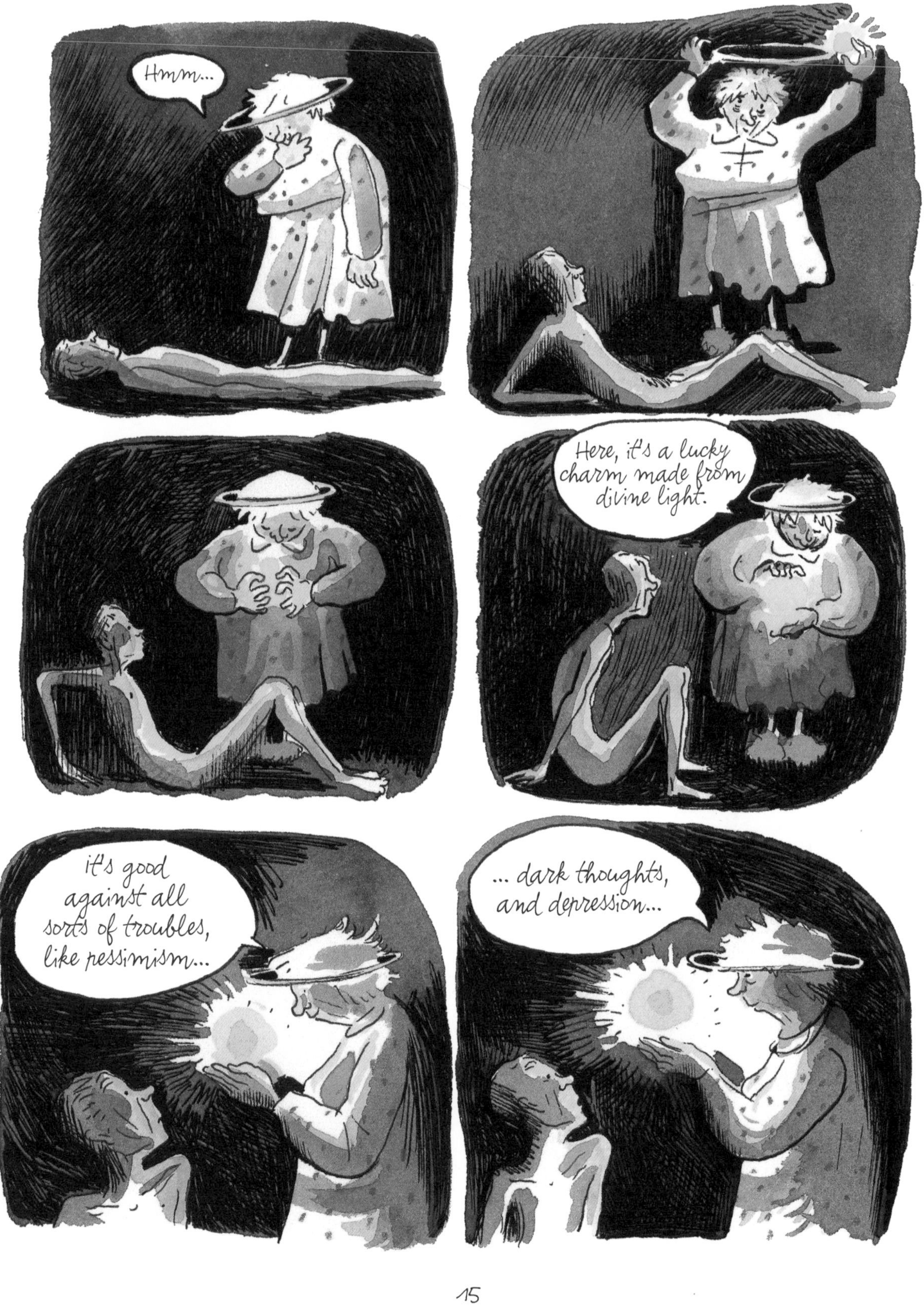
Hmm...
Here, it's a lucky charm made from divine light.
it's good against all sorts of troubles, like pessimism...
... dark thoughts, and depression...

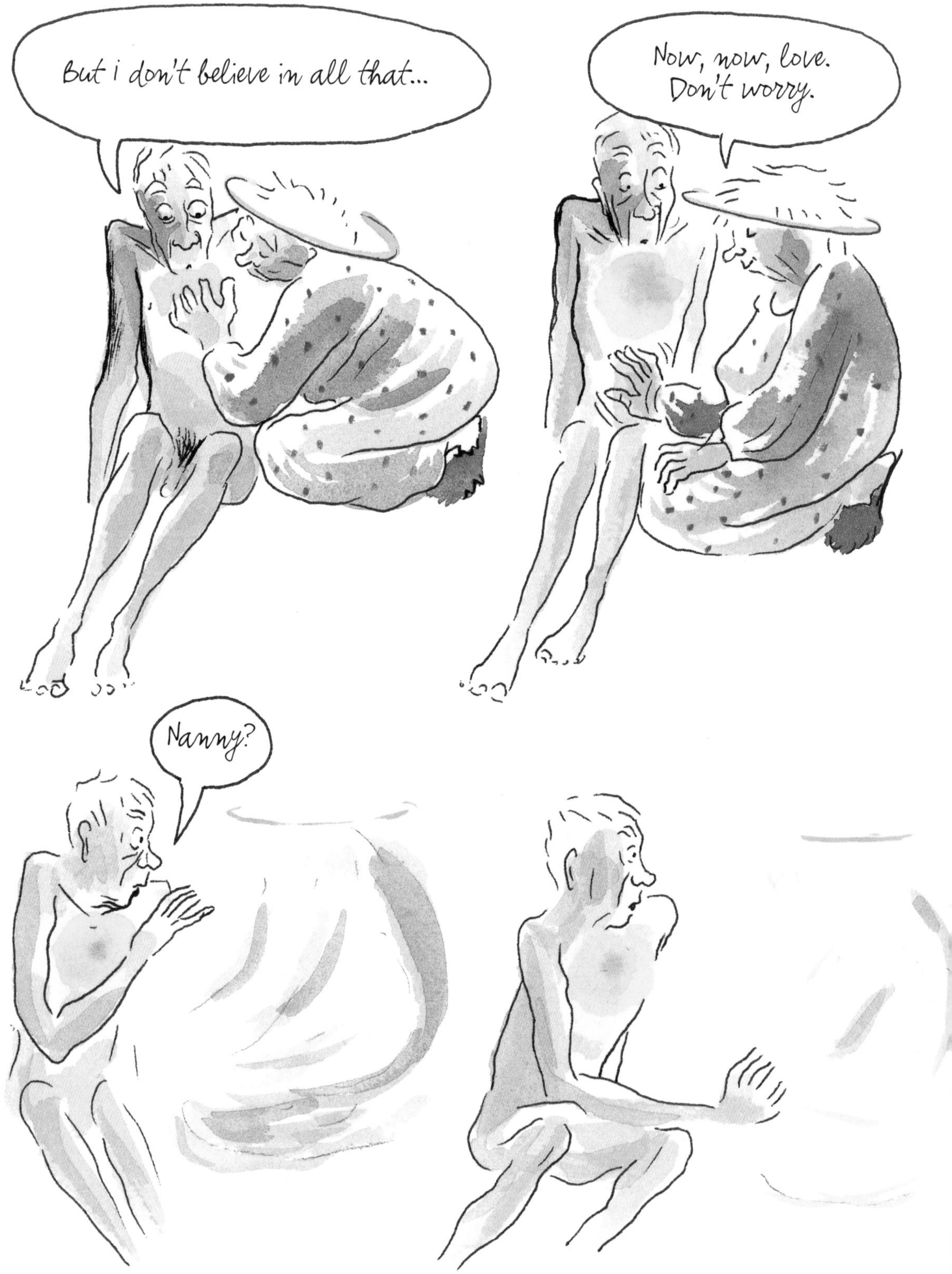
But i don't believe in all that...
Now, now, love. Don't worry.
Nanny?

BY ANTONIO GALA, FROM "YA NUNCA MÁS DIRÉ" IN
POEMAS DE AMOR. PLANETA, 2ND ED., 1998.
TRANSLATED BY JETHRO SOUTAR.

MIRIAM

No more will I say: "Everything has its end",
but: "Smile, darling, and let's begin."
New hands I put new oars in,
And new towers from ruins ascend.

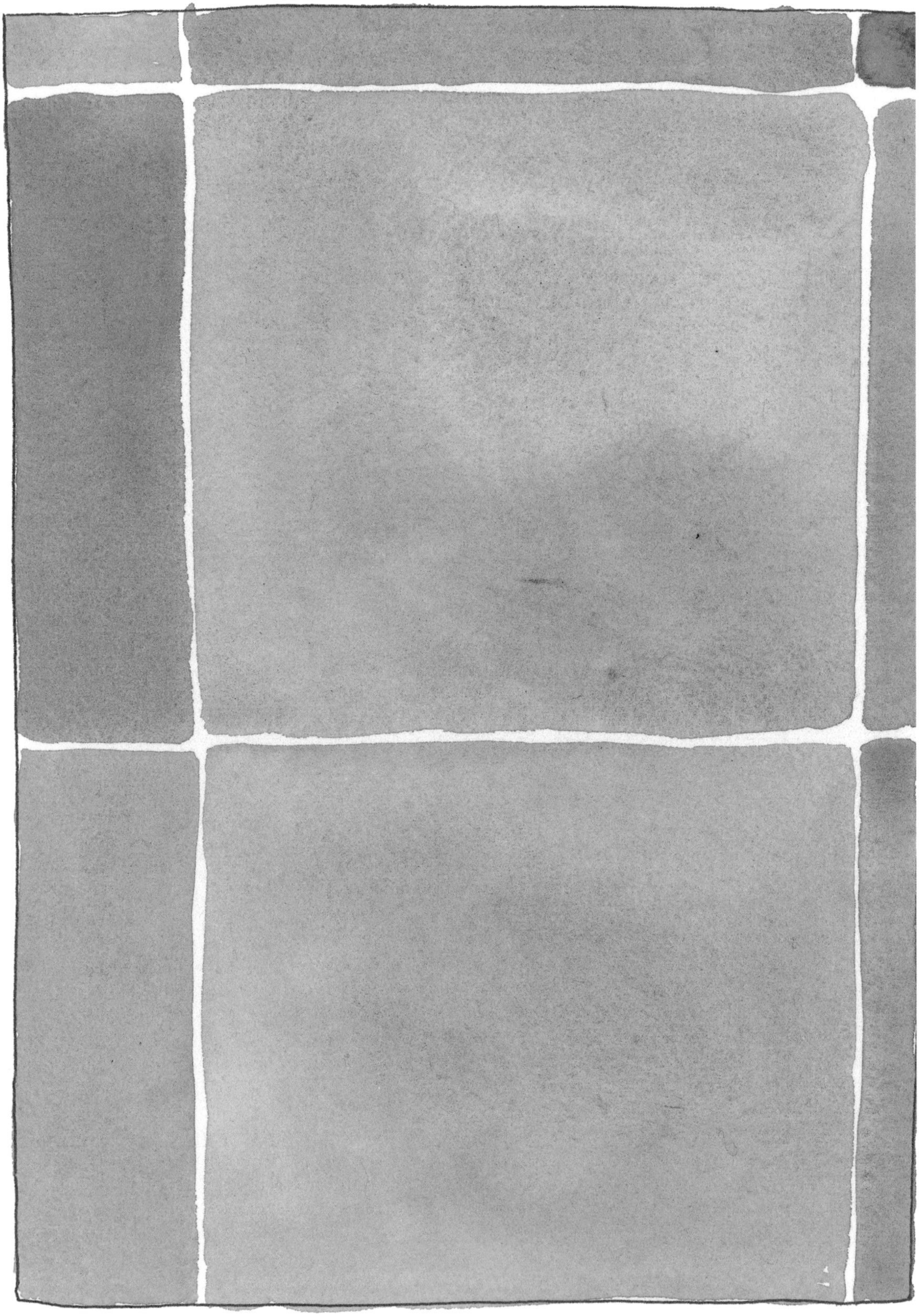

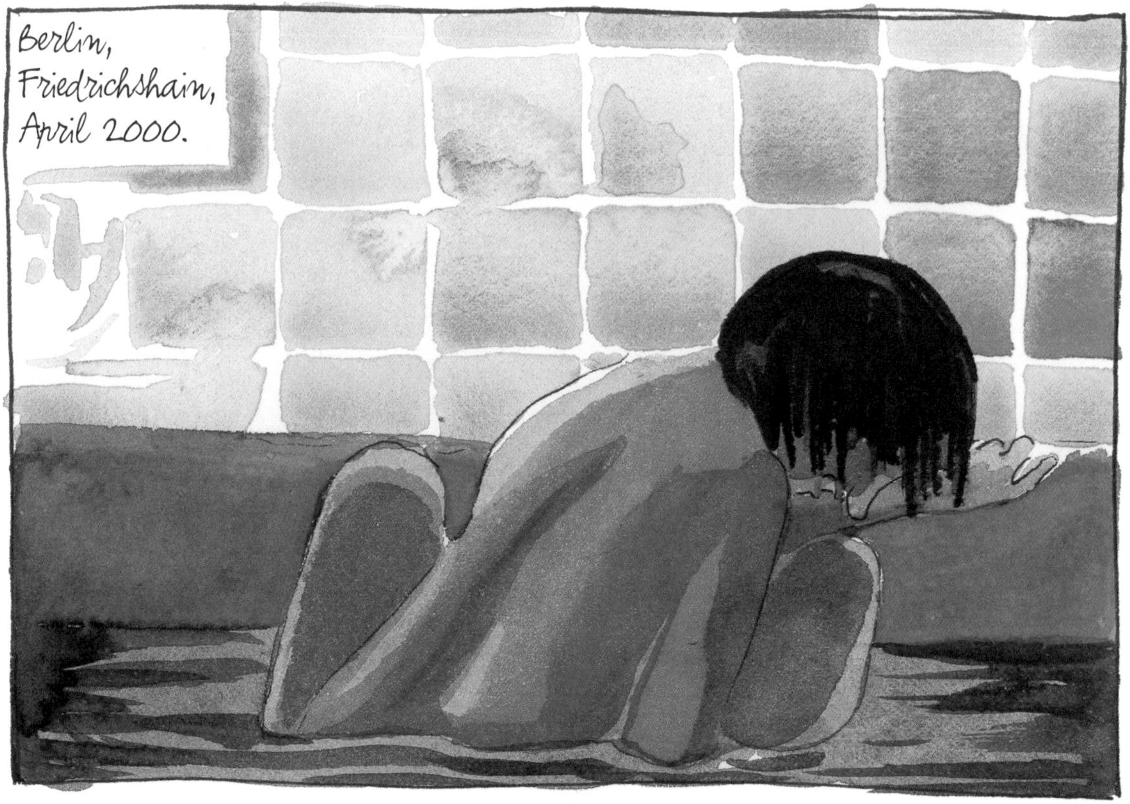
Berlin,
Friedrichshain,
April 2000.

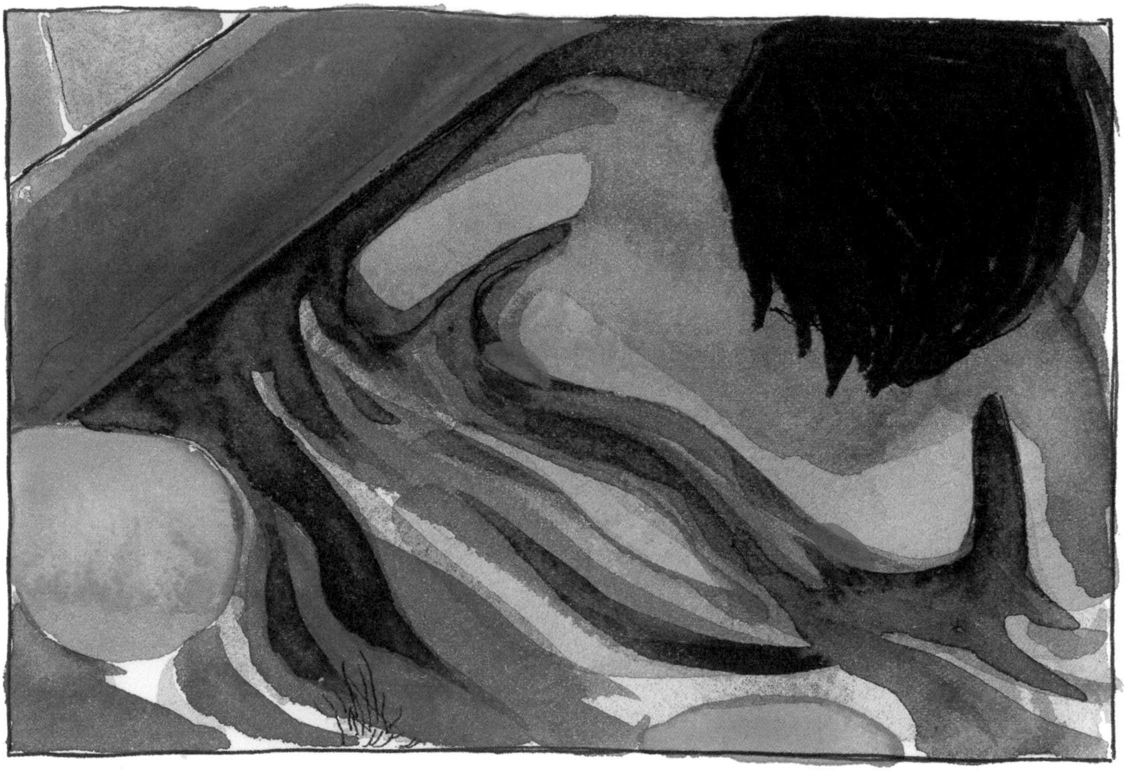

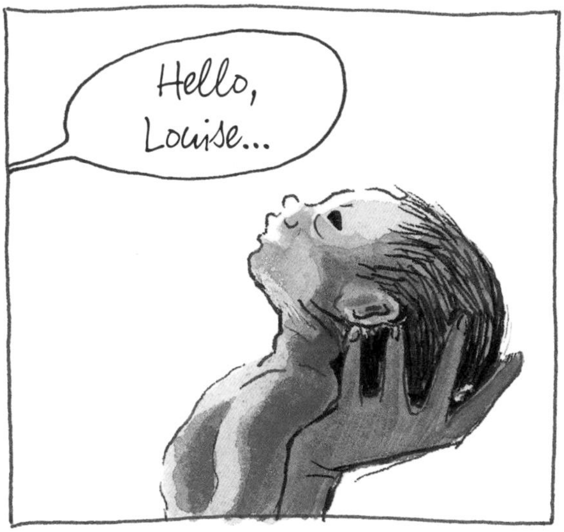
Hello, Louise...

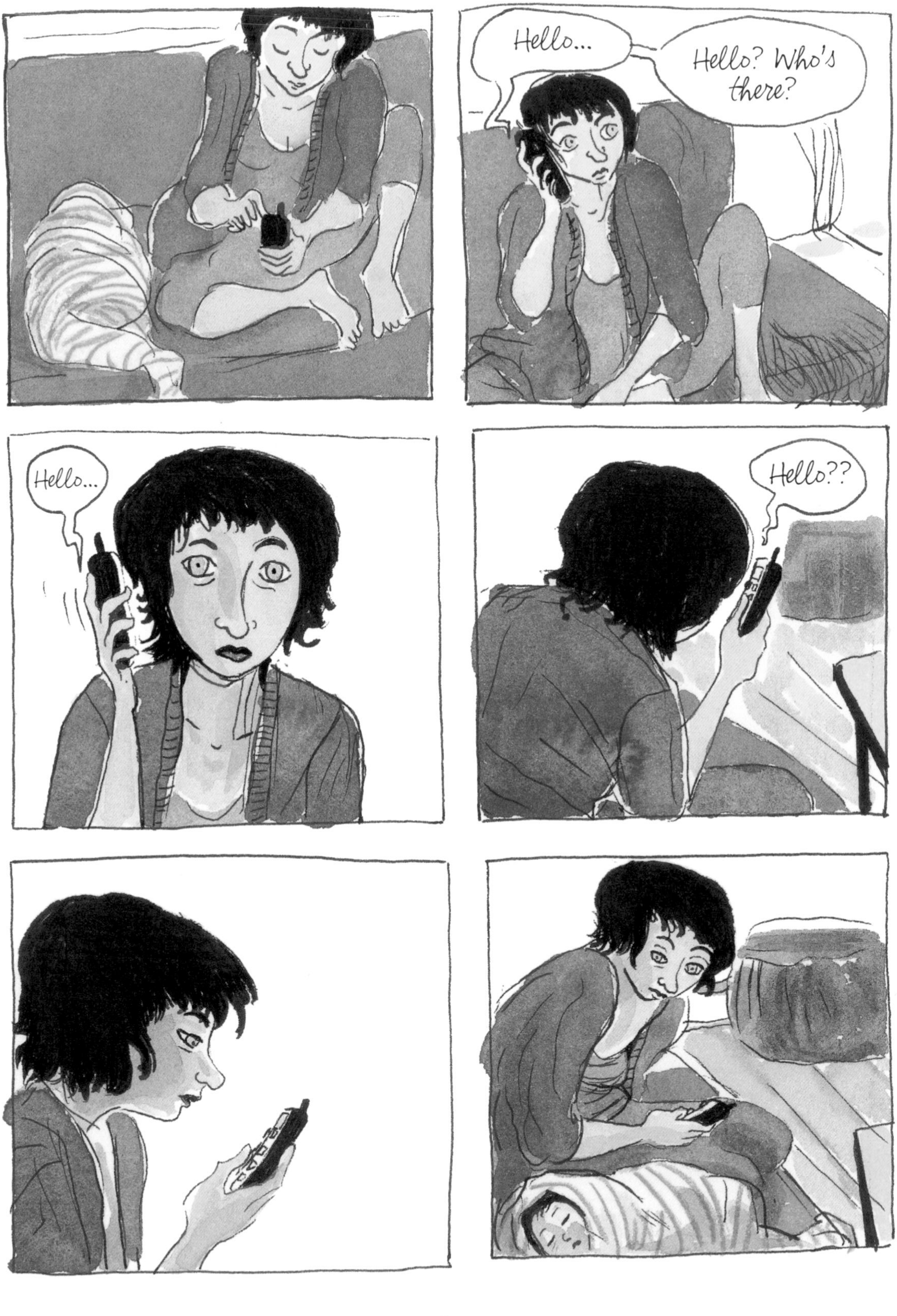
Hello...
Hello? Who's there?
Hello...
Hello??

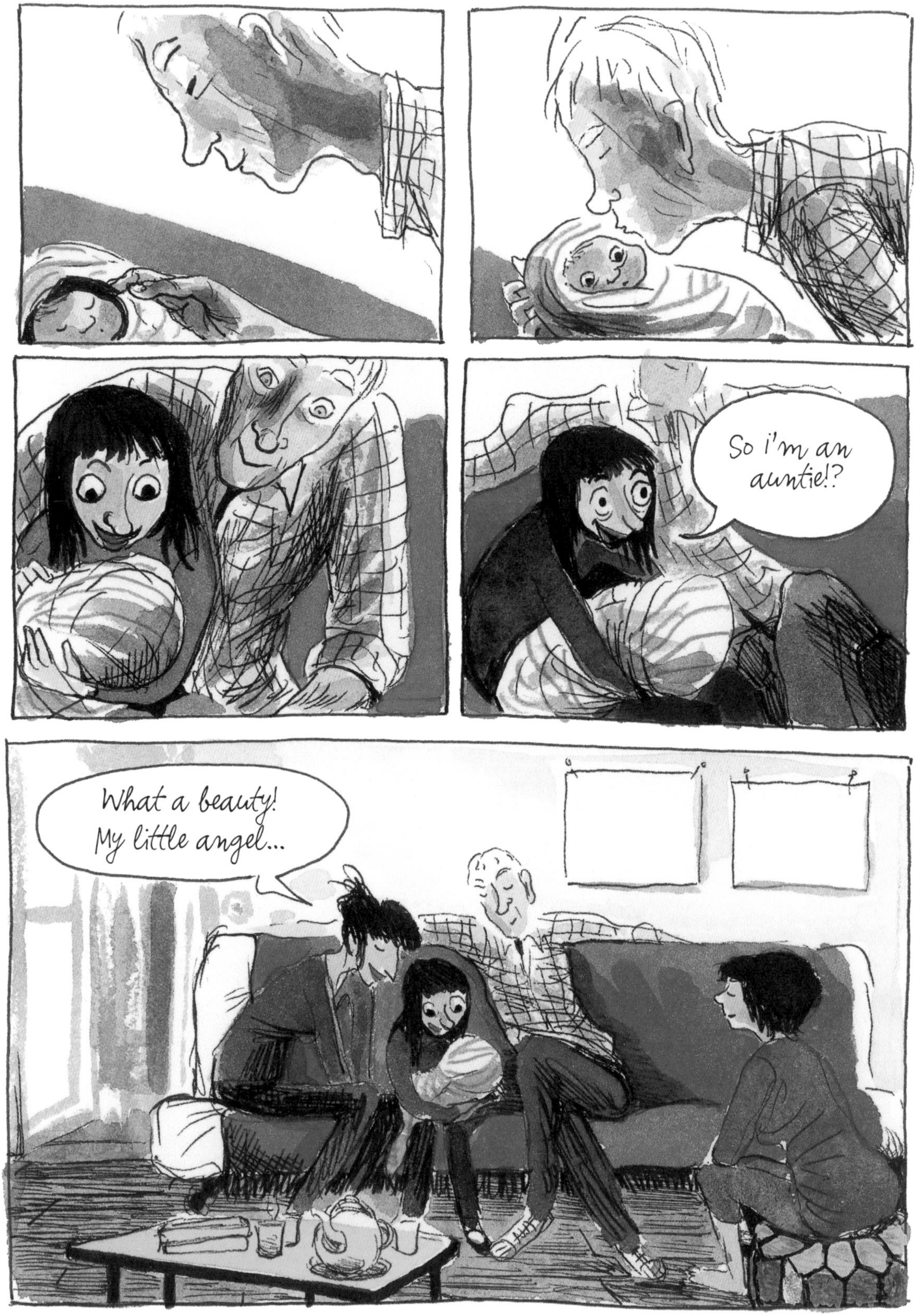
So i'm an auntie!?
What a beauty! My little angel...

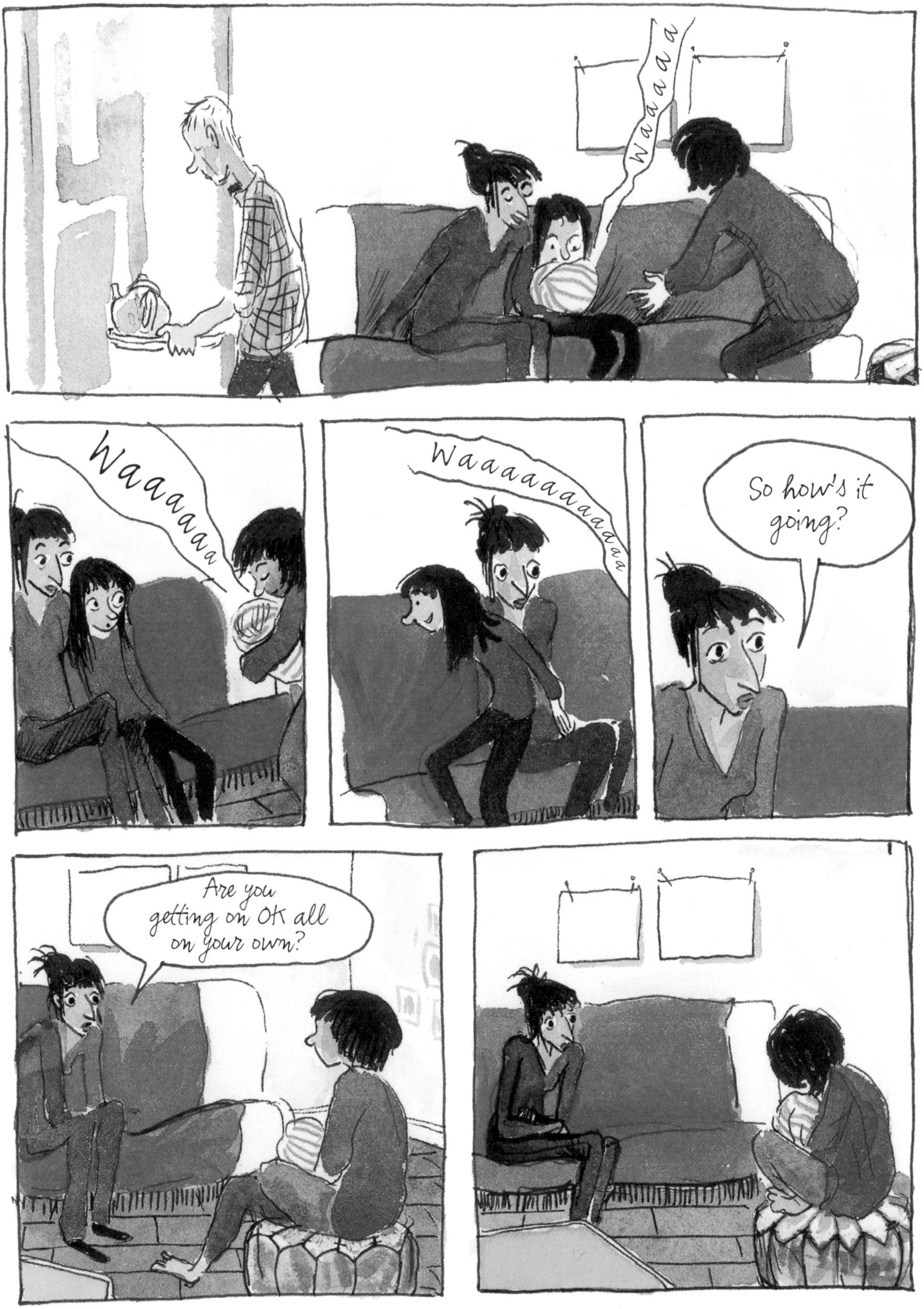
Waaaaa
Waaaaaaa
Waaaaaaaaaaaaa
So how's it going?
Are you getting on OK all on your own?

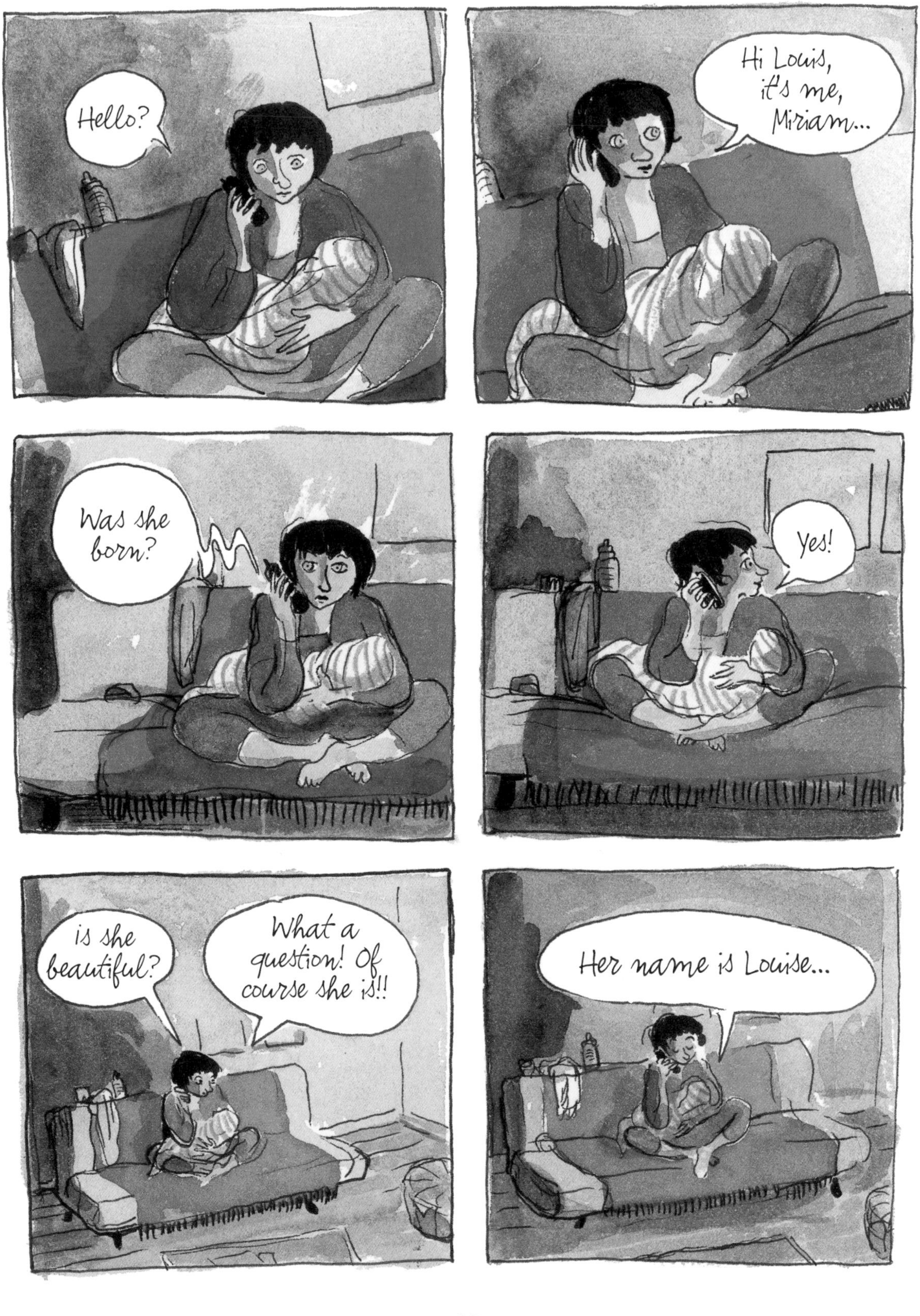
Hello?
Hi Louis, it's me, Miriam...
Was she born?
Yes!
is she beautiful?
What a question! Of course she is!!
Her name is Louise...

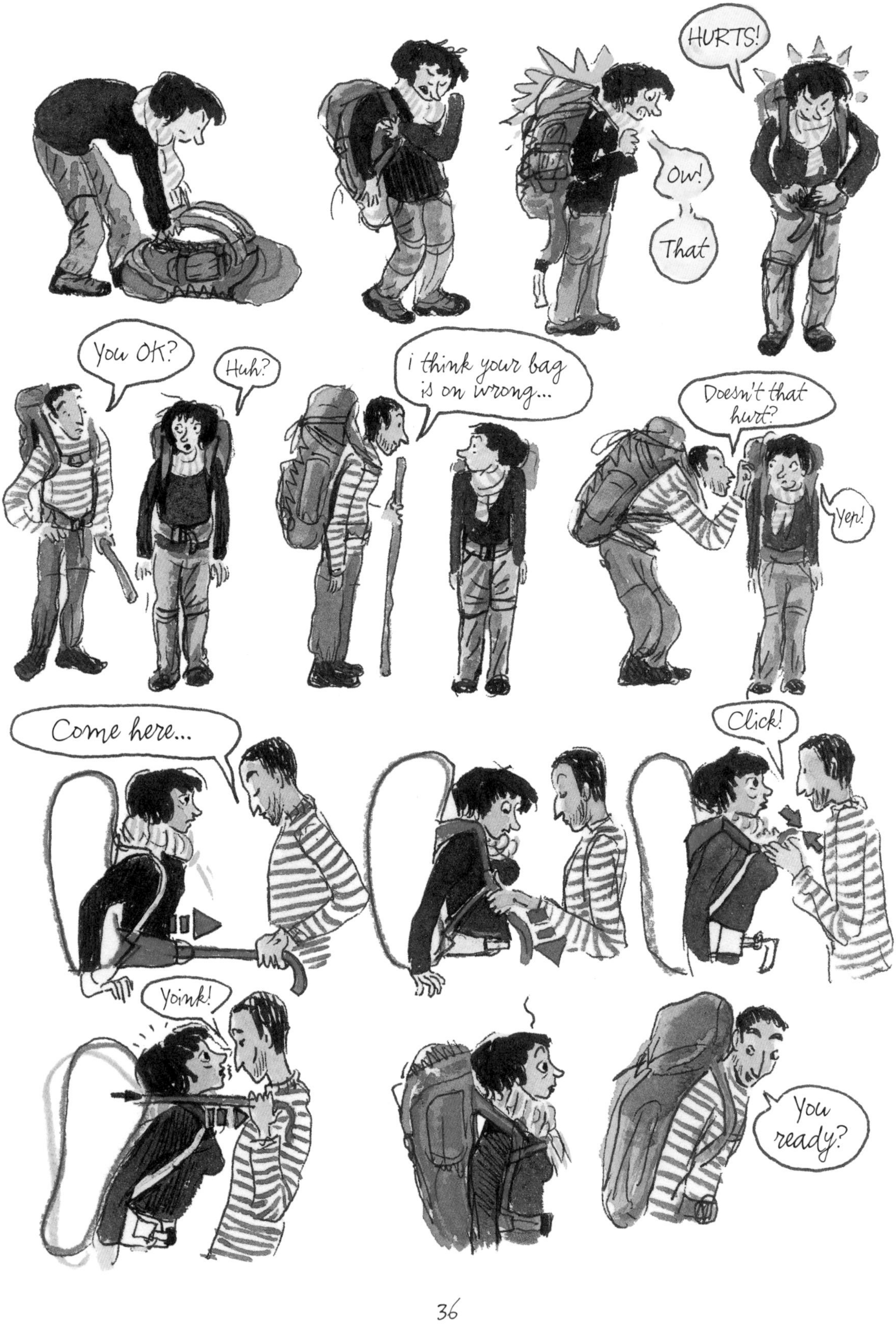
Ow!
That
HURTS!
You OK?
Huh?
i think your bag is on wrong...
Doesn't that hurt?
Yep!
Come here...
Click!
Yoink!
You ready?

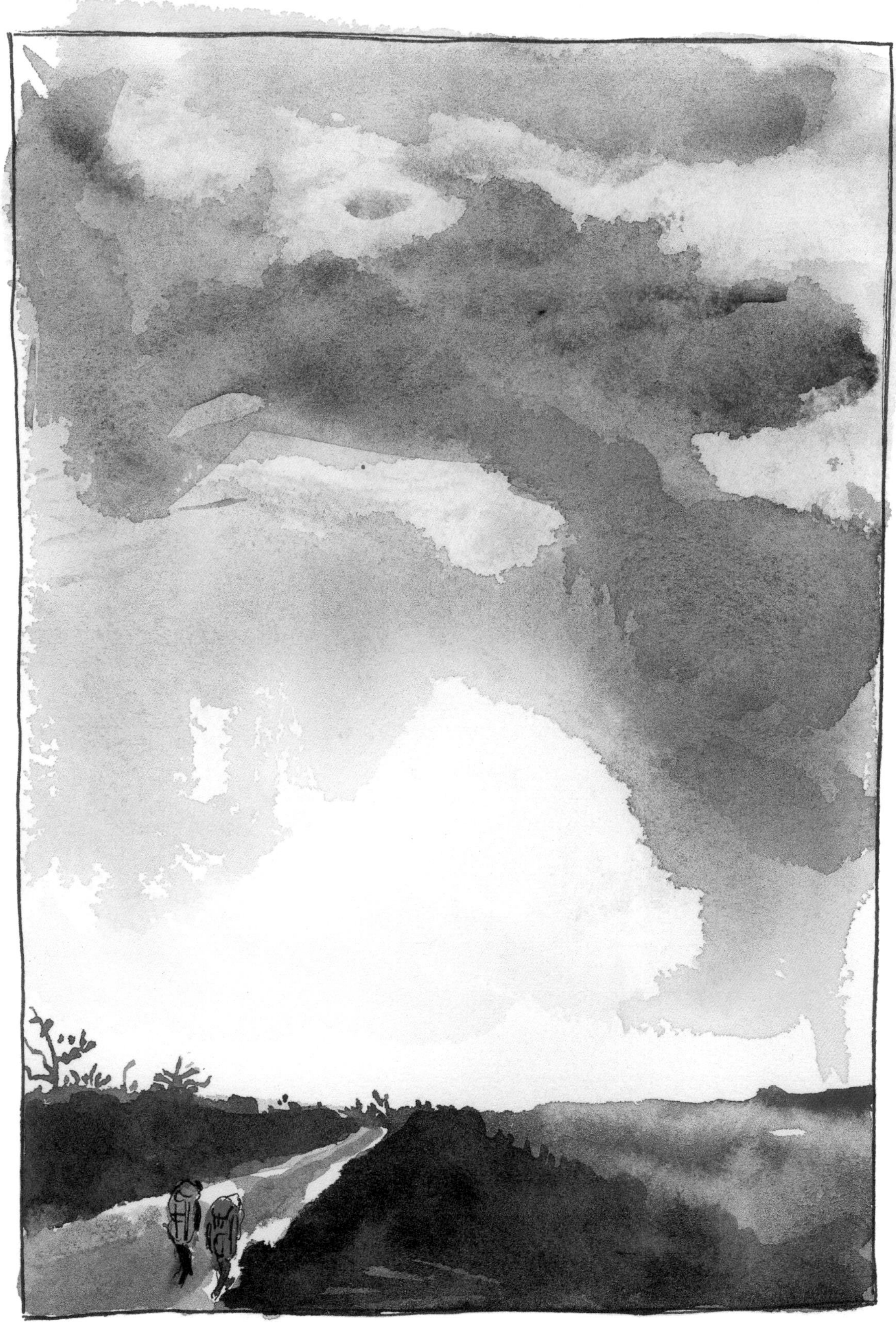

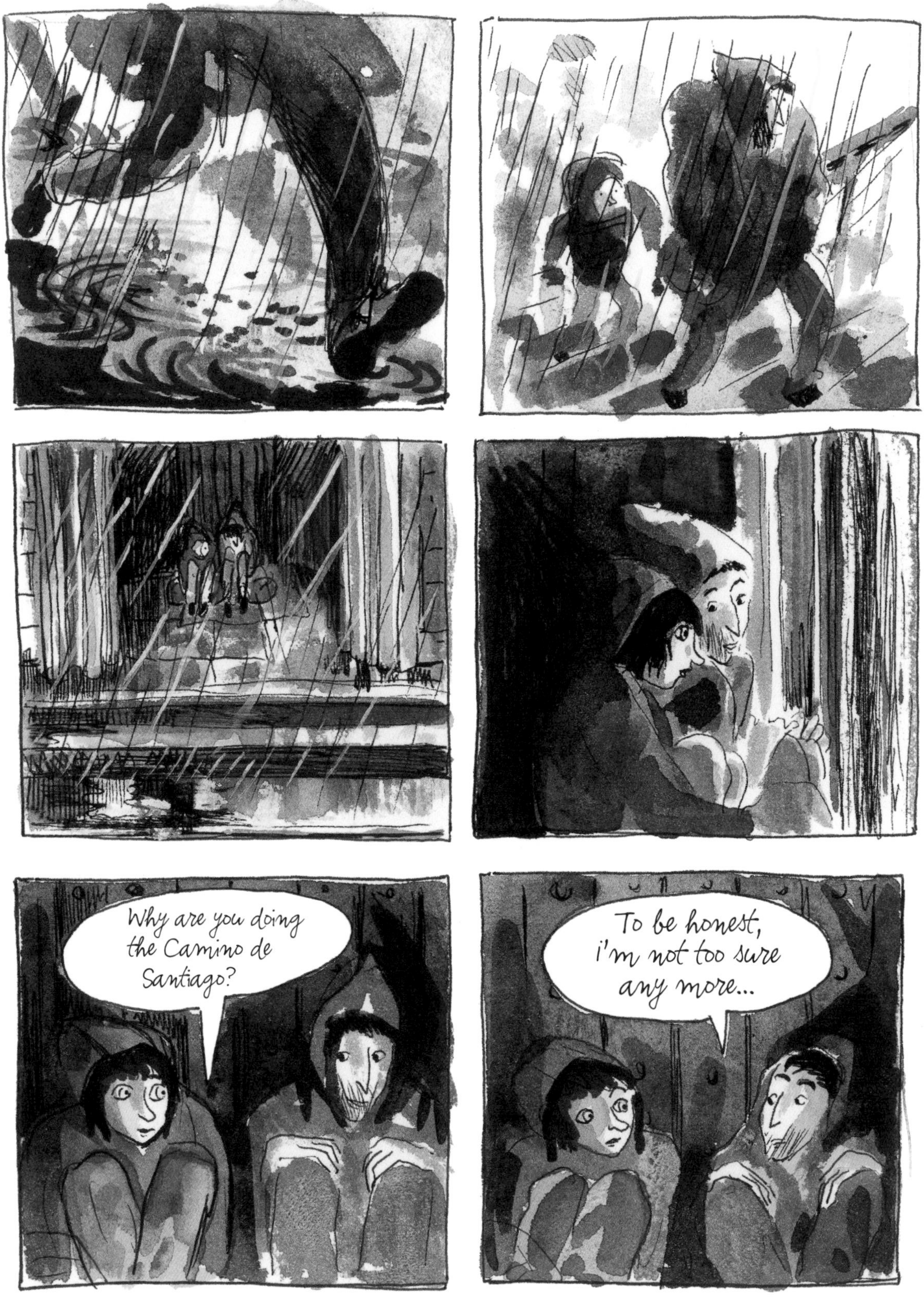
Why are you doing the Camino de Santiago?
To be honest, i'm not too sure any more...

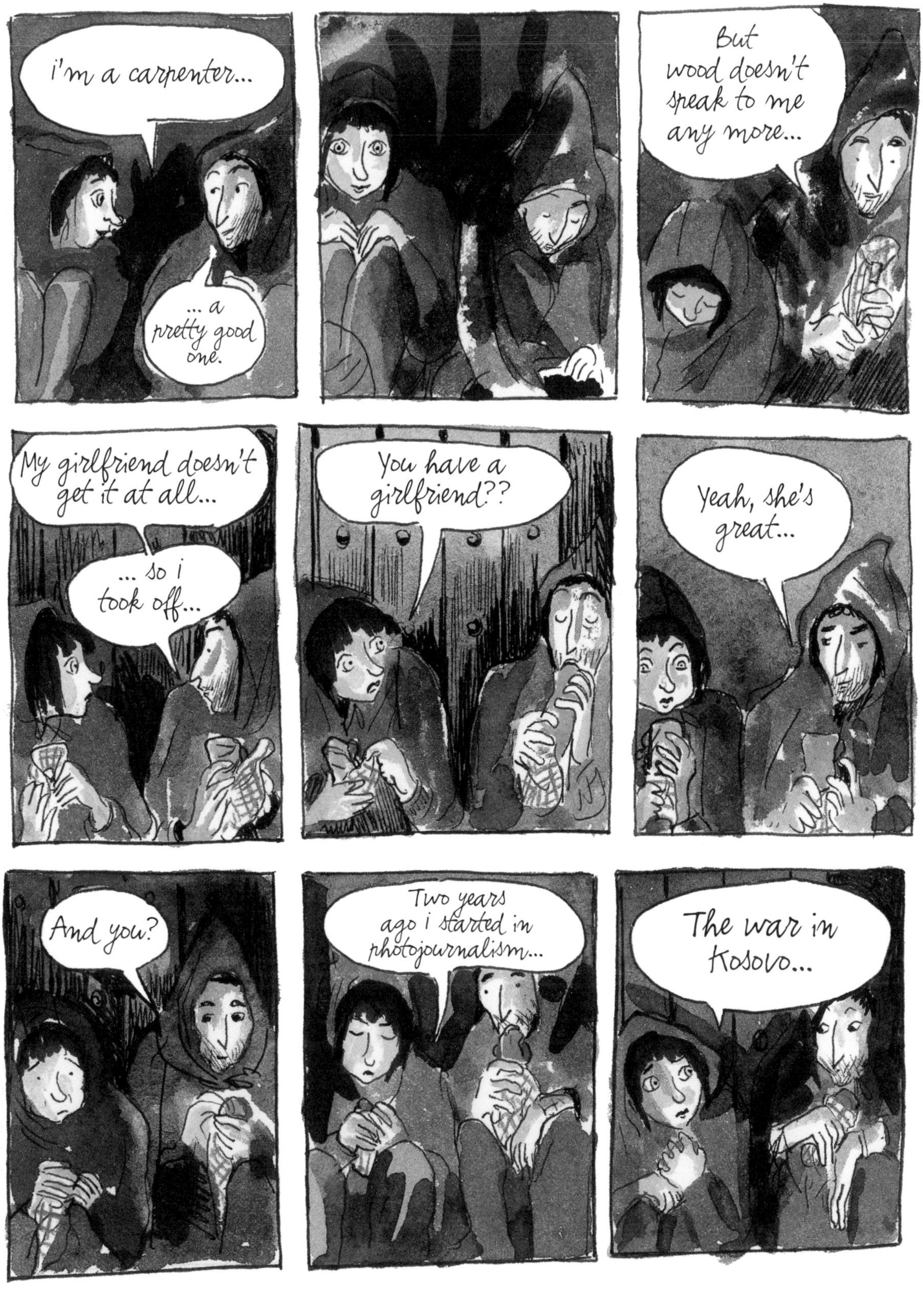
i'm a carpenter...
... a pretty good one.
But wood doesn't speak to me any more...
My girlfriend doesn't get it at all...
... so i took off...
You have a girlfriend??
Yeah, she's great...
And you?
Two years ago i started in photojournalism...
The war in Kosovo...

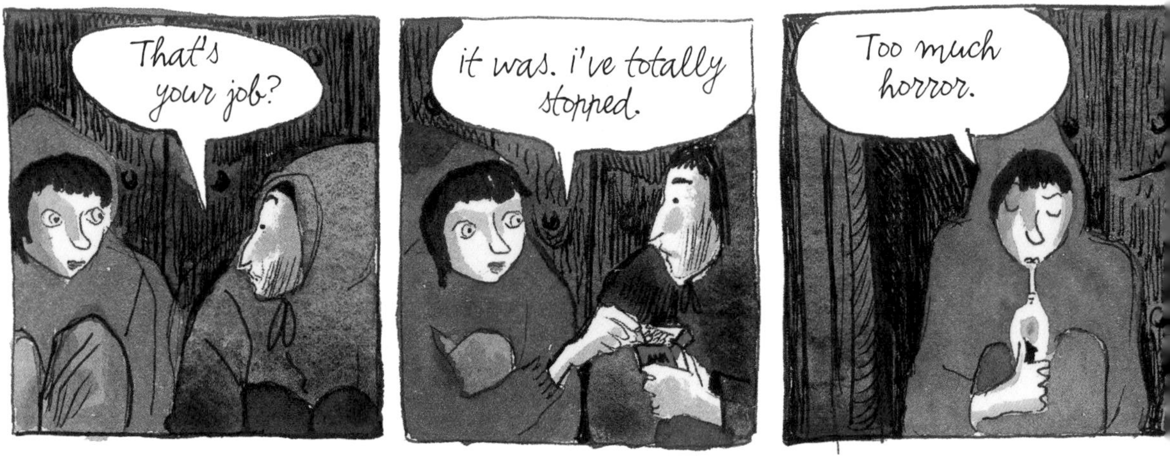
That's your job?
it was. i've totally stopped.
Too much horror.

A little girl was coming home one day... and found herself

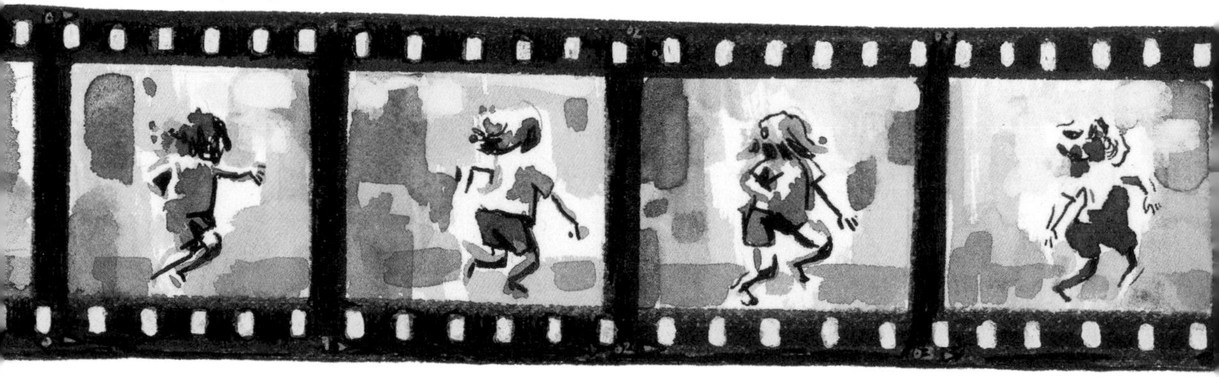

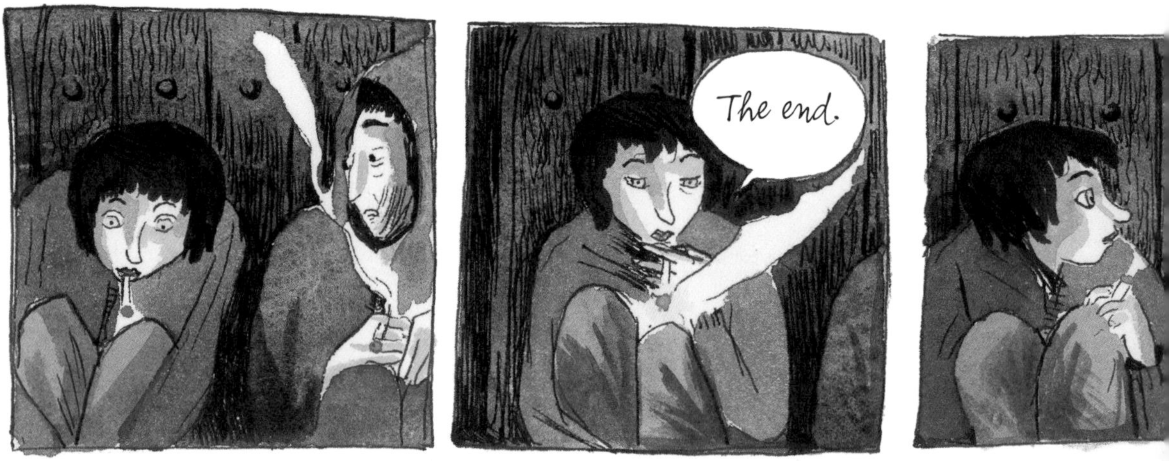
The end.

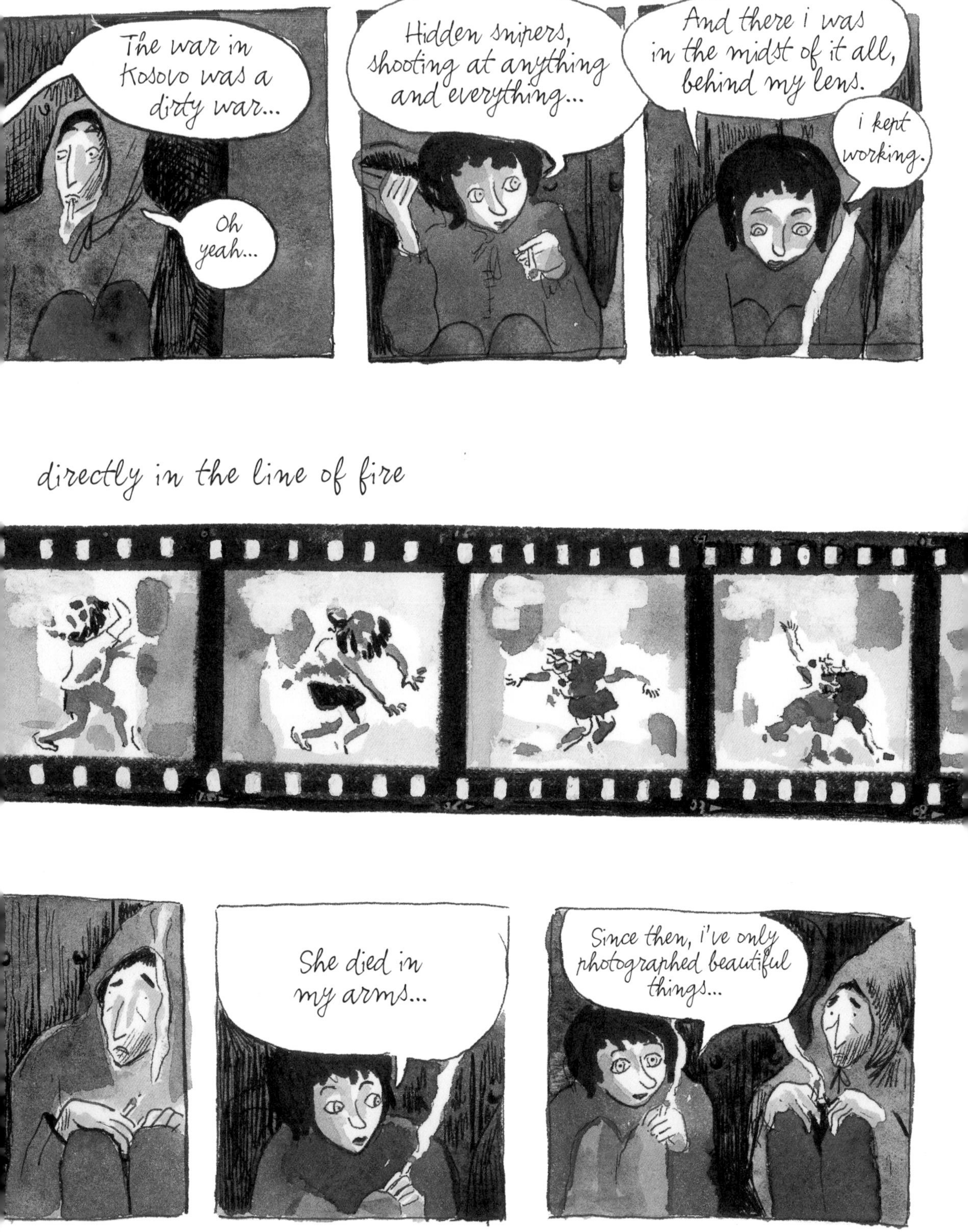
The war in Kosovo was a dirty war...
Oh yeah...
Hidden snipers, shooting at anything and everything...
And there i was in the midst of it all, behind my lens.
i kept working.
directly in the line of fire
She died in my arms...
Since then, i've only photographed beautiful things...

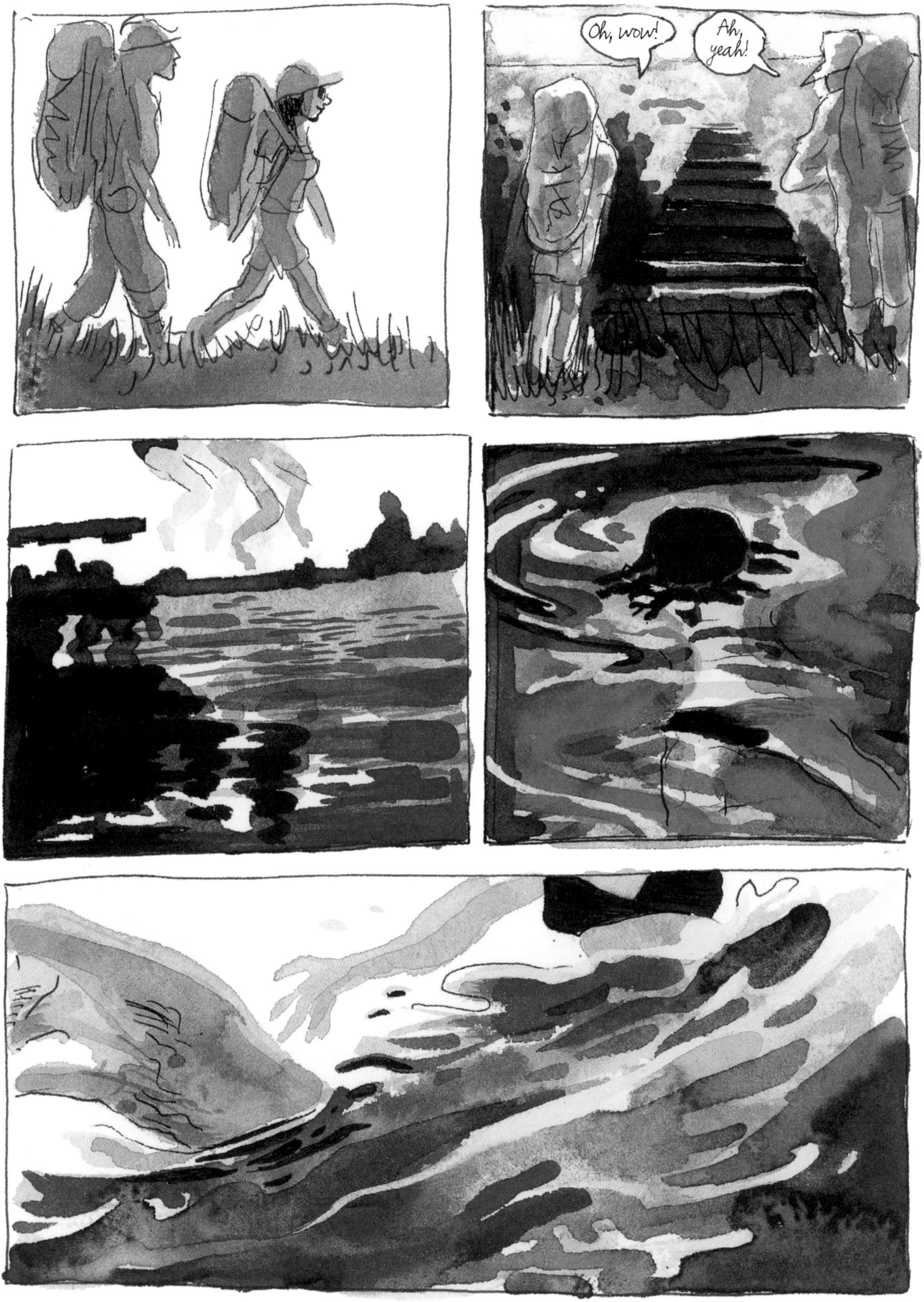
Oh, wow!
Ah, yeah!

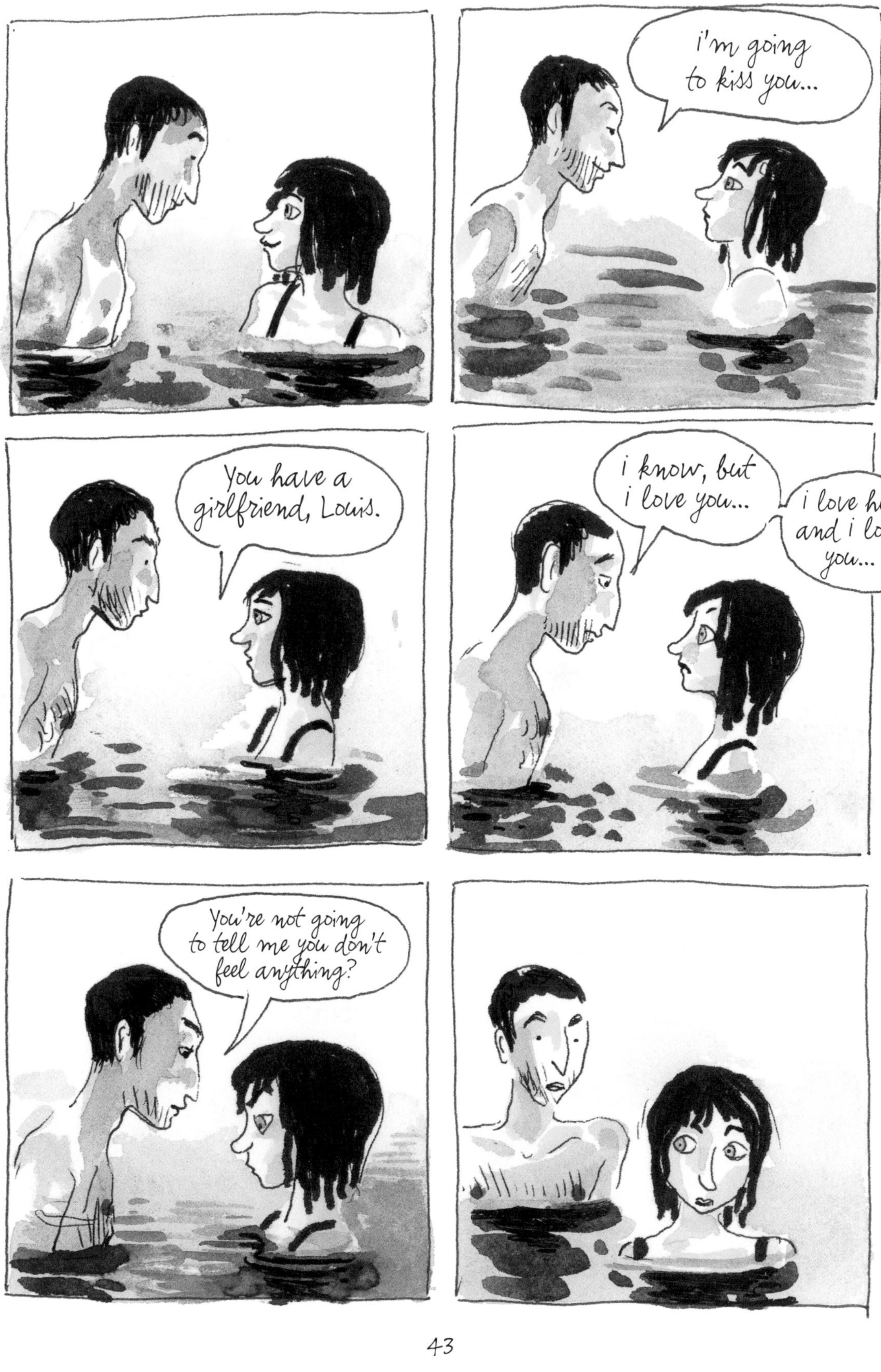
i'm going to kiss you...
You have a girlfriend, Louis.
i know, but i love you...
i love her and i love you...
You're not going to tell me you don't feel anything?

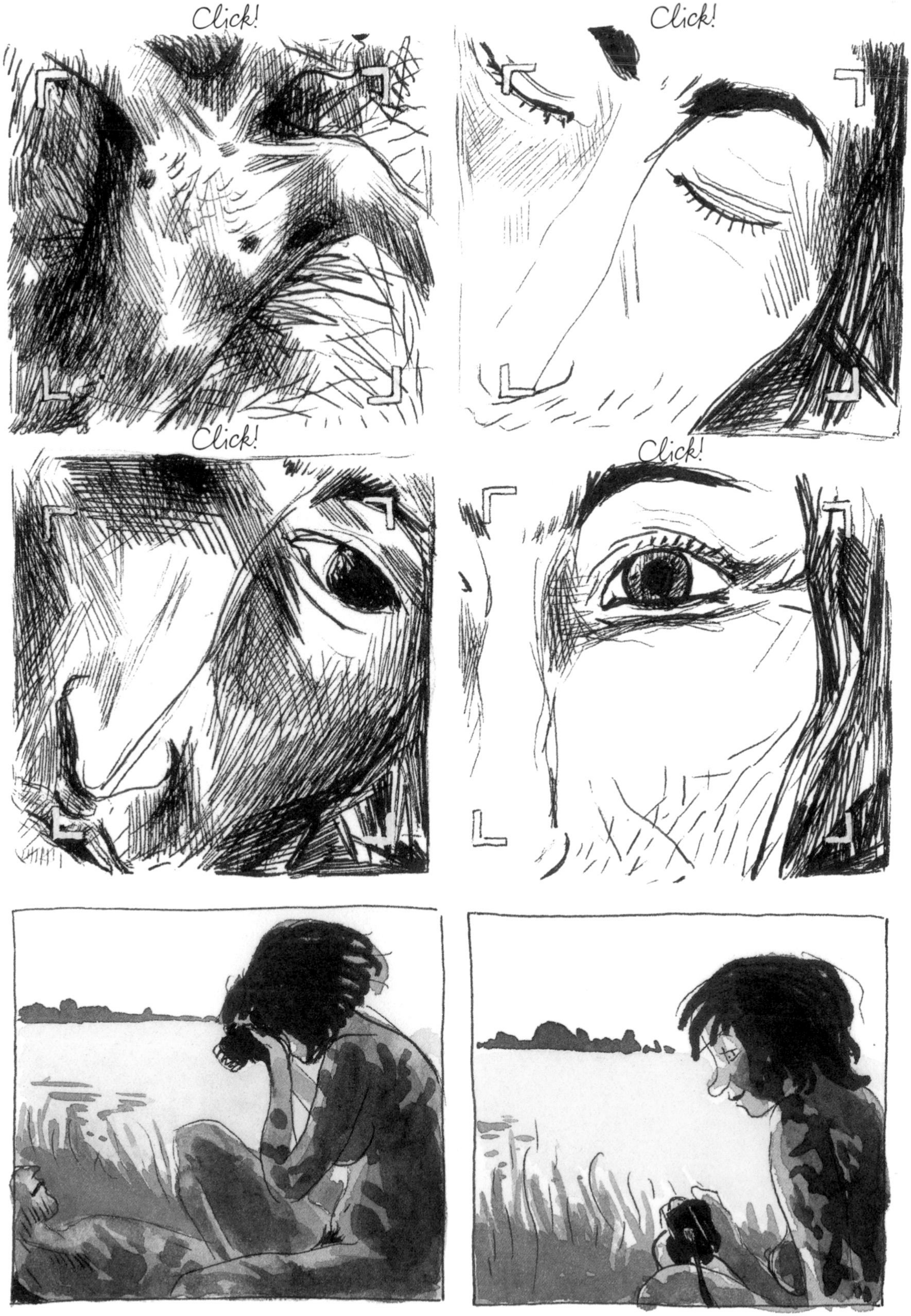
Click!
Click!
Click!
Click!

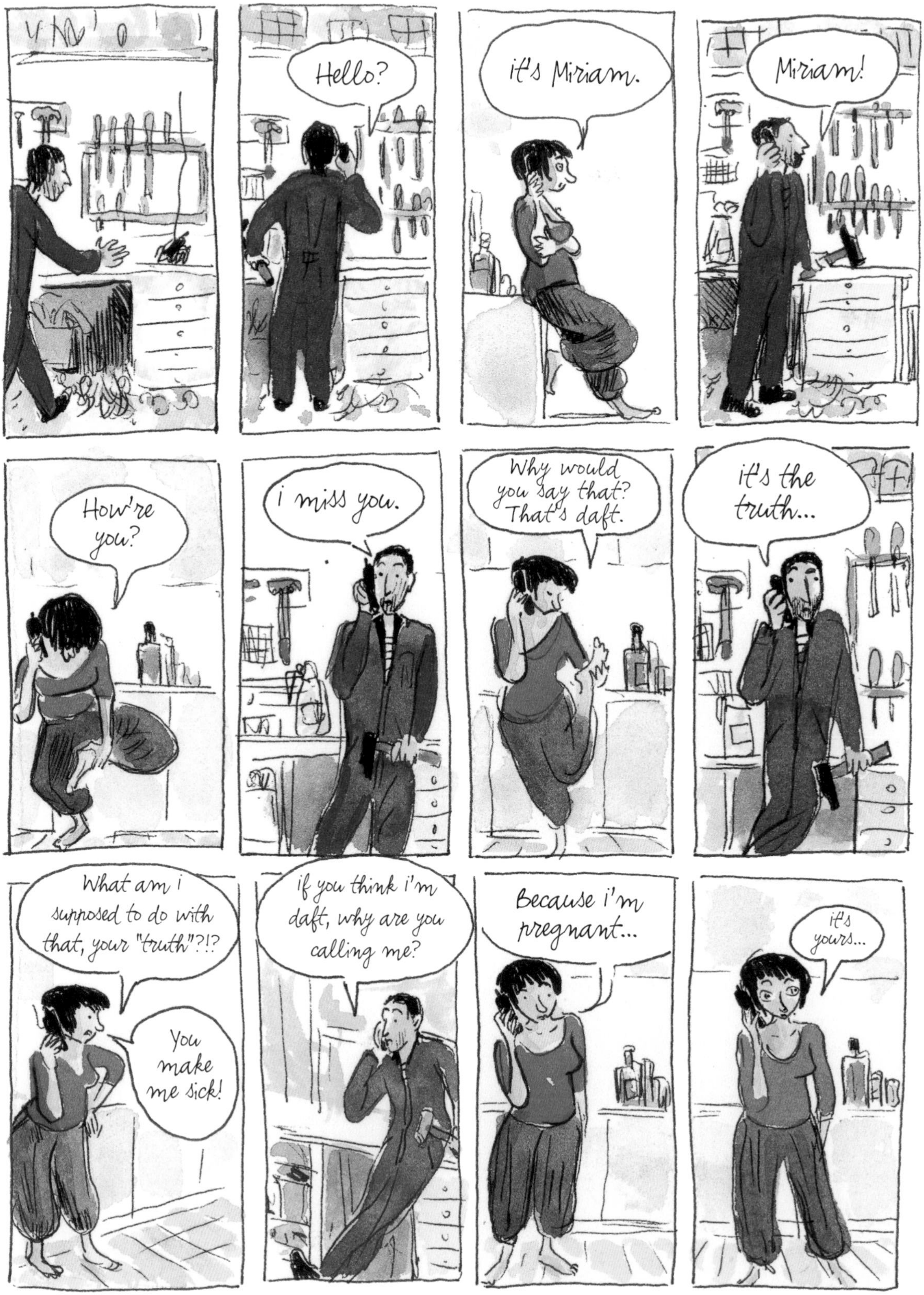
Hello?
it's Miriam.
Miriam!
How're you?
i miss you.
Why would you say that? That's daft.
it's the truth...
What am i supposed to do with that, your "truth"?!?
You make me sick!
if you think i'm daft, why are you calling me?
Because i'm pregnant...
it's yours...

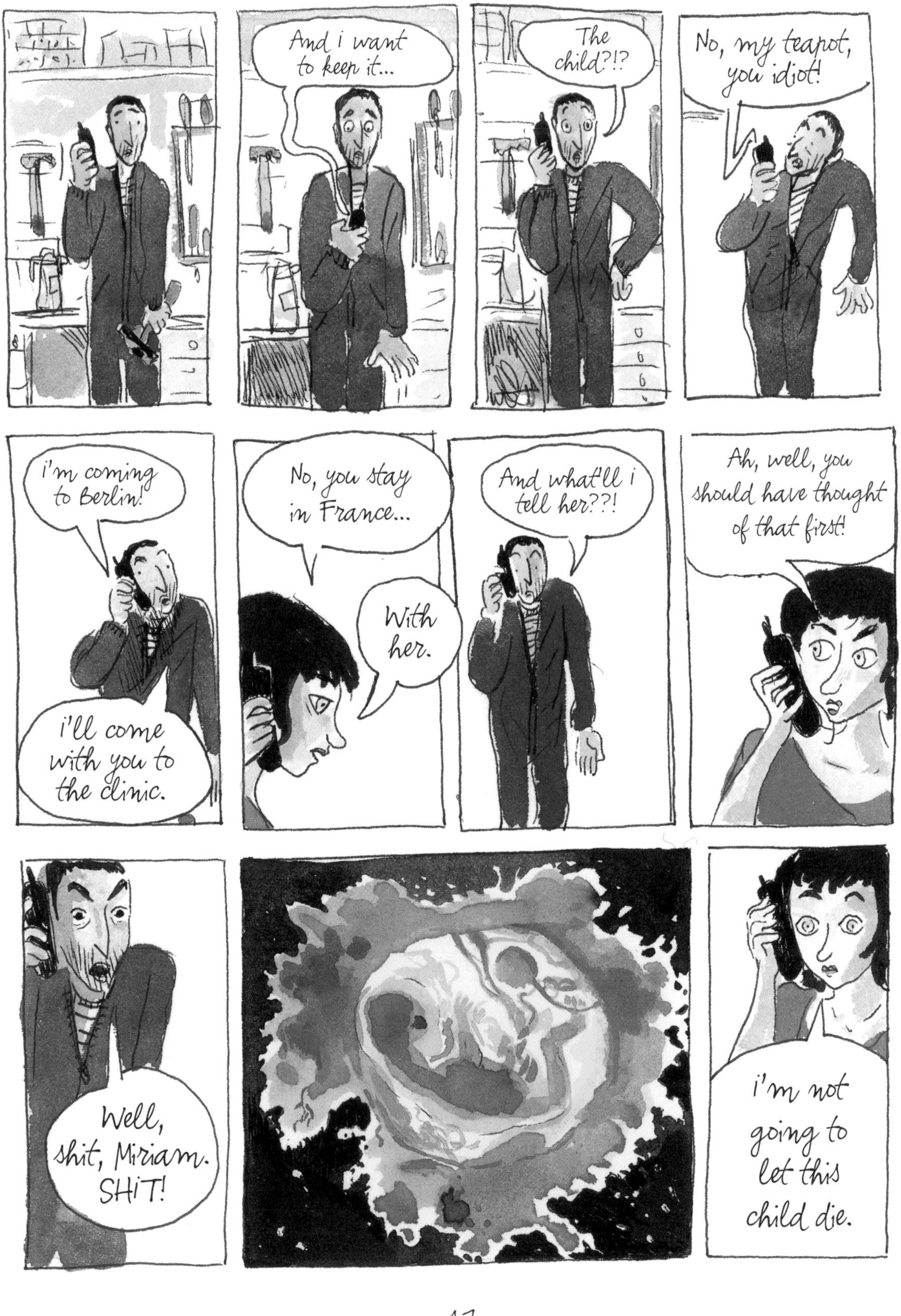
And i want to keep it...
The child?!?
No, my teapot, you idiot!
i'm coming to Berlin!
i'll come with you to the clinic.
No, you stay in France...
With her.
And what'll i tell her??!
Ah, well, you should have thought of that first!
Well, shit, Miriam. SHIT!
i'm not going to let this child die.

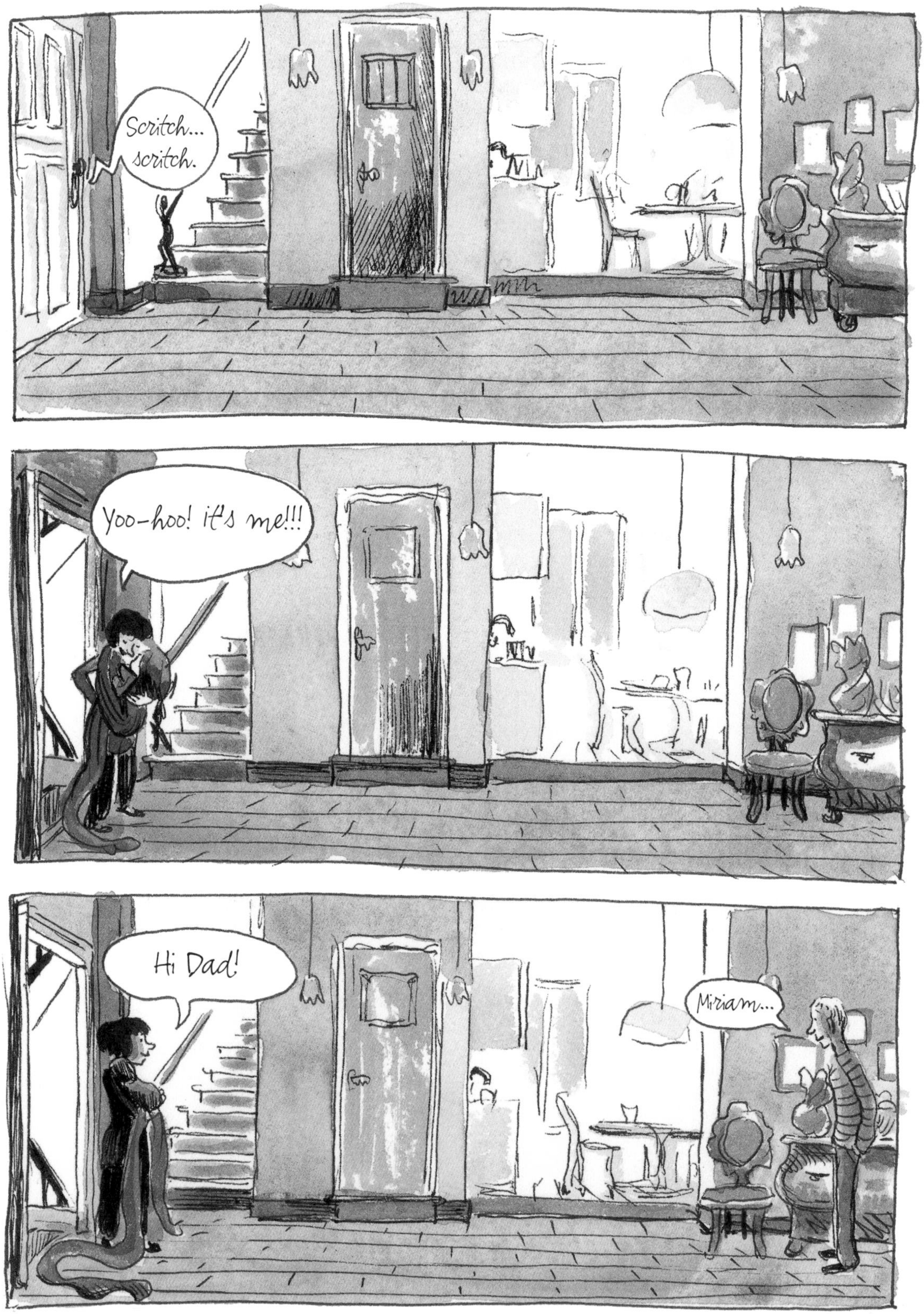
Scritch... scritch.
Yoo-hoo! it's me!!!
Hi Dad!
Miriam...

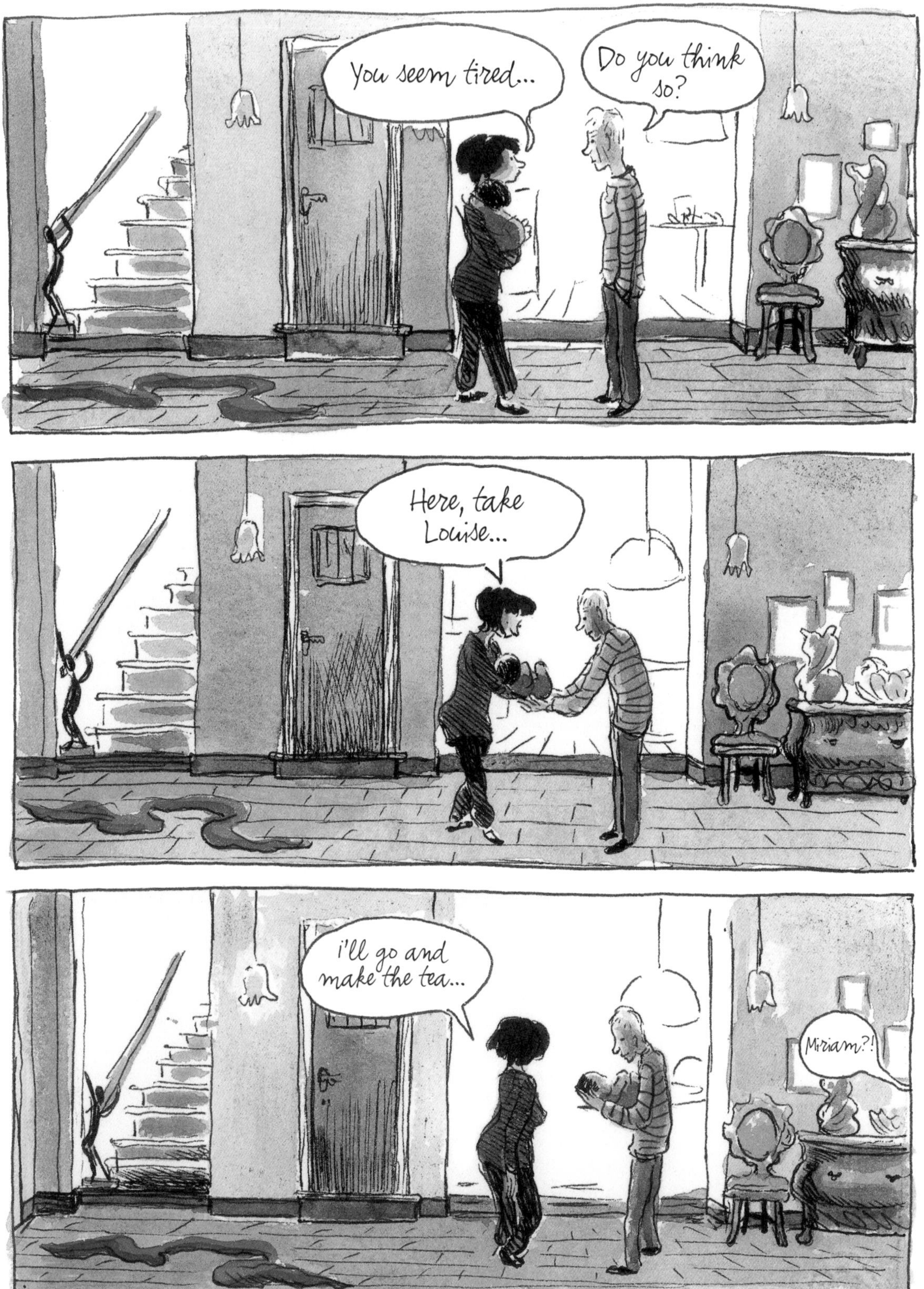
You seem tired...
Do you think so?
Here, take Louise...
i'll go and make the tea...
Miriam?!

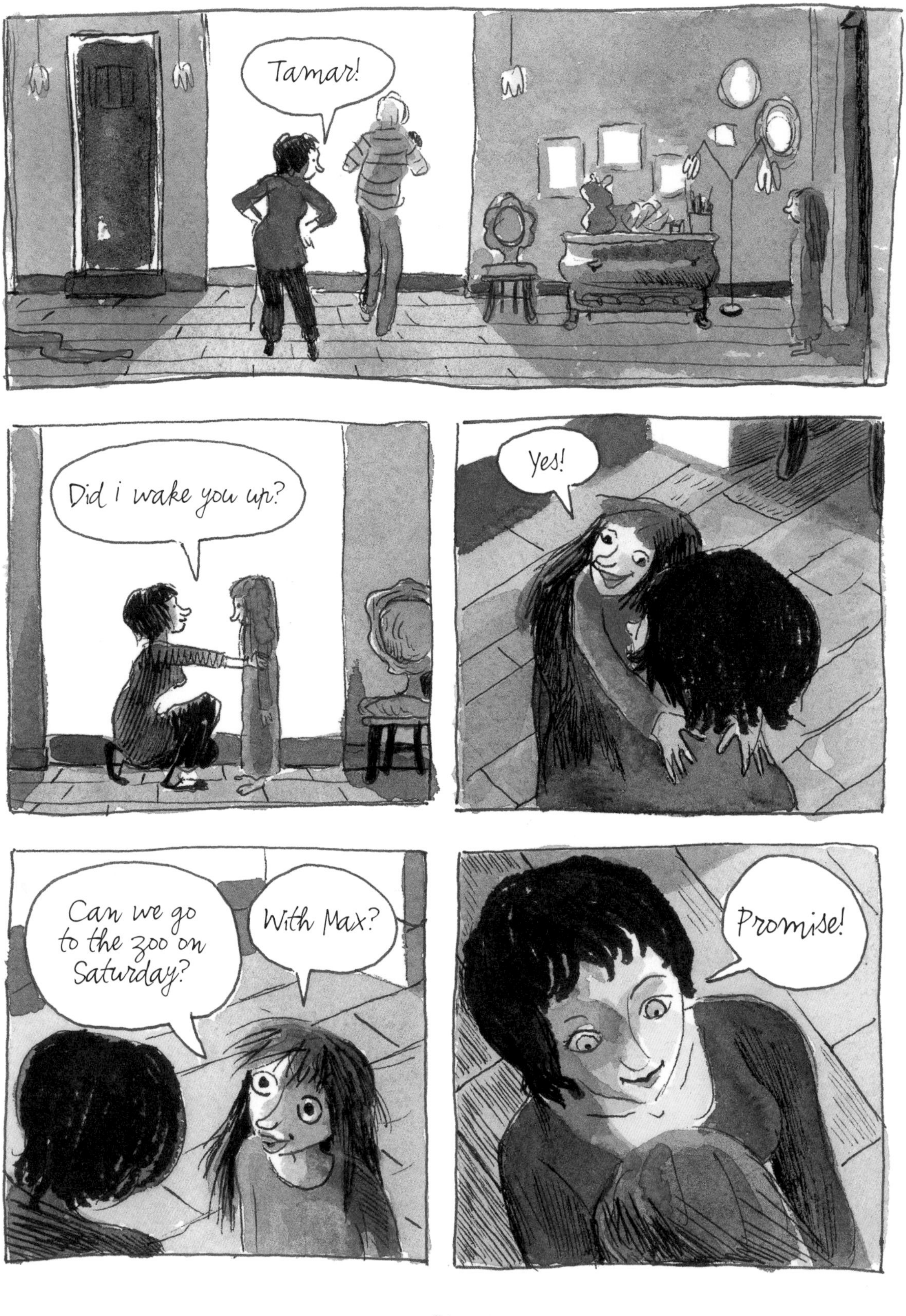
Tamar!
Did i wake you up?
Yes!
Can we go to the zoo on Saturday?
With Max?
Promise!

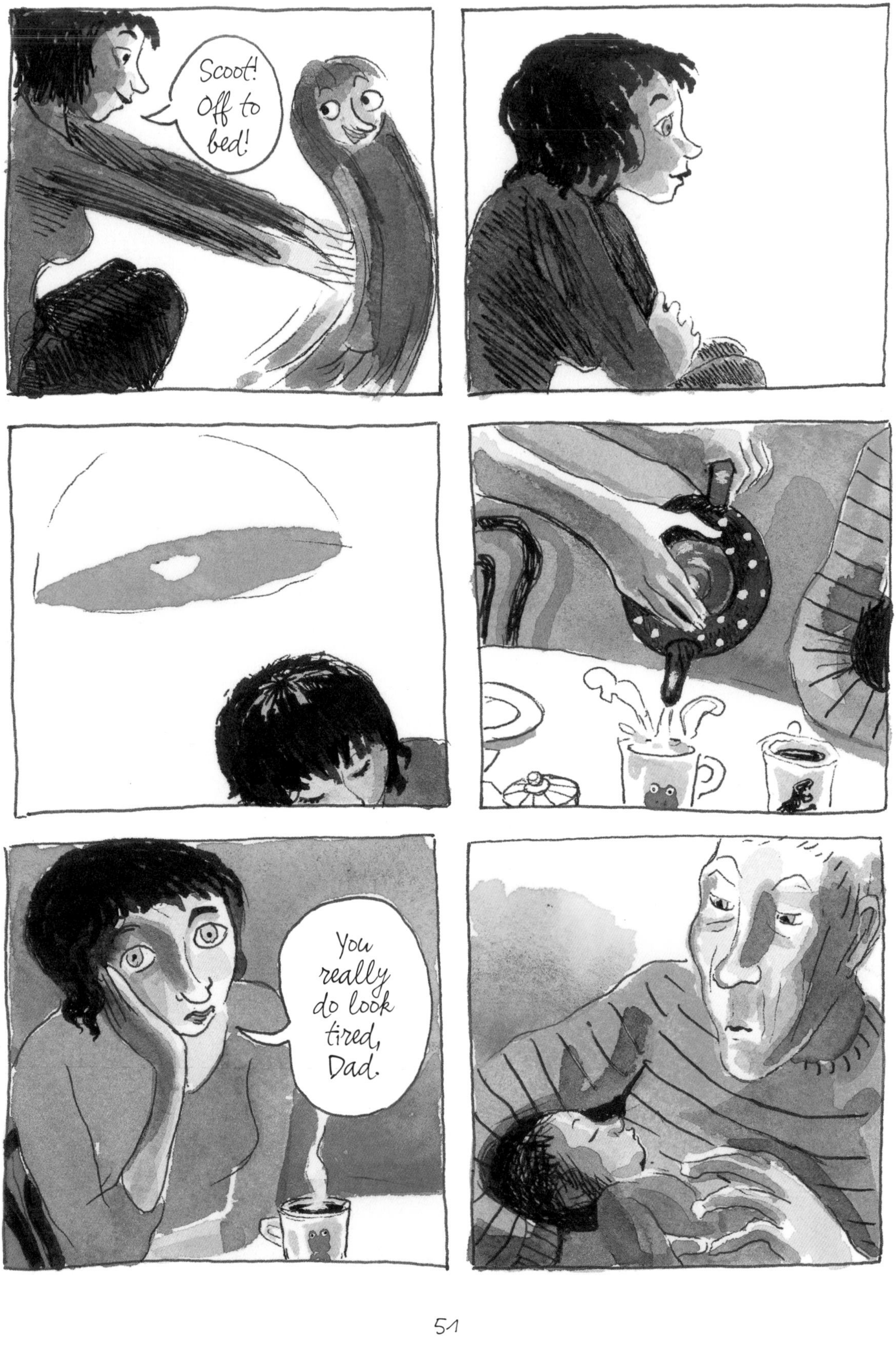
Scoot! Off to bed!
You really do look tired, Dad.

i'm undergoing chemotherapy.

Chemotherapy???

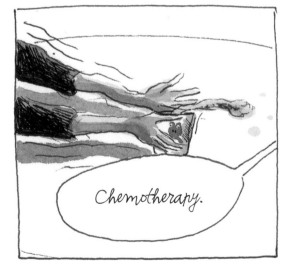

Chemotherapy.

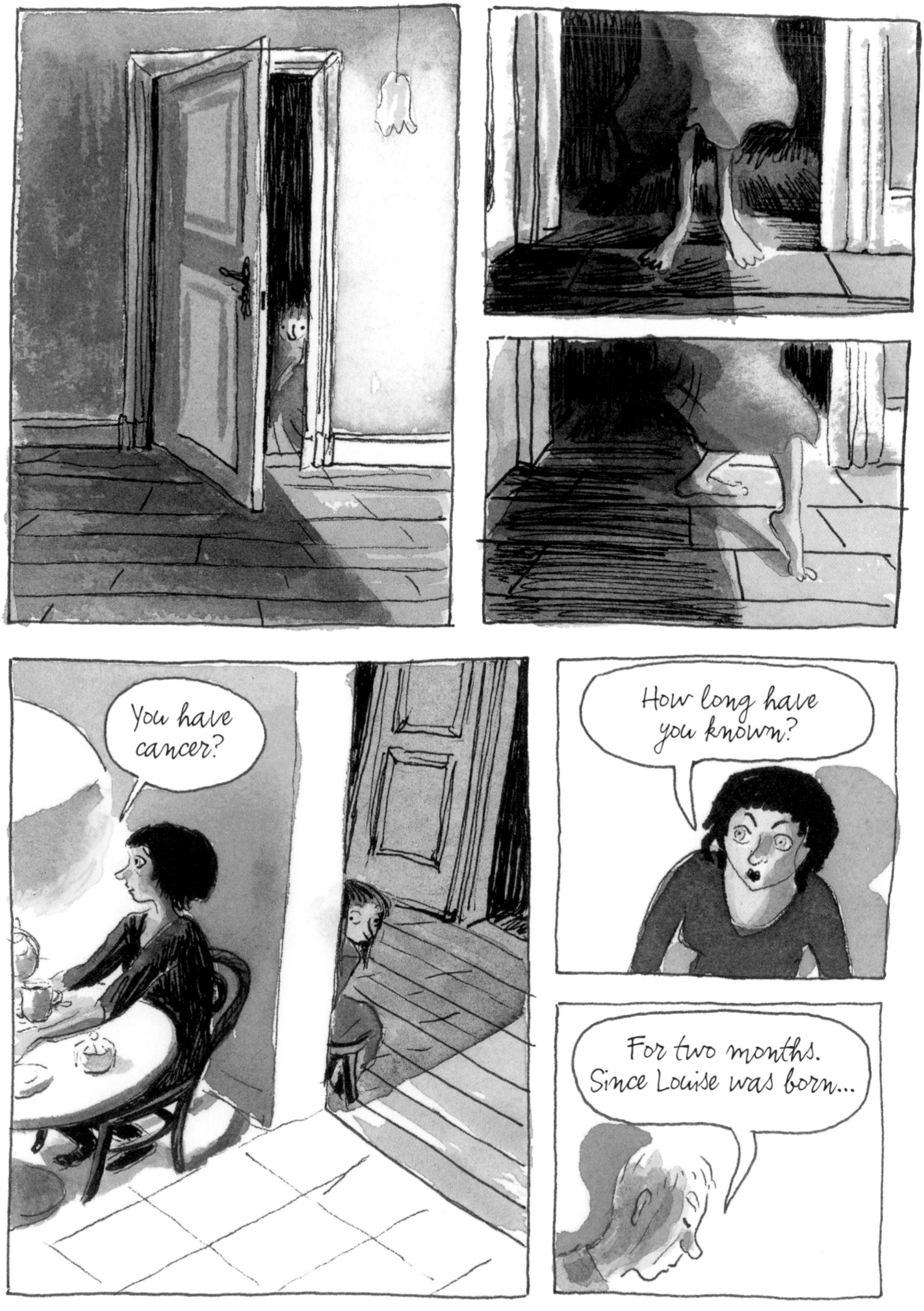
You have cancer?
How long have you known?
For two months. Since Louise was born...

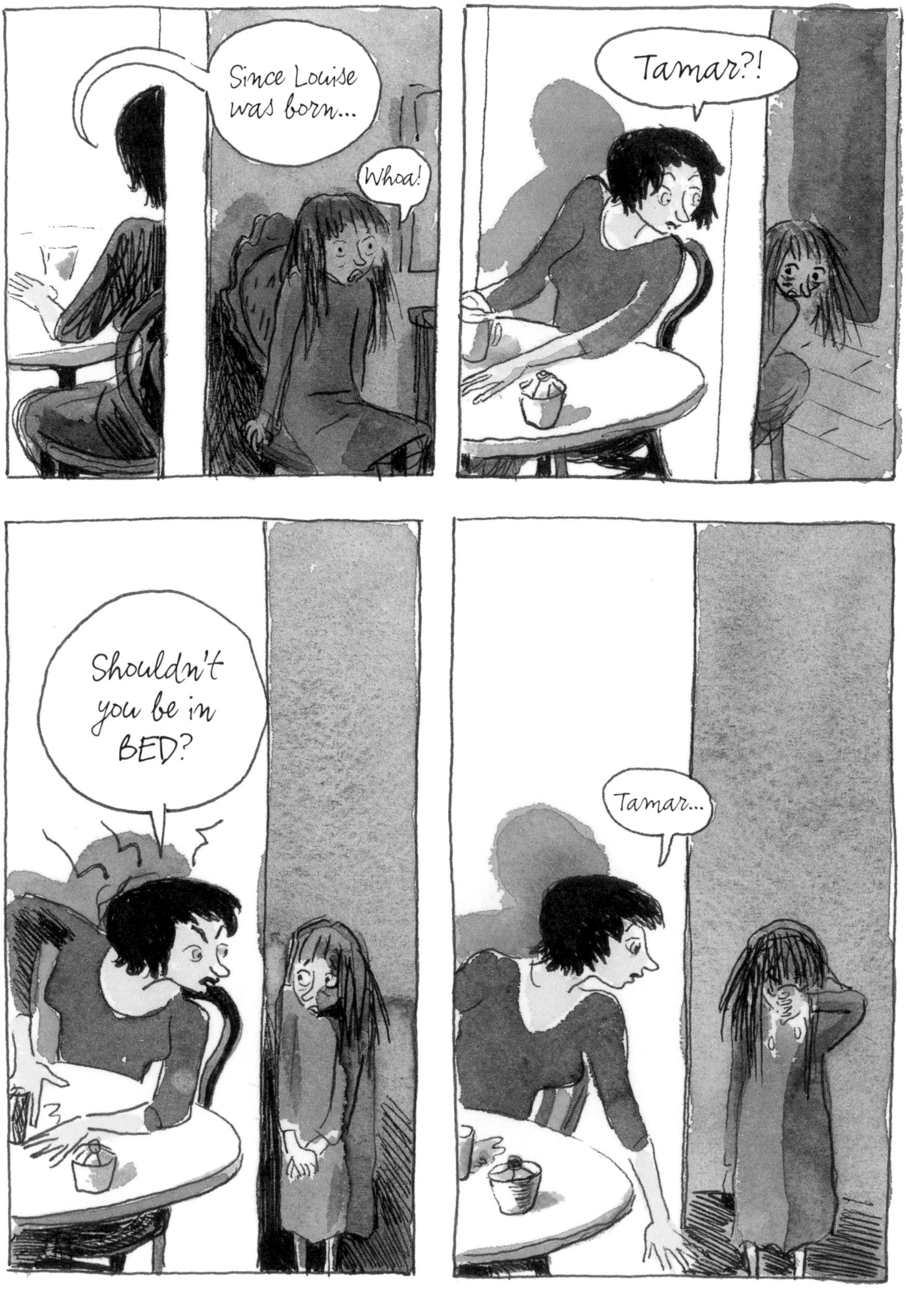
Since Louise was born...
Whoa!
Tamar?!
Shouldn't you be in BED?
Tamar...

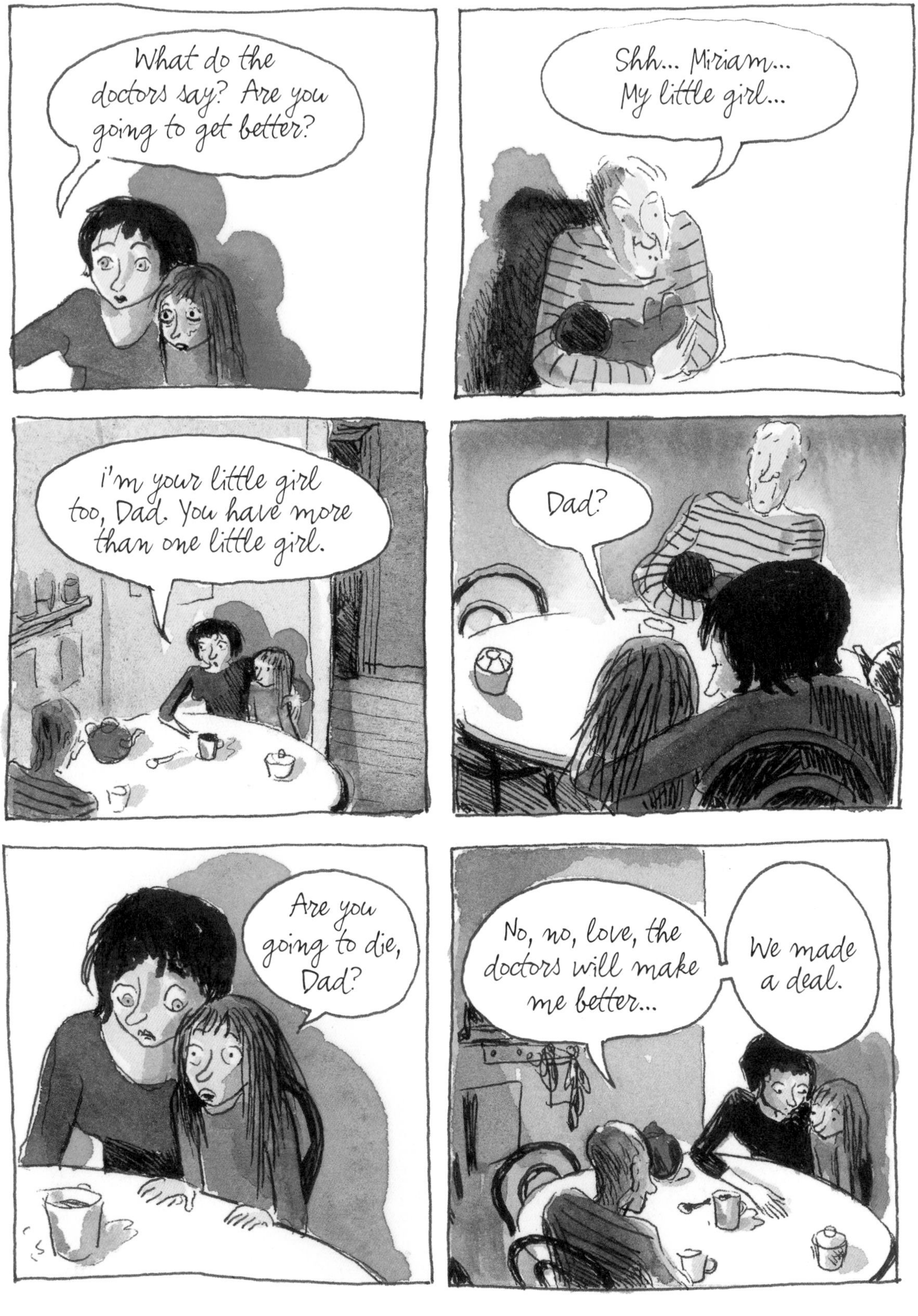
What do the doctors say? Are you going to get better?
Shh... Miriam... My little girl...
i'm your little girl too, Dad. You have more than one little girl.
Dad?
Are you going to die, Dad?
No, no, love, the doctors will make me better...
We made a deal.

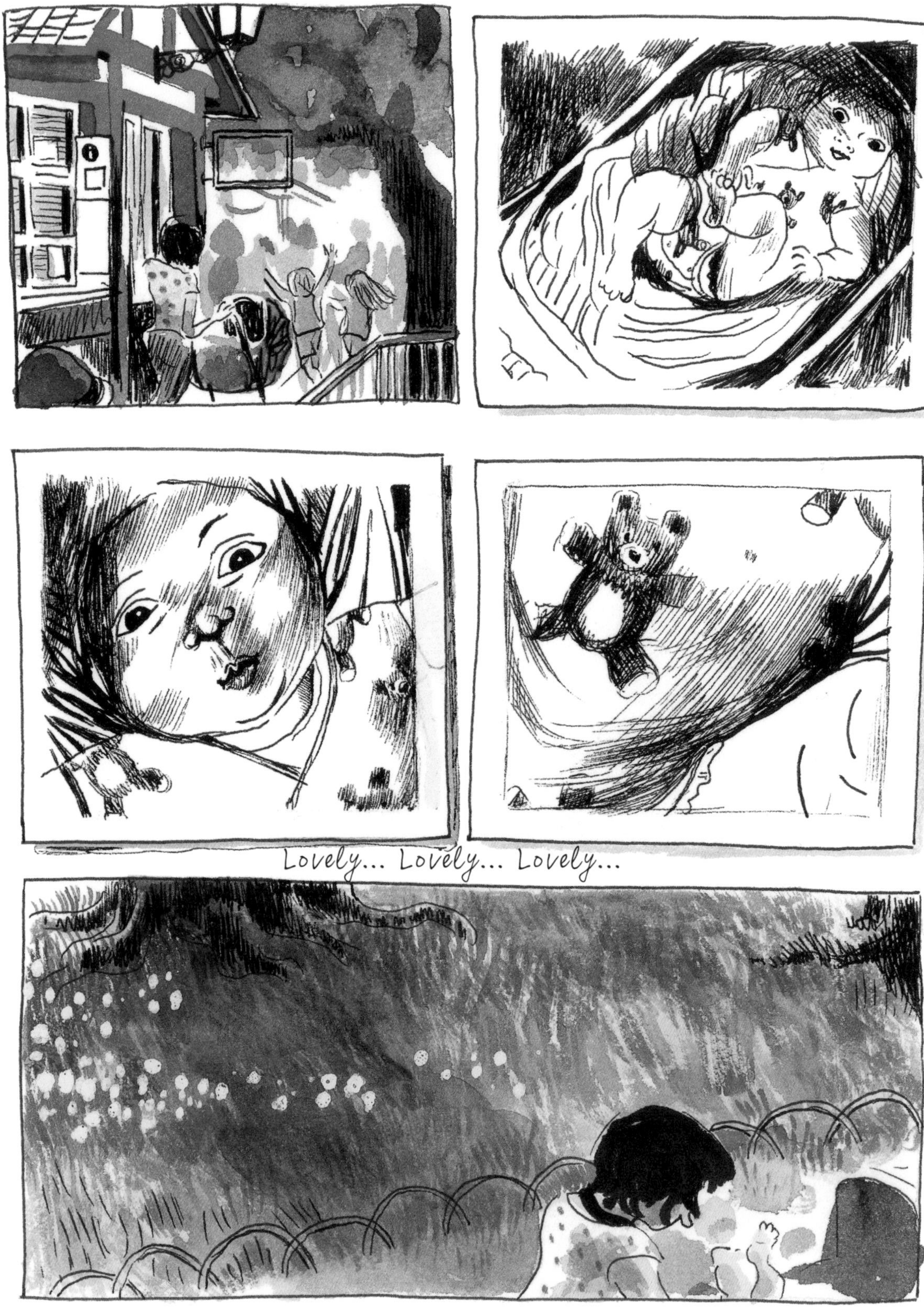
Lovely... Lovely... Lovely...

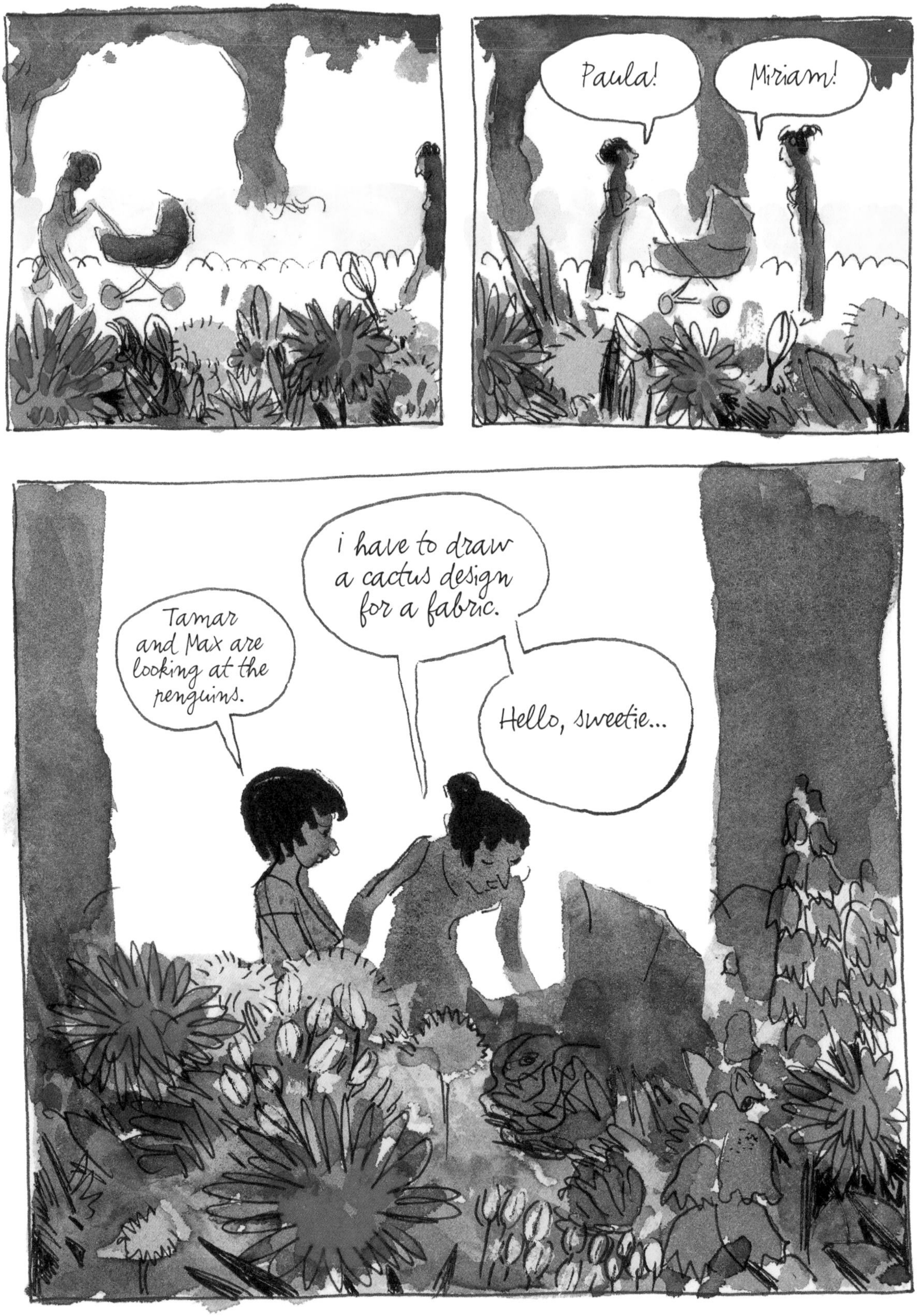
Paula!
Miriam!
Tamar and Max are looking at the penguins.
i have to draw a cactus design for a fabric.
Hello, sweetie...

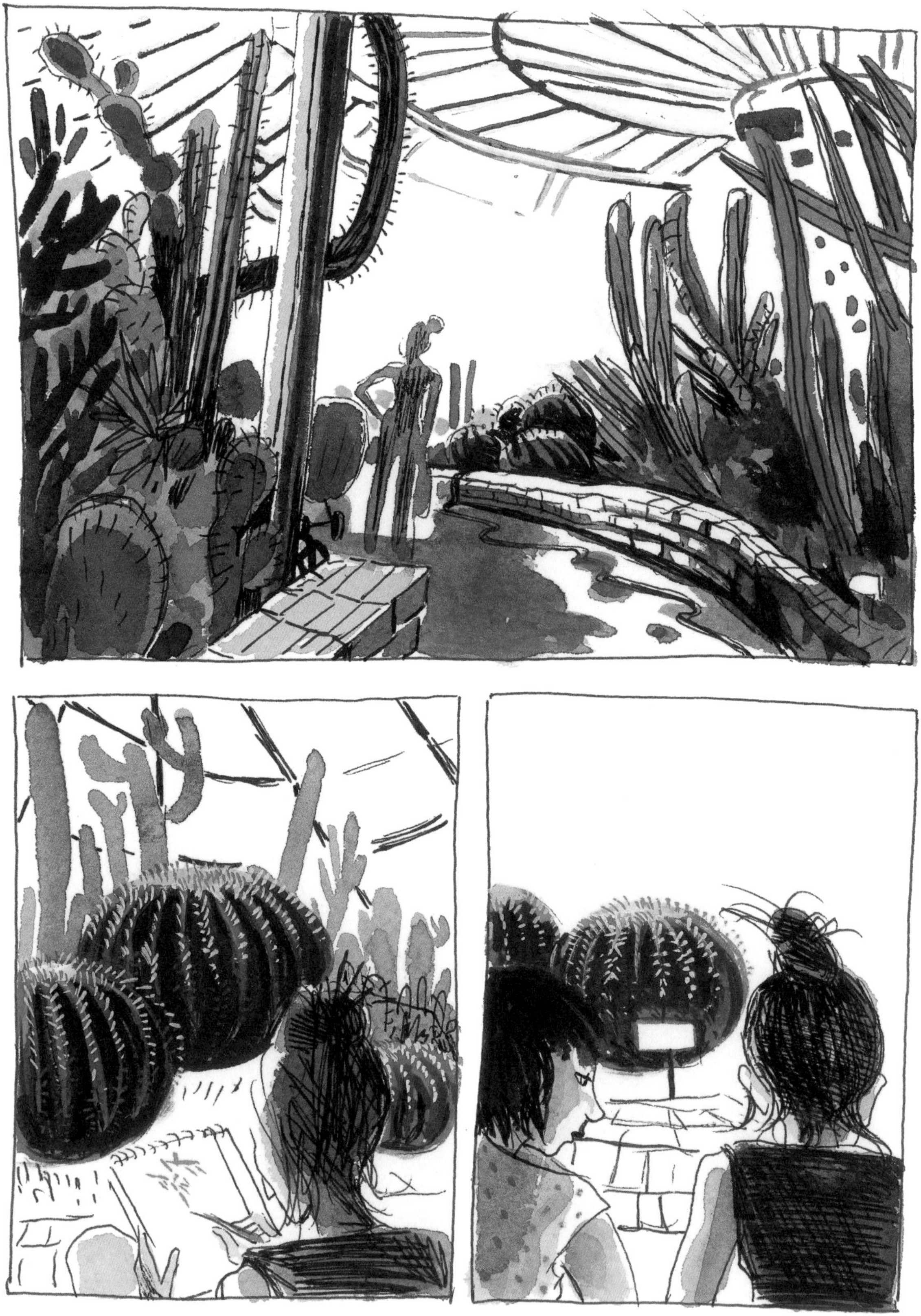

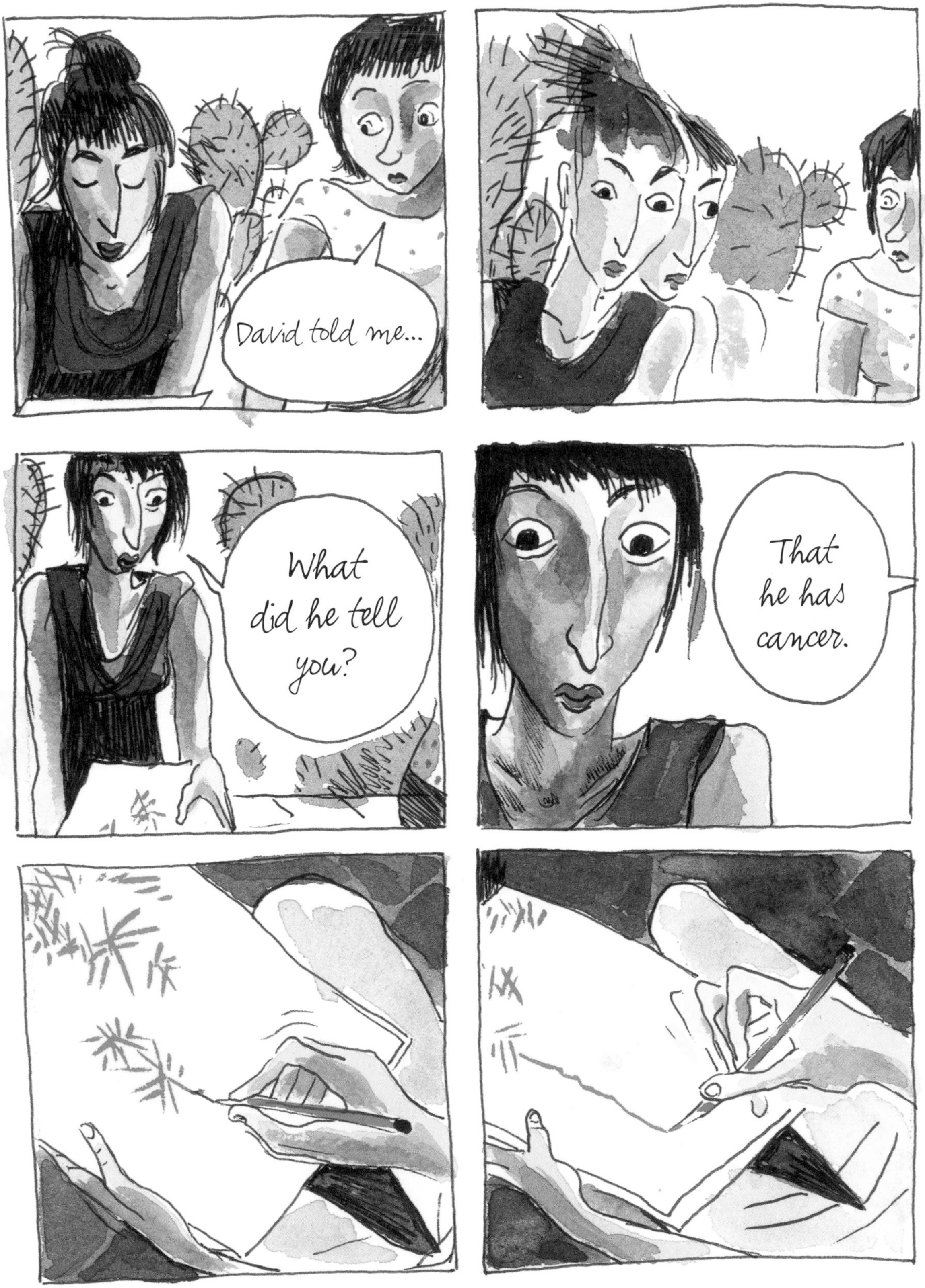
David told me...
What did he tell you?
That he has cancer.

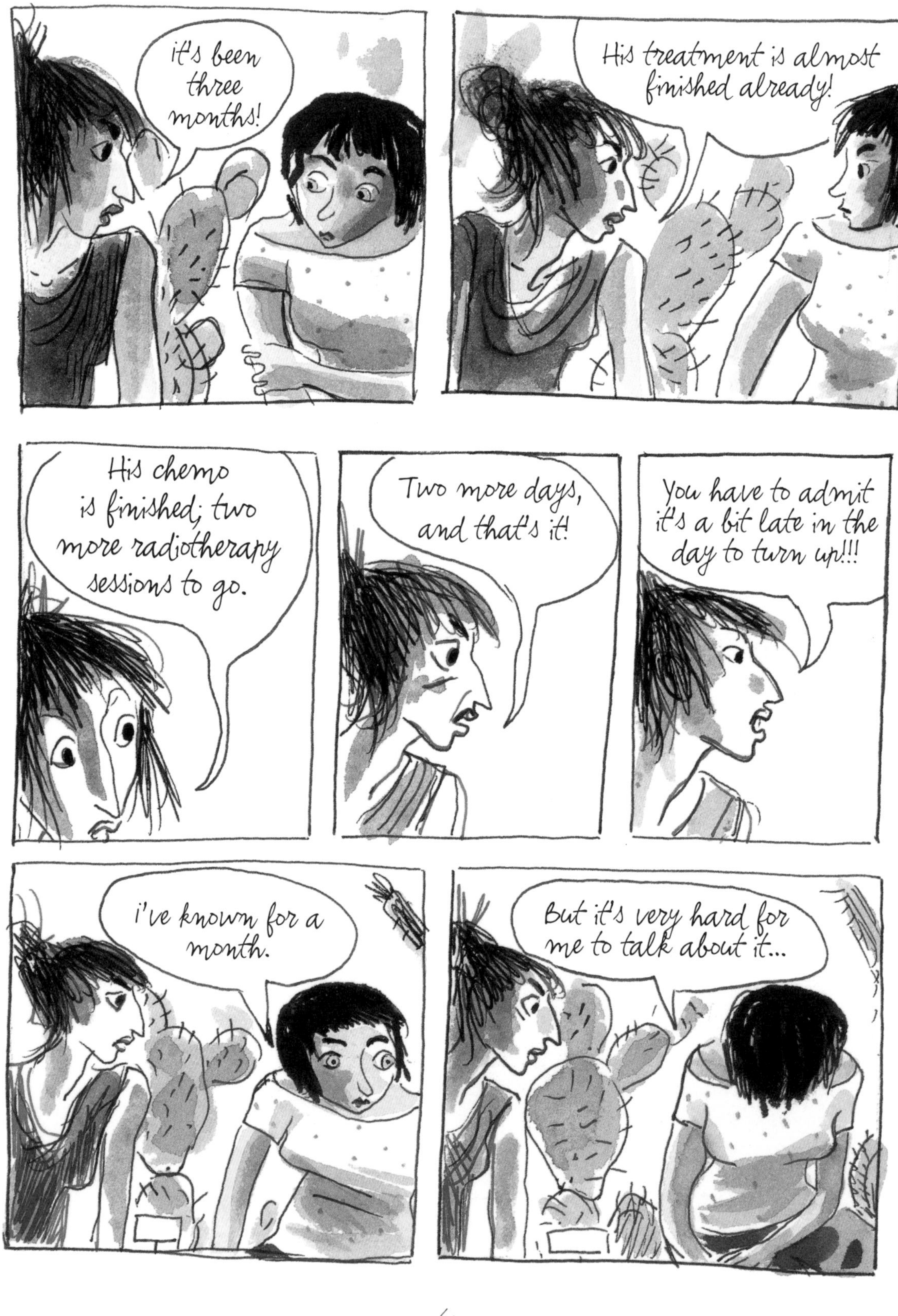
it's been three months!
His treatment is almost finished already!
His chemo is finished; two more radiotherapy sessions to go.
Two more days, and that's it!
You have to admit it's a bit late in the day to turn up!!!
i've known for a month.
But it's very hard for me to talk about it...

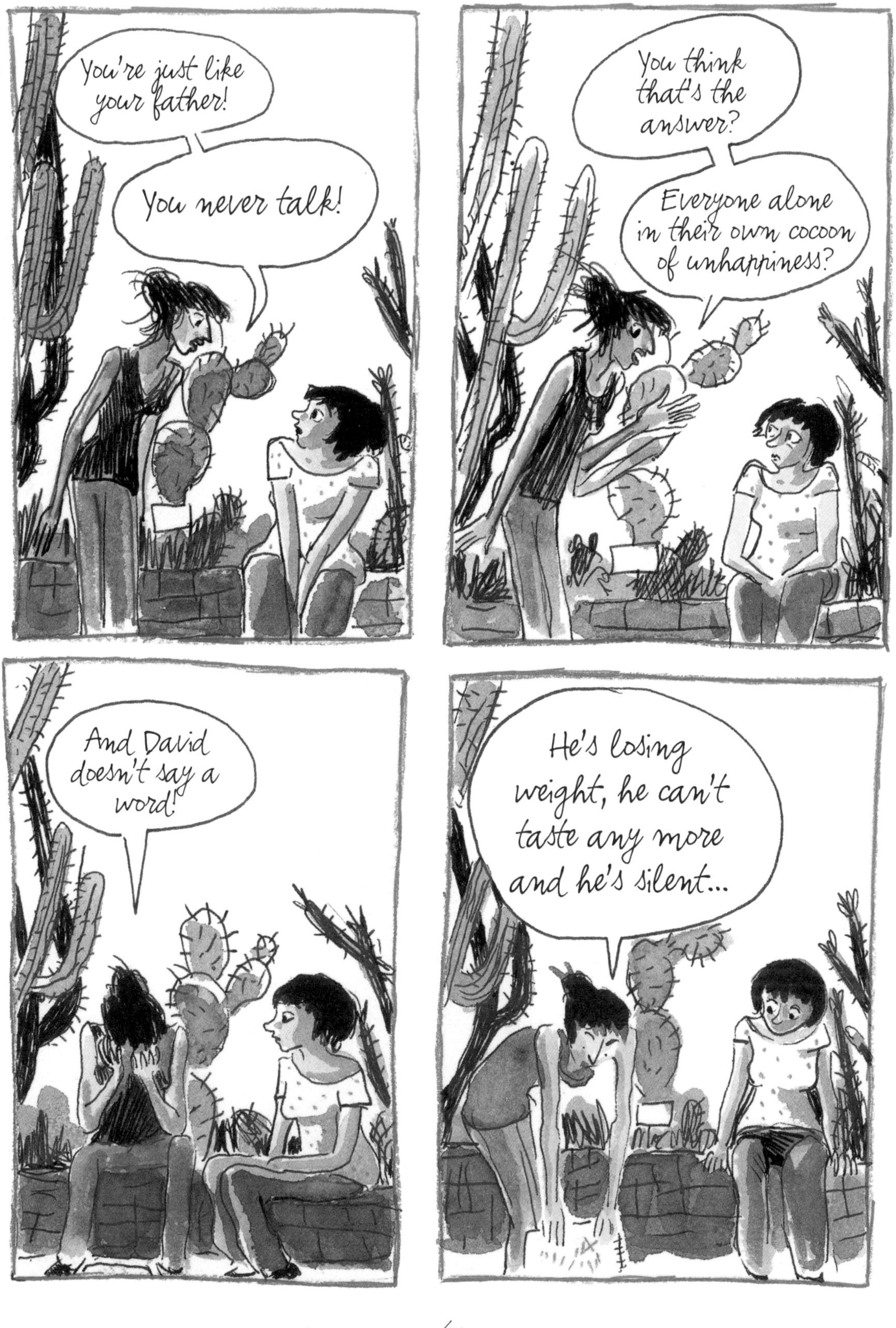
You're just like your father!
You never talk!
You think that's the answer?
Everyone alone in their own cocoon of unhappiness?
And David doesn't say a word!
He's losing weight, he can't taste any more and he's silent...

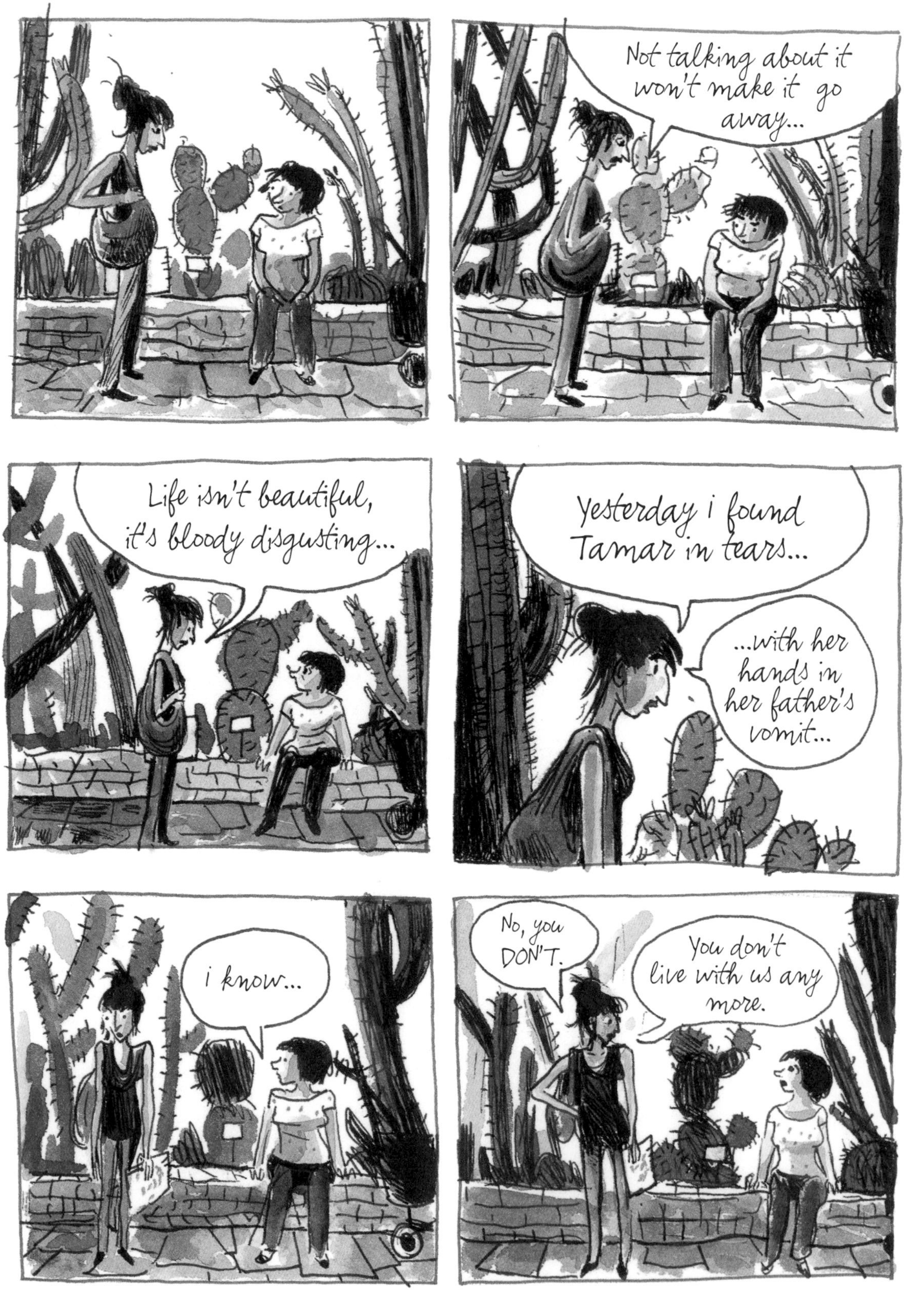
Not talking about it won't make it go away...
Life isn't beautiful, it's bloody disgusting...
Yesterday i found Tamar in tears...
...with her hands in her father's vomit...
i know...
No, you DON'T.
You don't live with us any more.

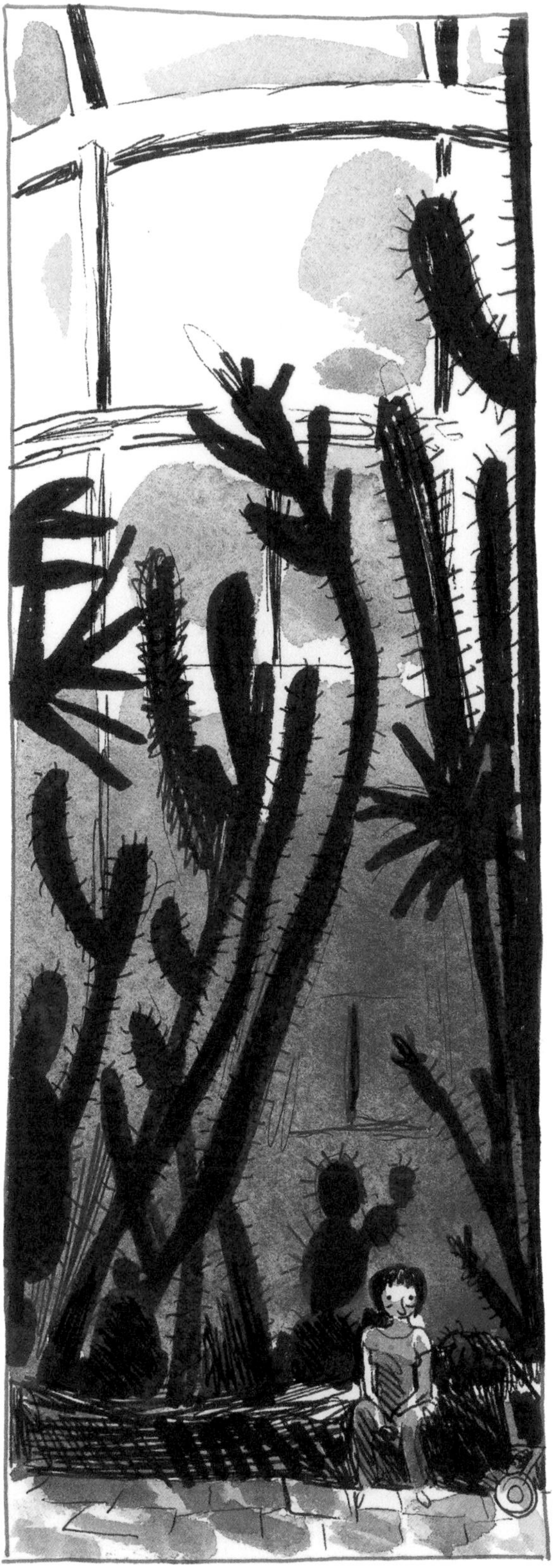

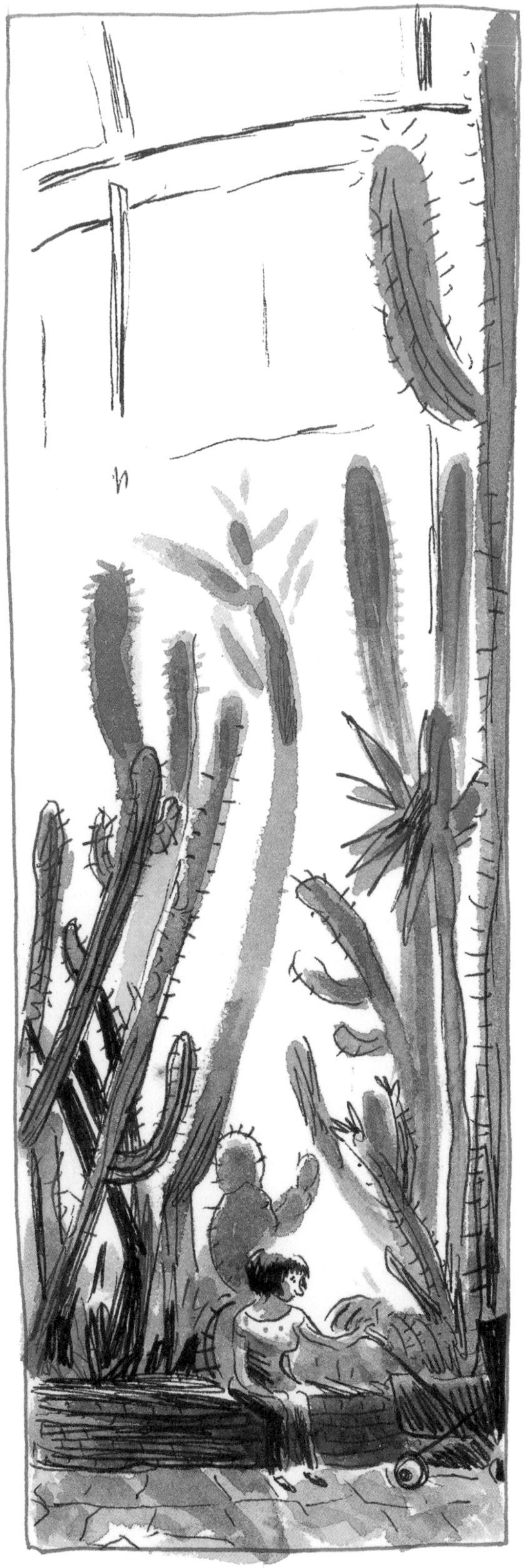

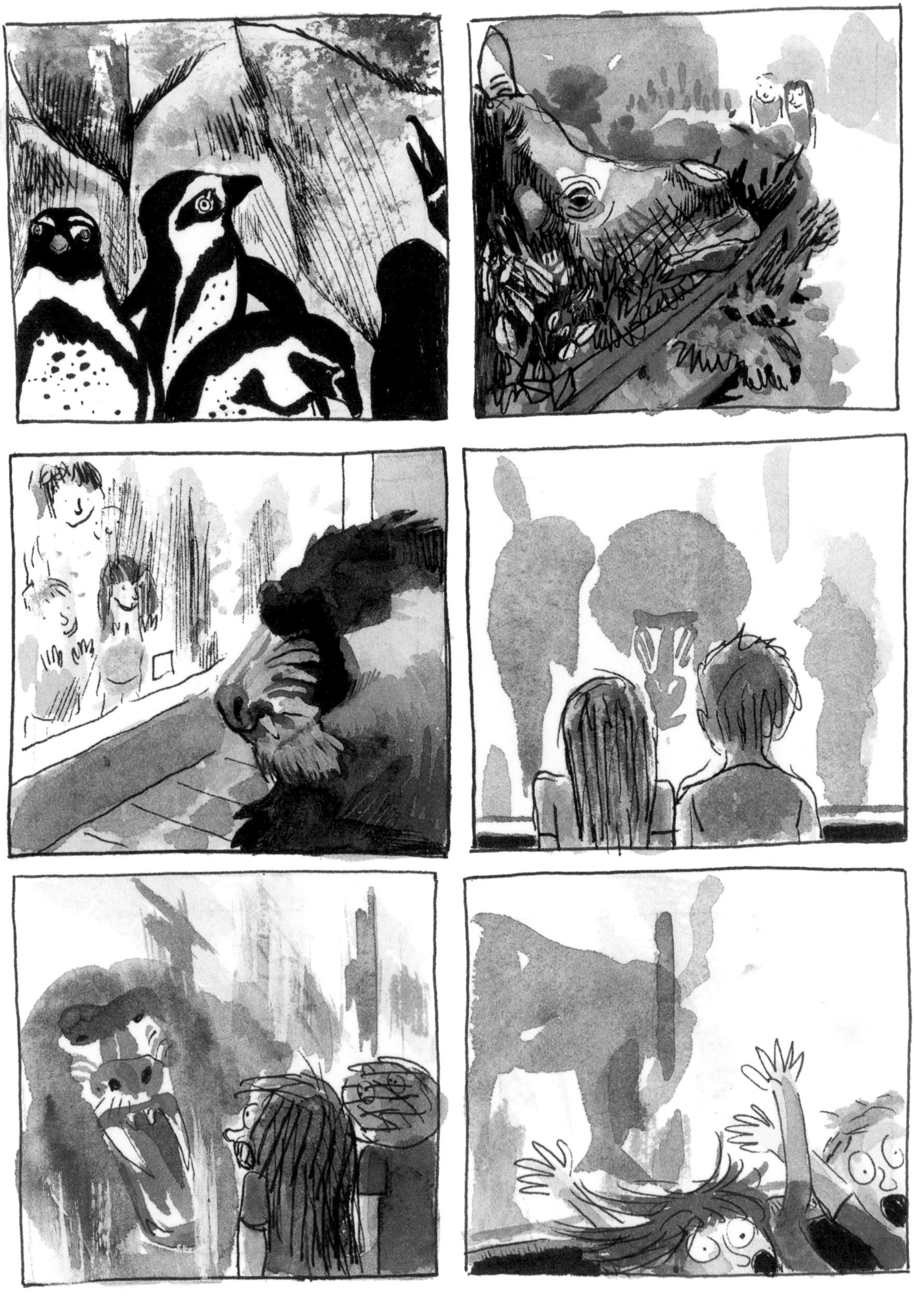

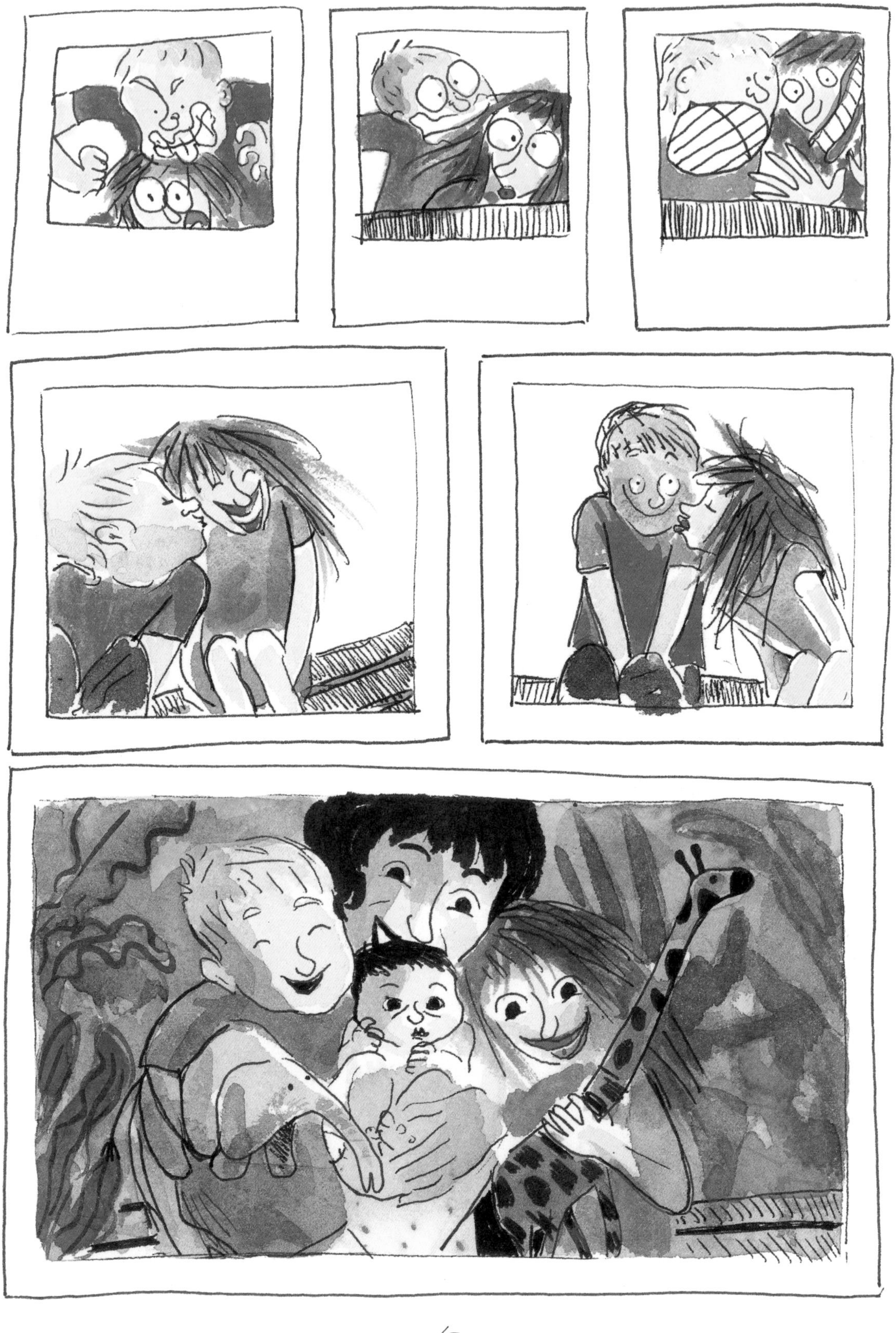

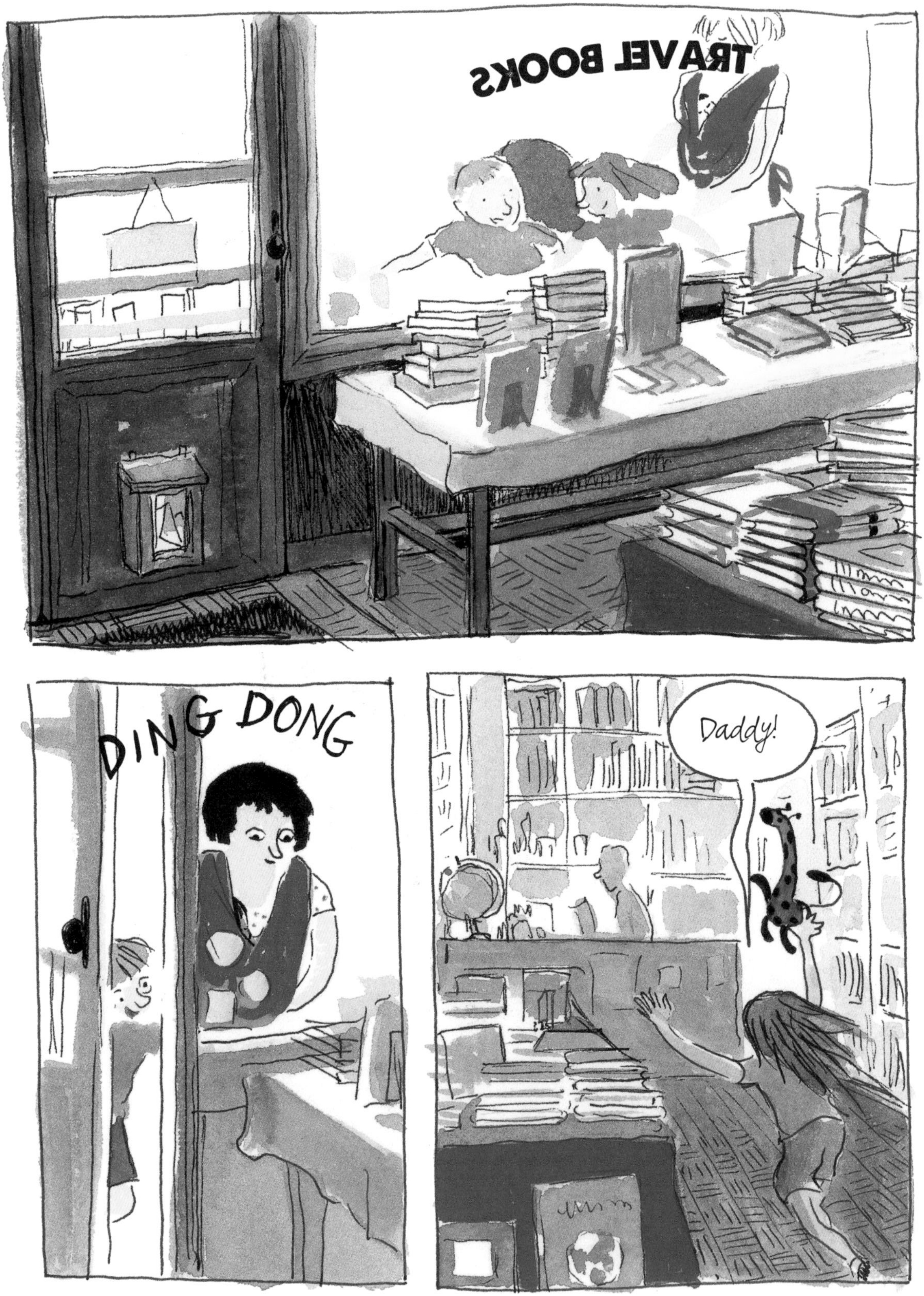
TRAVEL BOOKS
DING DONG
Daddy!

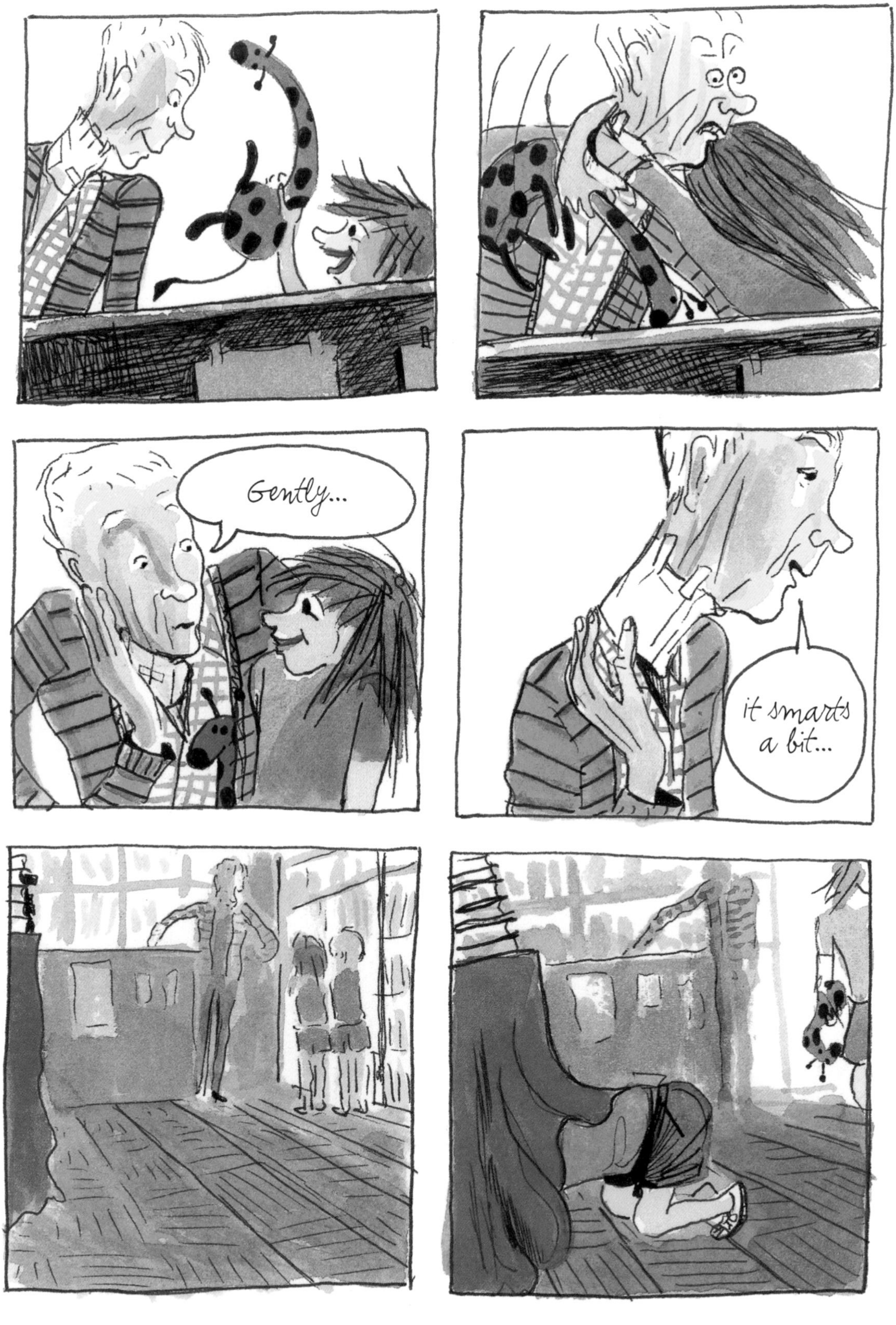
Gently...
it smarts a bit...

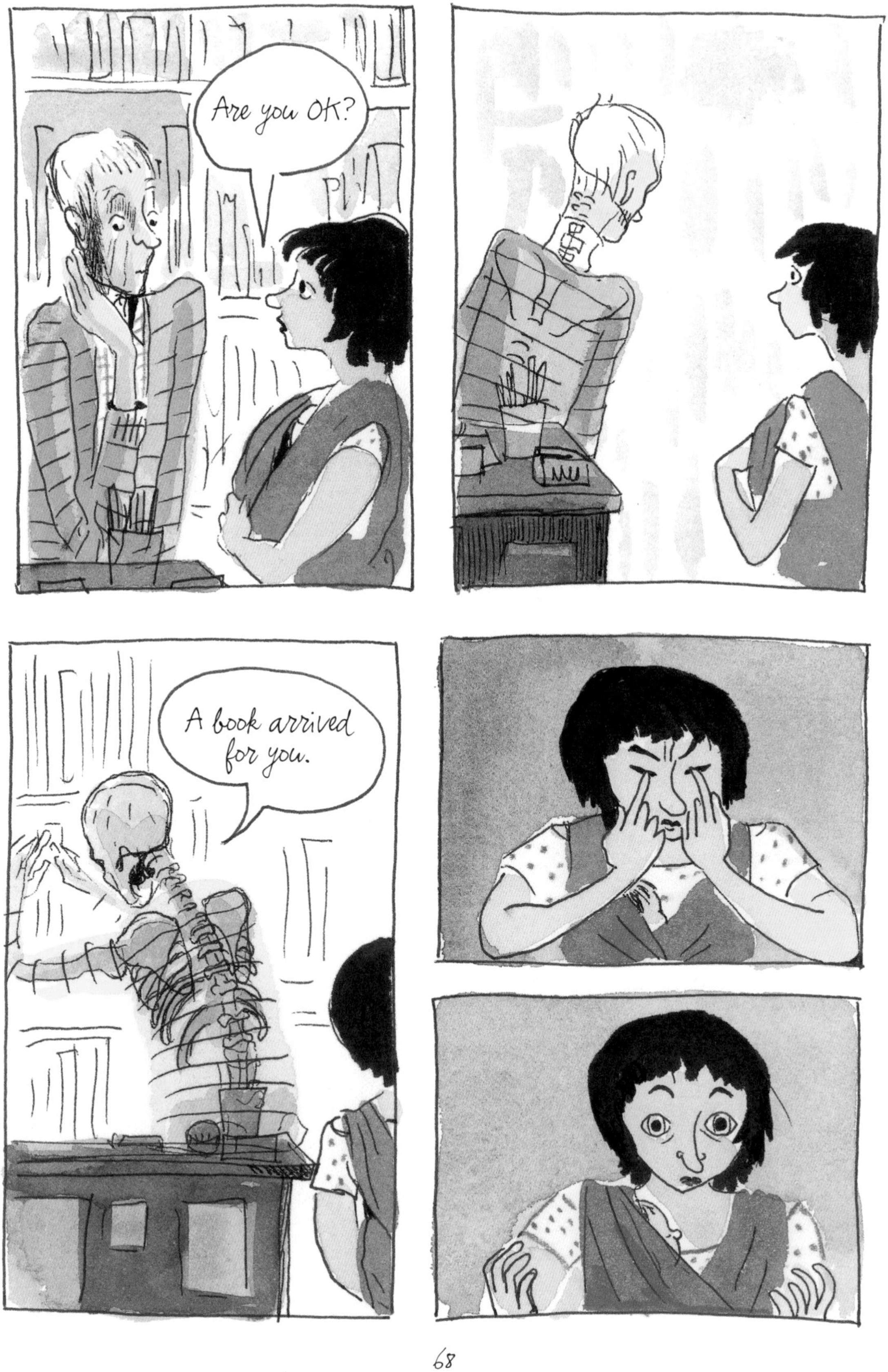
Are you OK?
A book arrived for you.

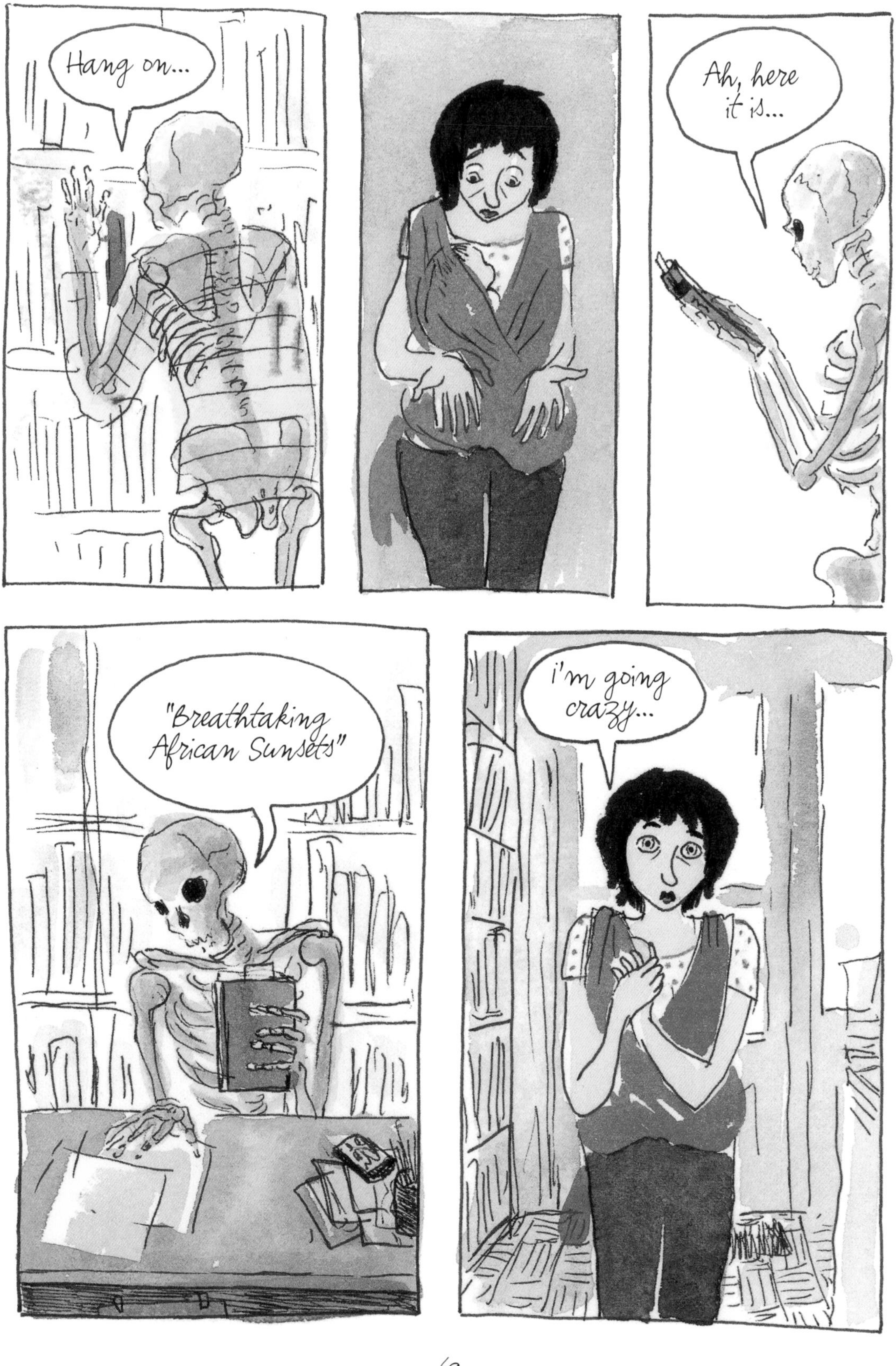
Hang on...
Ah, here it is...
"Breathtaking African Sunsets"
i'm going crazy...

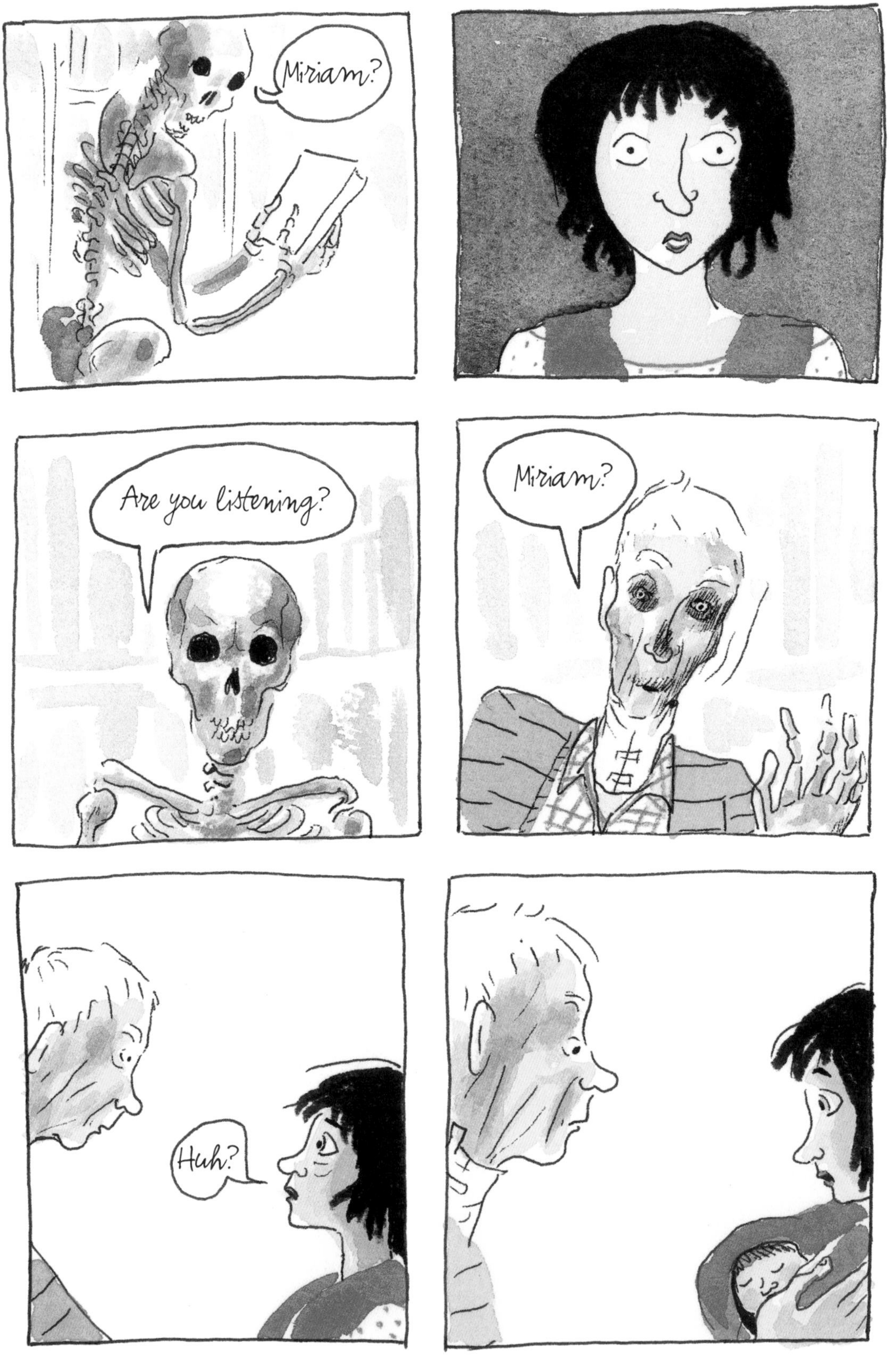
Miriam?
Are you listening?
Miriam?
Huh?

You must be very, very tired...
Don't worry about me...
it'll be OK....
You used to say that when i was little, too...
And look...

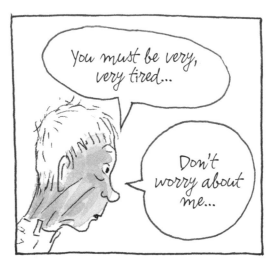

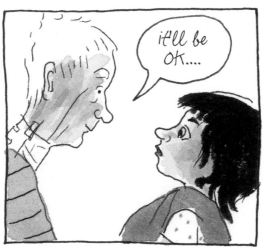

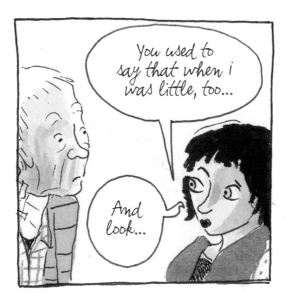

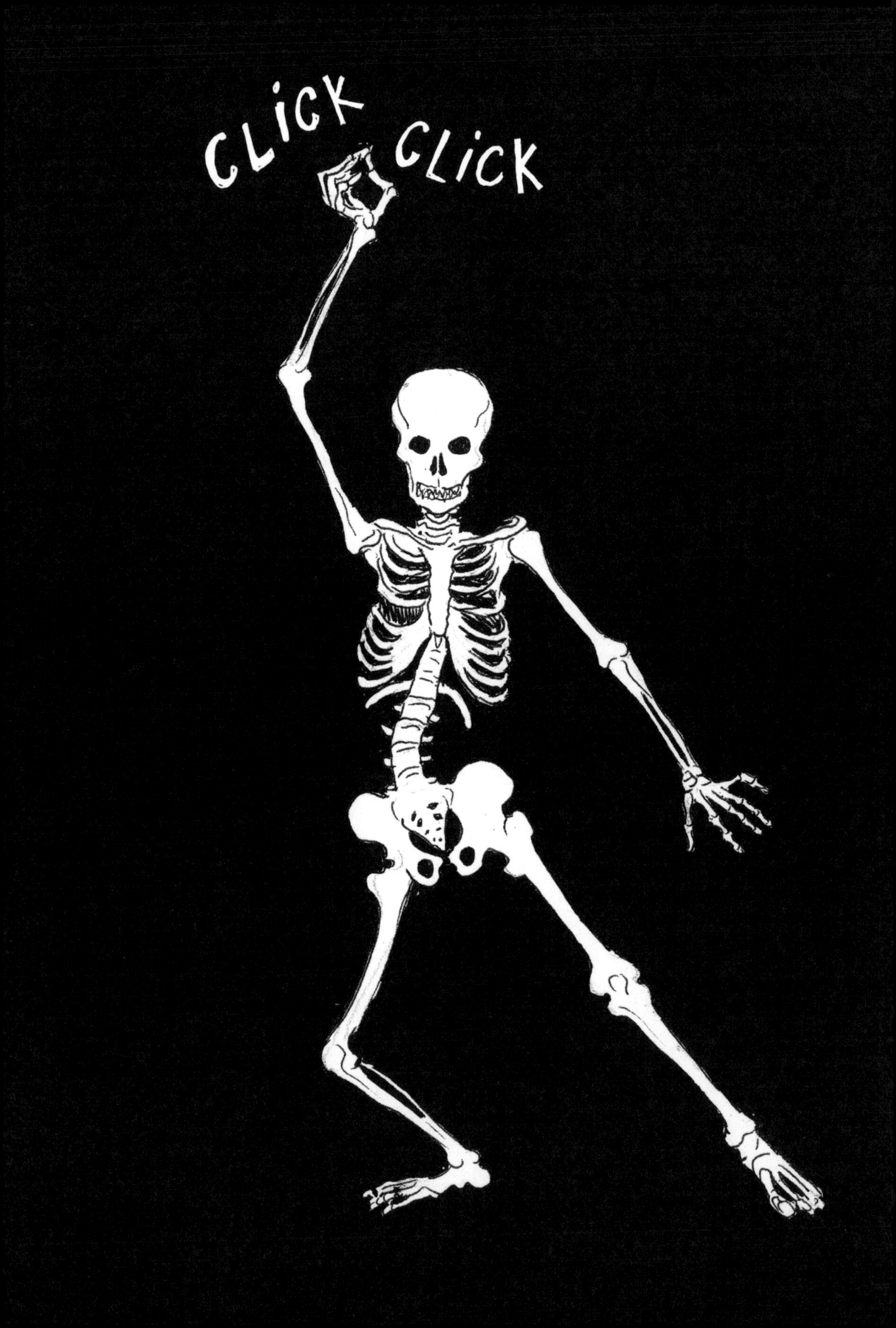
CLICK CLICK

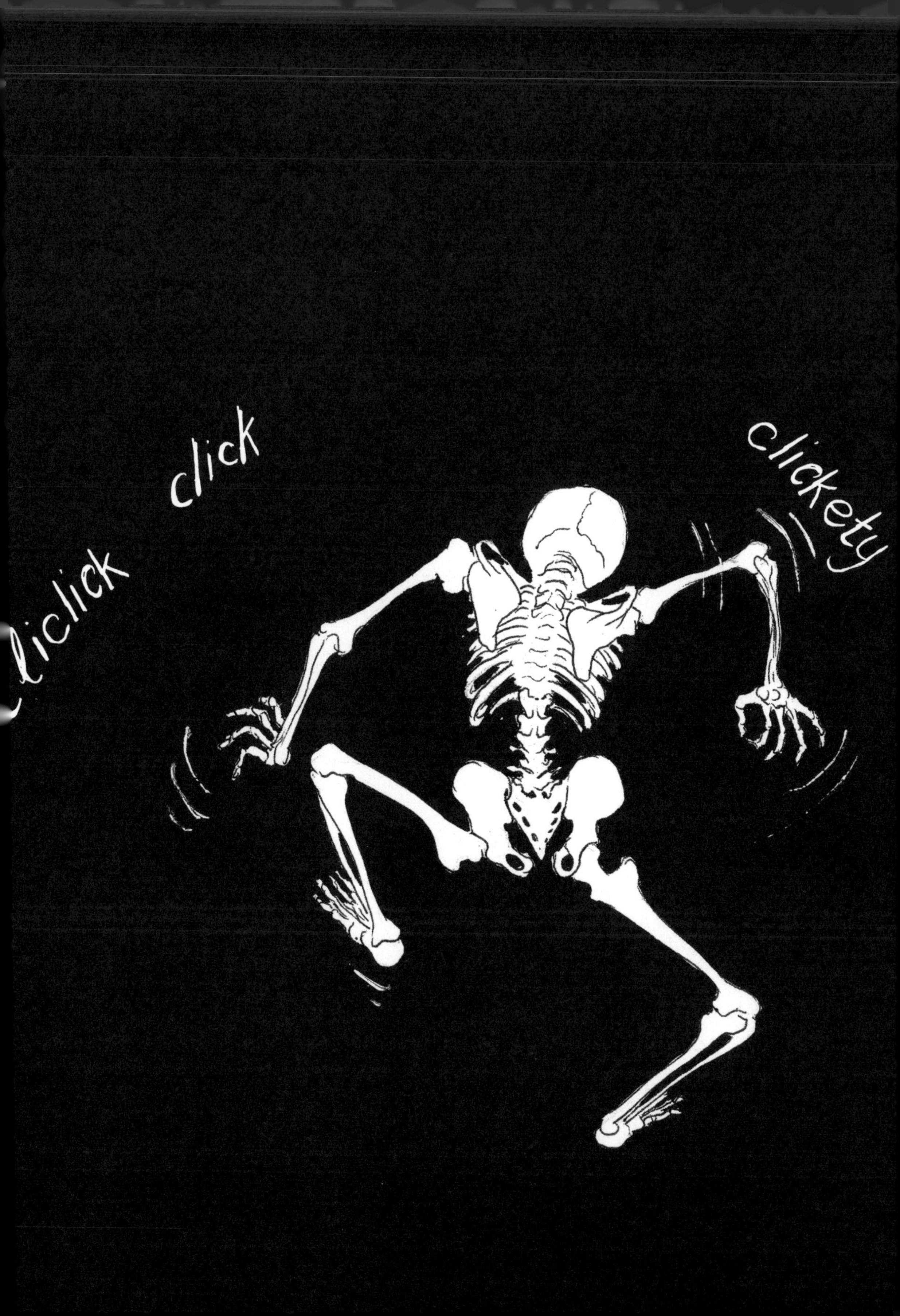

liclick
click
clickety

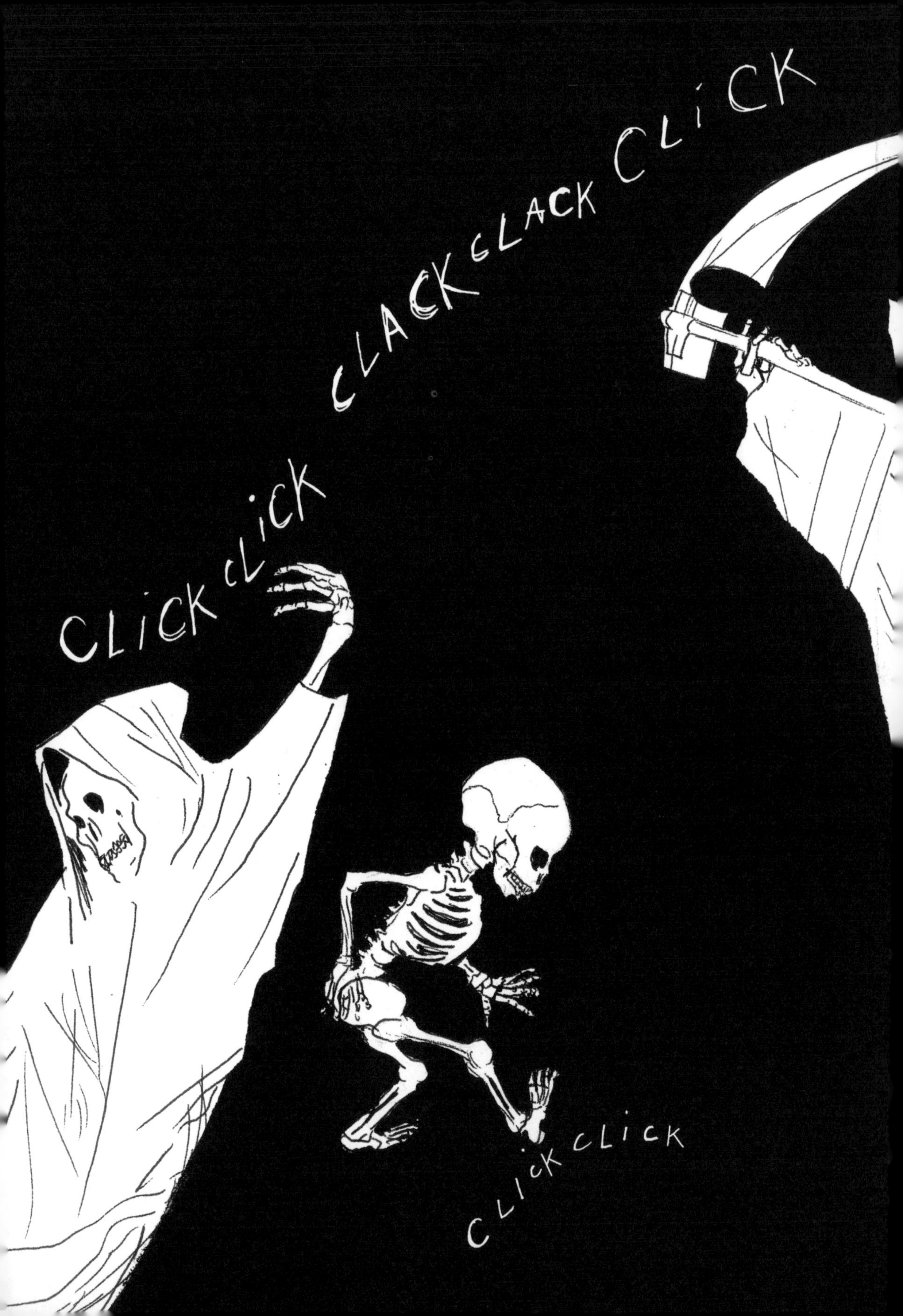
CLICK CLICK
CLACK CLACK CLICK
CLICK CLICK

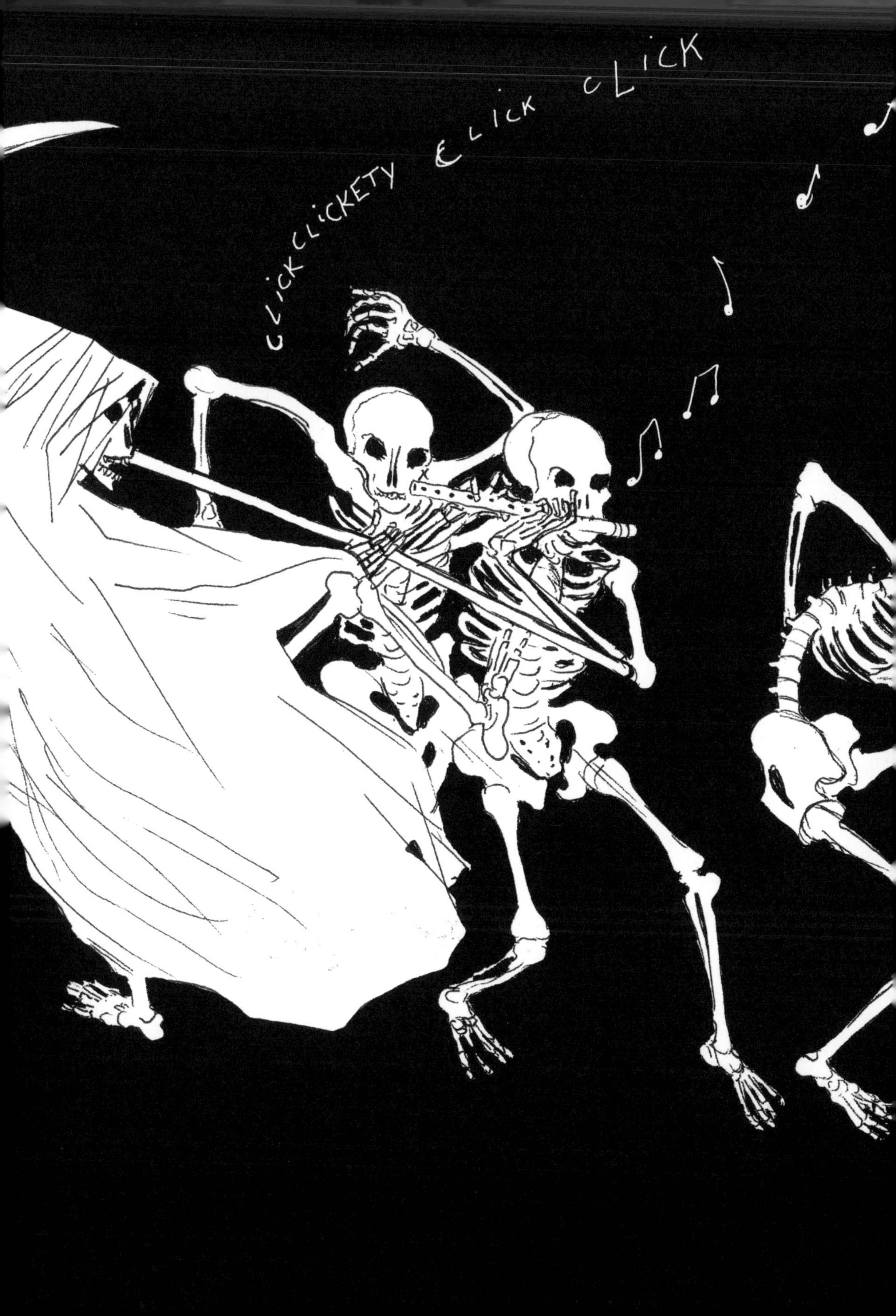
CLICK CLICKETY CLICK CLICK

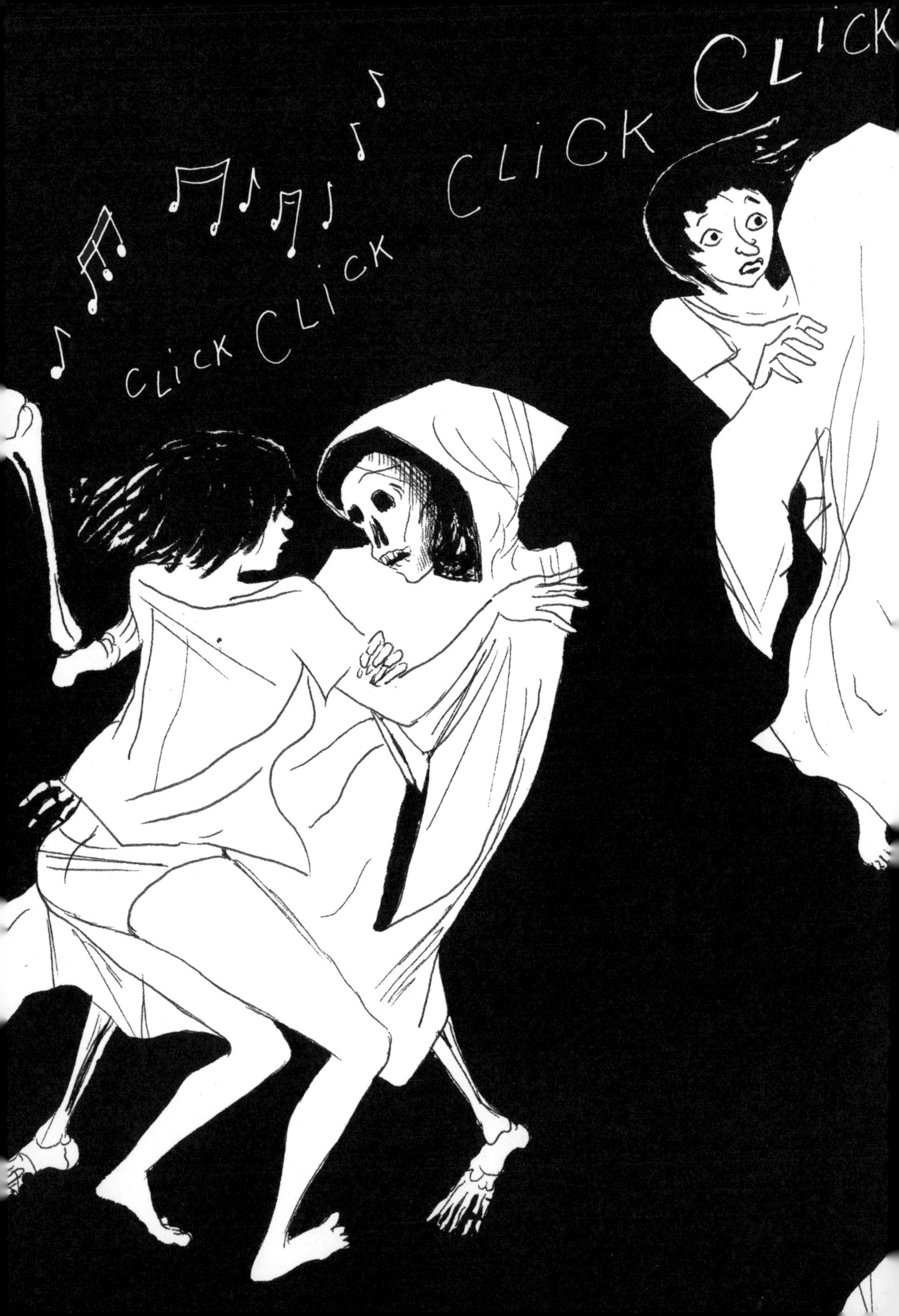
CLICK CLICK
CLICK CLICK

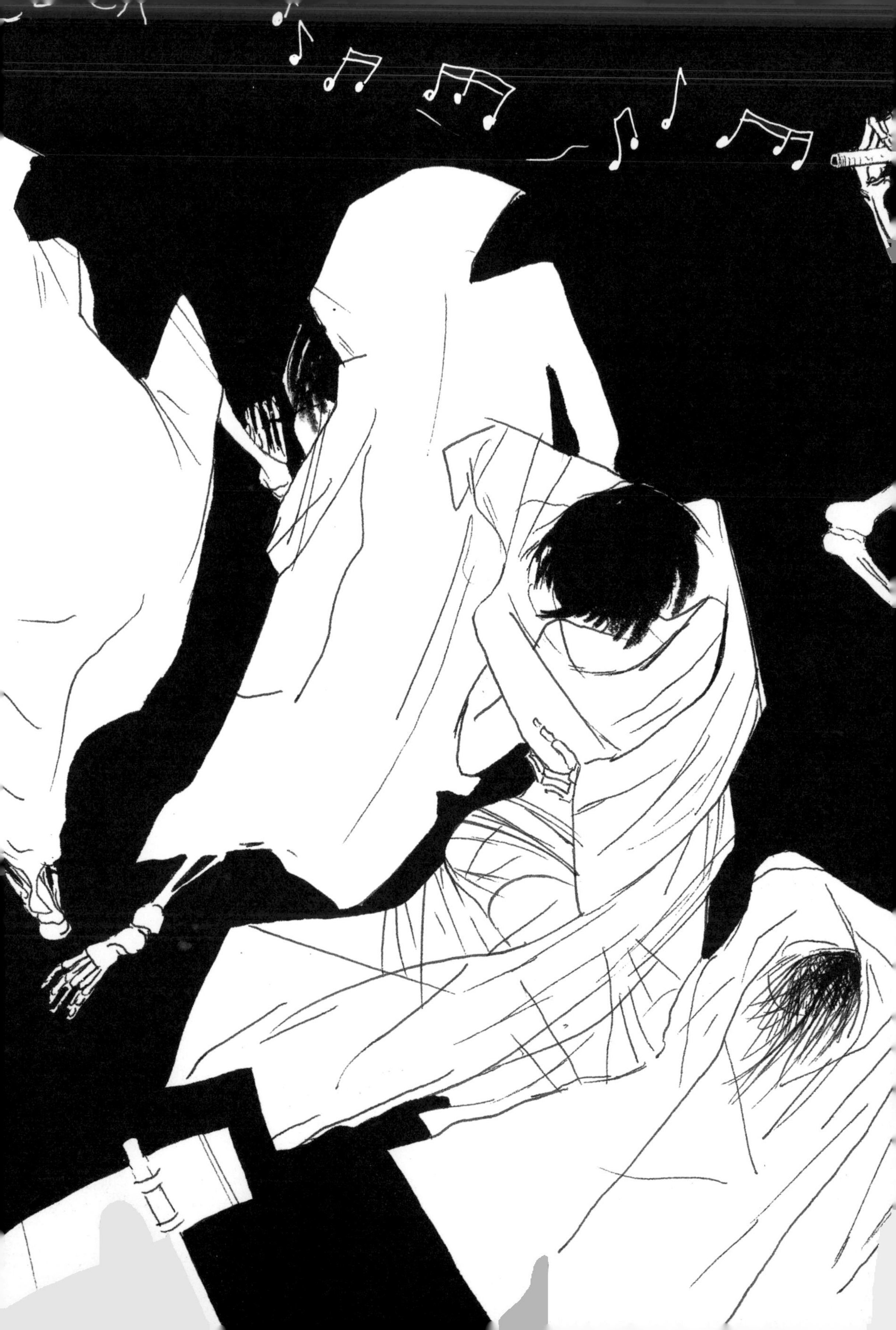

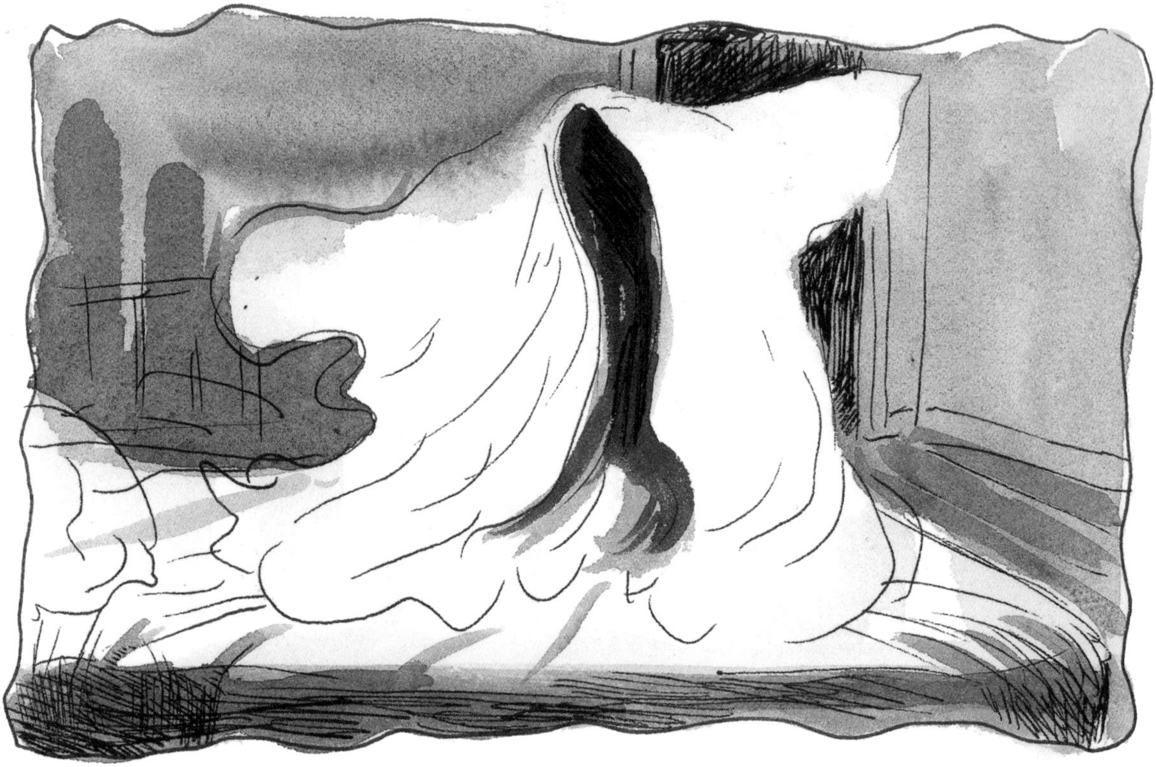

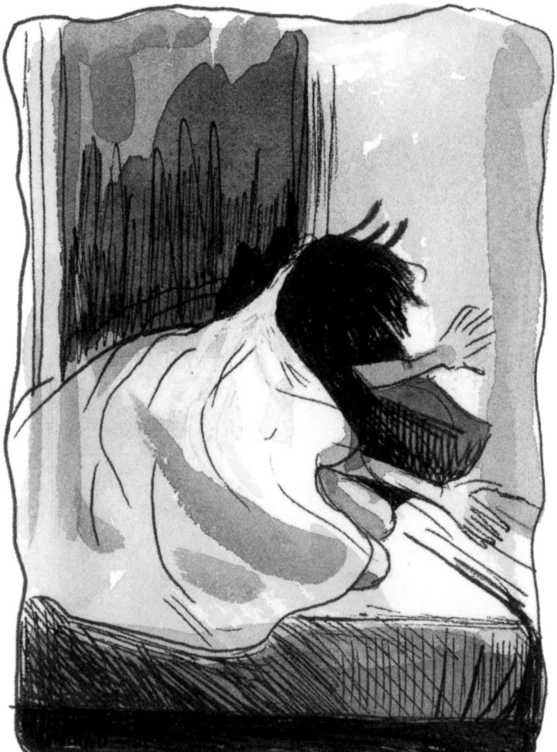

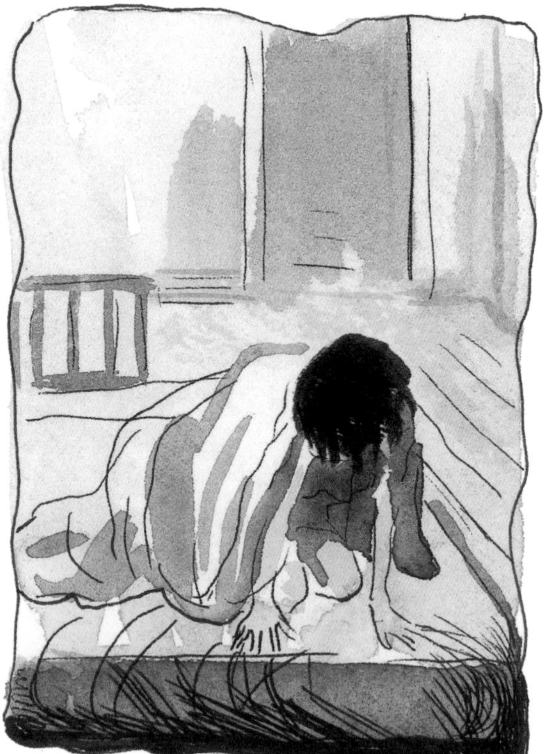

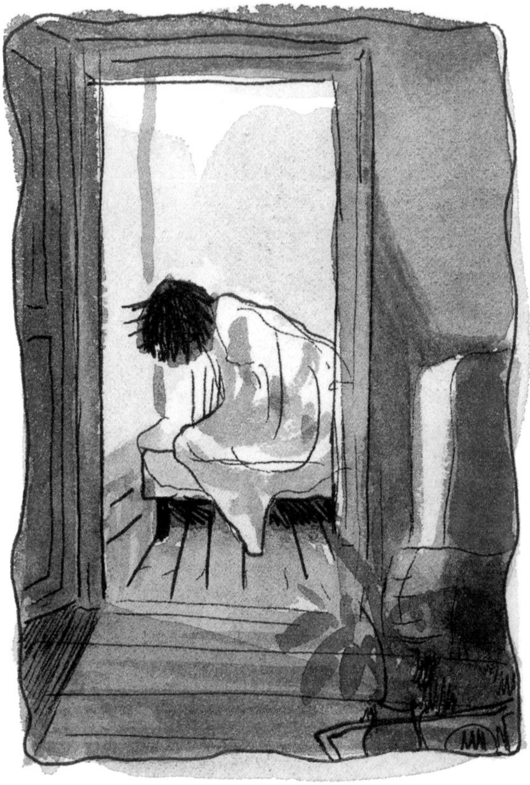

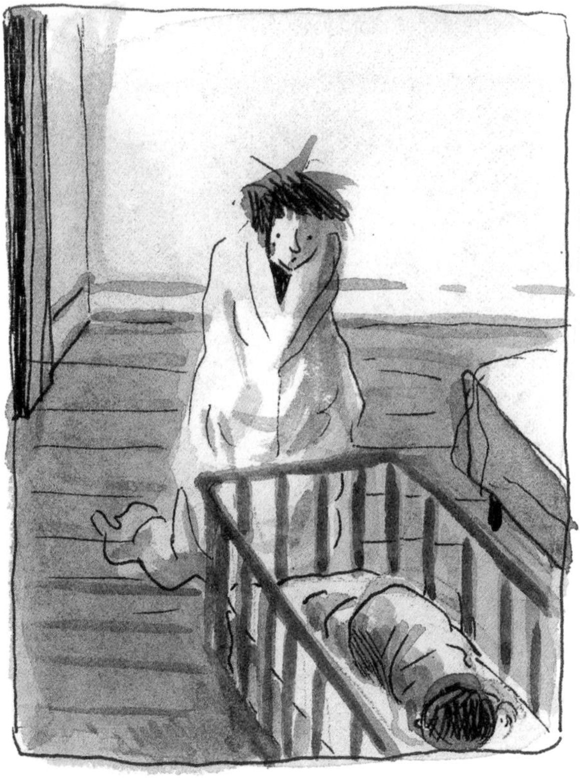

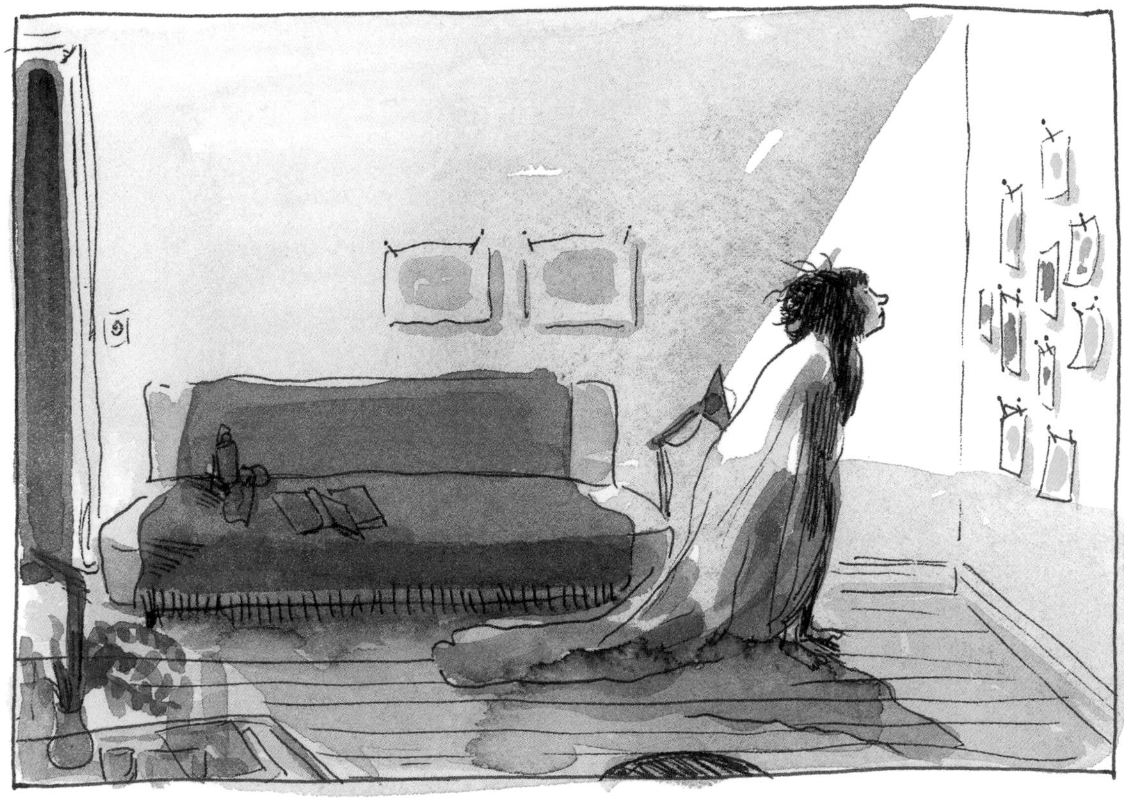

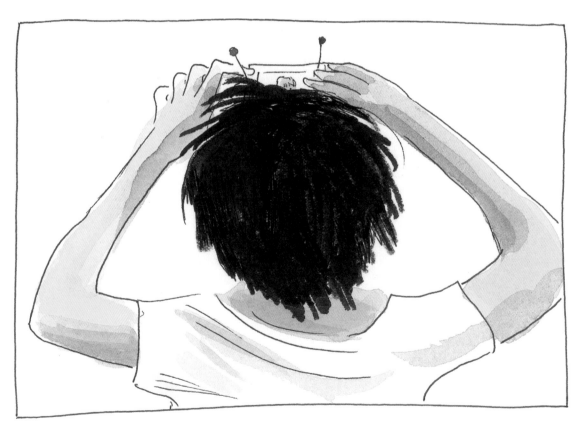

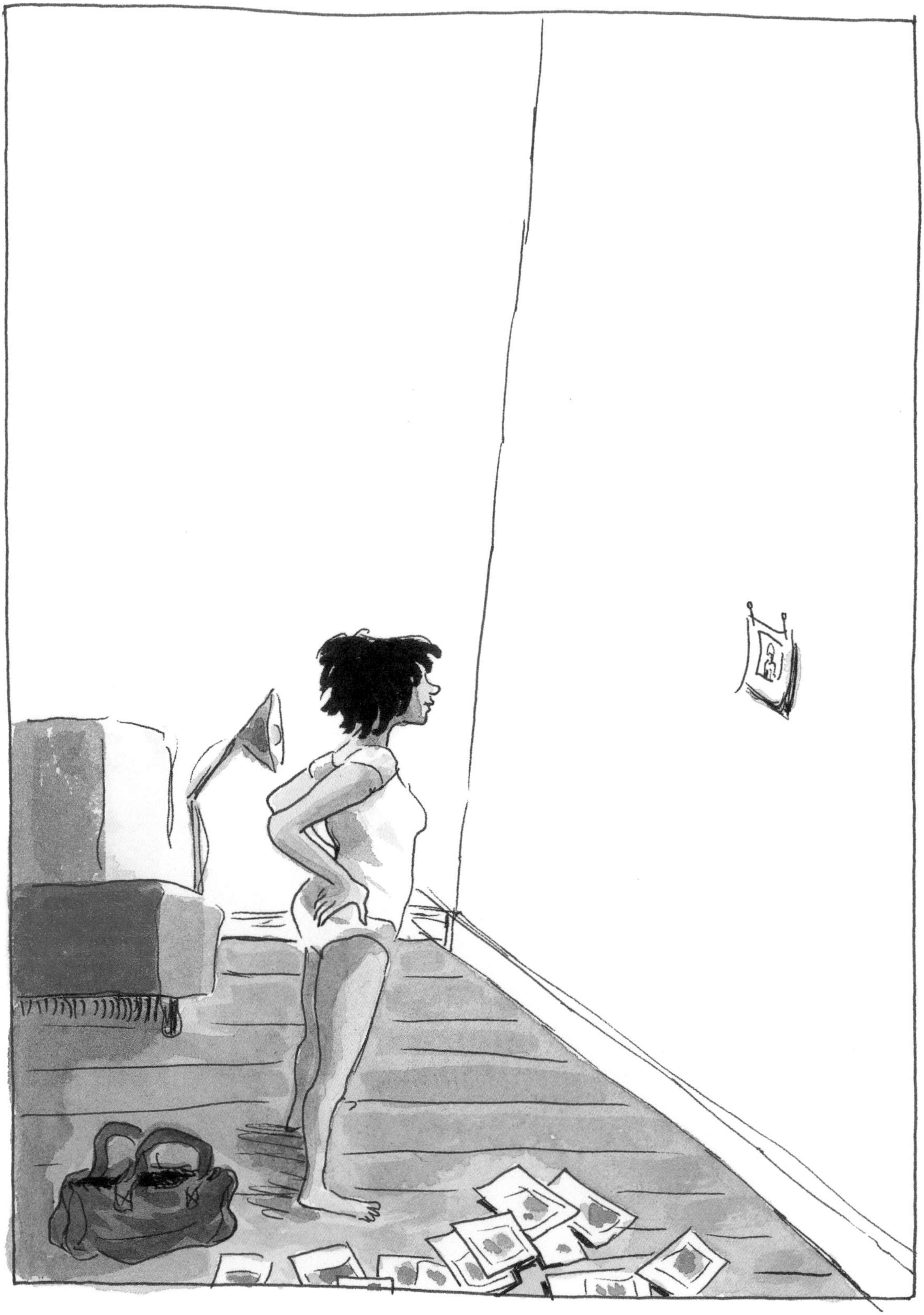

BY BENNO BARNARD, "HET MEER IN MIJ". ARBEIDERSPERS, 1986.
AUTHORIZED TRANSLATION BY WOUTER MULDERS

TAMAR

My inner lake pours from another lake
out into me. It is not comparable in size:
it is a word whose depth is different.
Maybe you drown, but you will always rise.

Can origins be switched? Everything flows
upwards too, since waters are in turn
their source's source. And in between,
from its mouth to its beginning, a river goes.

My lake is not below. Below is the reflection
of the sun, the sparkle of the past. Your name,
in water written, can now still be seen.

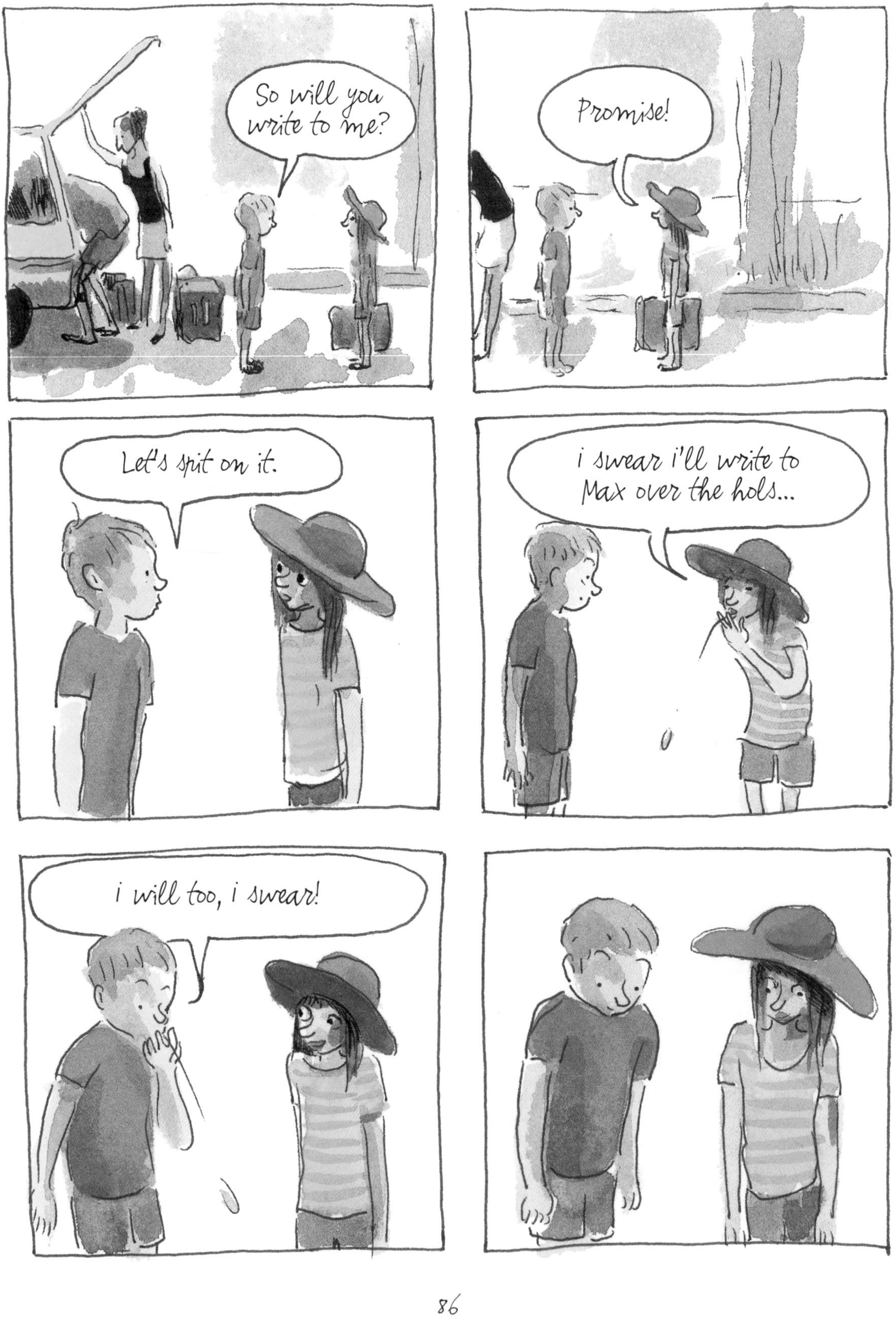
So will you write to me?
Promise!
Let's spit on it.
i swear i'll write to Max over the hols...
i will too, i swear!

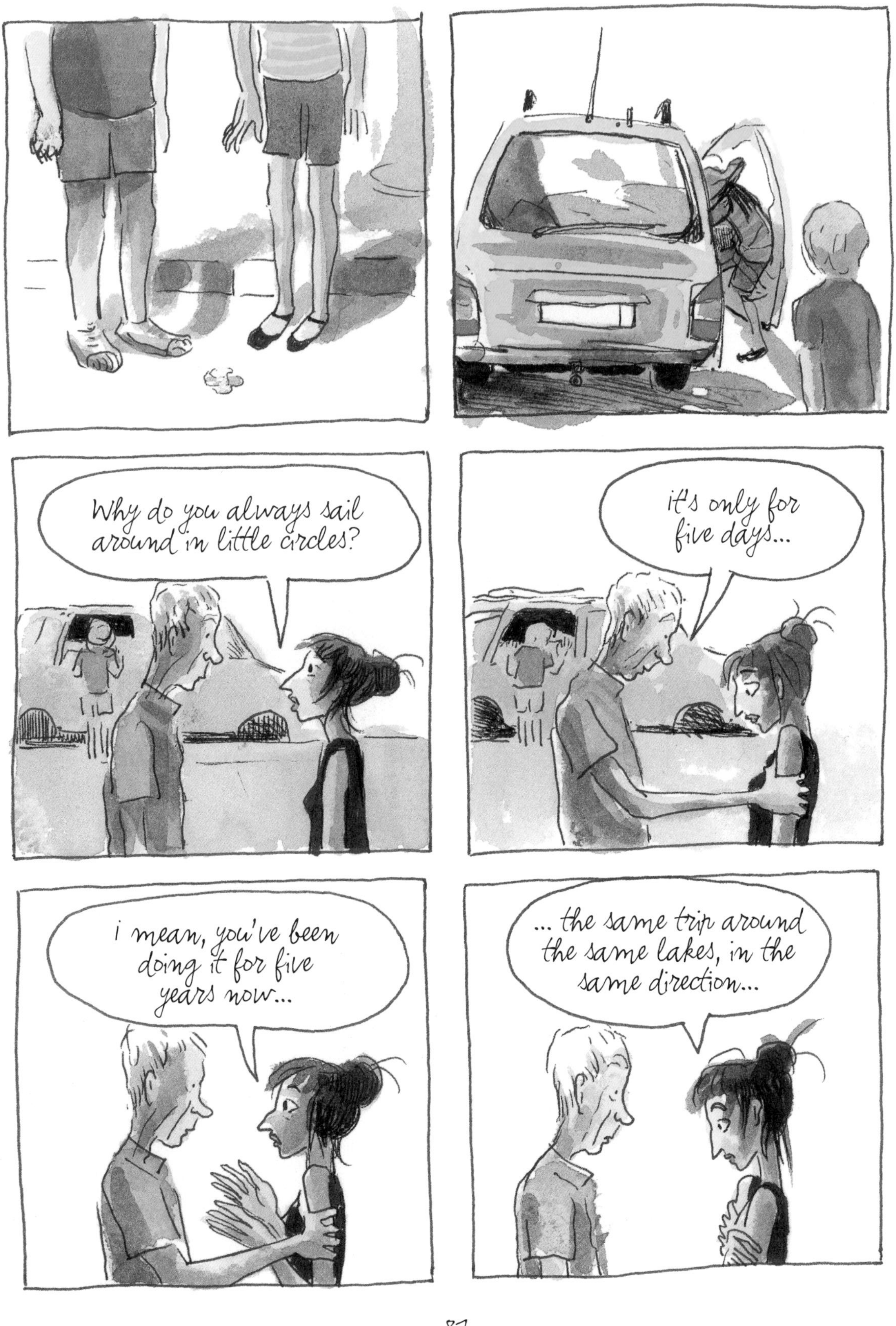
Why do you always sail around in little circles?
it's only for five days...
i mean, you've been doing it for five years now...
... the same trip around the same lakes, in the same direction...

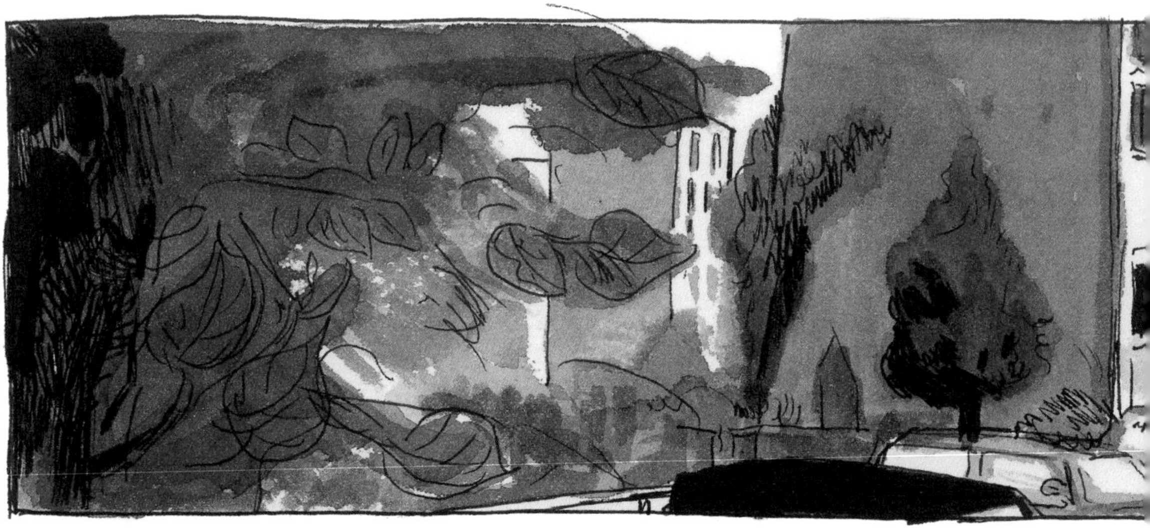

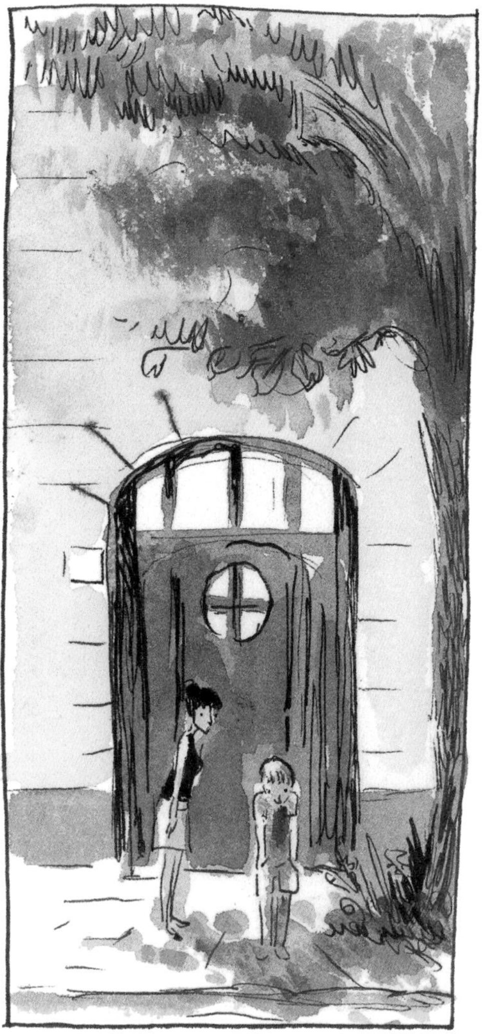

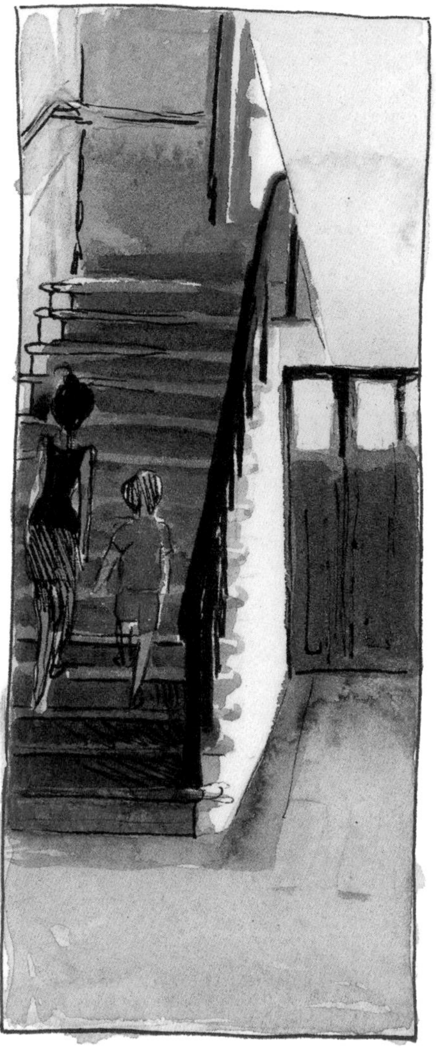

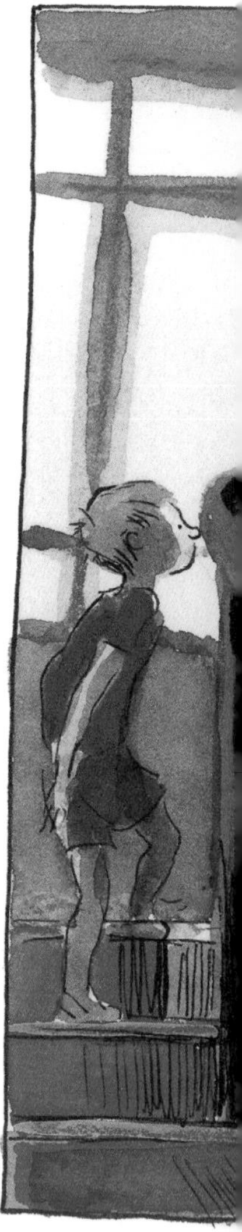

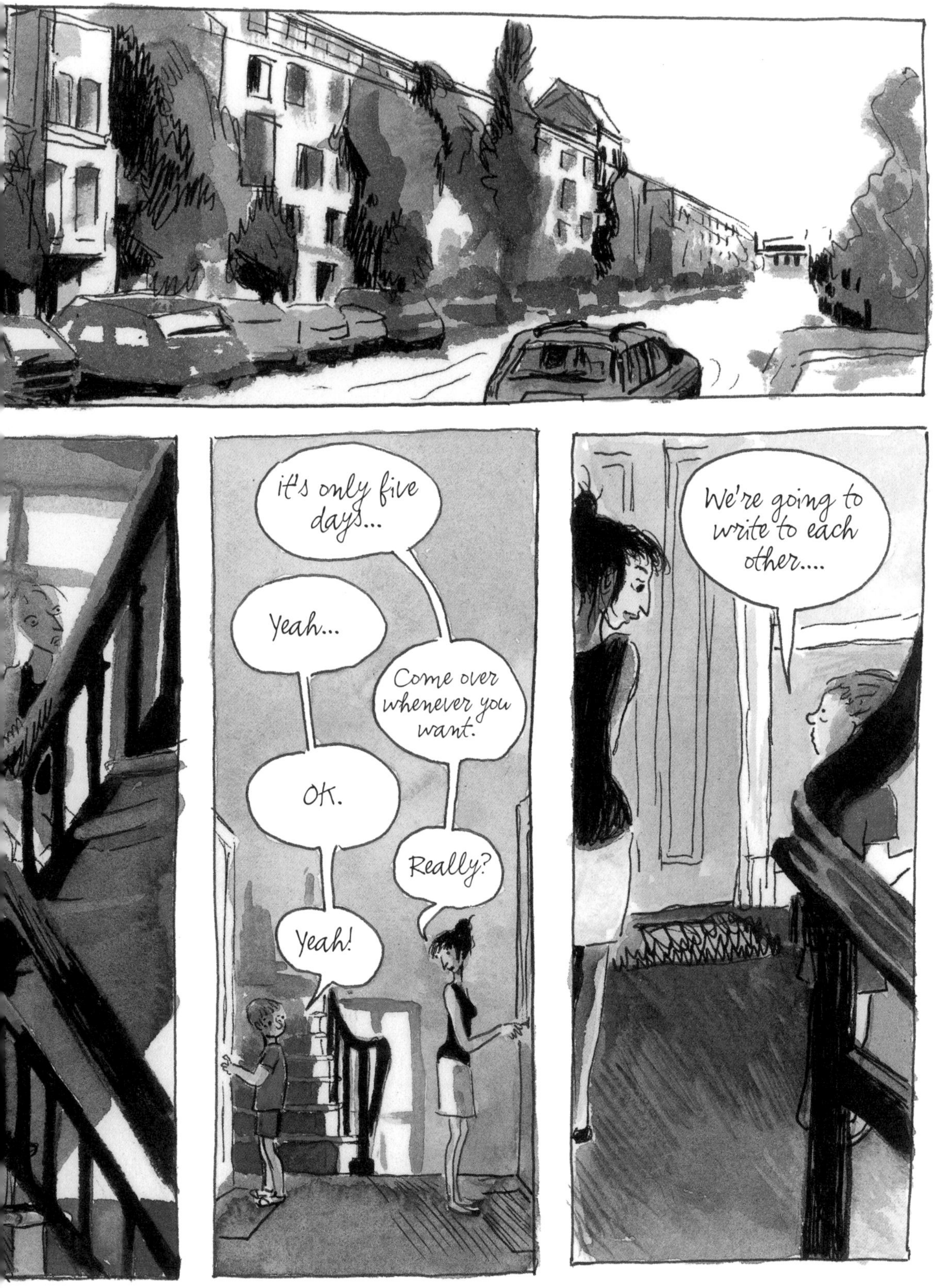
it's only five days...
Yeah...
Come over whenever you want.
OK.
Really?
Yeah!
We're going to write to each other....

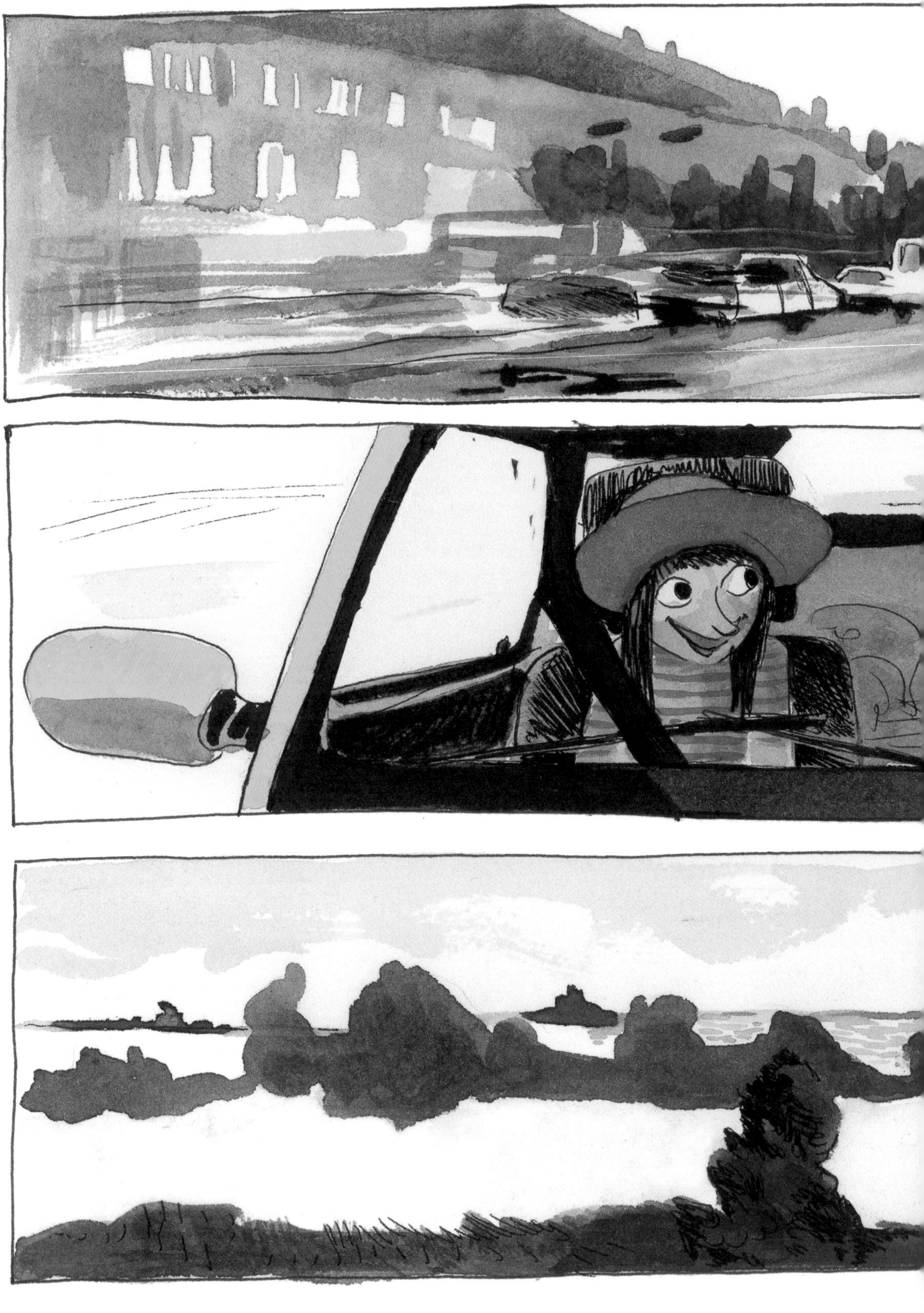

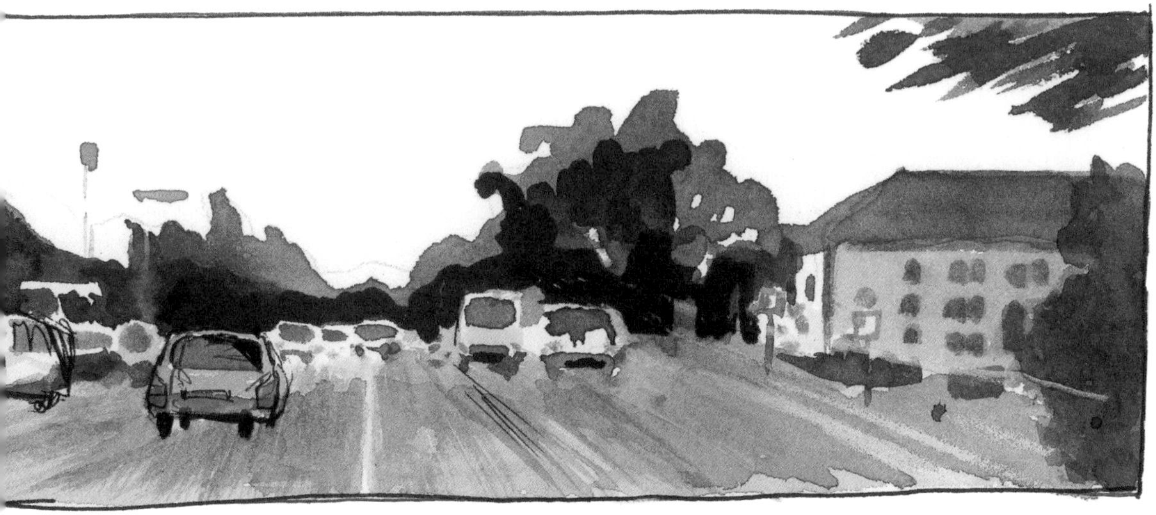

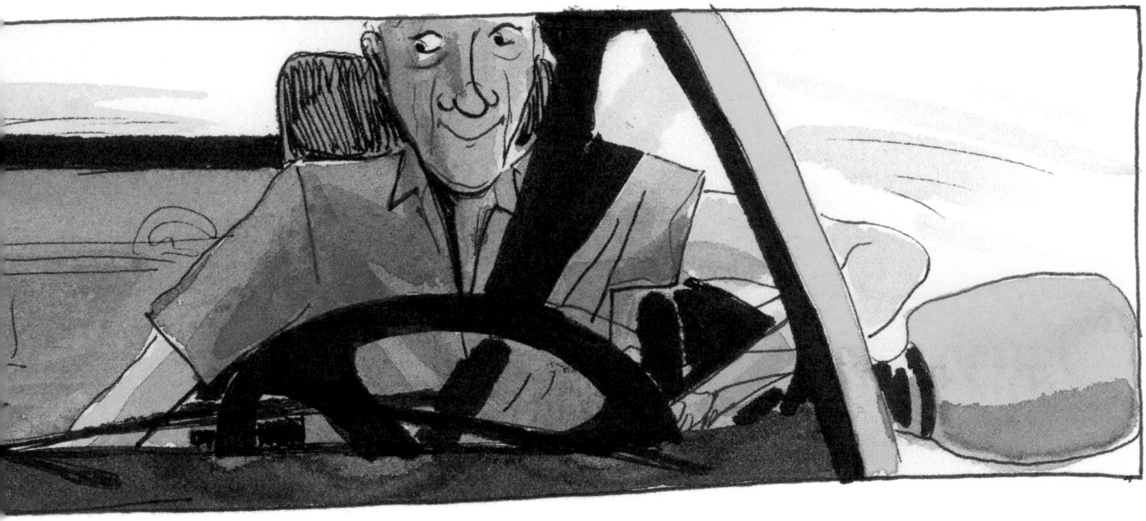

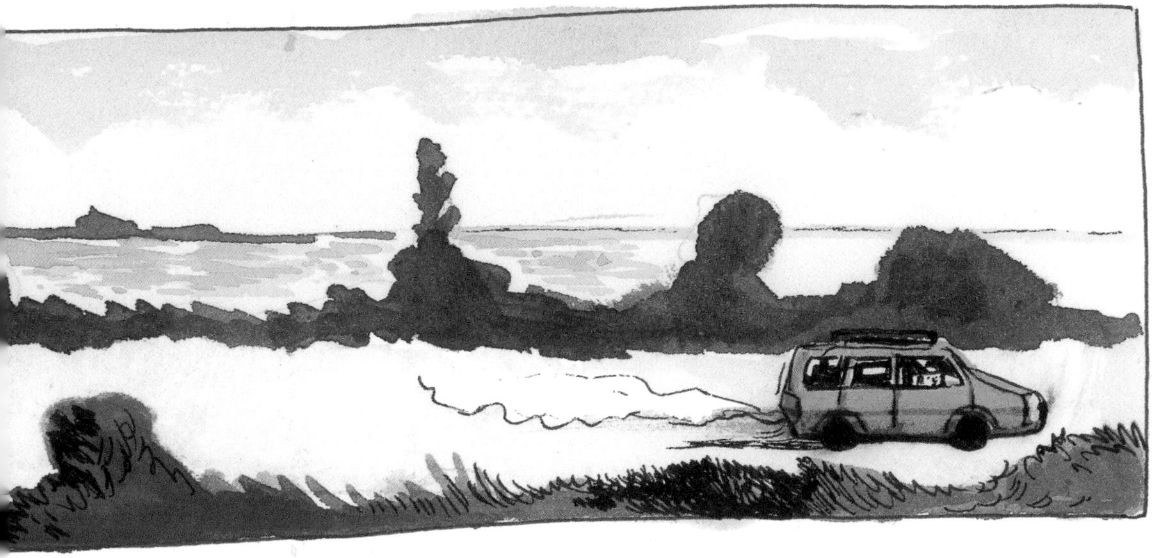

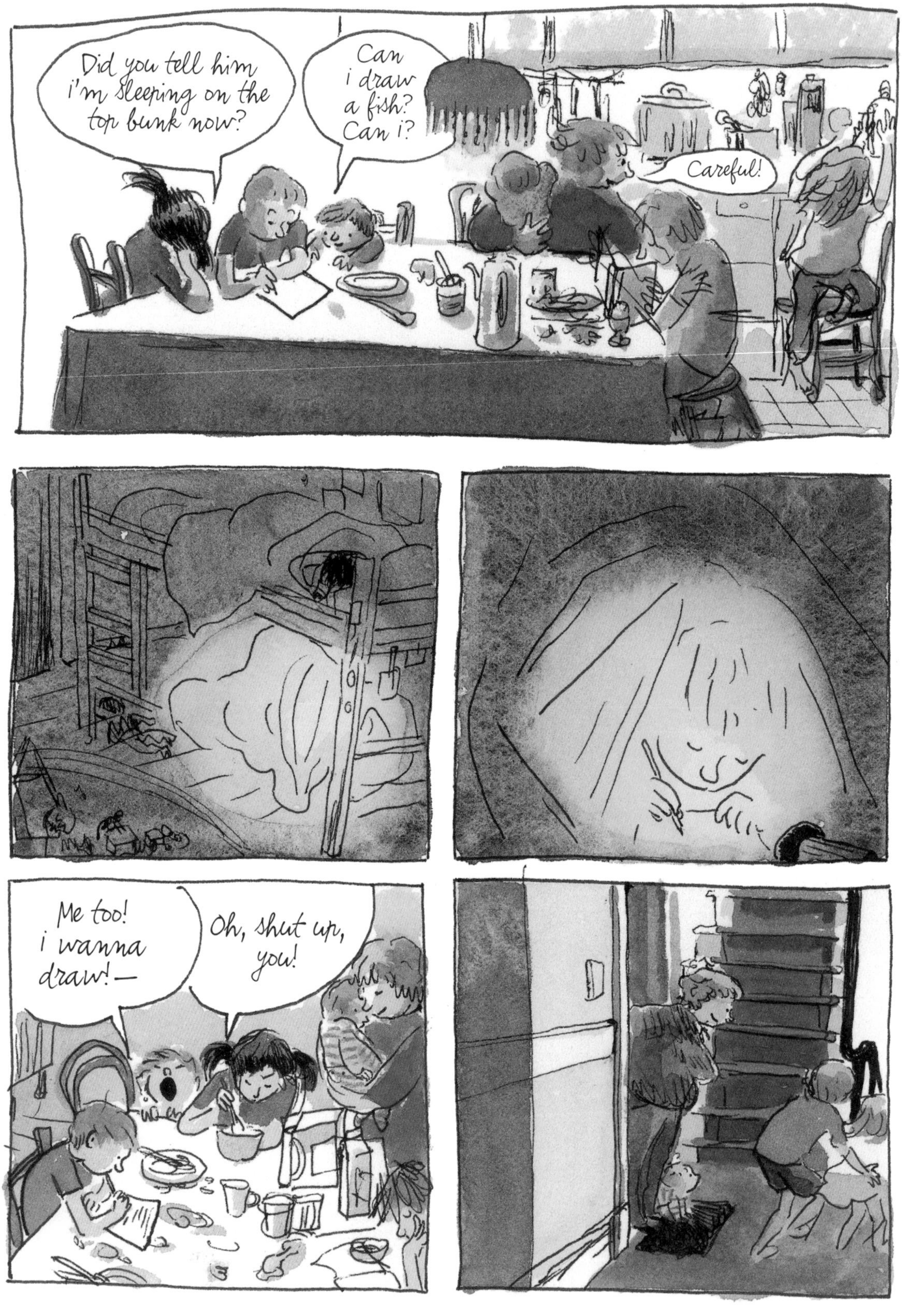
Did you tell him i'm sleeping on the top bunk now?
Can i draw a fish? Can i?
Careful!
Me too! i wanna draw!—
Oh, shut up, you!

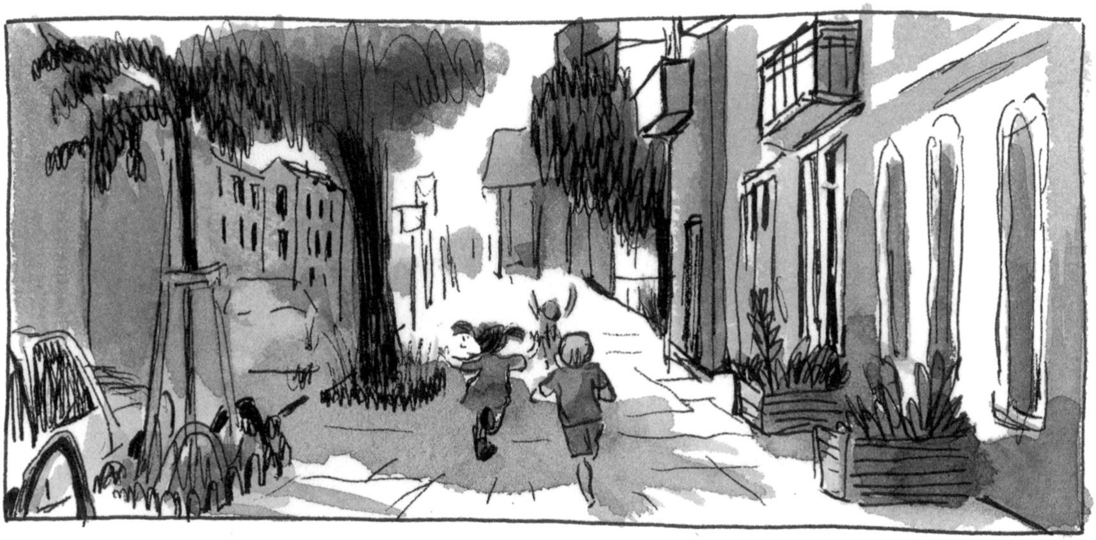

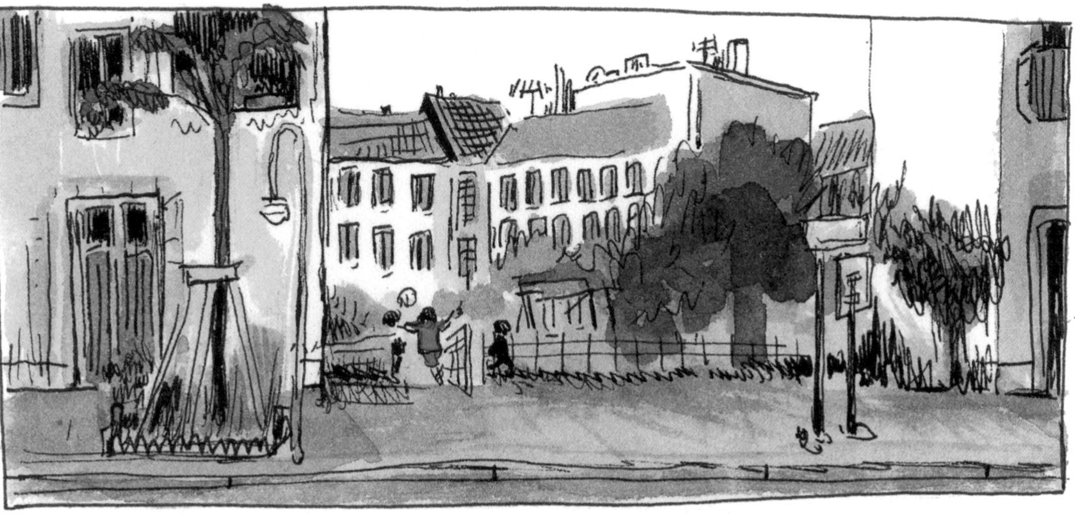

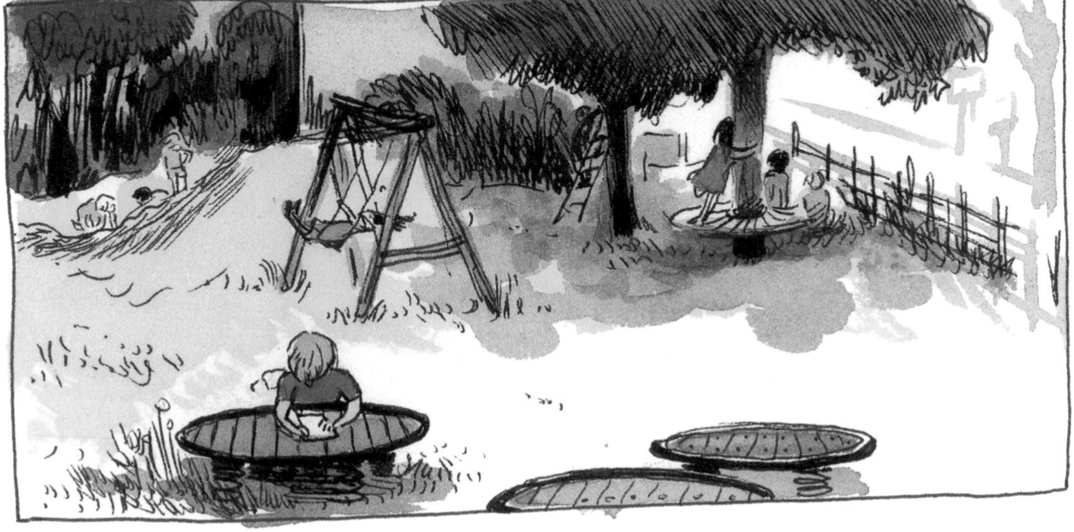

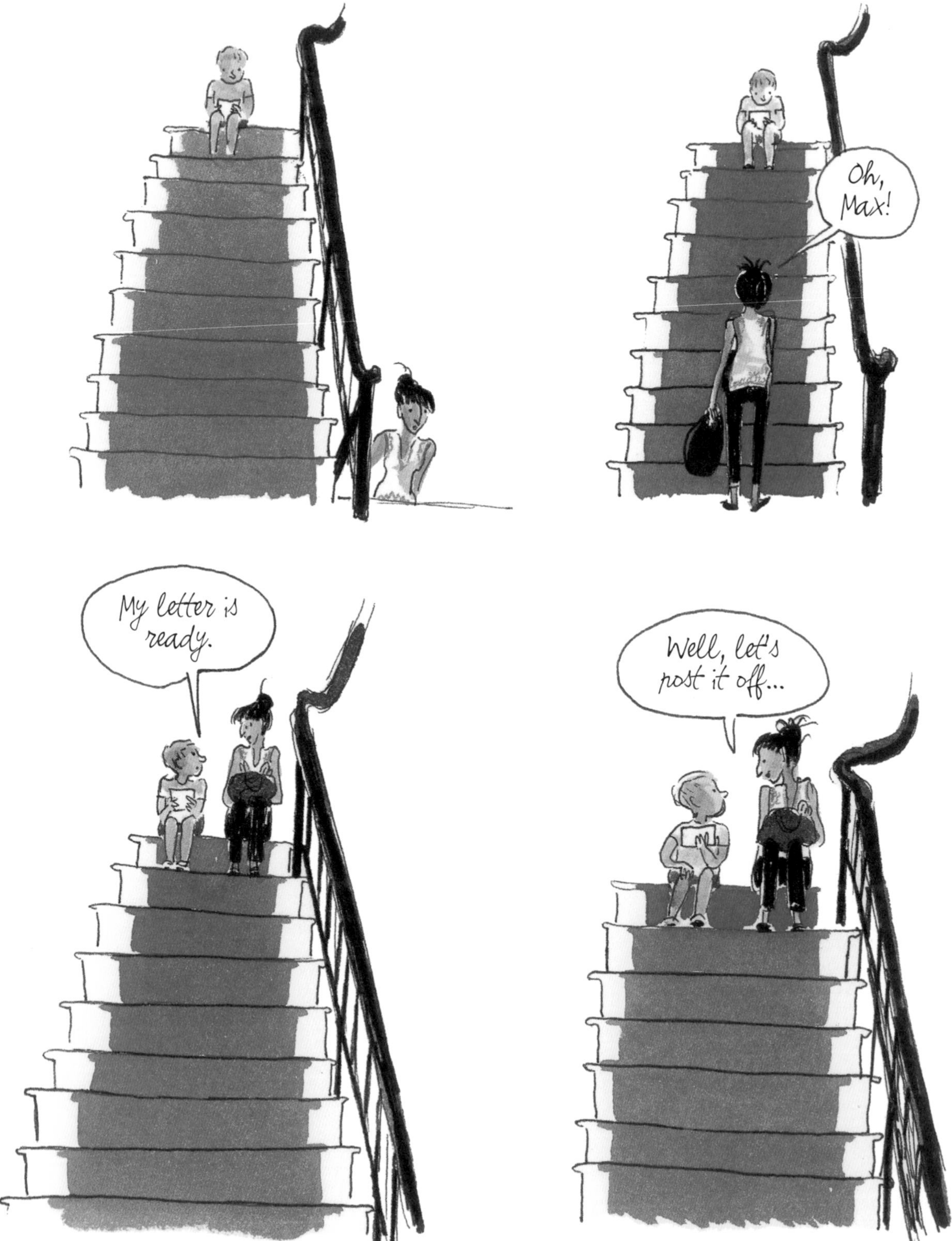
Oh, Max!
My letter is ready.
Well, let's post it off...

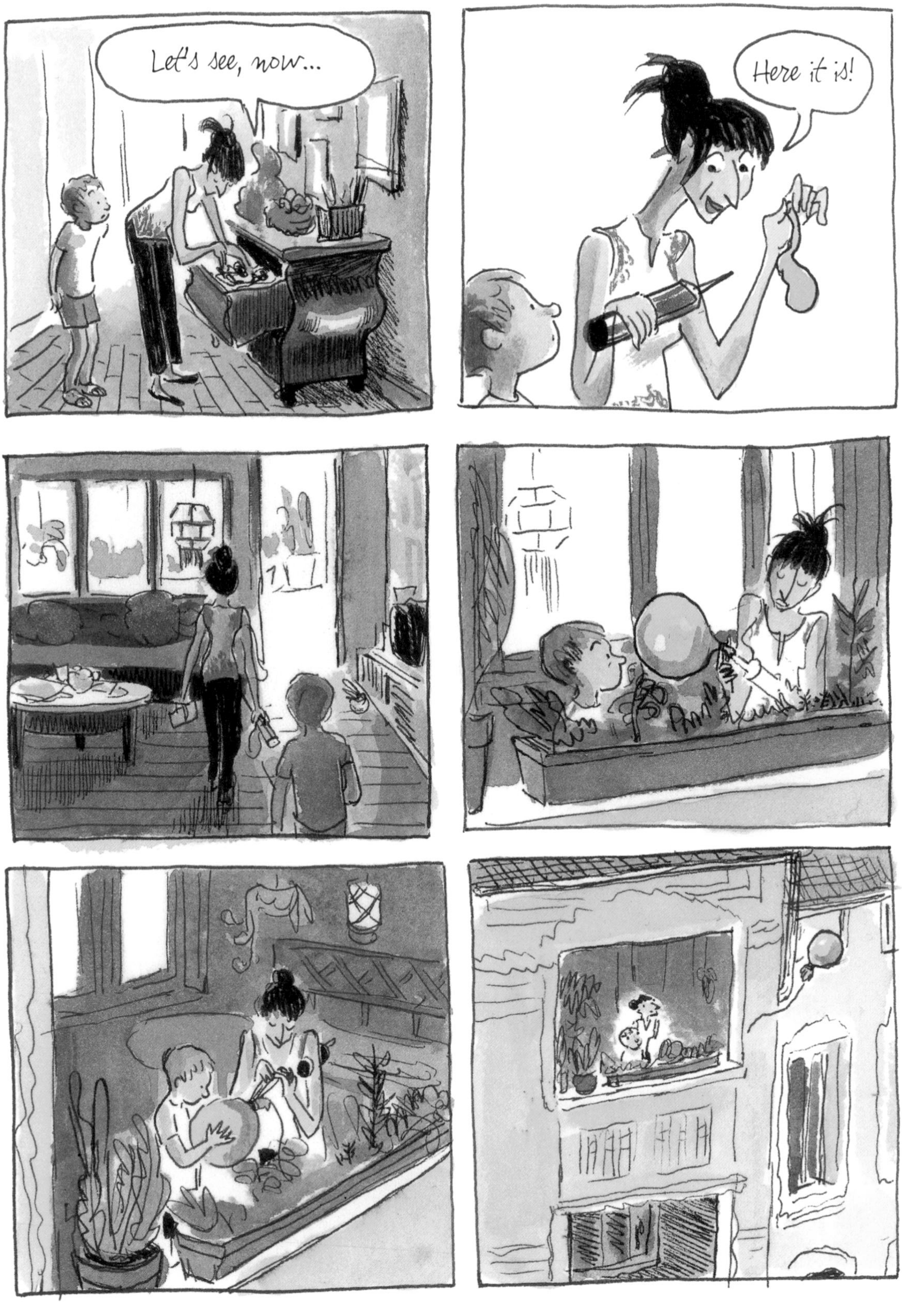
Let's see, now...
Here it is!

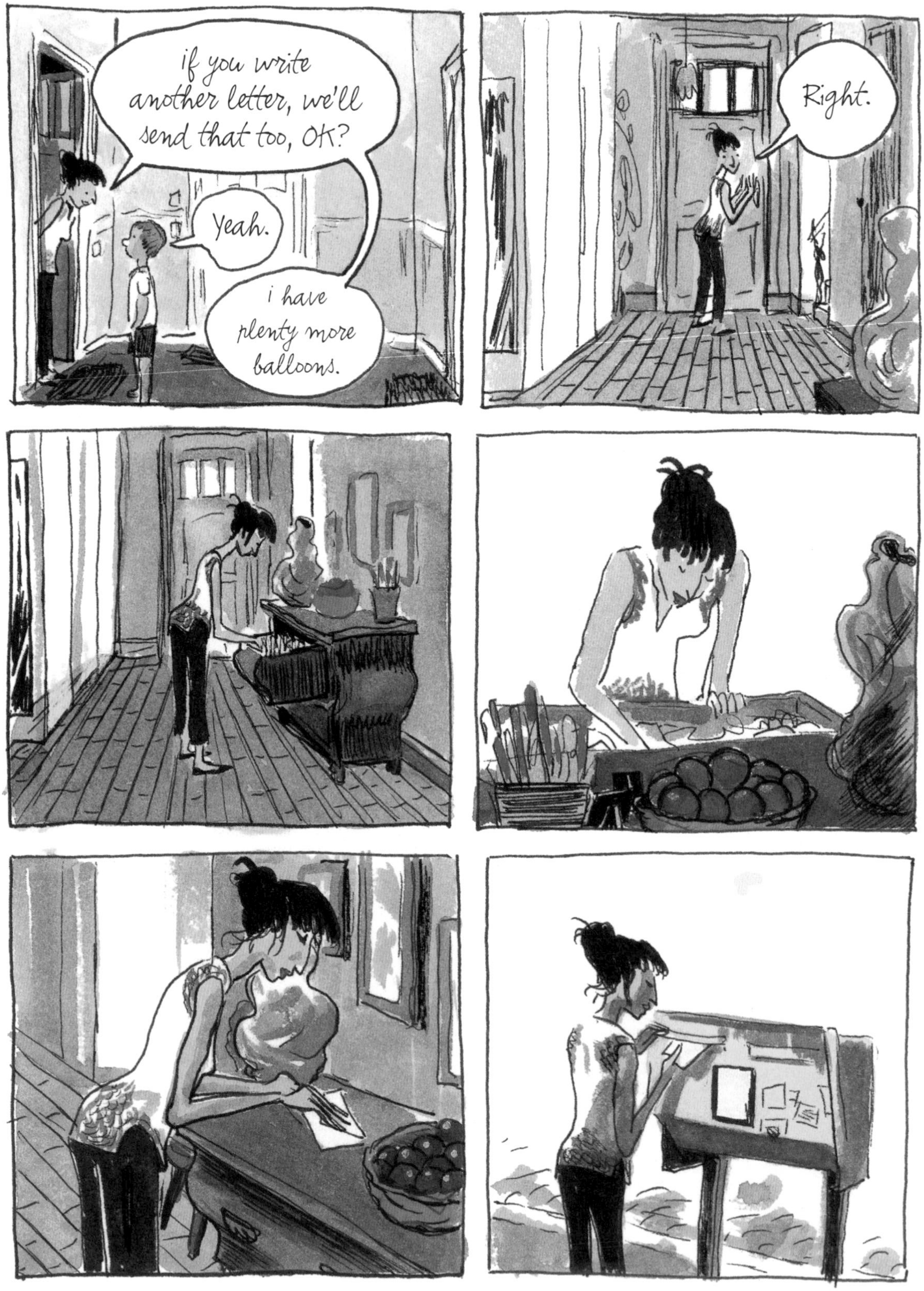
if you write another letter, we'll send that too, OK?
Yeah.
i have plenty more balloons.
Right.

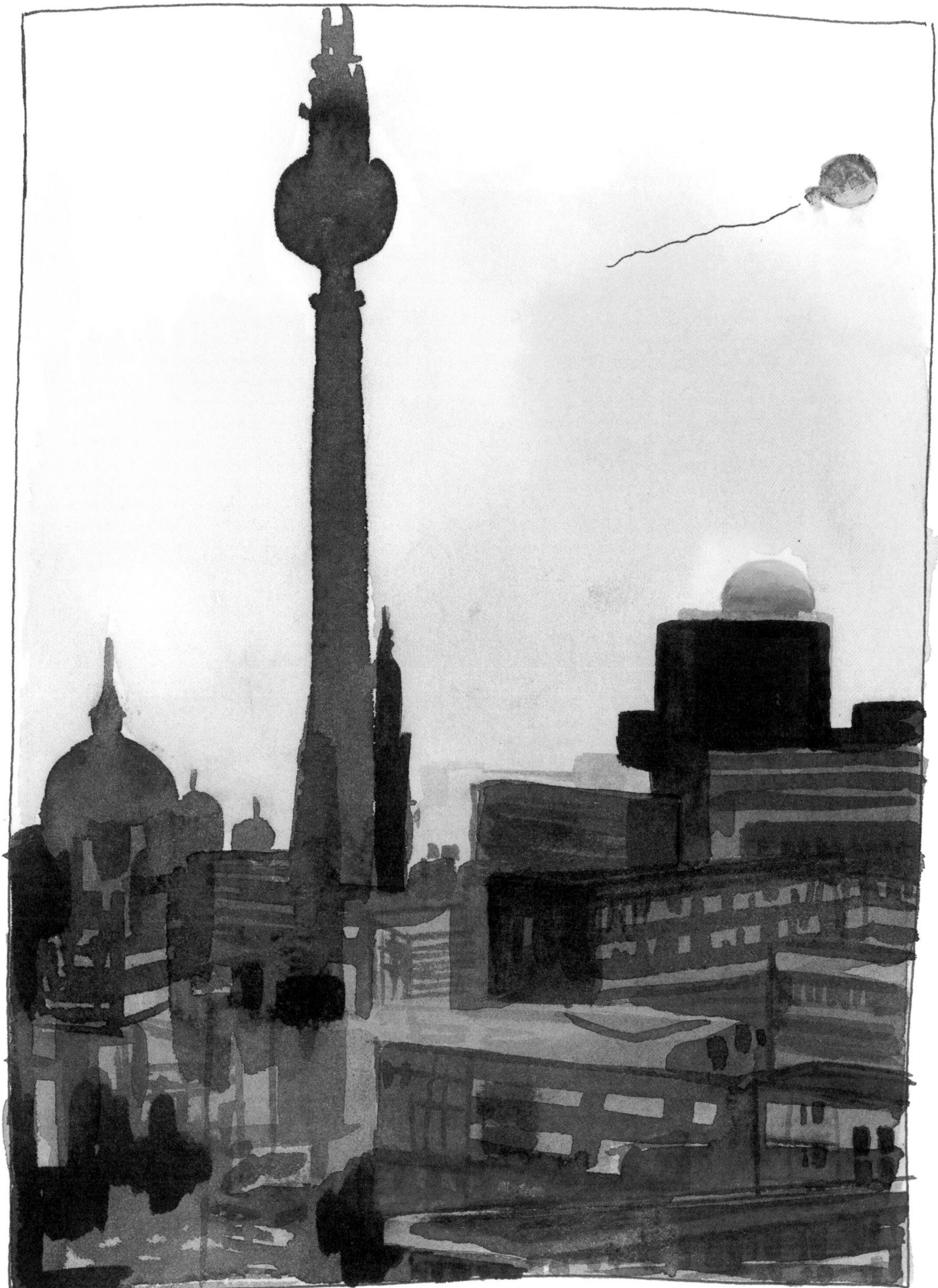

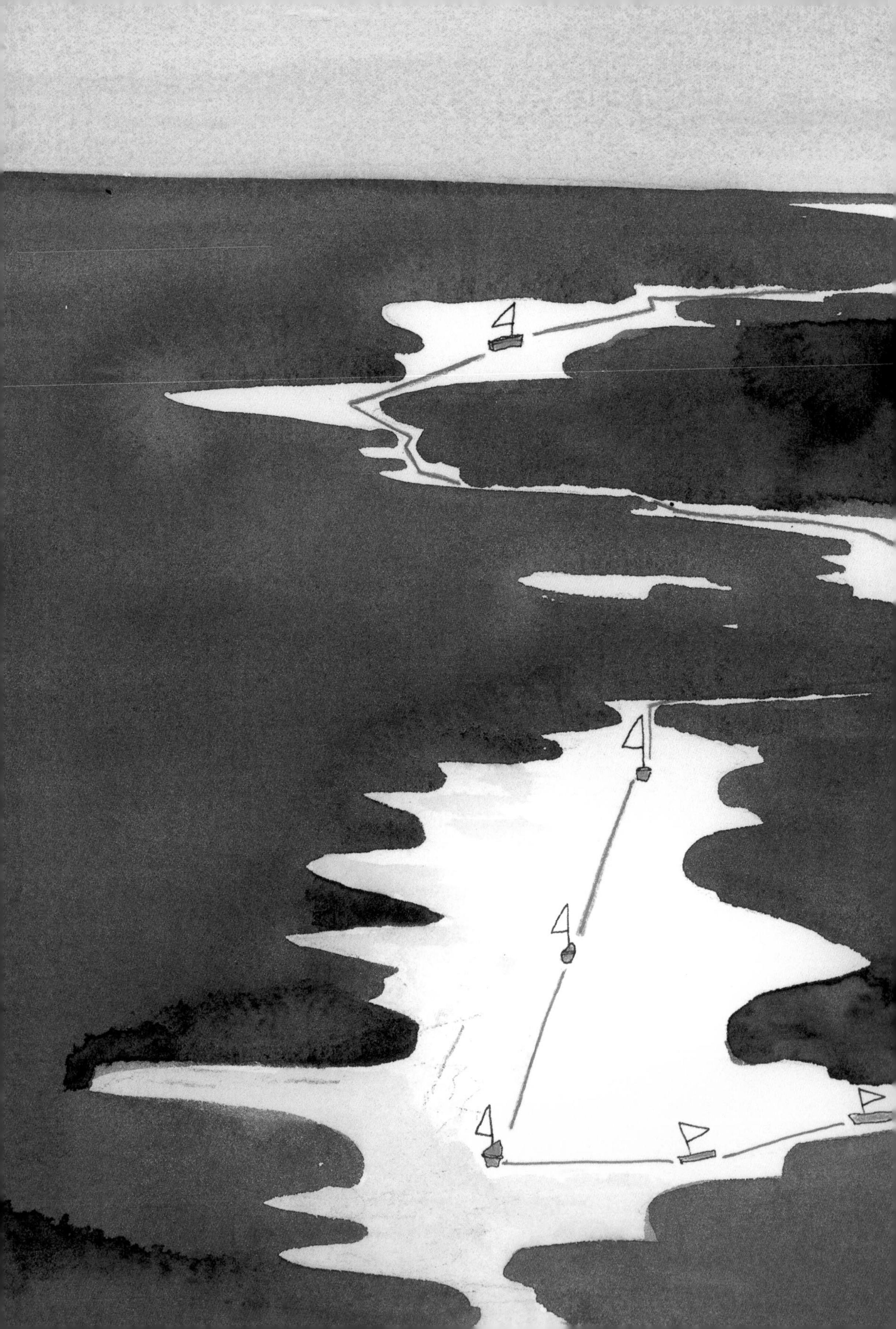

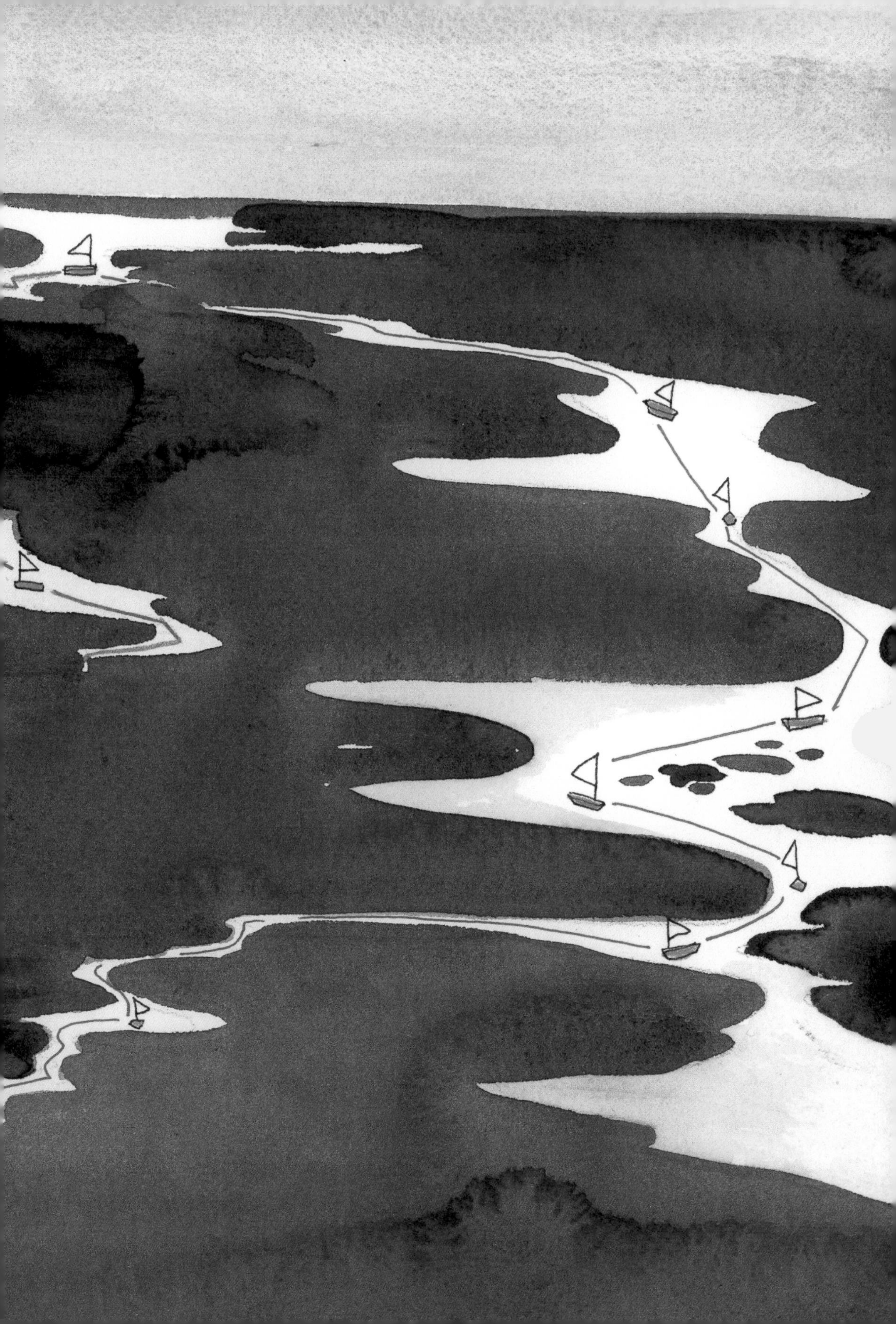

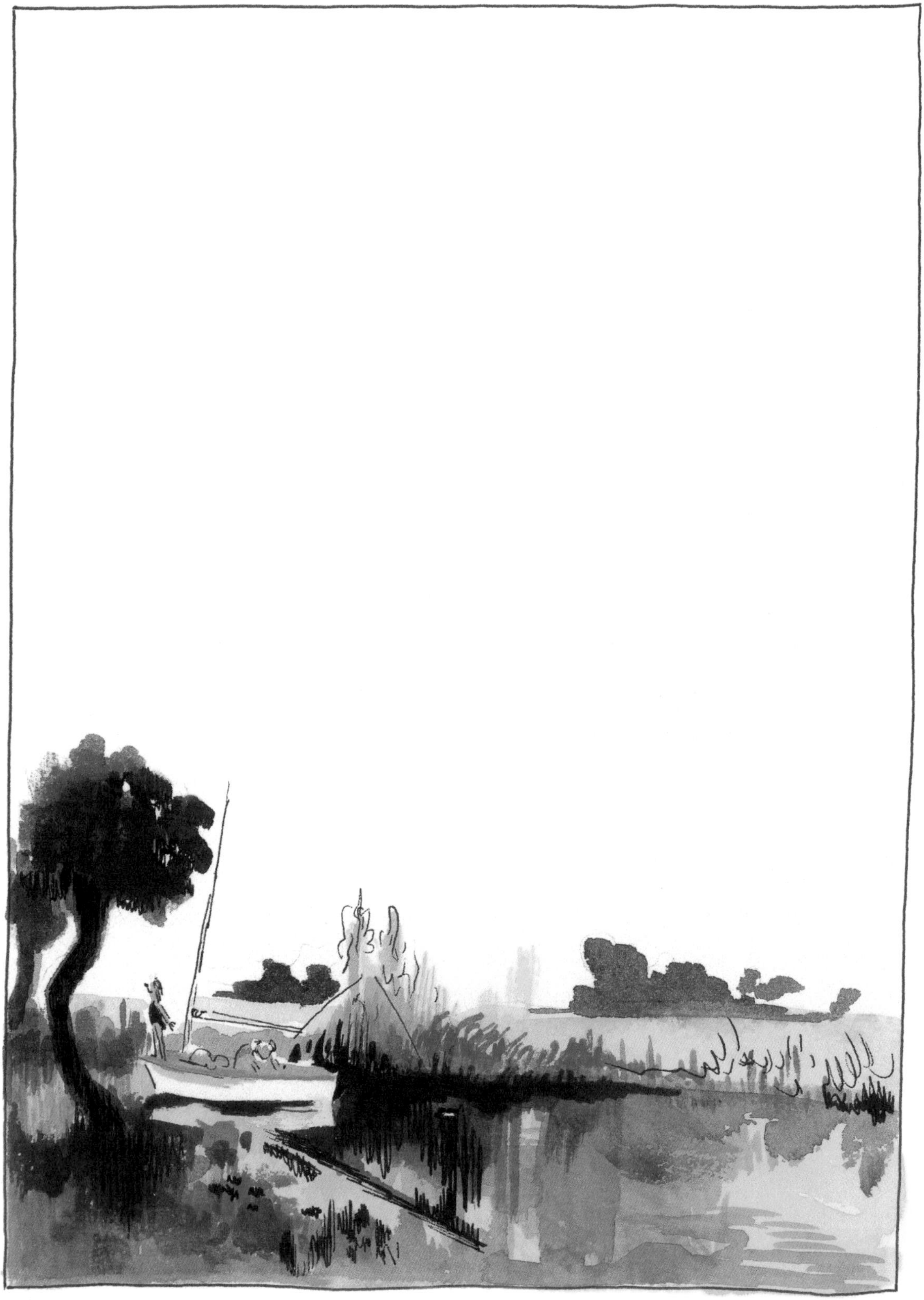

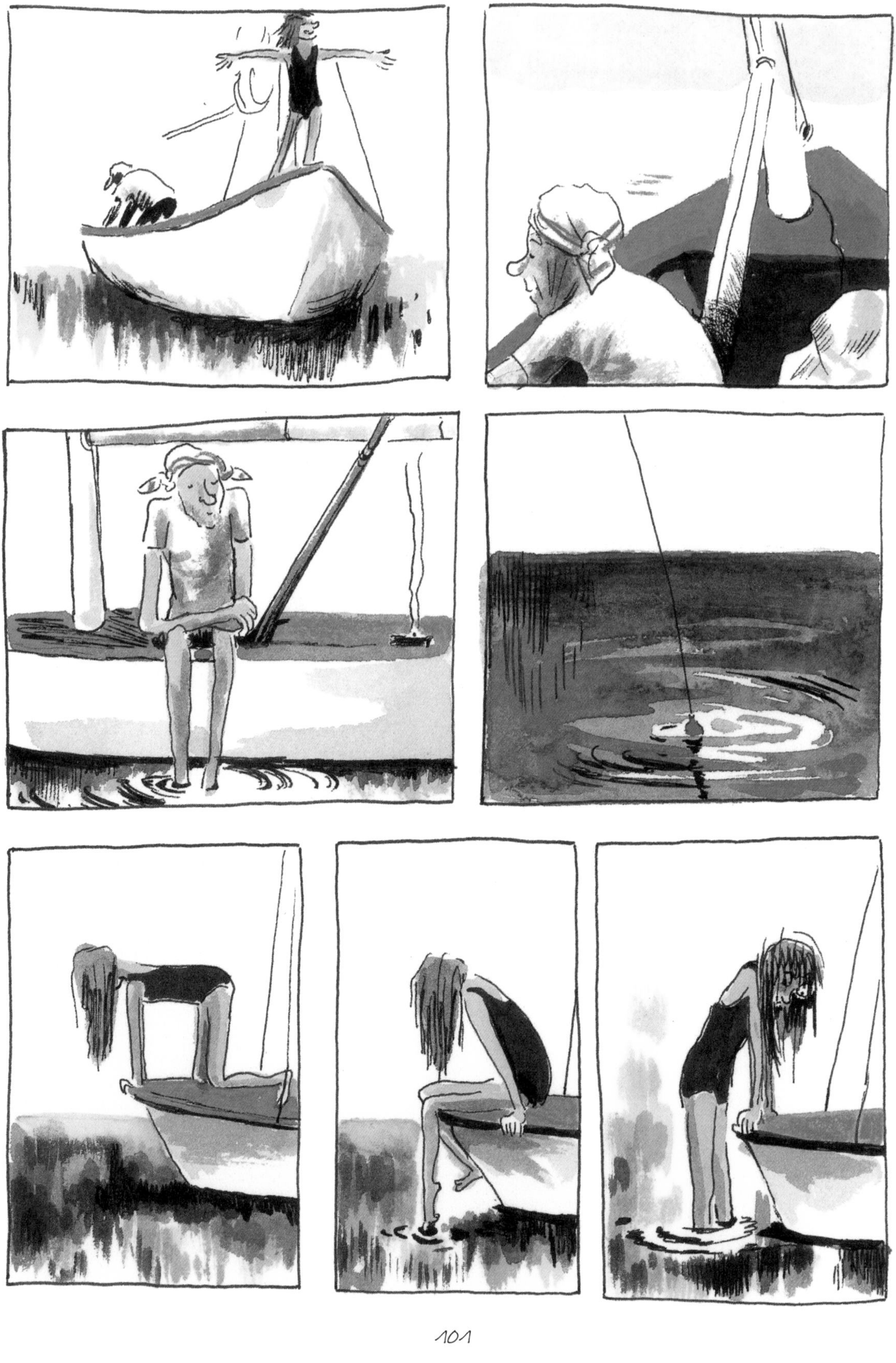

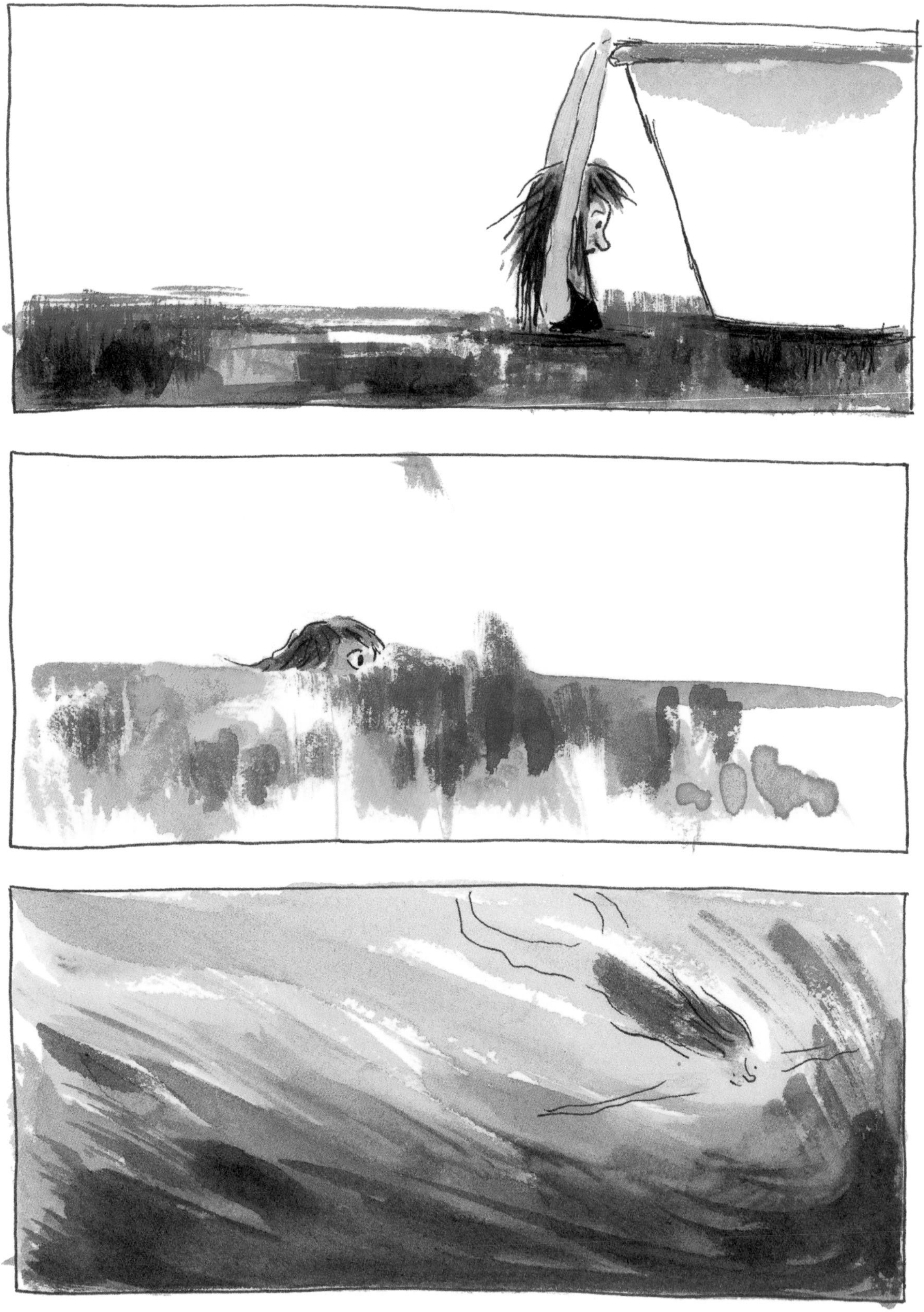

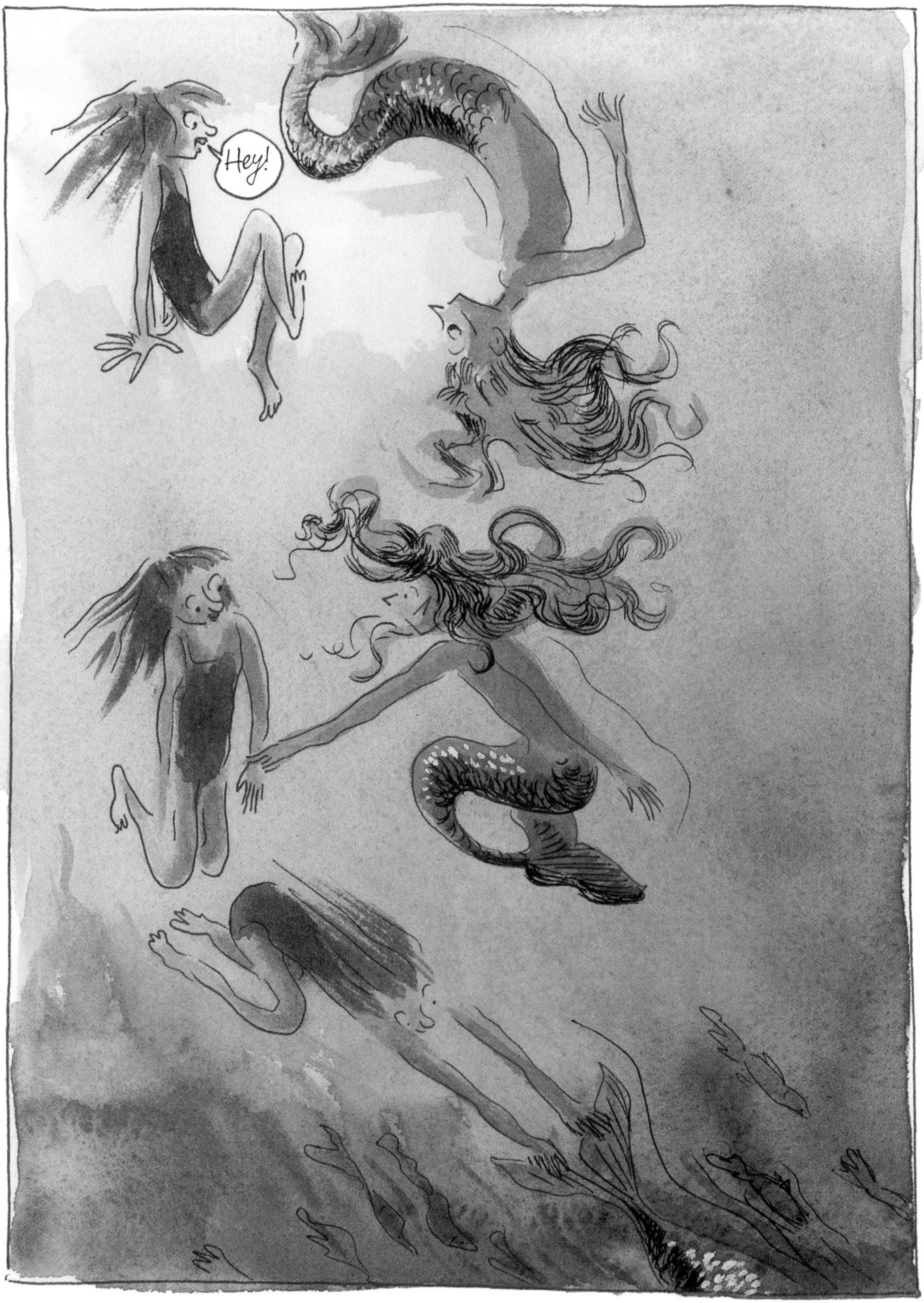
Hey!

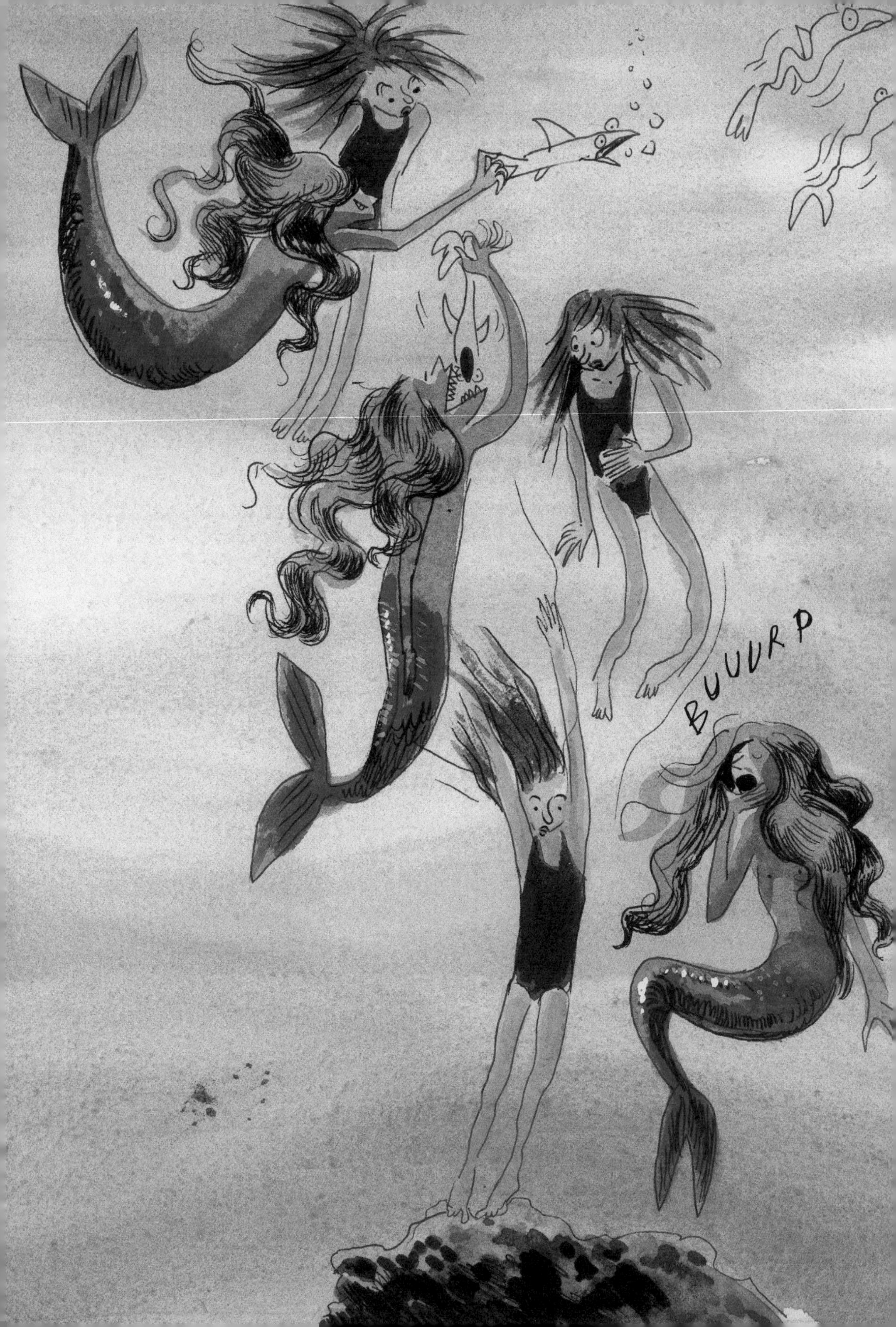
BUUURP

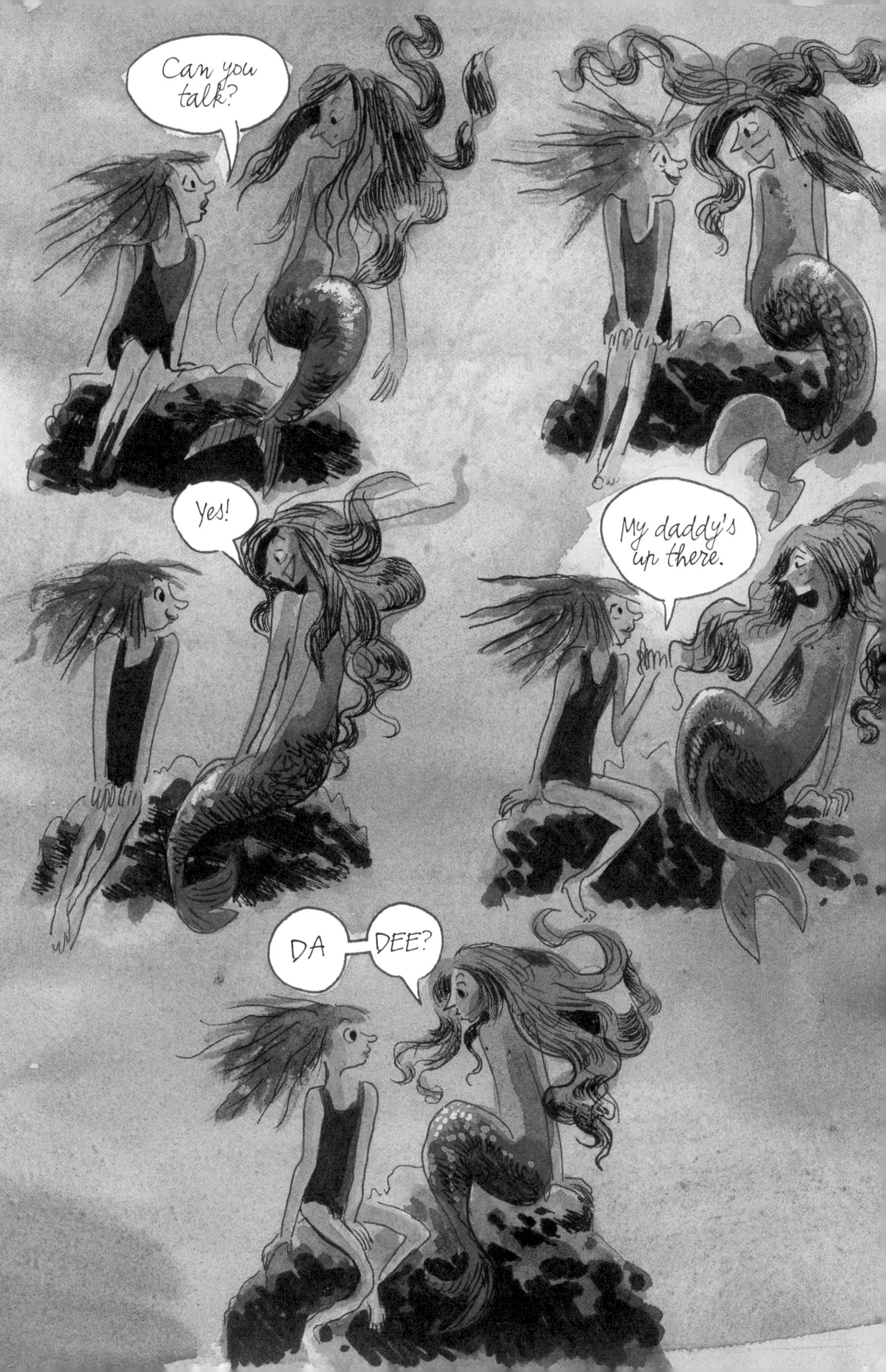
Can you talk?
Yes!
My daddy's up there.
DA
DEE?

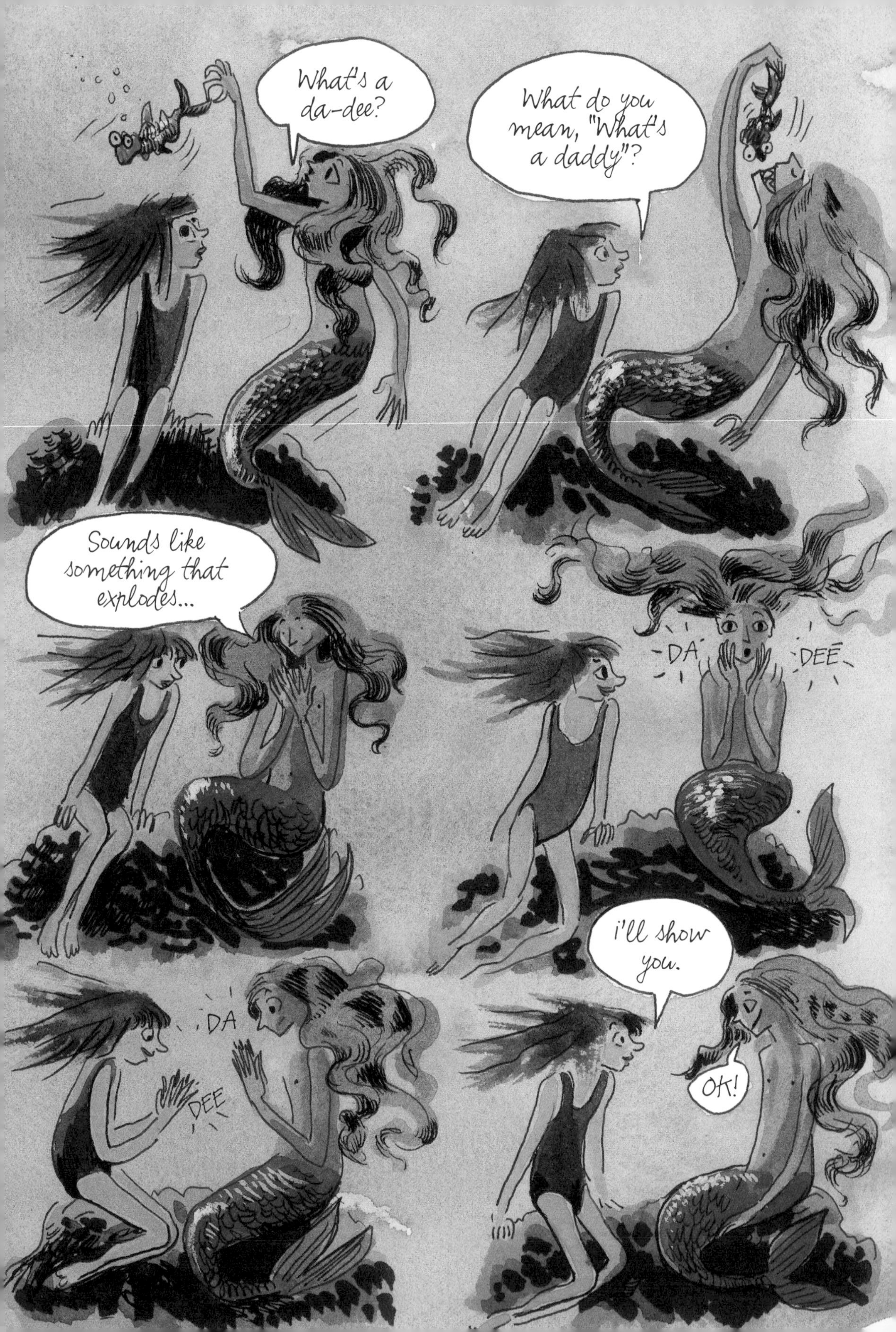
What's a da-dee?
What do you mean, "What's a daddy"?
Sounds like something that explodes...
DA
DEE
DA
DEE
i'll show you.
OK!

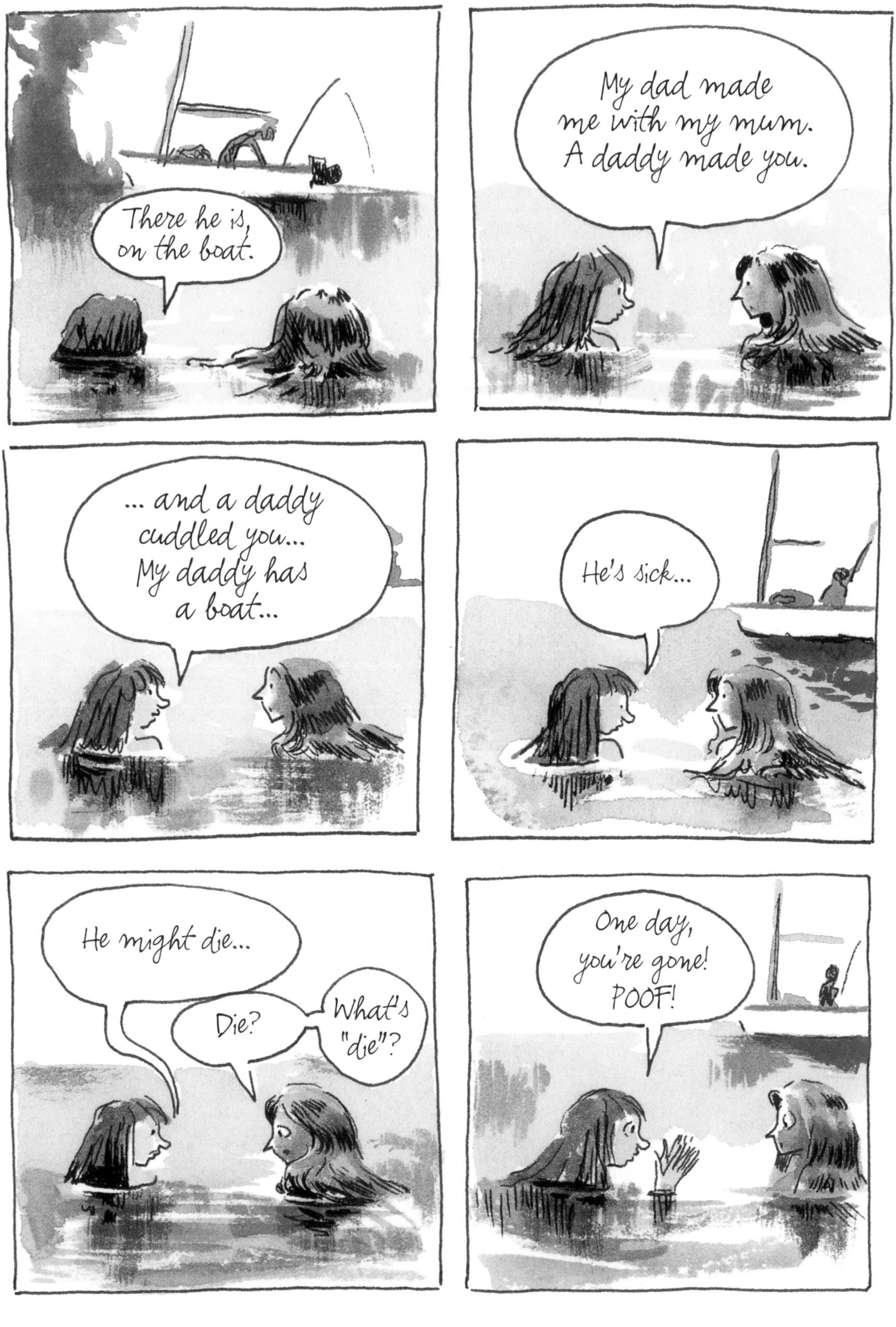
There he is, on the boat.
My dad made me with my mum. A daddy made you.
... and a daddy cuddled you... My daddy has a boat...
He's sick...
He might die...
Die?
What's "die"?
One day, you're gone! POOF!

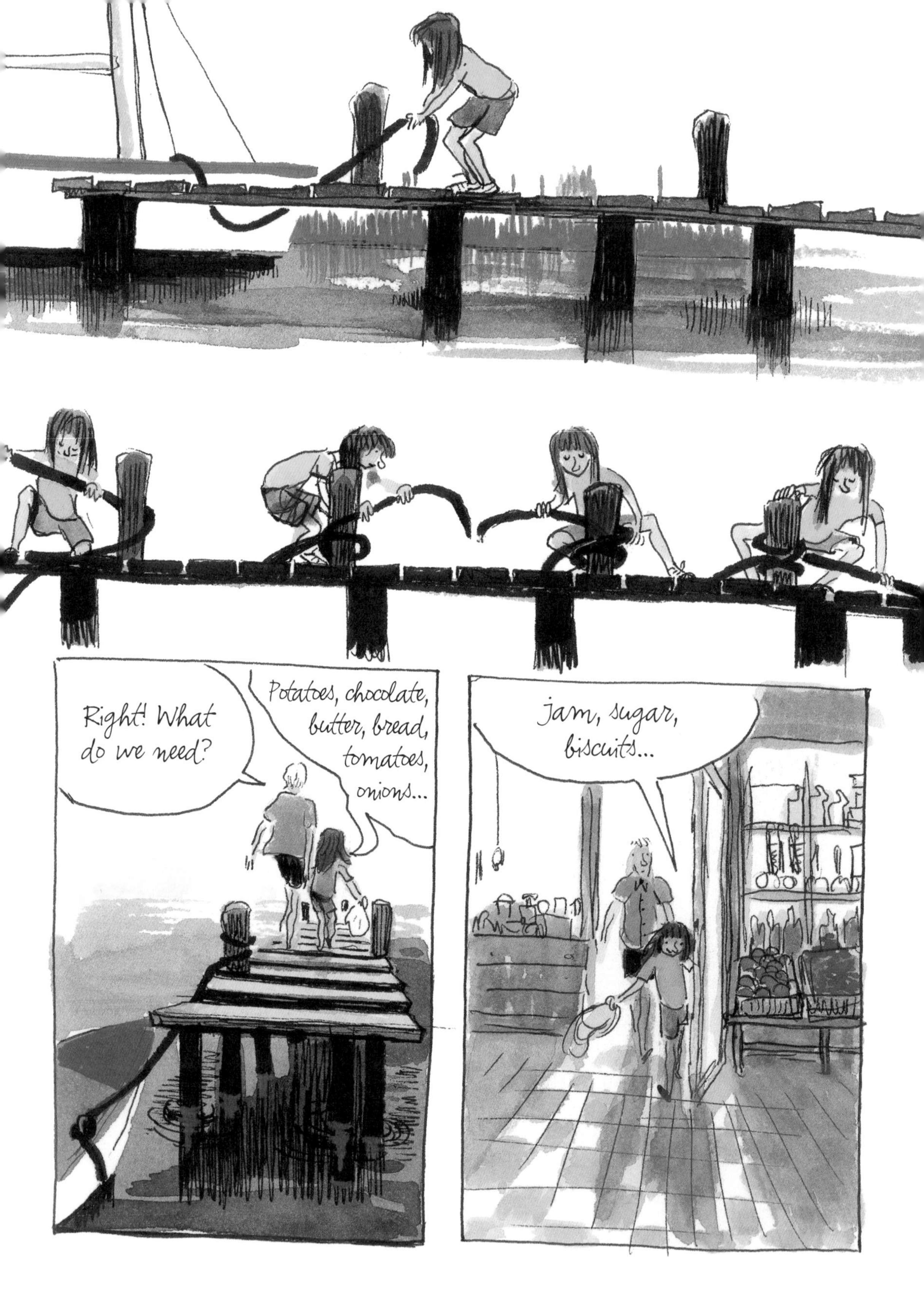
Right! What do we need?
Potatoes, chocolate, butter, bread, tomatoes, onions...
jam, sugar, biscuits...

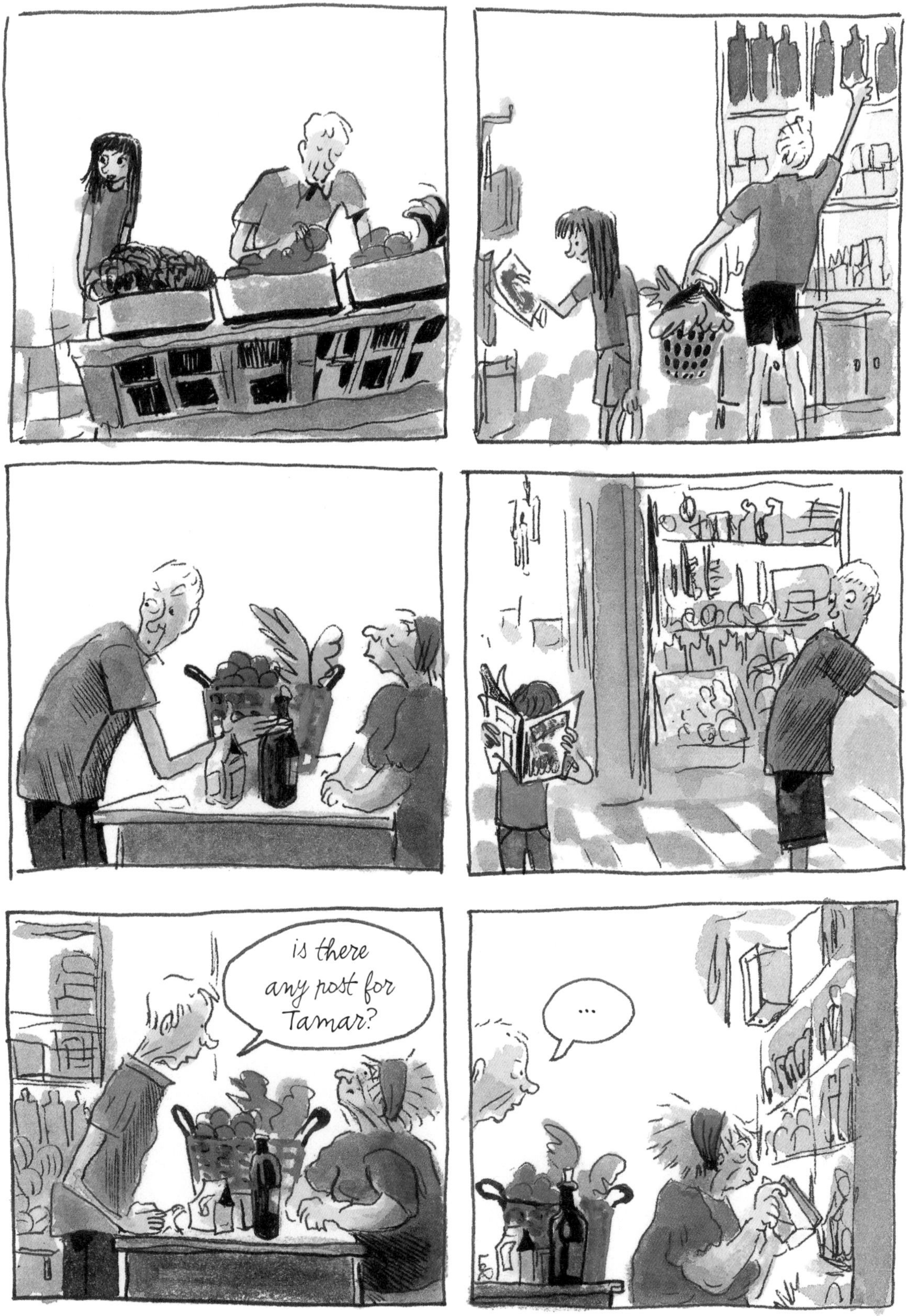
is there any post for Tamar?
...

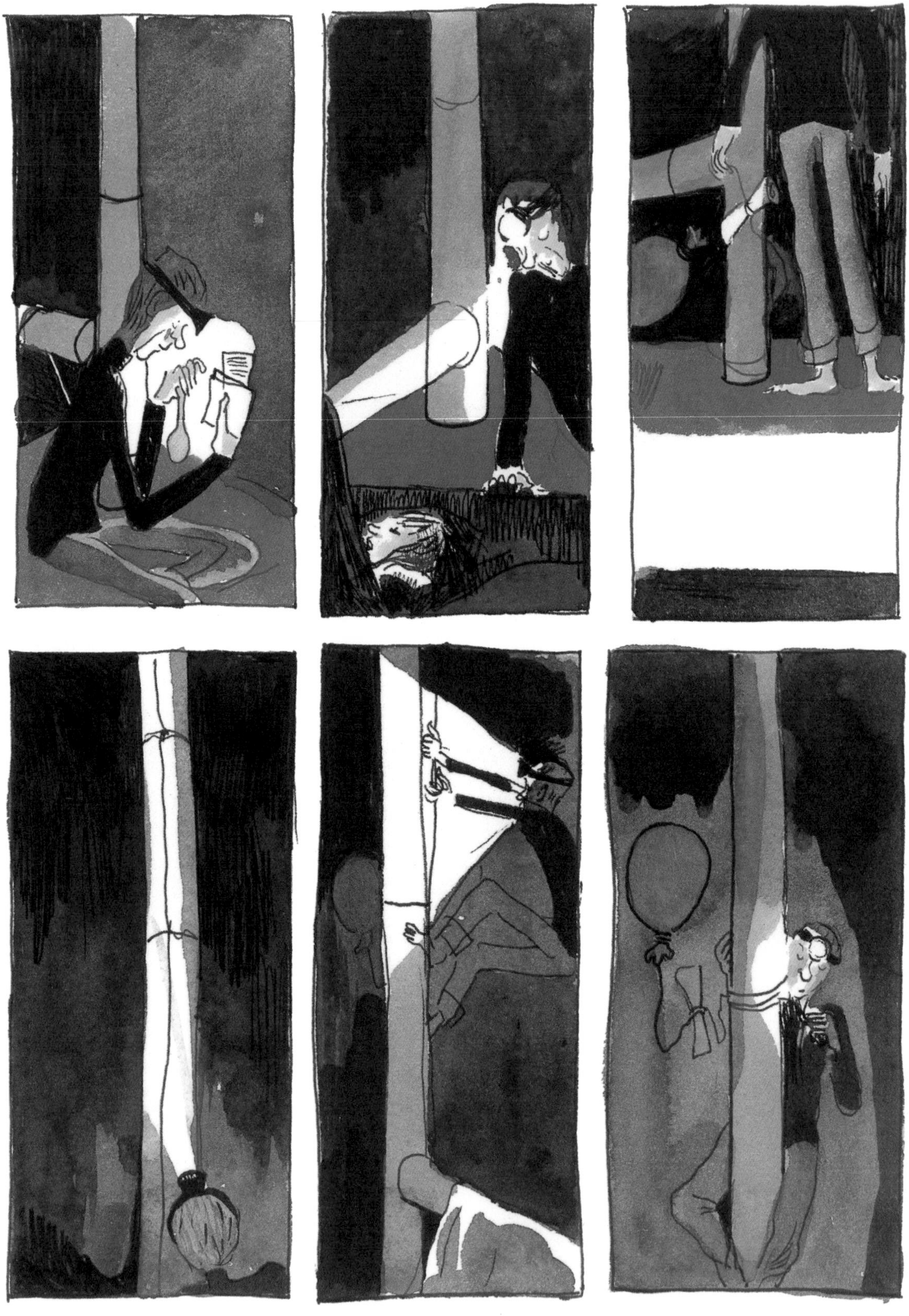

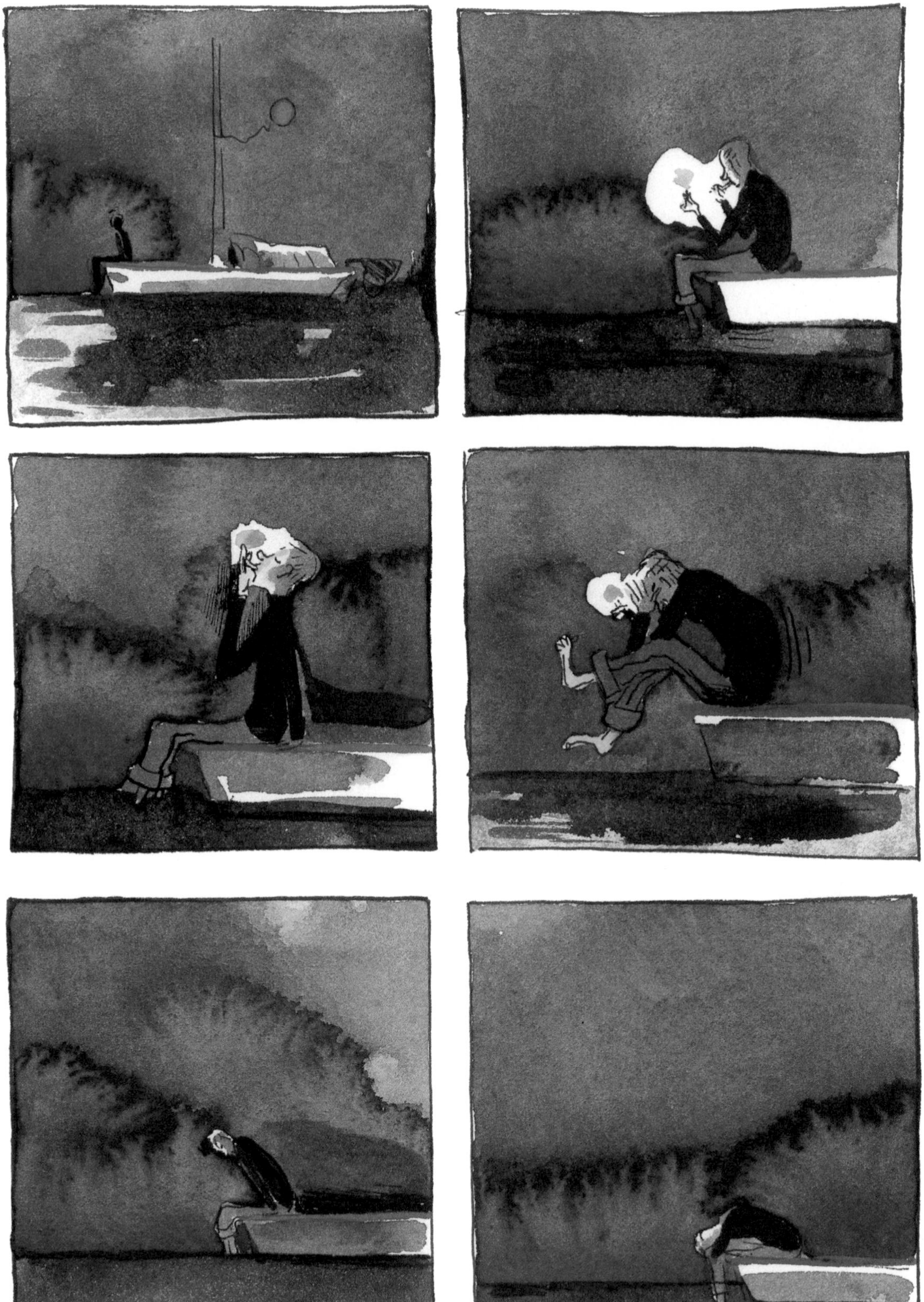

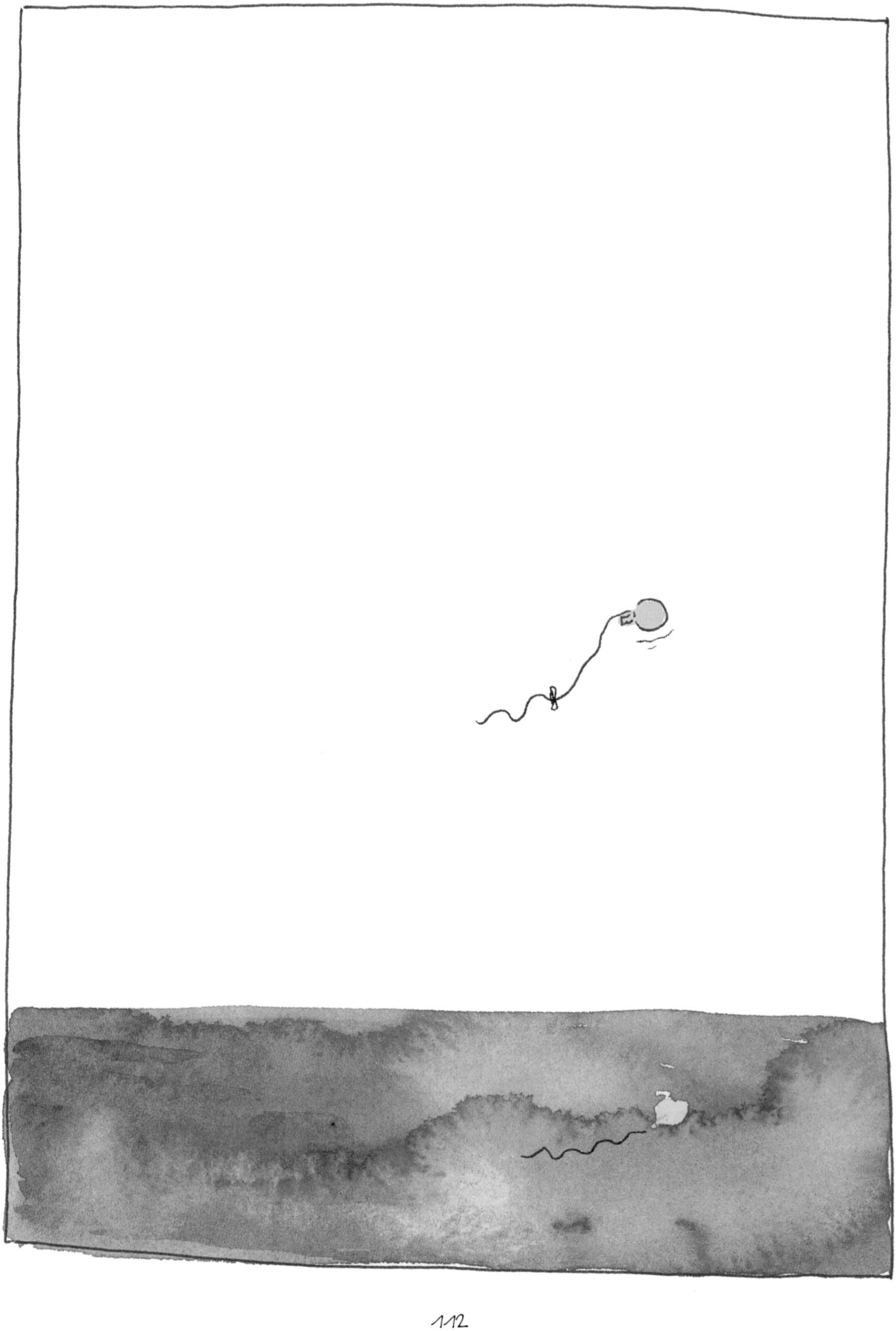

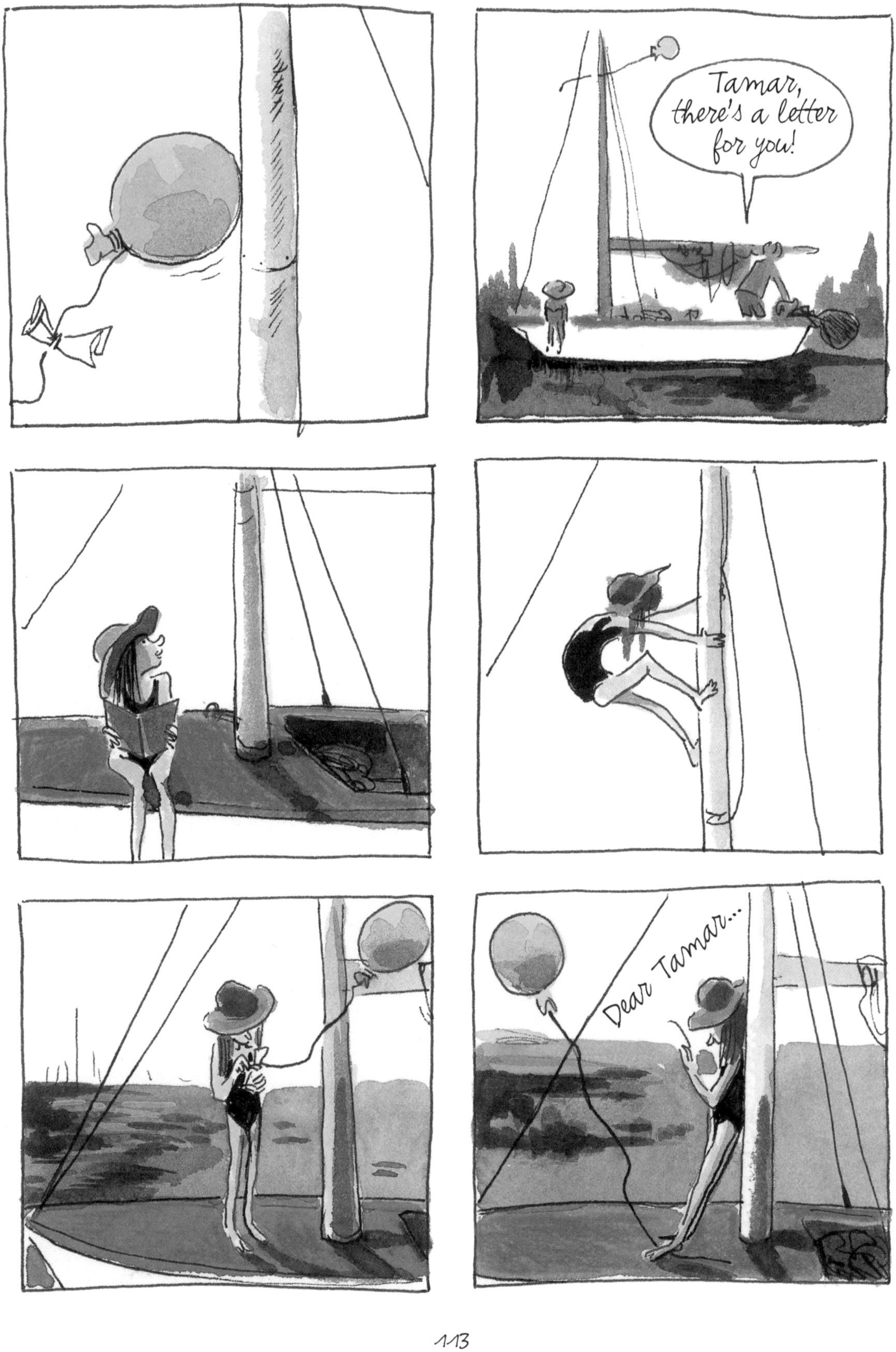
Tamar, there's a letter for you!
Dear Tamar...

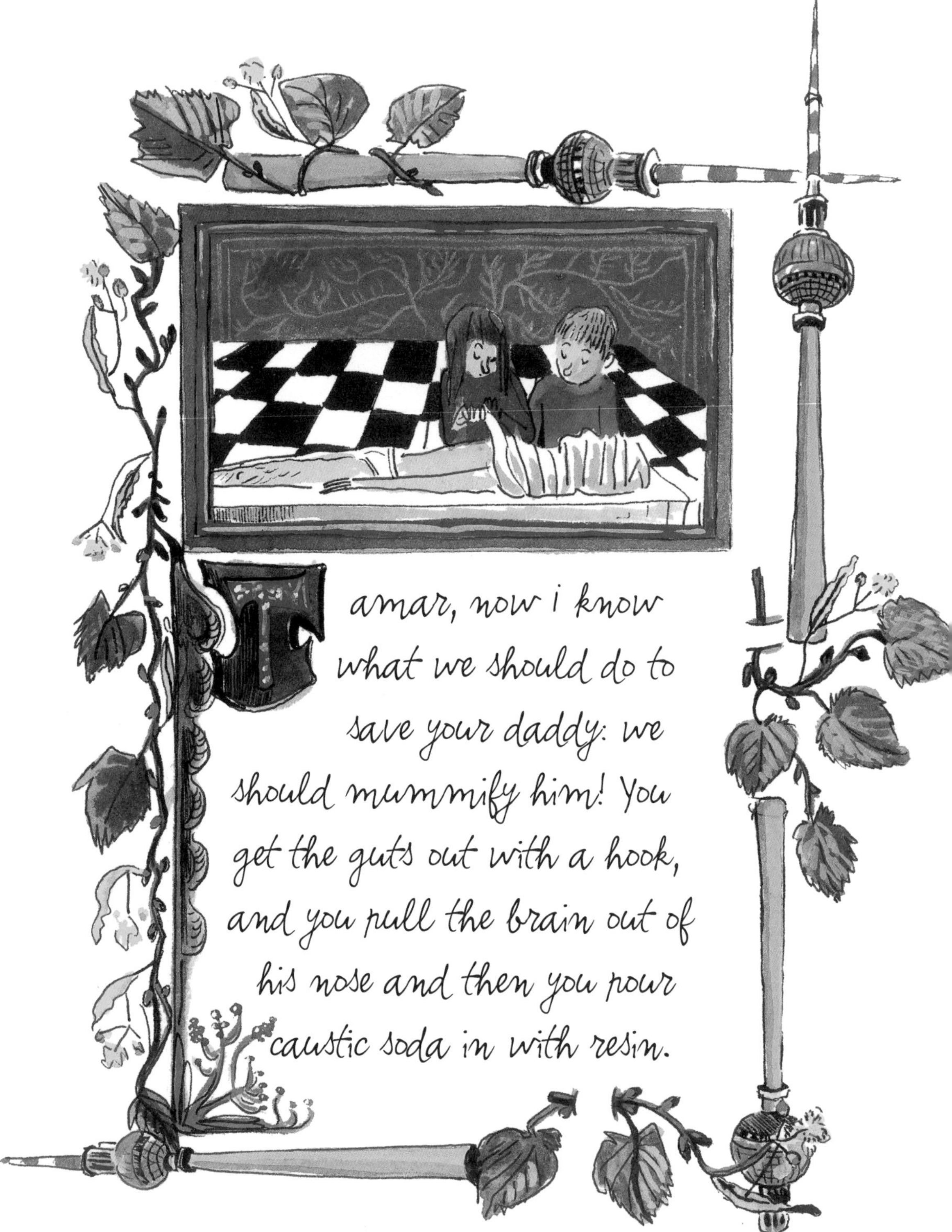

Tamar, now i know what we should do to save your daddy: we should mummify him! You get the guts out with a hook, and you pull the brain out of his nose and then you pour caustic soda in with resin.

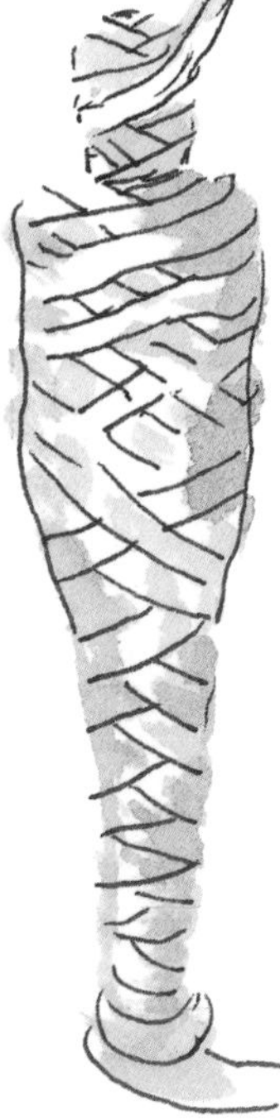

Then you put him in the bathtub with the soda and then he dries out. You take some bed sheets and wrap him up. And then it's a mummy! And then you can tidy him away under your bed.

MAX

P.S.: The soda is in a lake in Egypt. You'd have to go there first. But it's very far away. So you'd have to take the boat to get there.

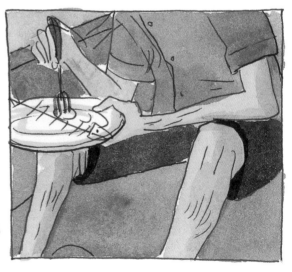

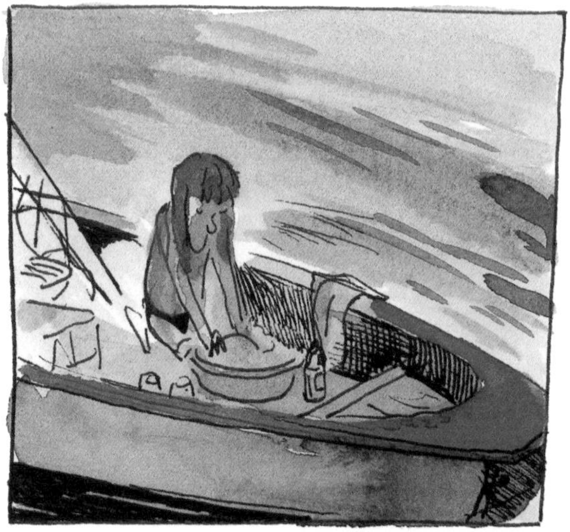

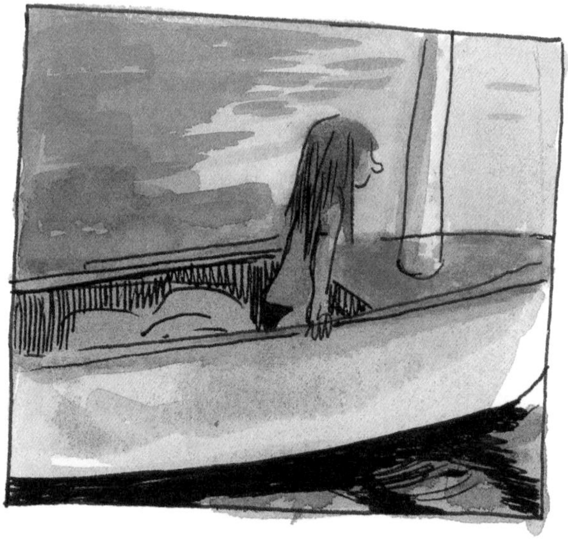

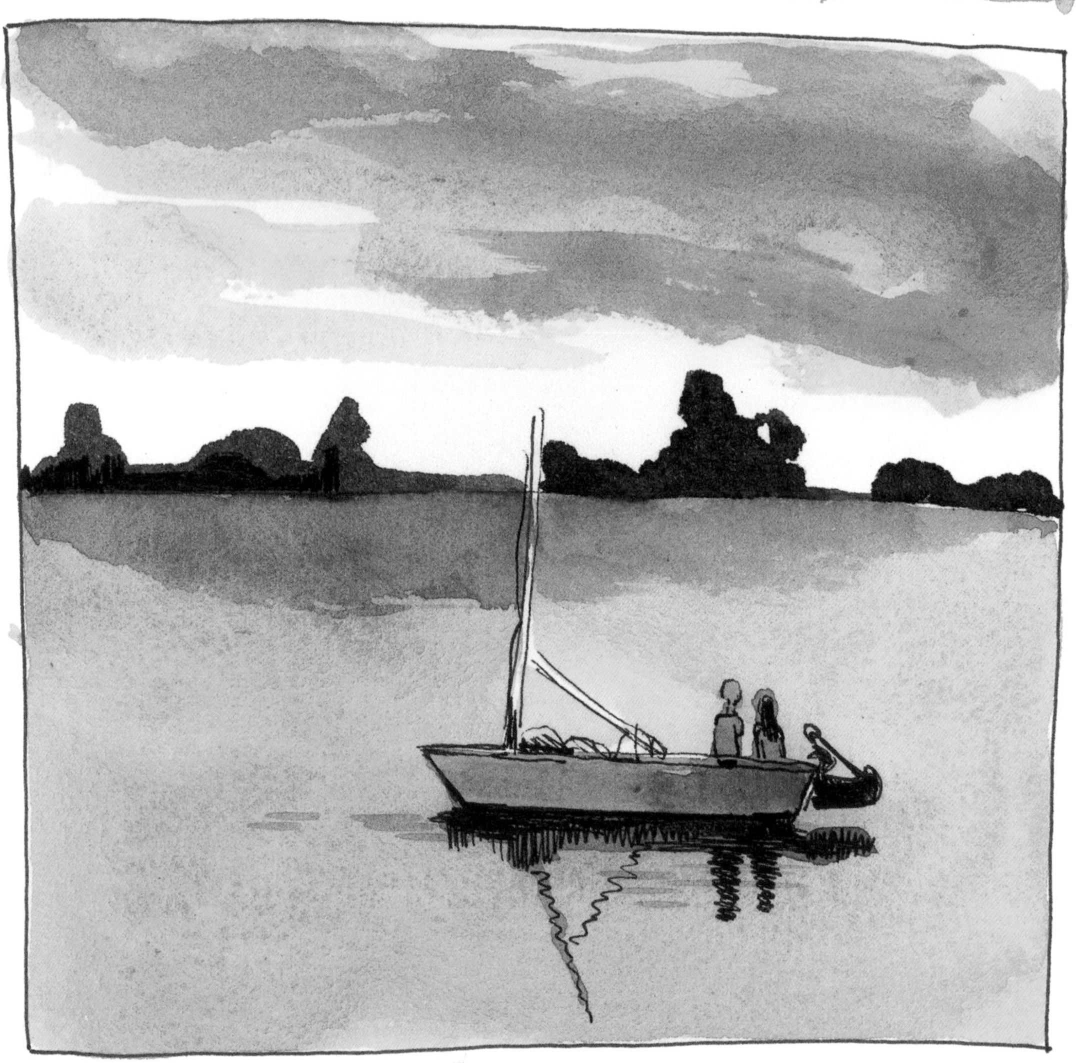

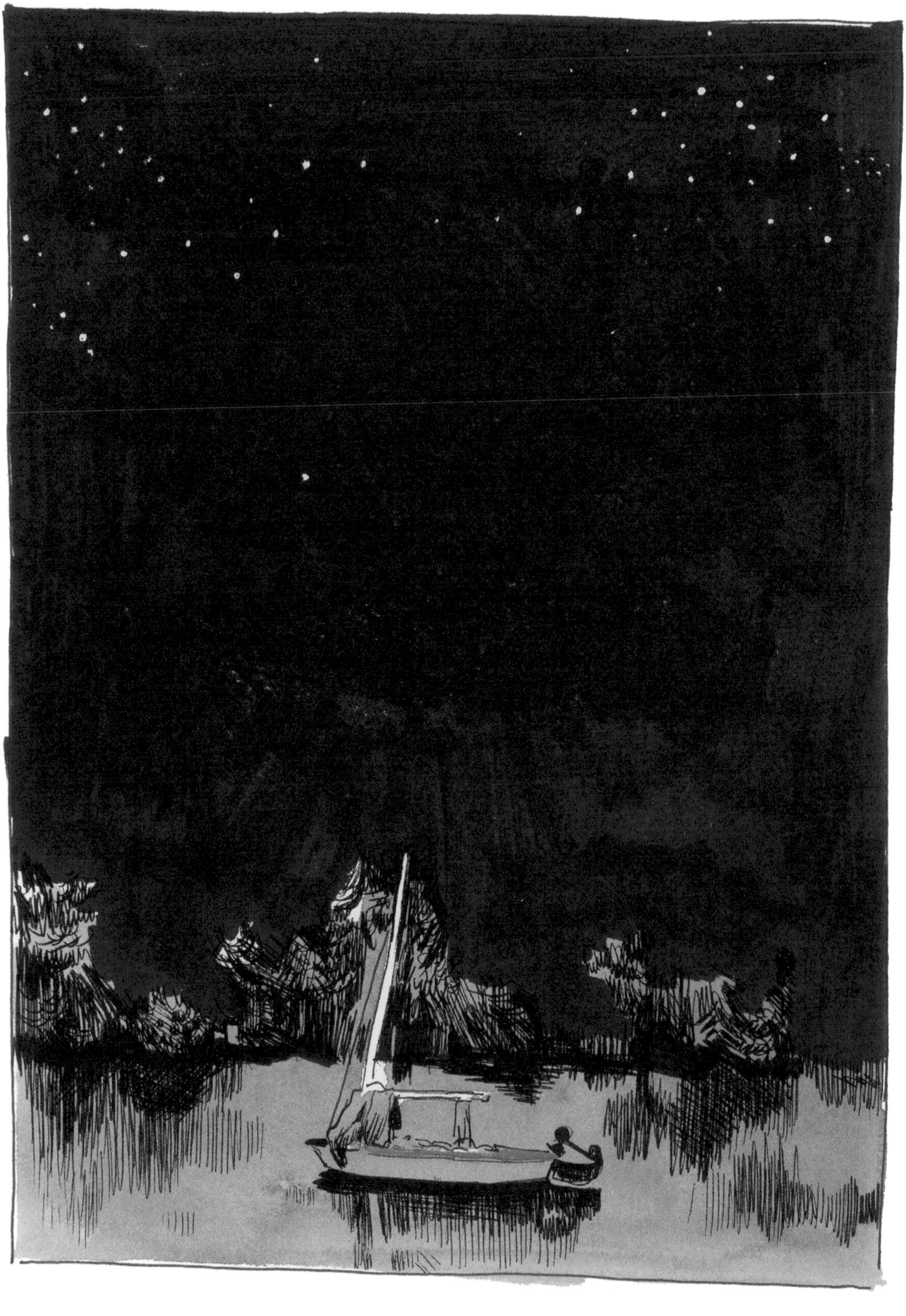

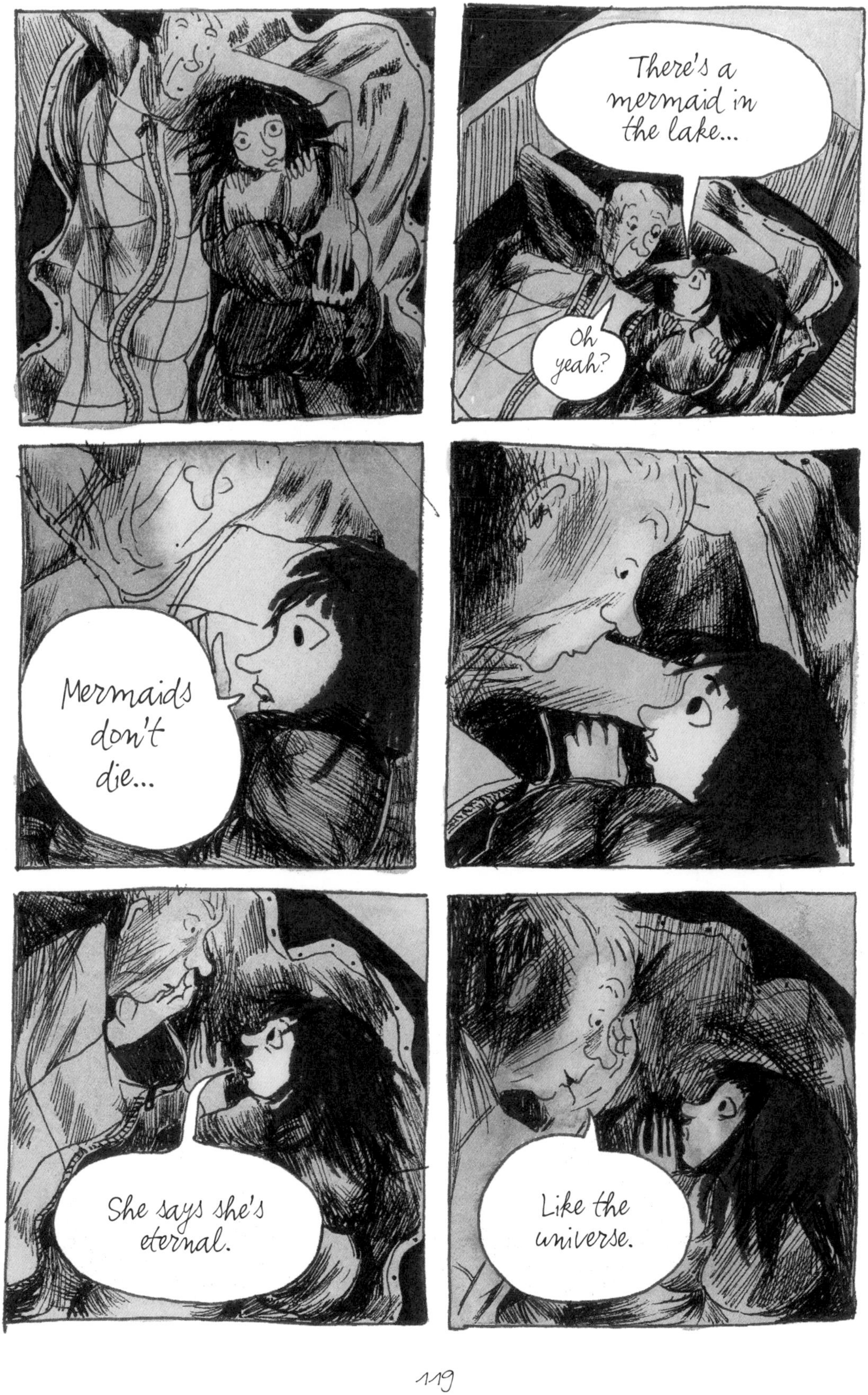
There's a mermaid in the lake...
Oh yeah?
Mermaids don't die...
She says she's eternal.
Like the universe.

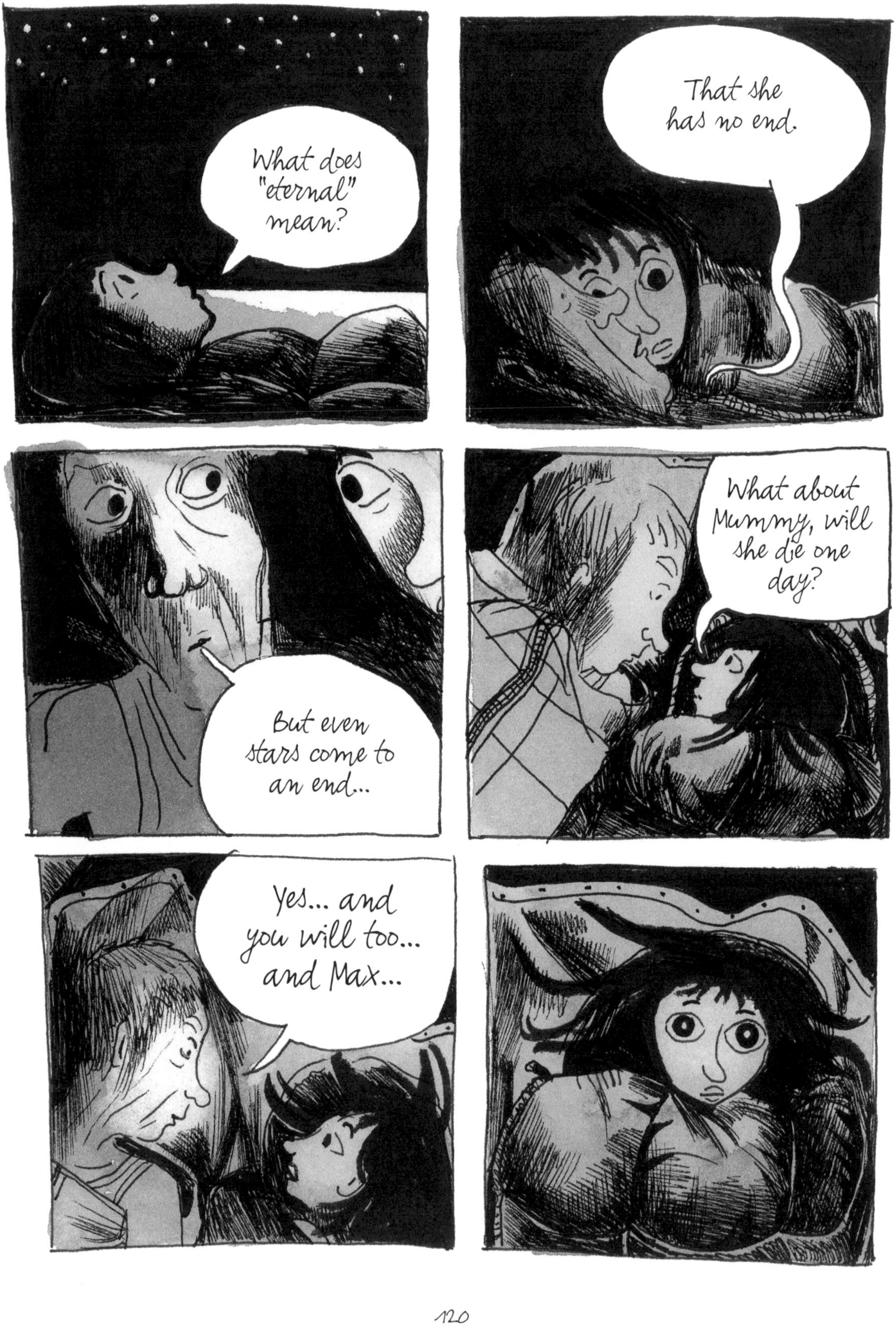
What does "eternal" mean?
That she has no end.
But even stars come to an end...
What about Mummy, will she die one day?
Yes... and you will too... and Max...

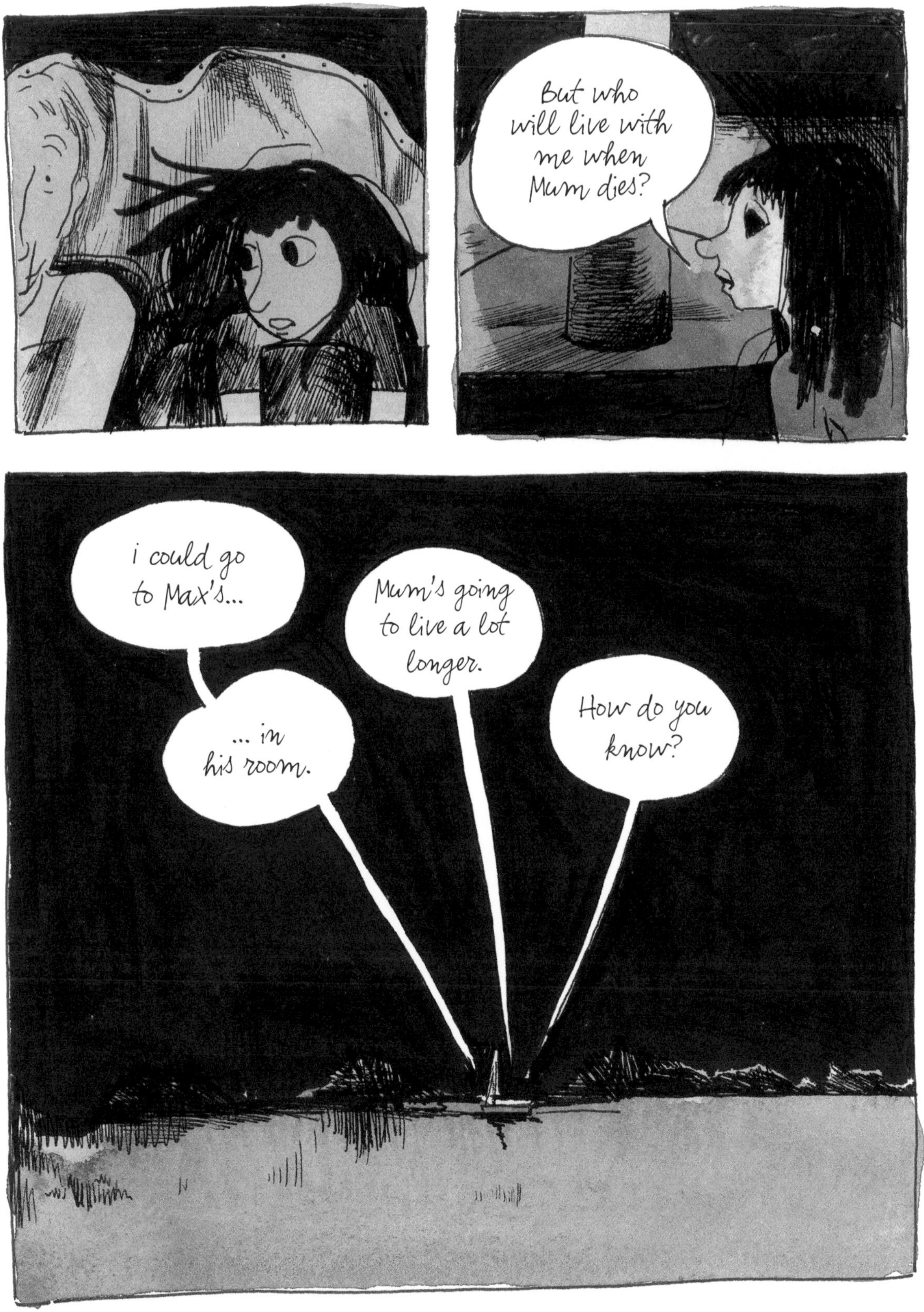
But who will live with me when Mum dies?
i could go to Max's...
... in his room.
Mum's going to live a lot longer.
How do you know?

Do you want me to put it in an envelope?

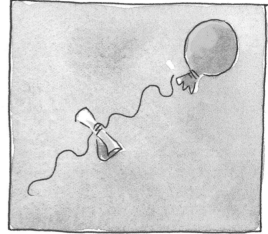

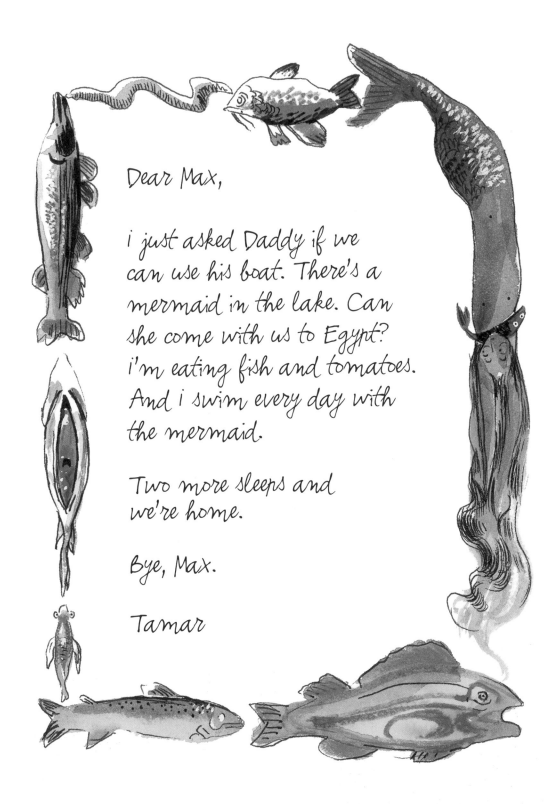

Dear Max,

i just asked Daddy if we
can use his boat. There's a
mermaid in the lake. Can
she come with us to Egypt?
i'm eating fish and tomatoes.
And i swim every day with
the mermaid.

Two more sleeps and
we're home.

Bye, Max.

Tamar

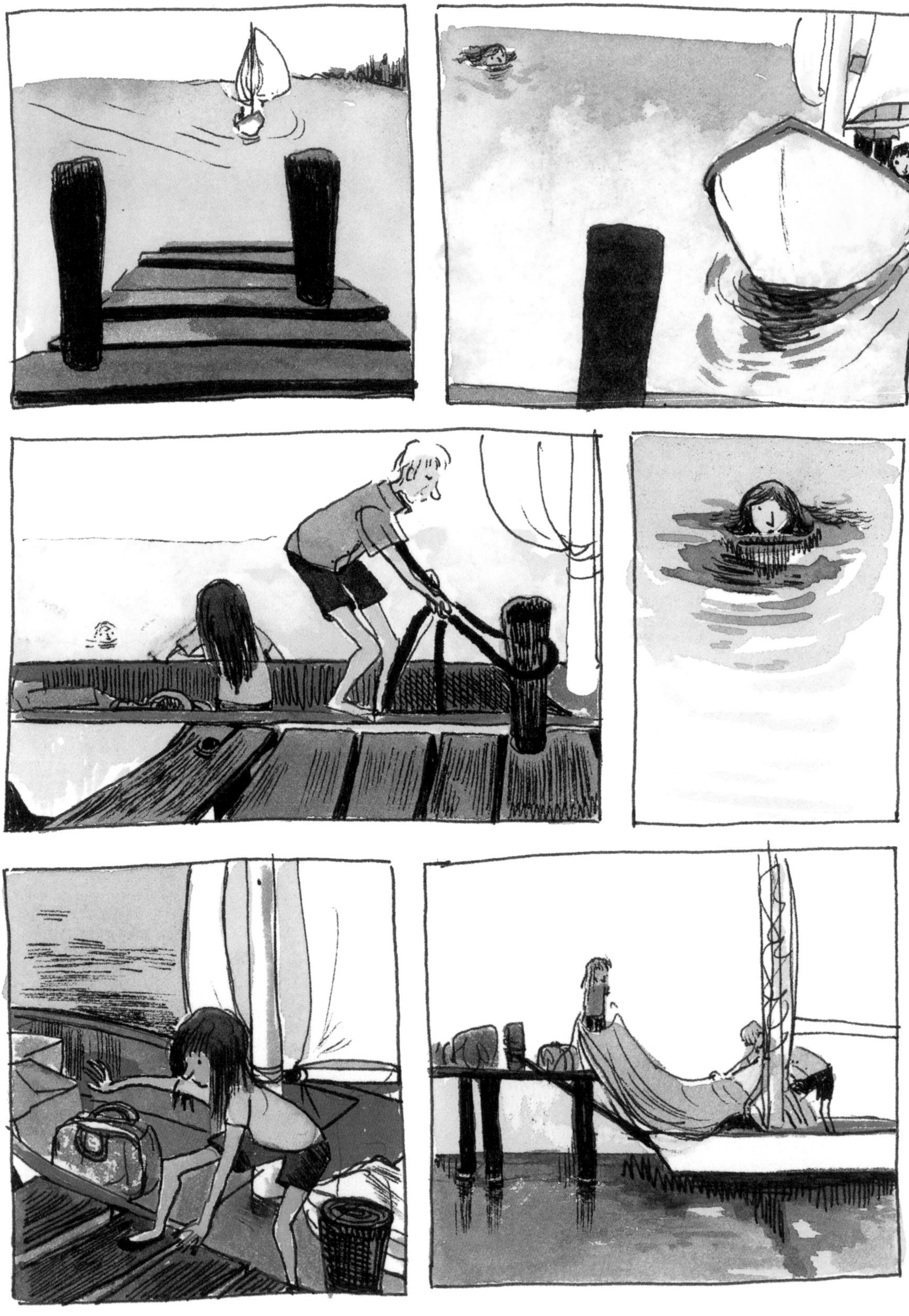

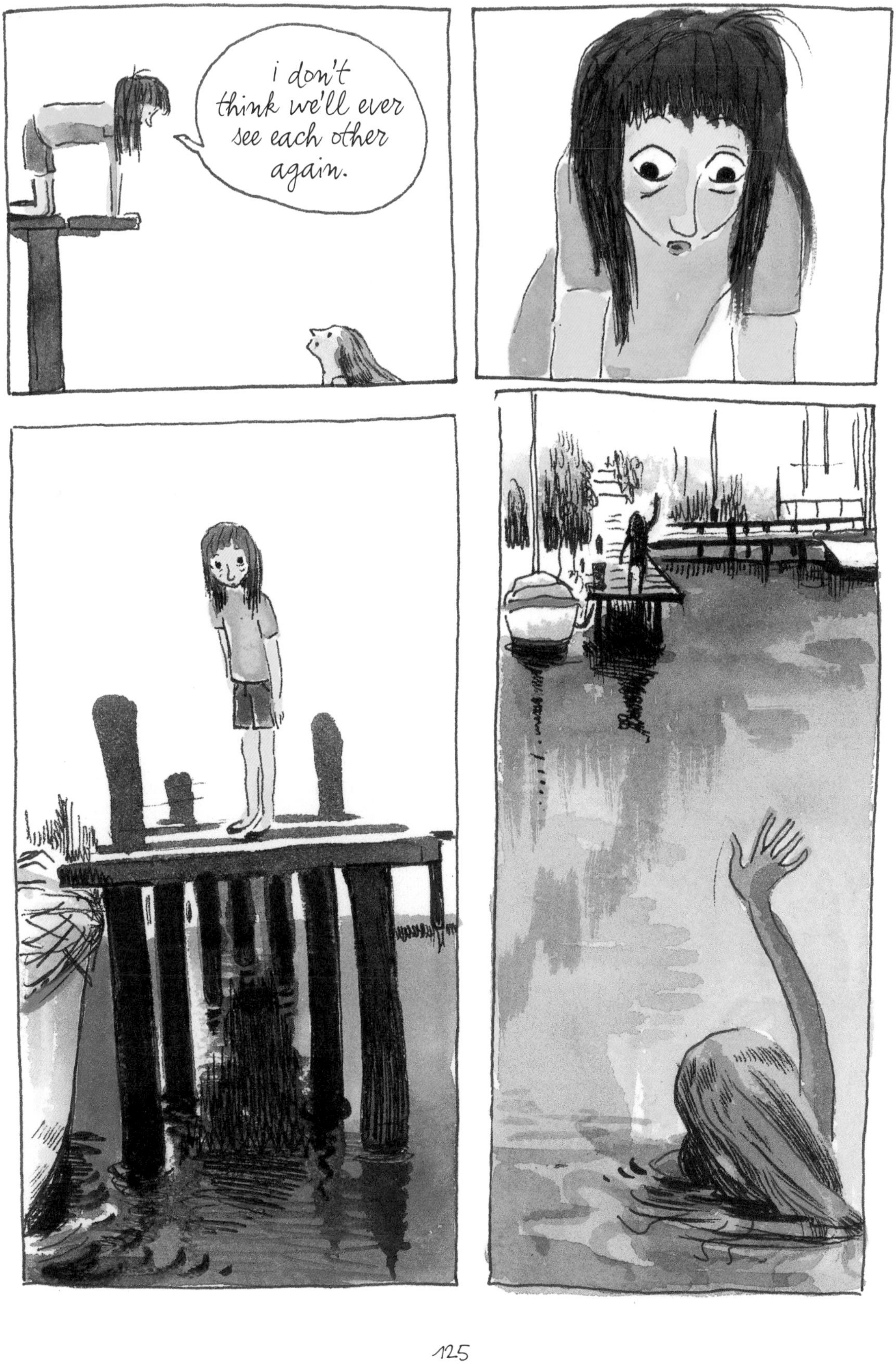
i don't think we'll ever see each other again.

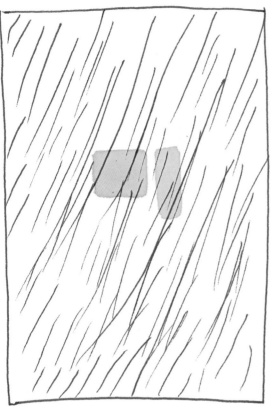

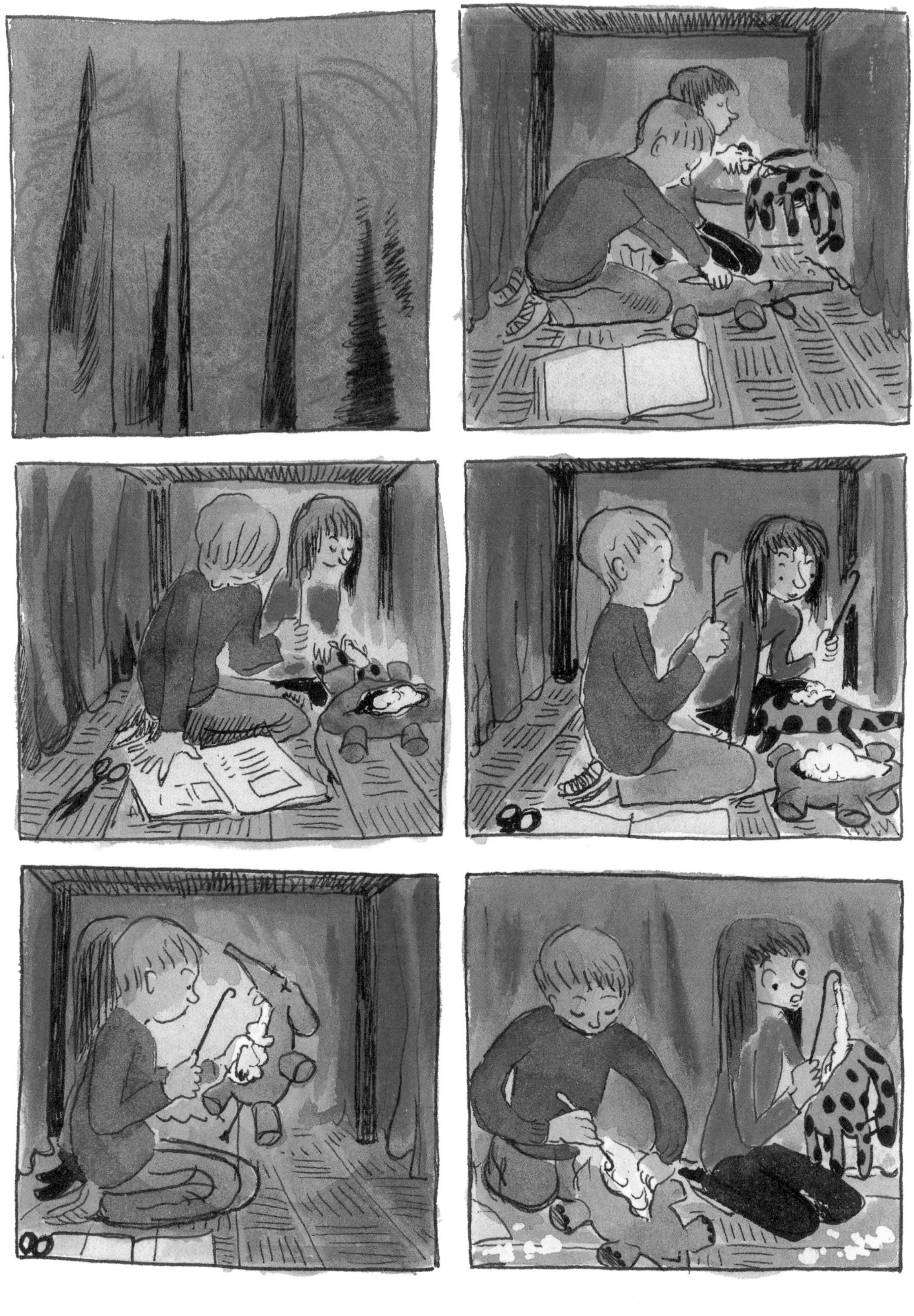

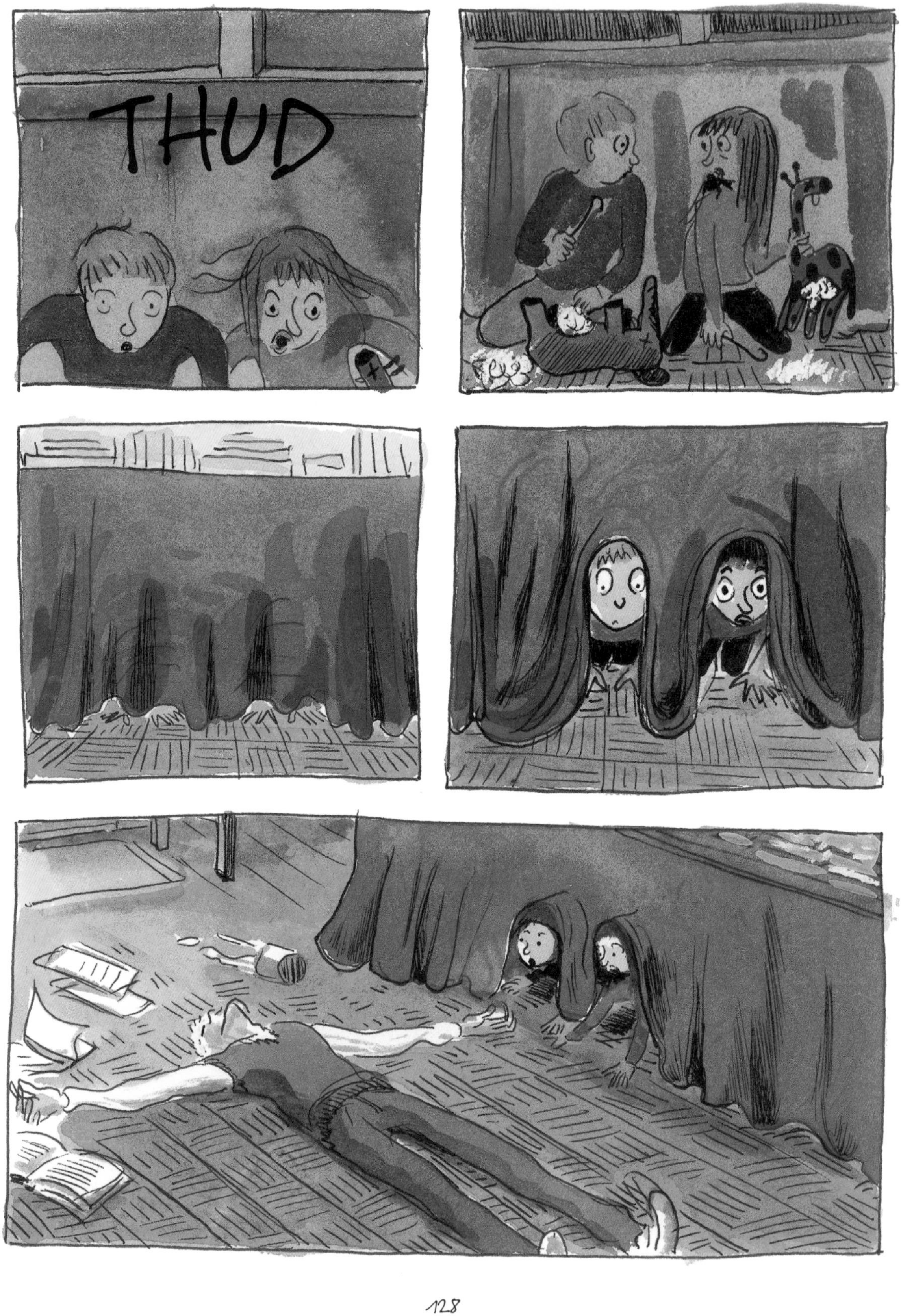
THUD

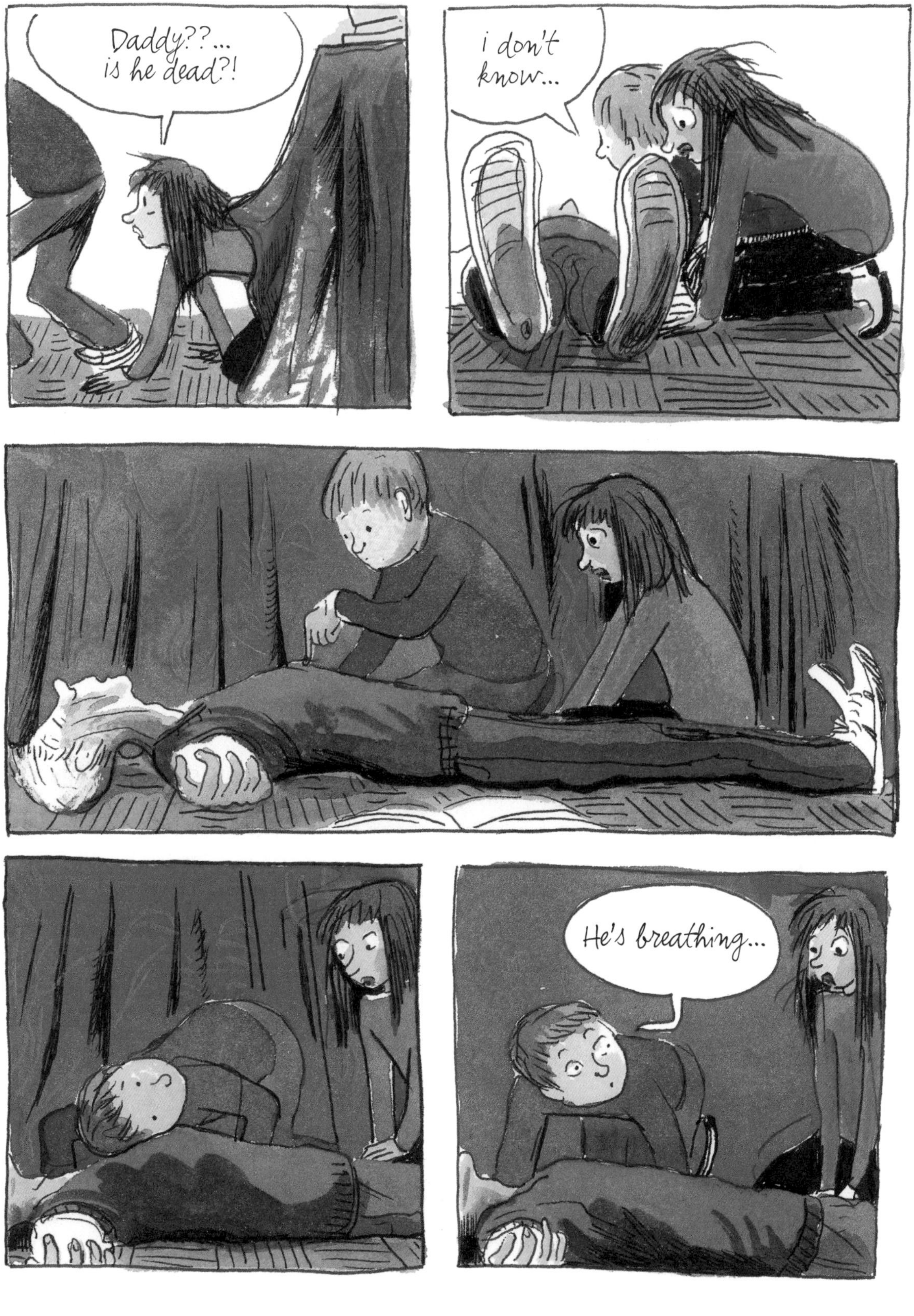
Daddy??... is he dead?!
i don't know...
He's breathing...

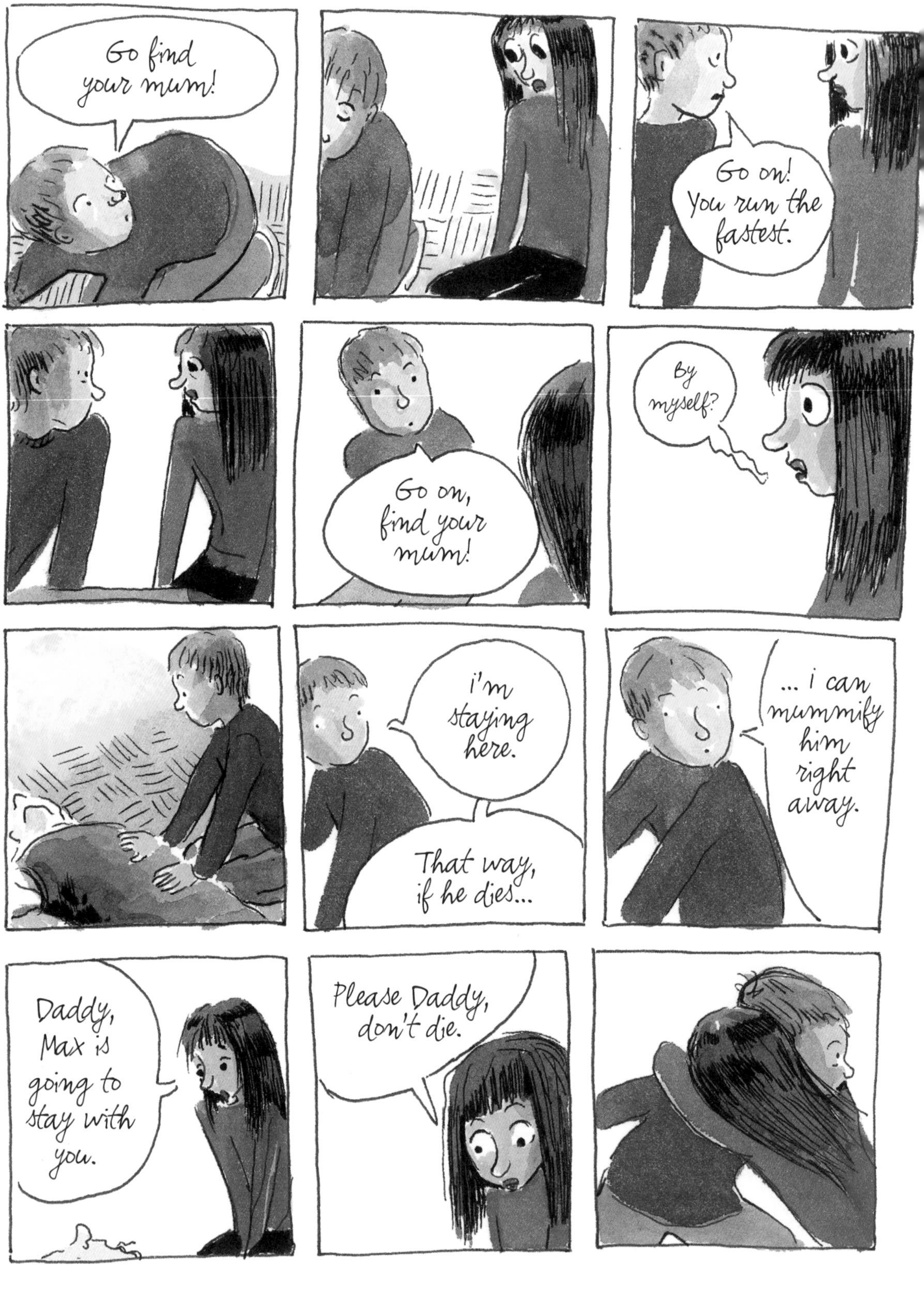
Go find your mum!
Go on! You run the fastest.
Go on, find your mum!
By myself?
i'm staying here.
That way, if he dies...
... i can mummify him right away.
Daddy, Max is going to stay with you.
Please Daddy, don't die.

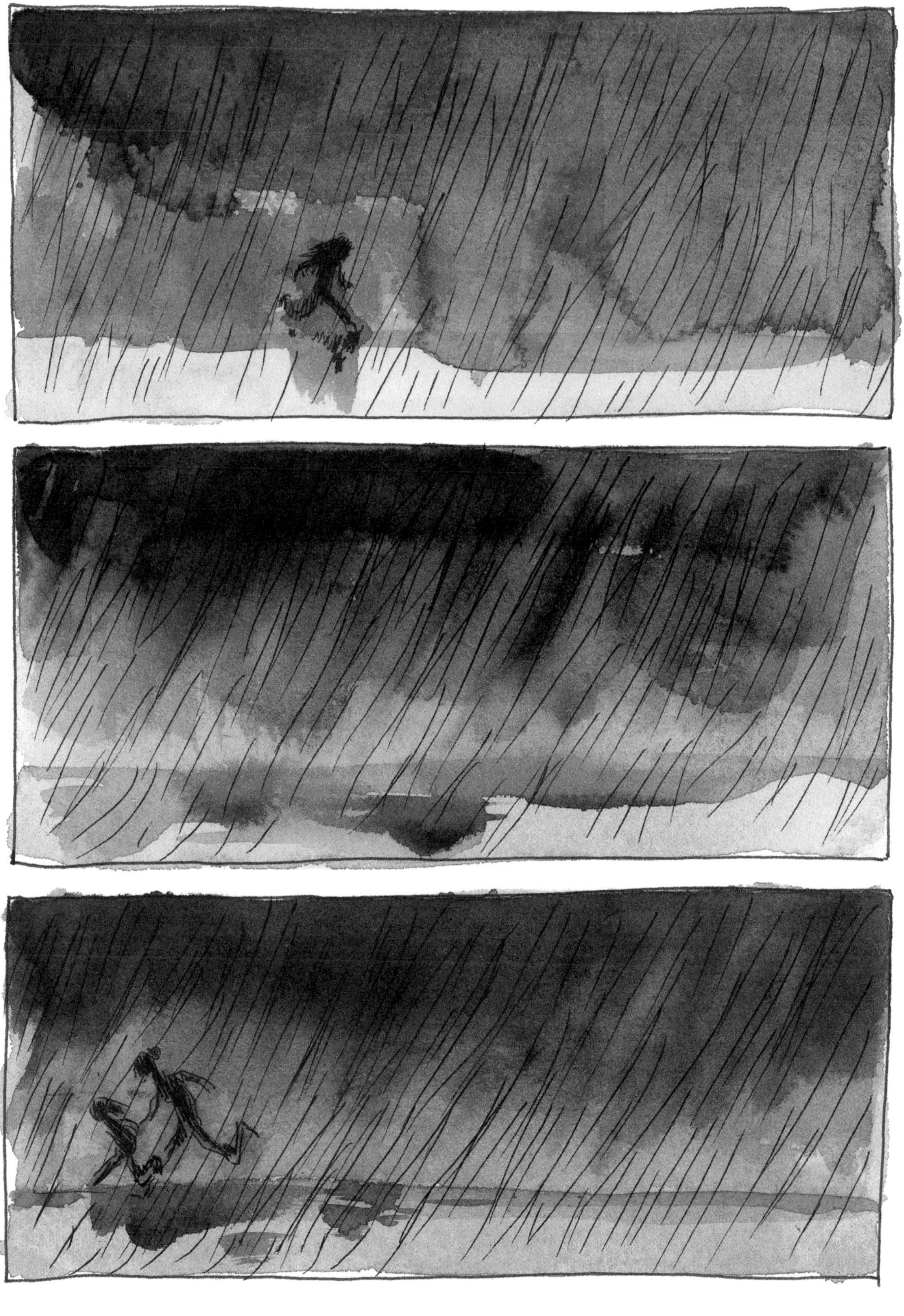

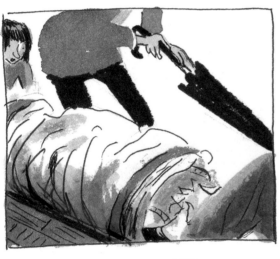

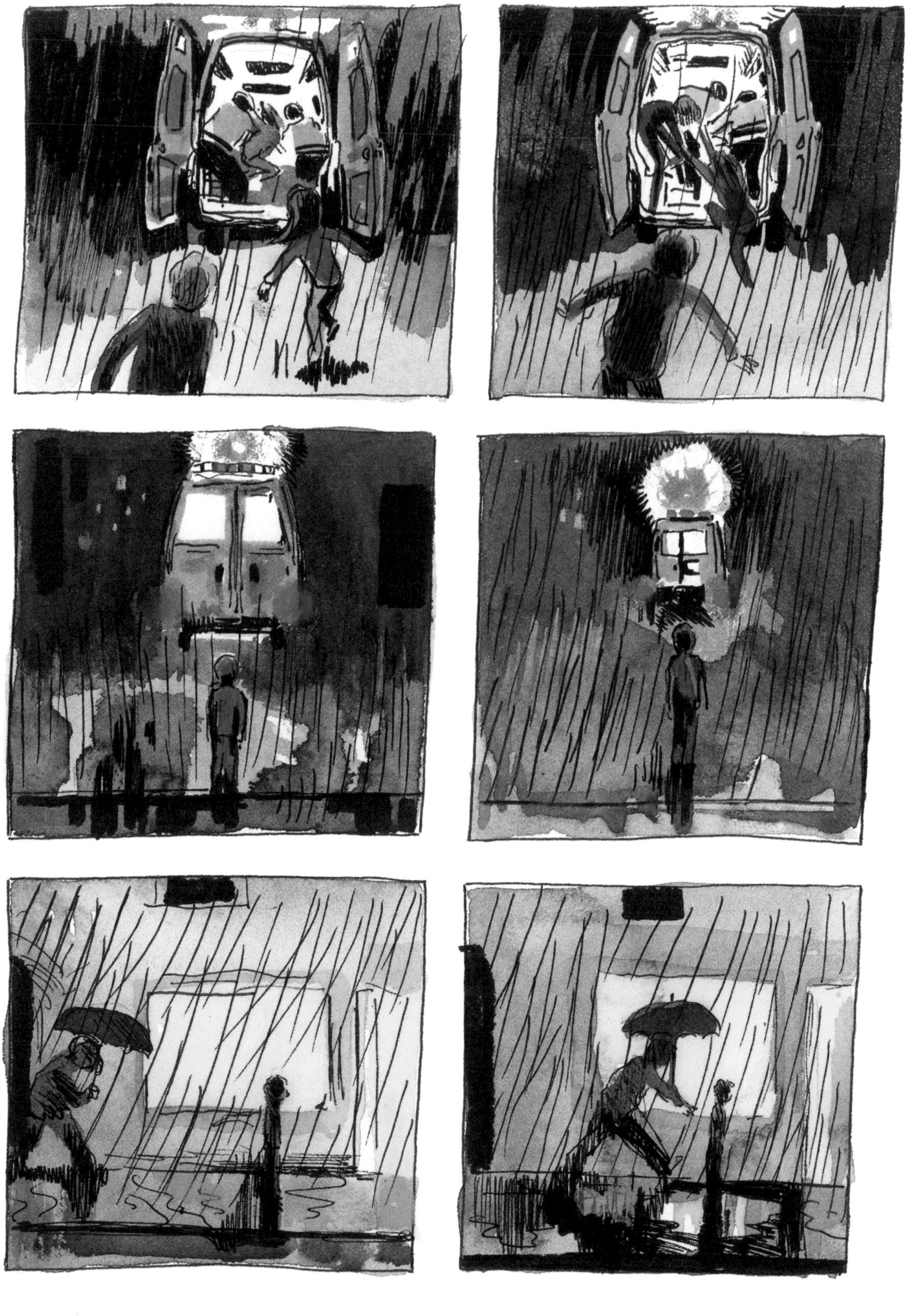

BY VASALIS, FROM "SOTTO VOCE" IN
VERGEZICHTEN EN GEZICHTEN. VAN OORSCHOT, 1954
TRANSLATION BY WOUTER MULDERS.

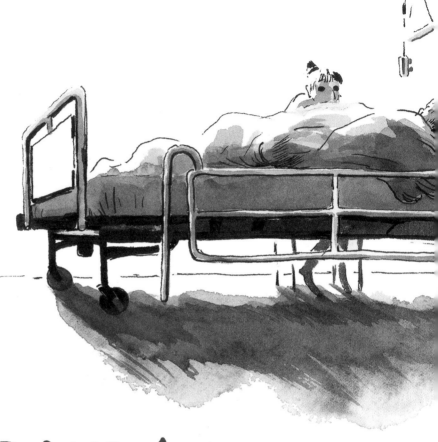

PAULA

Sorrow knows so many shapes,
I name them not.
But one, renouncing, parting.
And it's not the cut that's rough,
but the having been cut off.

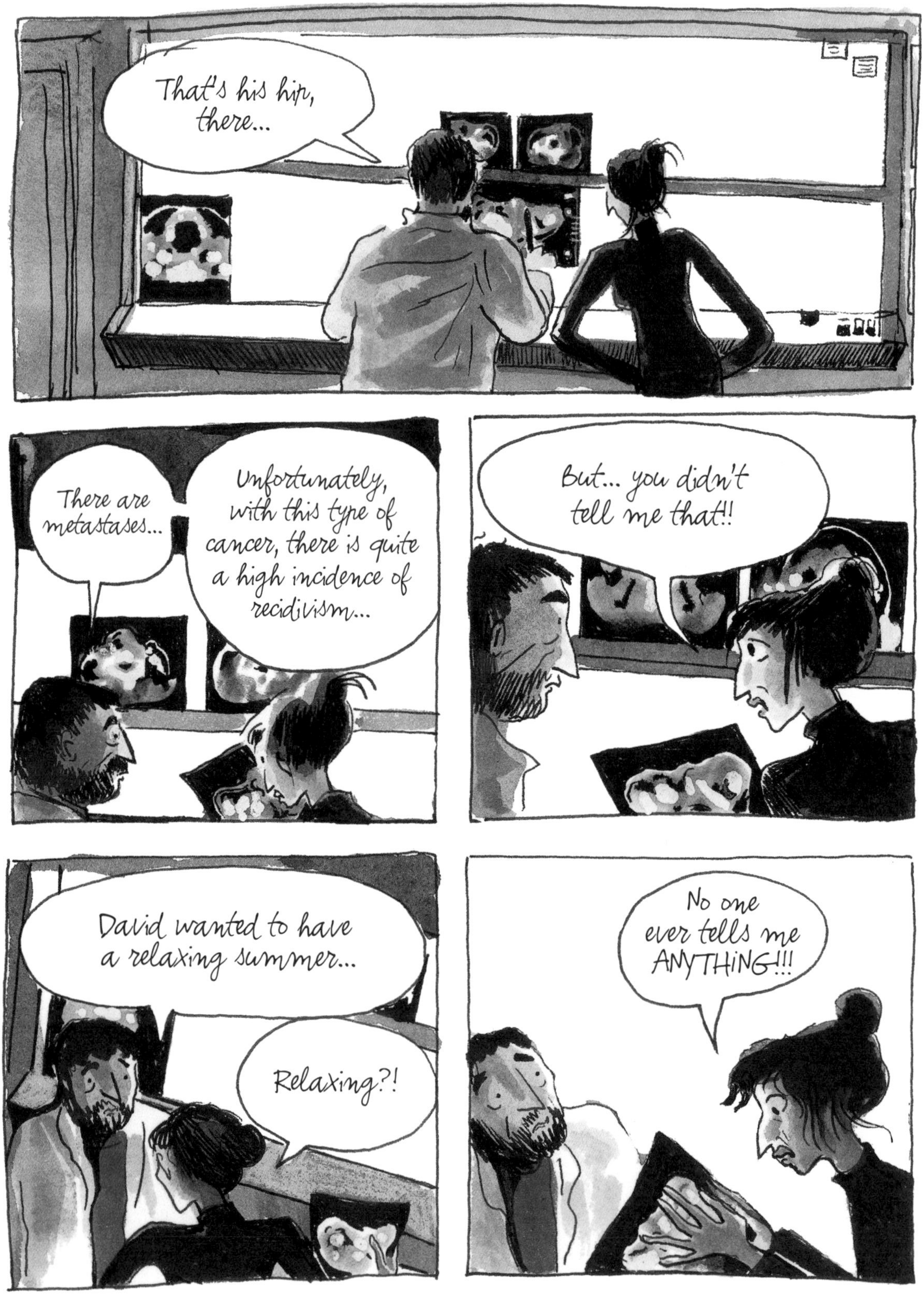
That's his hip, there...
There are metastases...
Unfortunately, with this type of cancer, there is quite a high incidence of recidivism...
But... you didn't tell me that!!
David wanted to have a relaxing summer...
Relaxing?!
No one ever tells me ANYTHING!!!

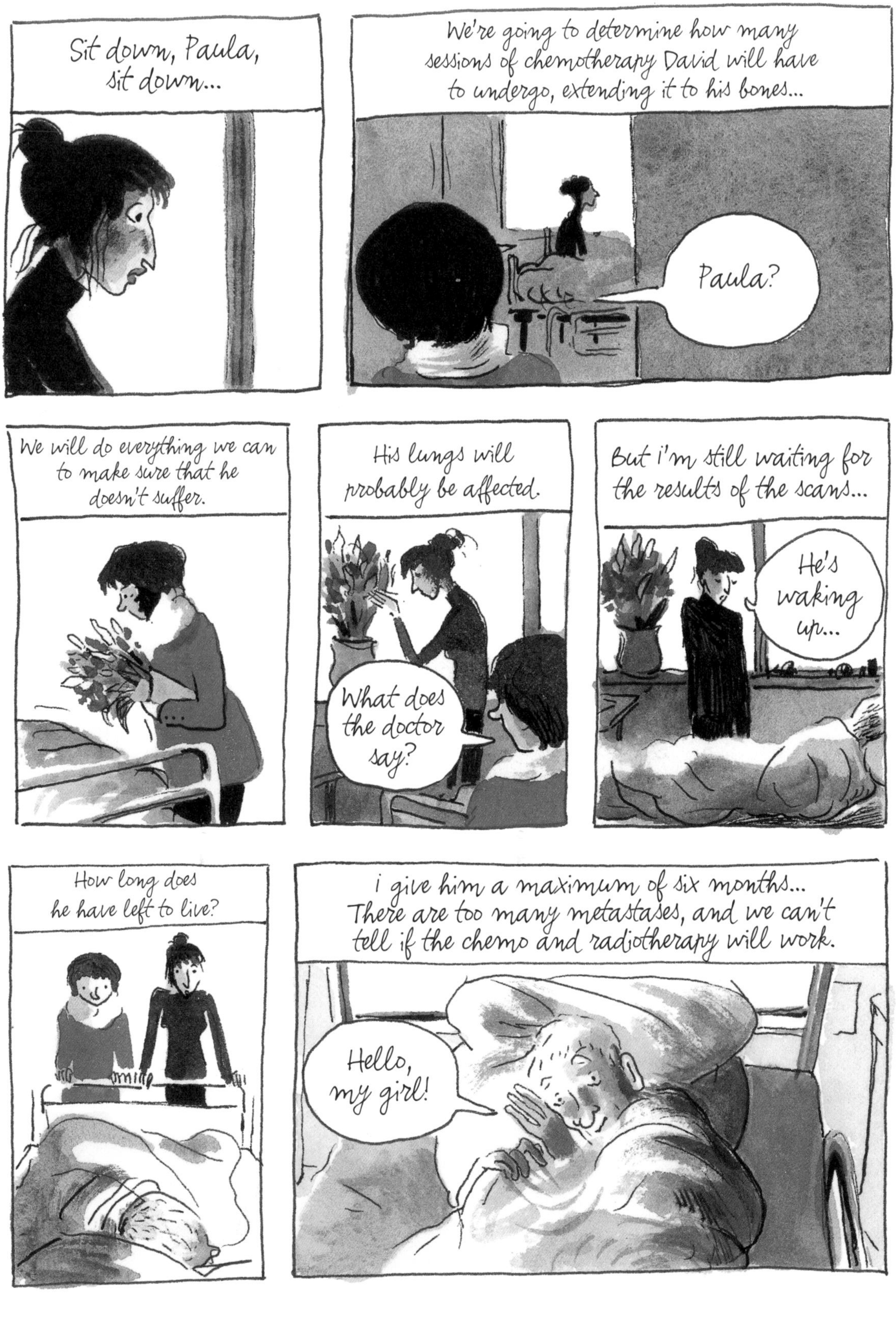
Sit down, Paula, sit down...
We're going to determine how many sessions of chemotherapy David will have to undergo, extending it to his bones...
Paula?
We will do everything we can to make sure that he doesn't suffer.
His lungs will probably be affected.
What does the doctor say?
But i'm still waiting for the results of the scans...
He's waking up...
How long does he have left to live?
i give him a maximum of six months... There are too many metastases, and we can't tell if the chemo and radiotherapy will work.
Hello, my girl!

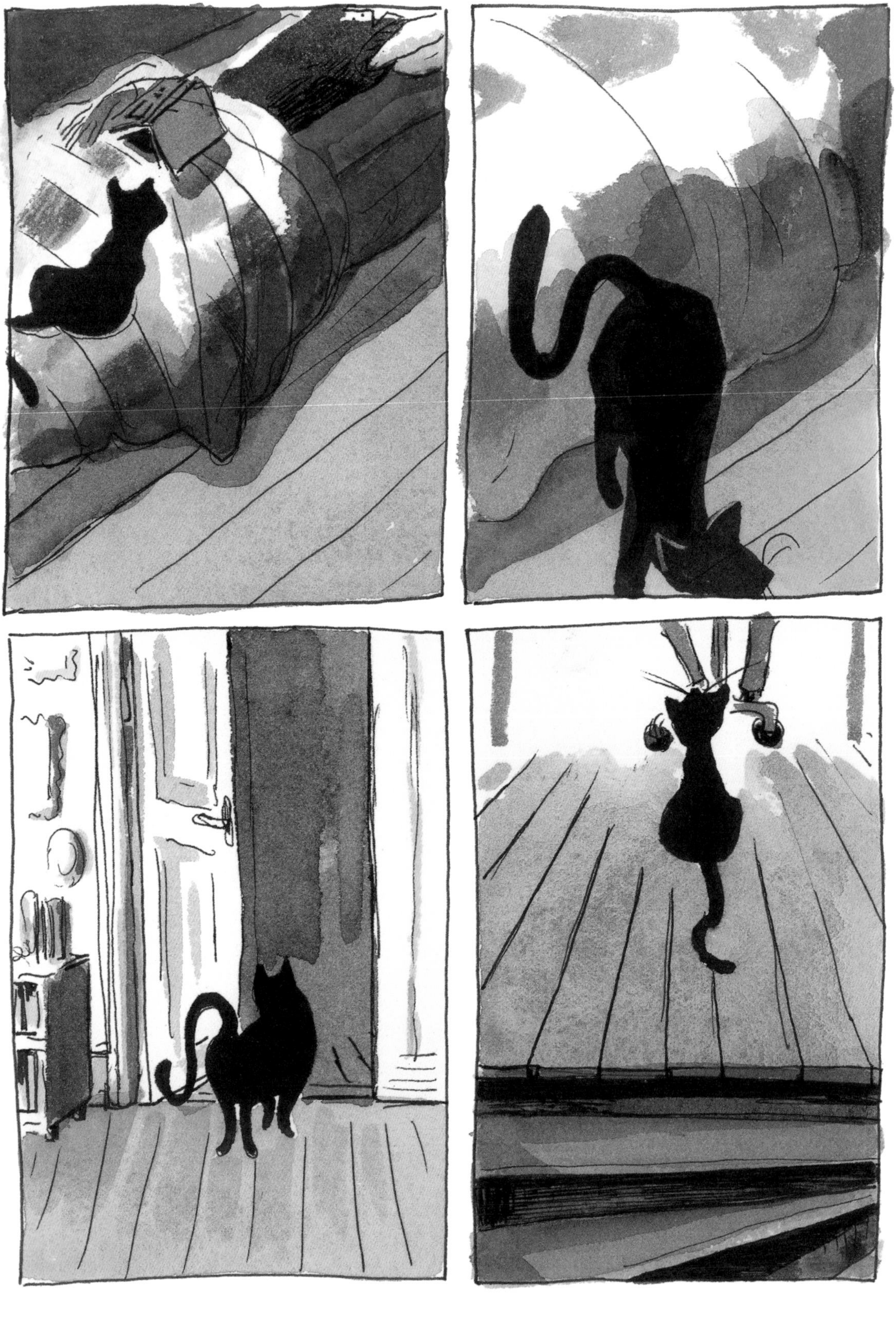

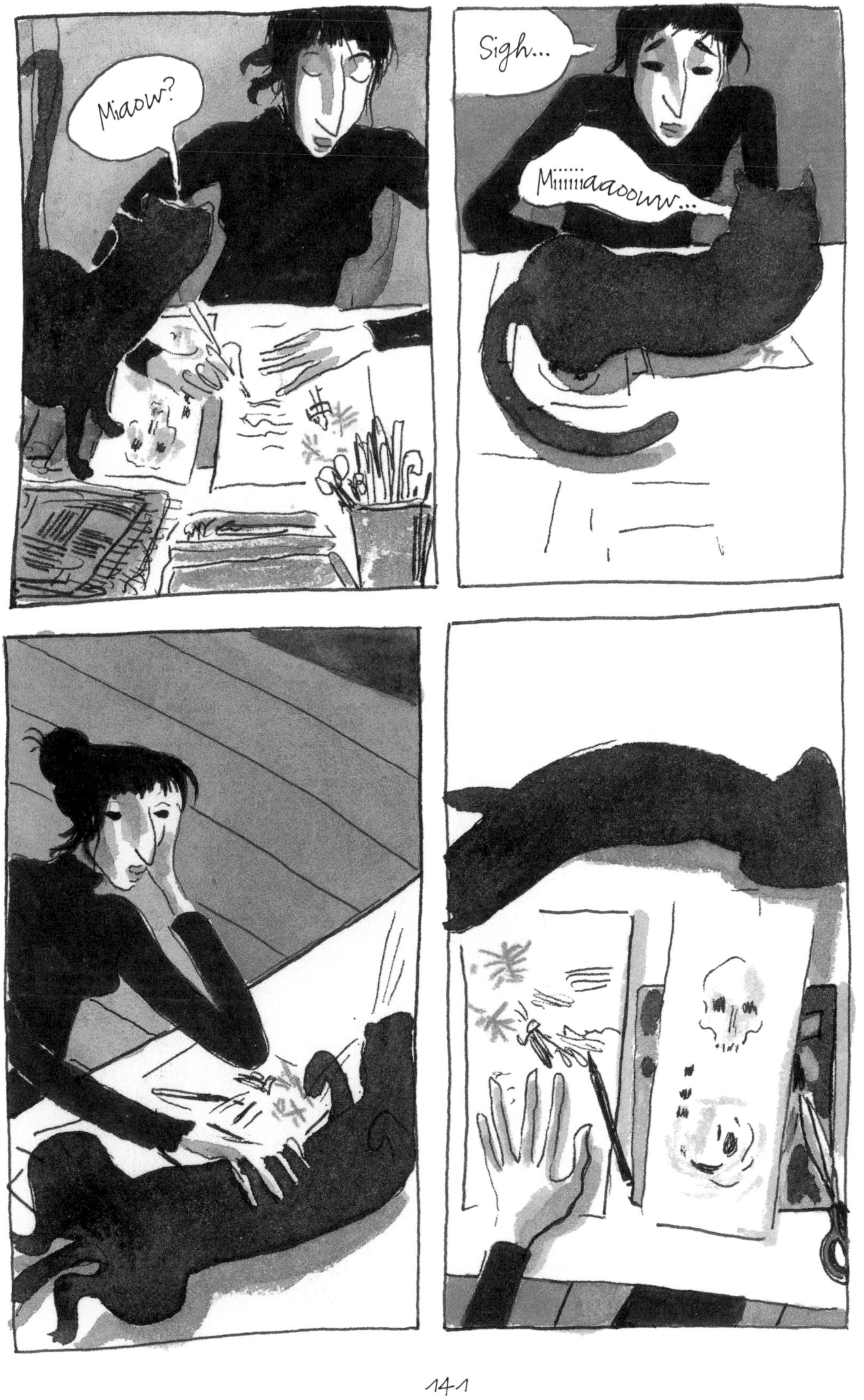
Miaow?
Sigh...
Miiiiiiaaoouw...

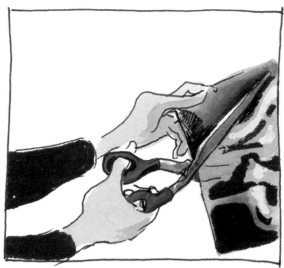
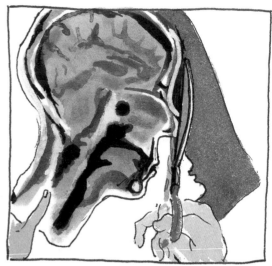

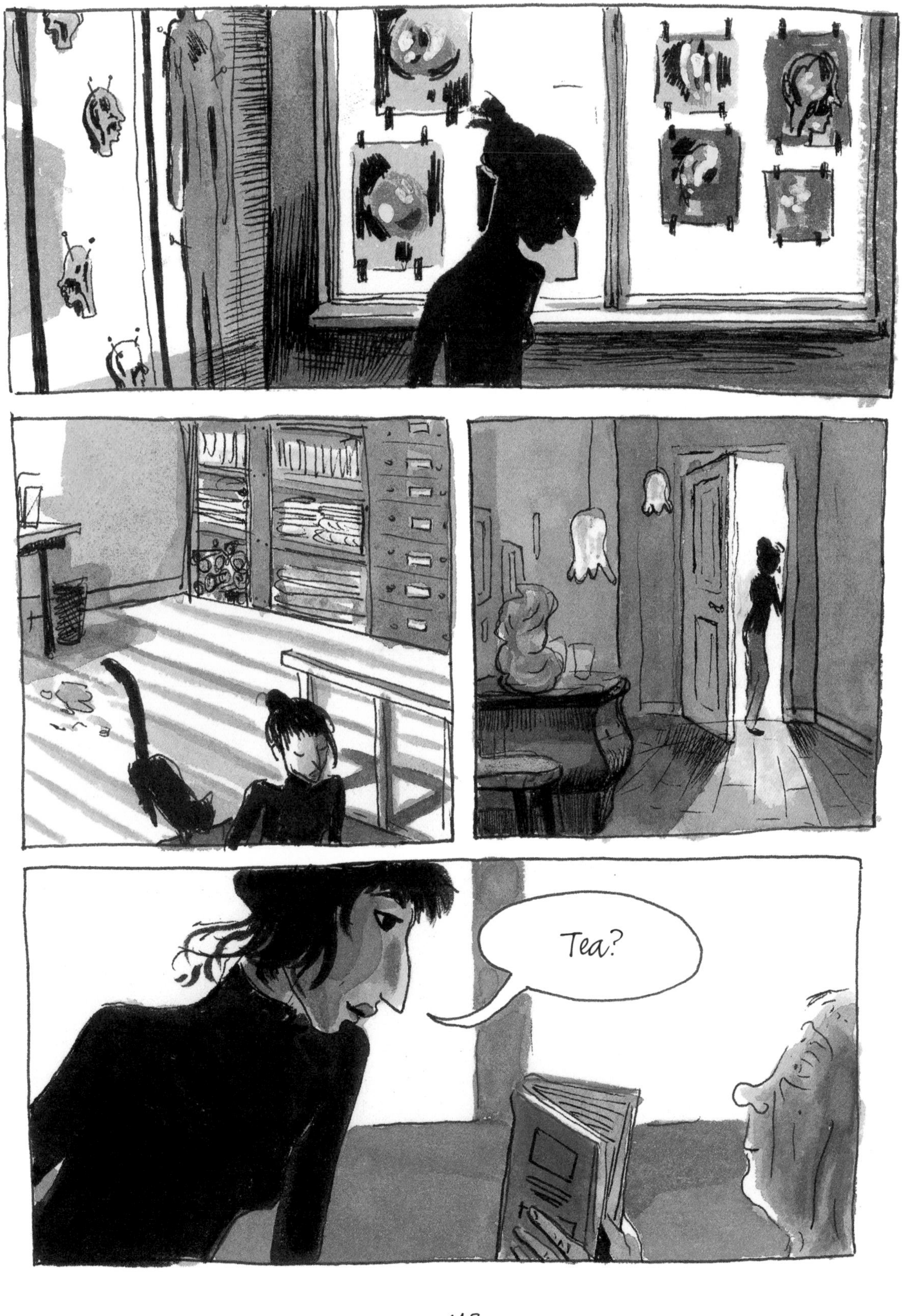
Tea?

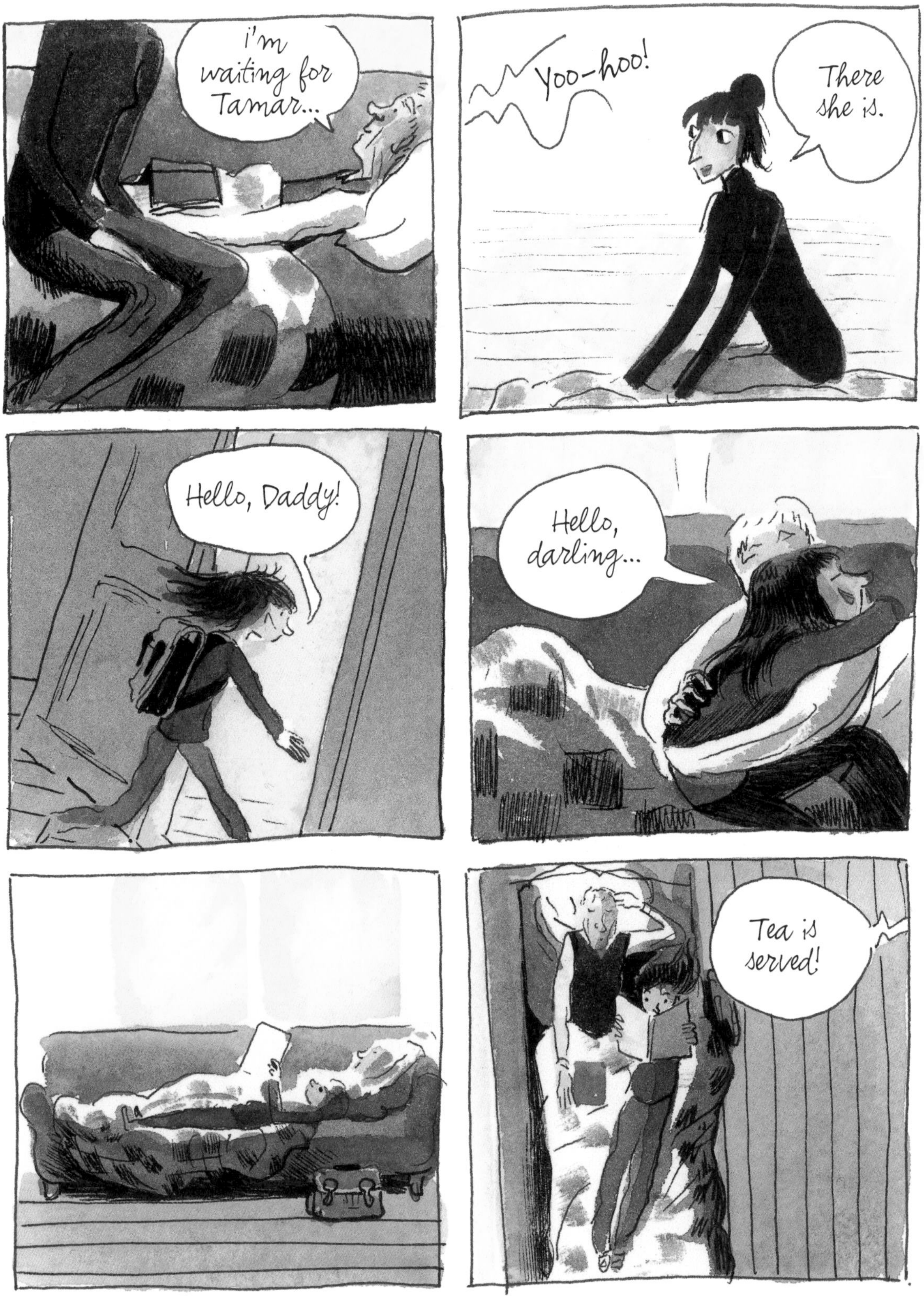
i'm waiting for Tamar...
Yoo-hoo!
There she is.
Hello, Daddy!
Hello, darling...
Tea is served!

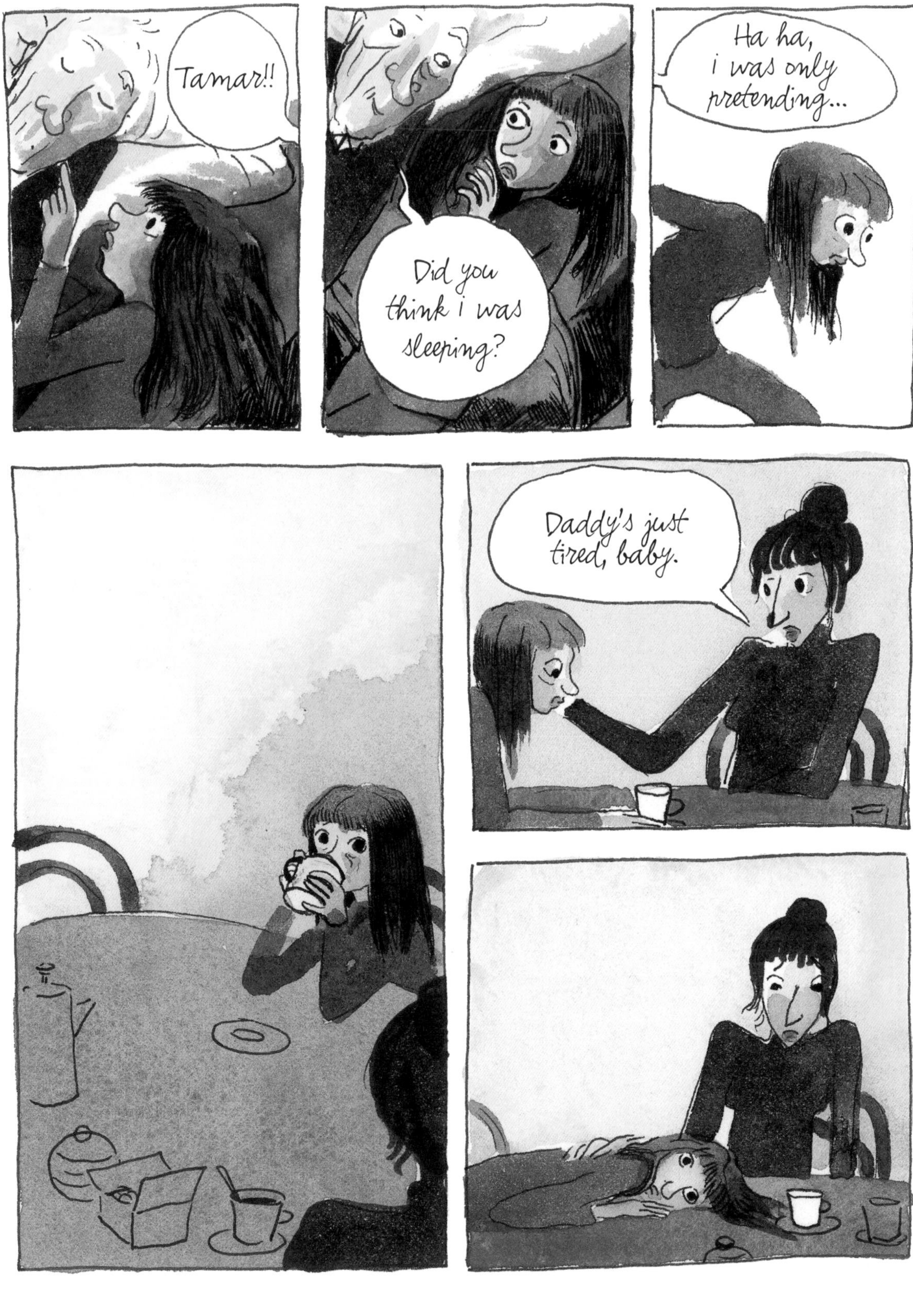
Tamar!!
Did you think i was sleeping?
Ha ha, i was only pretending...
Daddy's just tired, baby.

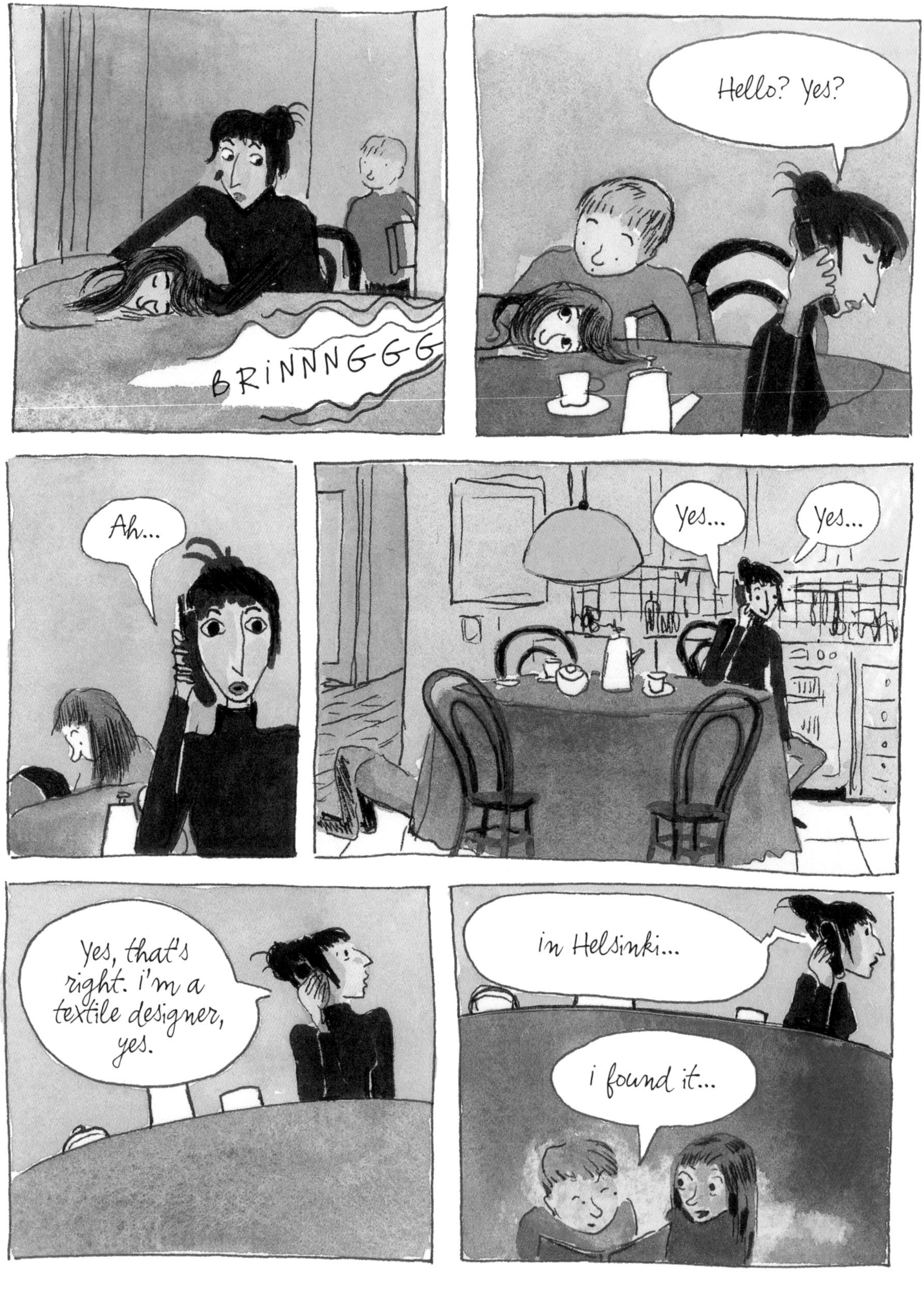
BRINNNGGG
Hello? Yes?
Ah...
Yes...
Yes...
Yes, that's right. i'm a textile designer, yes.
in Helsinki...
i found it...

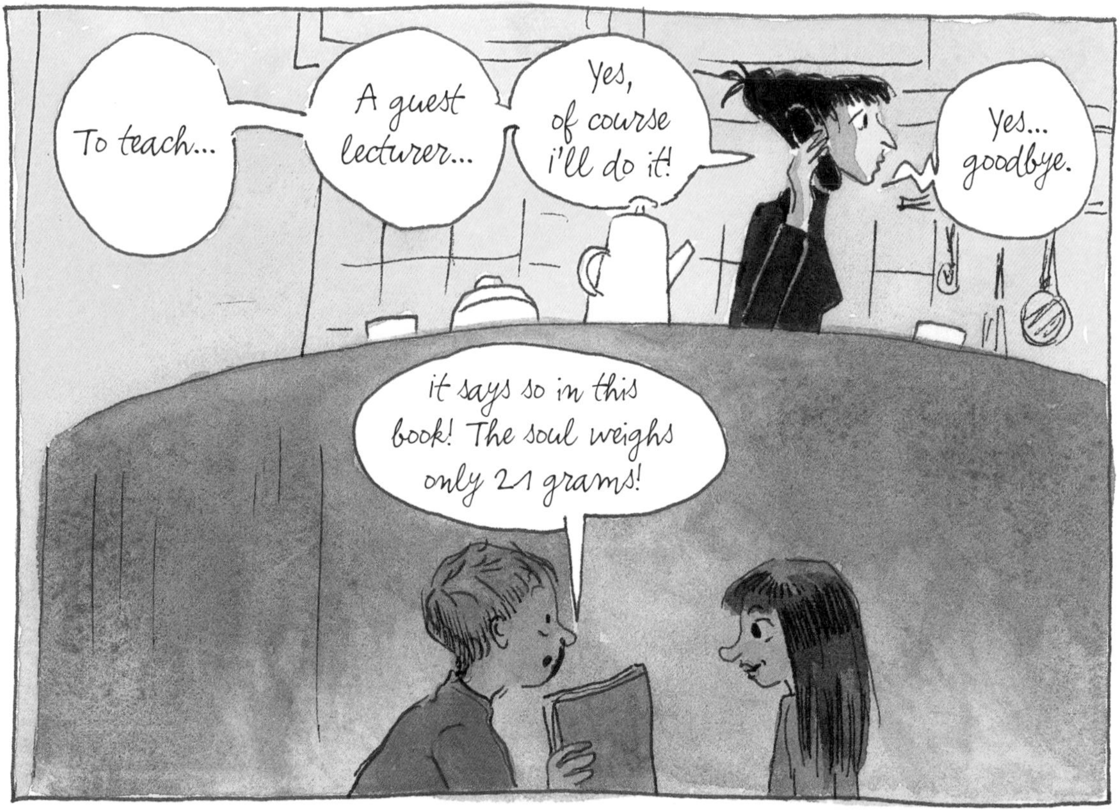
To teach...
A guest lecturer...
Yes, of course i'll do it!
Yes... goodbye.
it says so in this book! The soul weighs only 21 grams!

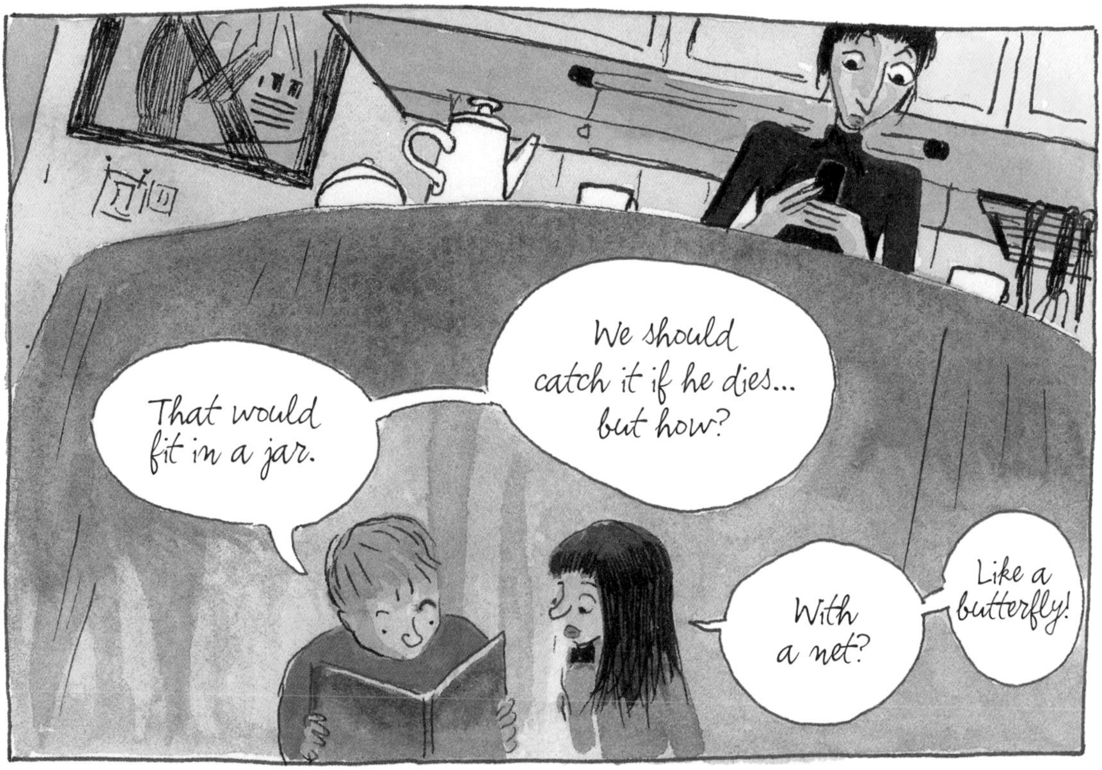
That would fit in a jar.
We should catch it if he dies... but how?
With a net?
Like a butterfly!

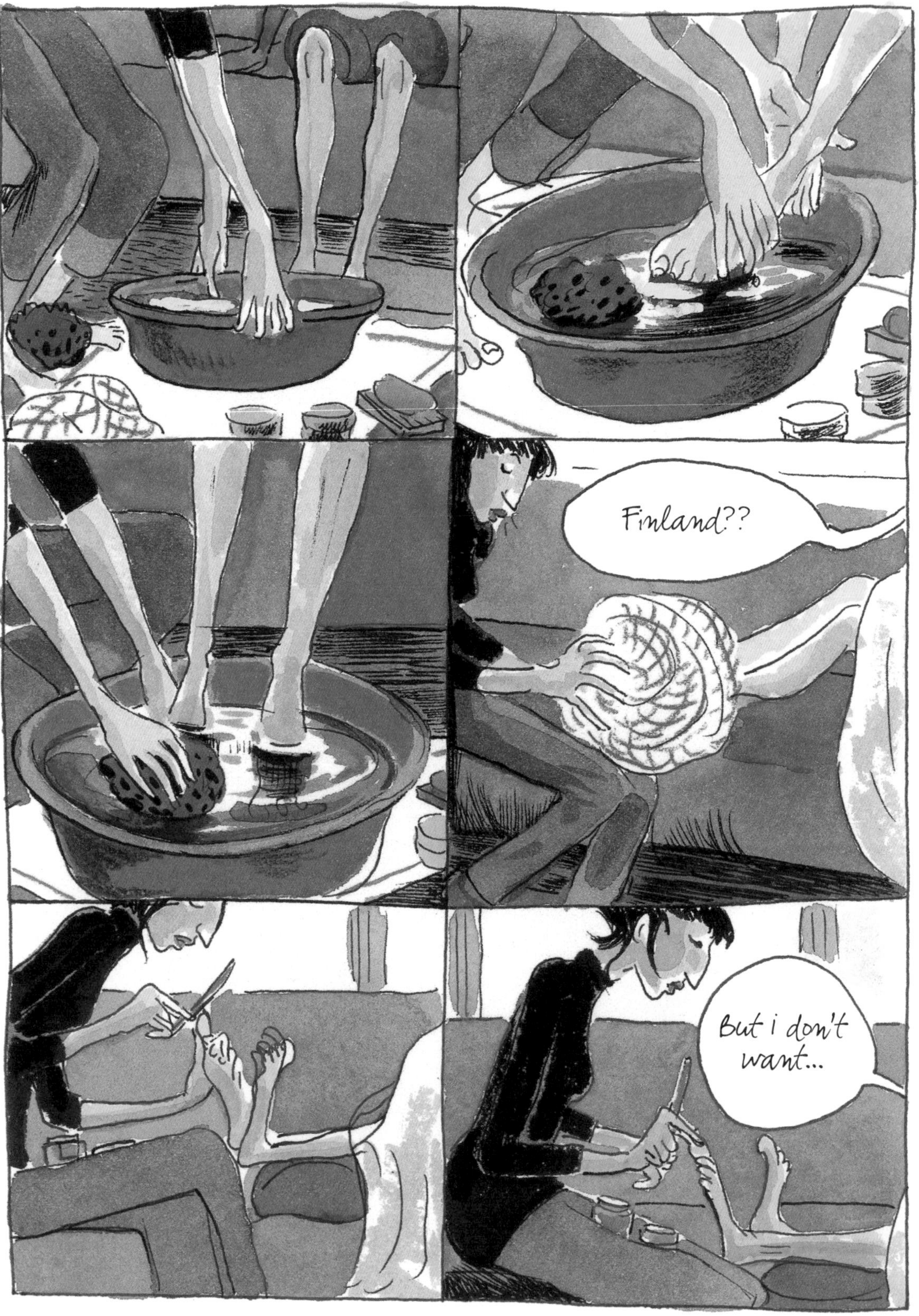
Finland??
But i don't want...

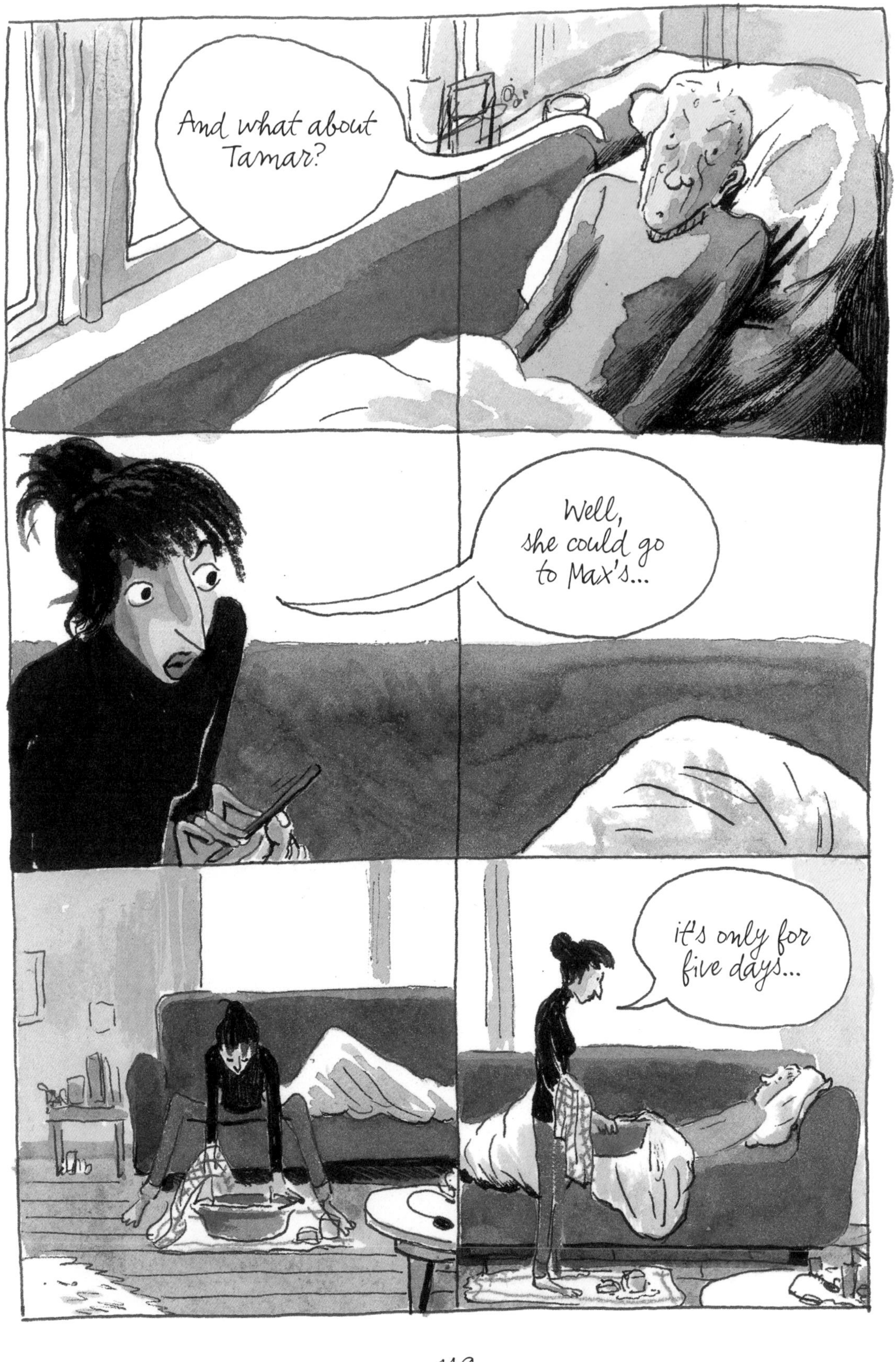
And what about Tamar?
Well, she could go to Max's...
it's only for five days...

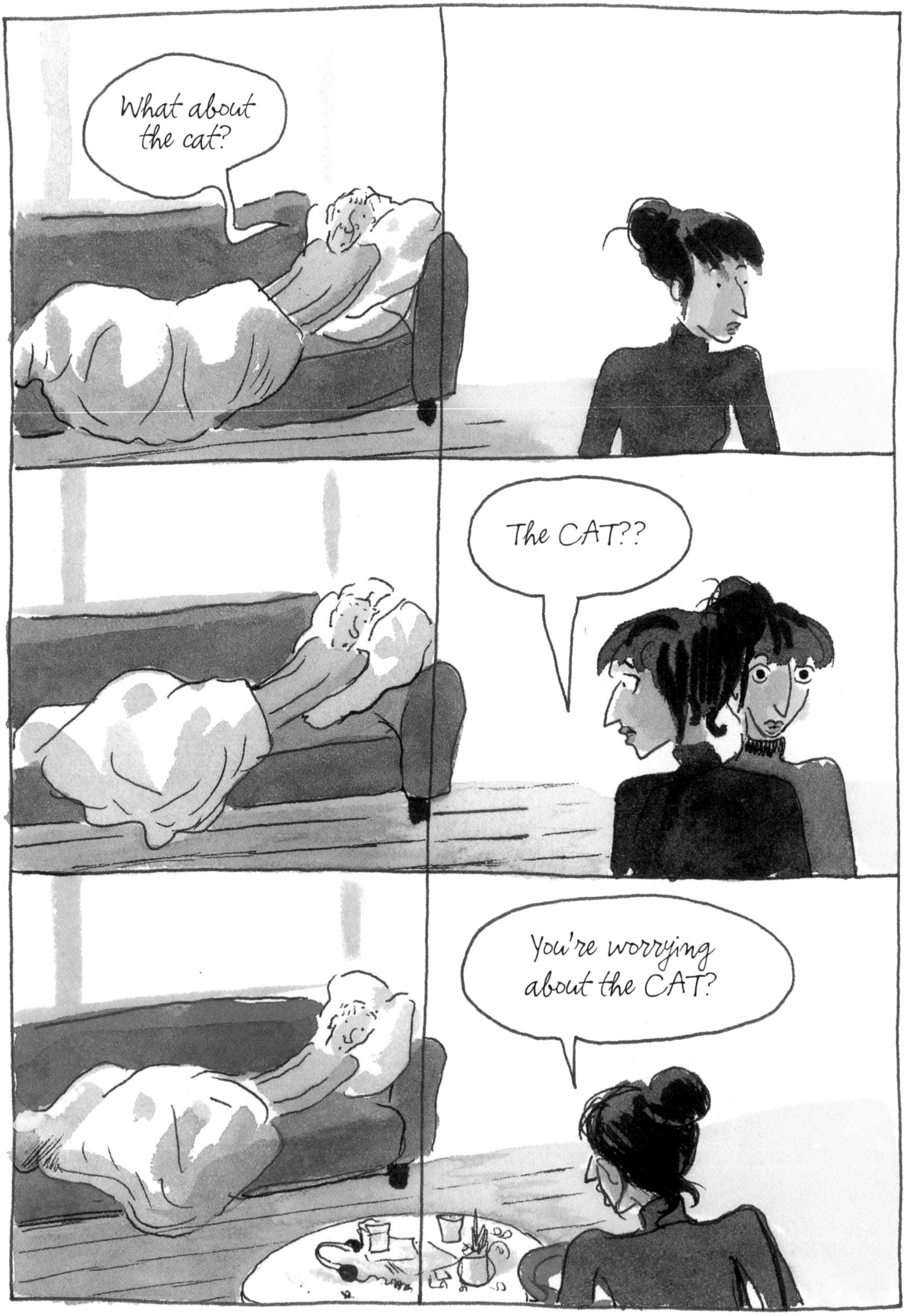
What about the cat?
The CAT??
You're worrying about the CAT?

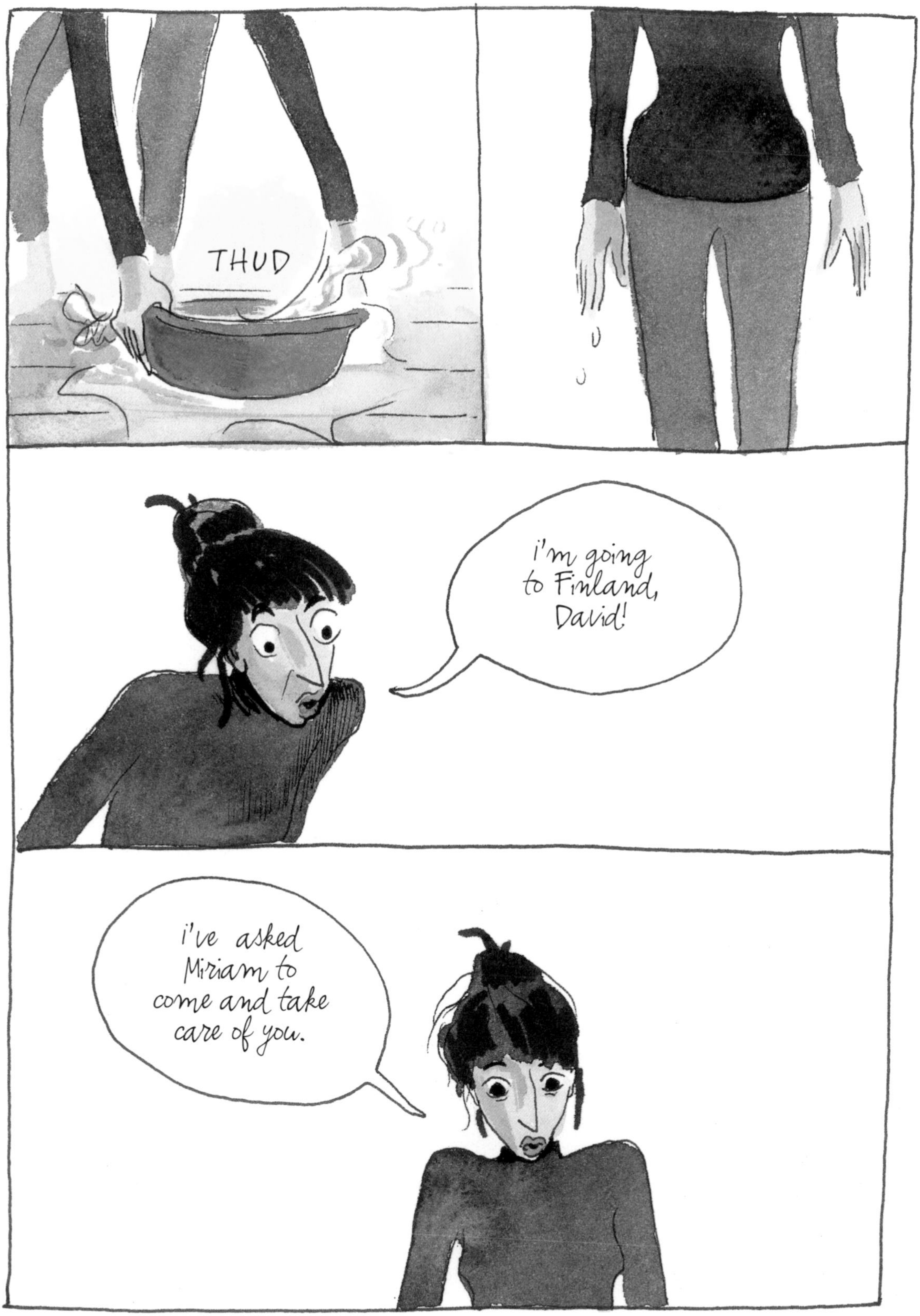
THUD
i'm going to Finland, David!
i've asked Miriam to come and take care of you.

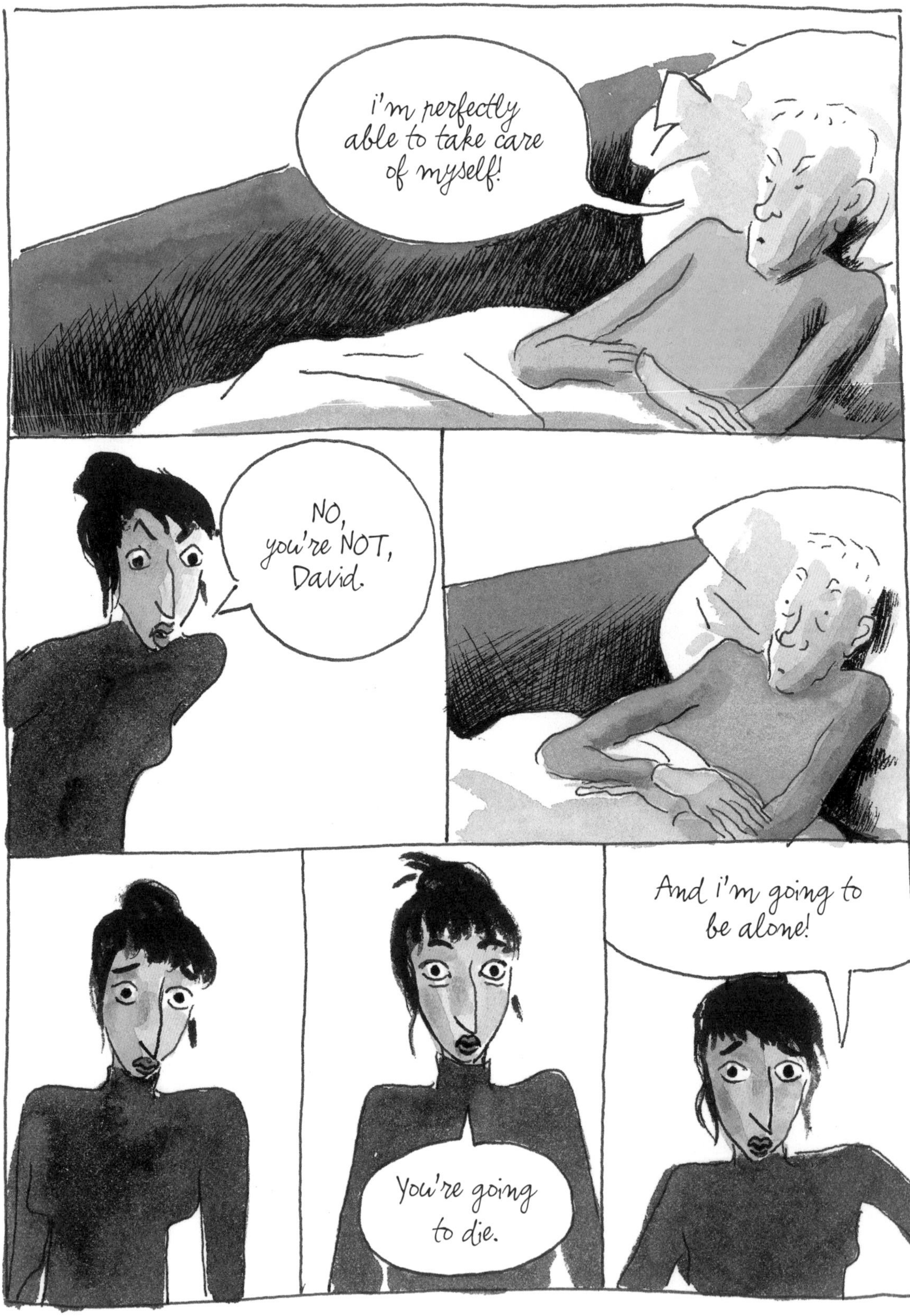
i'm perfectly able to take care of myself!
NO, you're NOT, David.
You're going to die.
And i'm going to be alone!

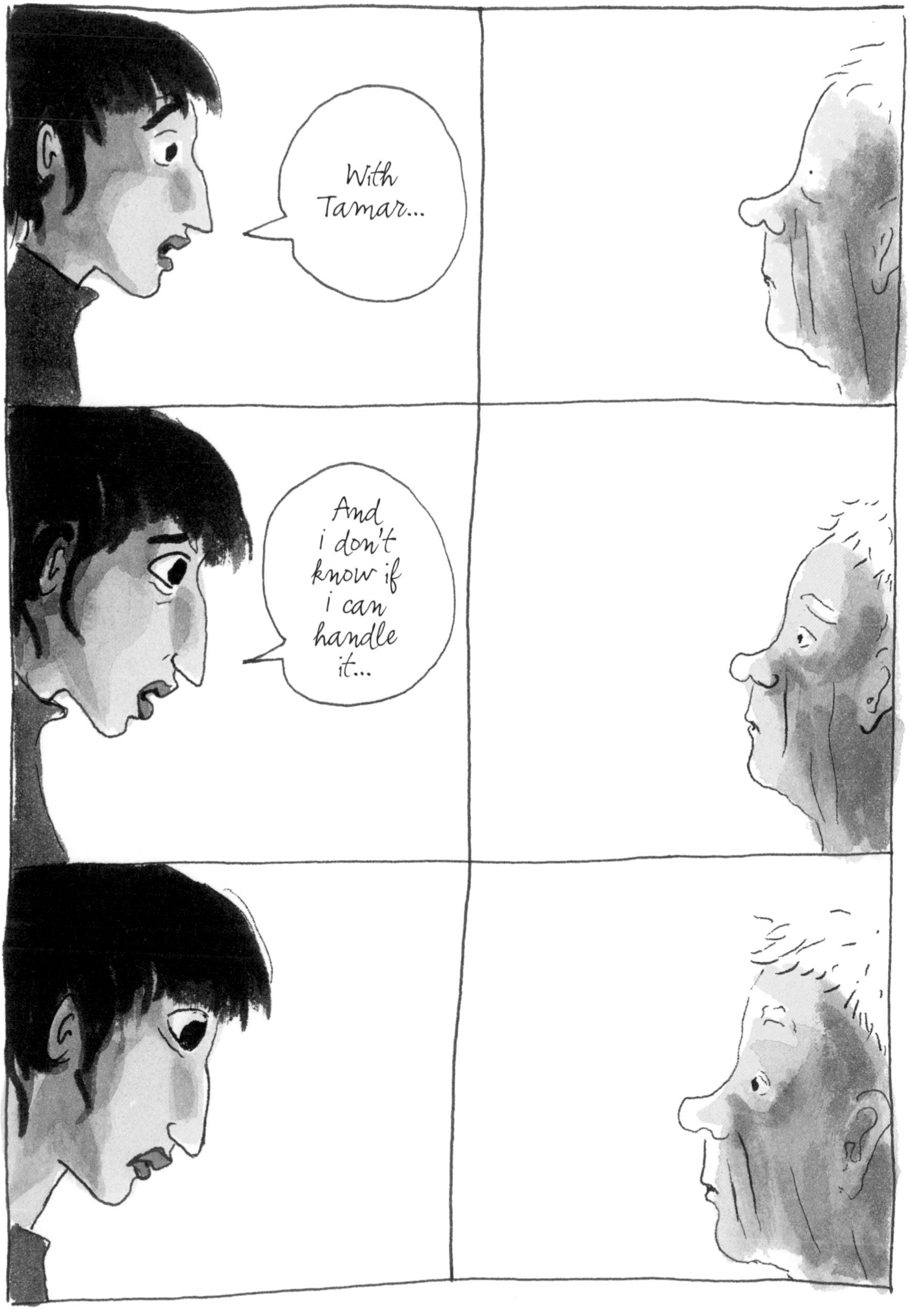
With Tamar...
And i don't know if i can handle it...

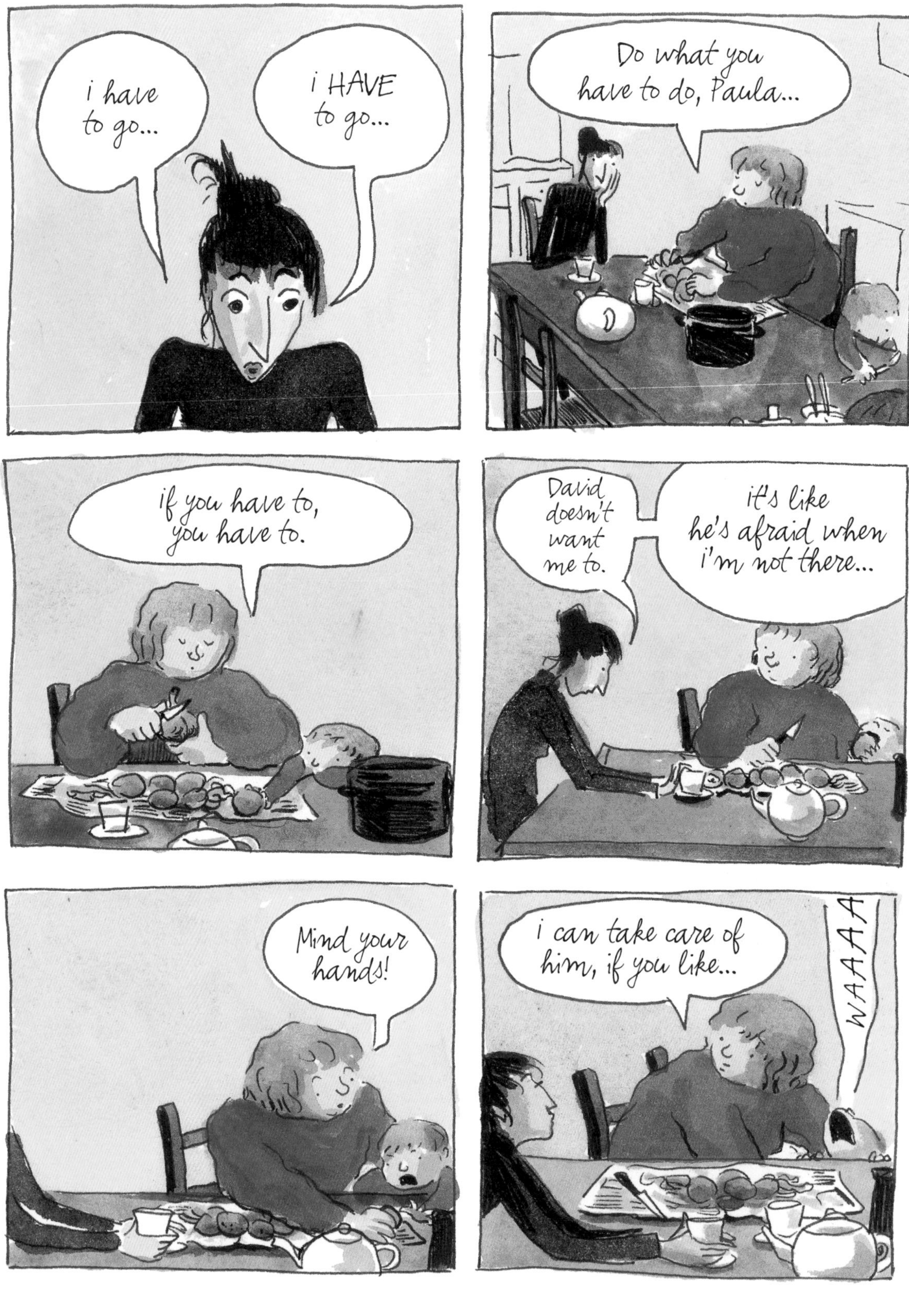
i have to go...
i HAVE to go...
Do what you have to do, Paula...
if you have to, you have to.
David doesn't want me to.
it's like he's afraid when i'm not there...
Mind your hands!
i can take care of him, if you like...
WAAAA

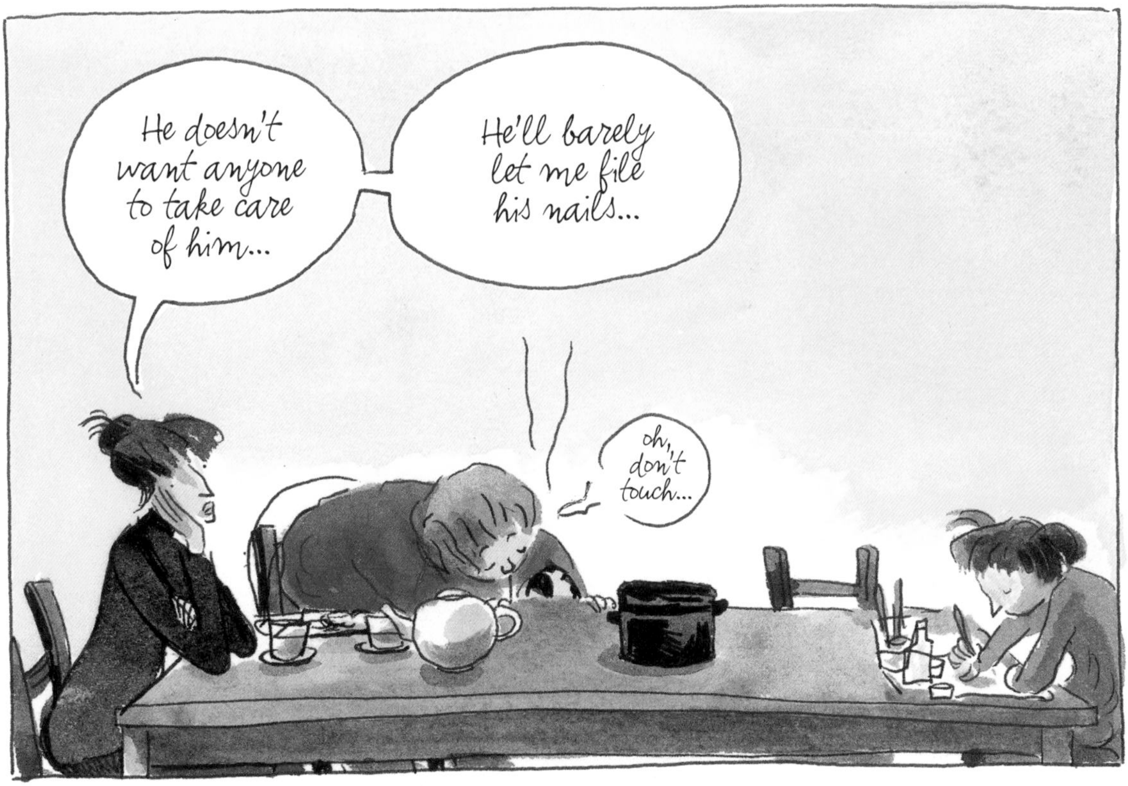
He doesn't want anyone to take care of him...
He'll barely let me file his nails...
oh, don't touch...

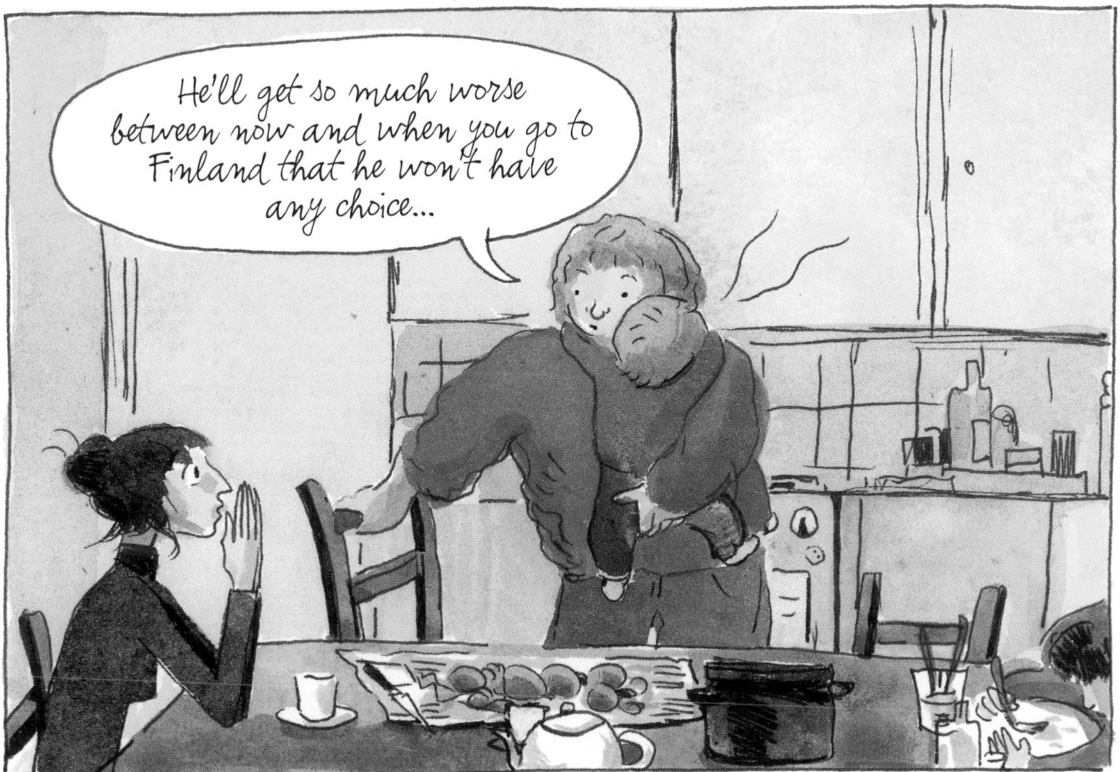
He'll get so much worse between now and when you go to Finland that he won't have any choice...

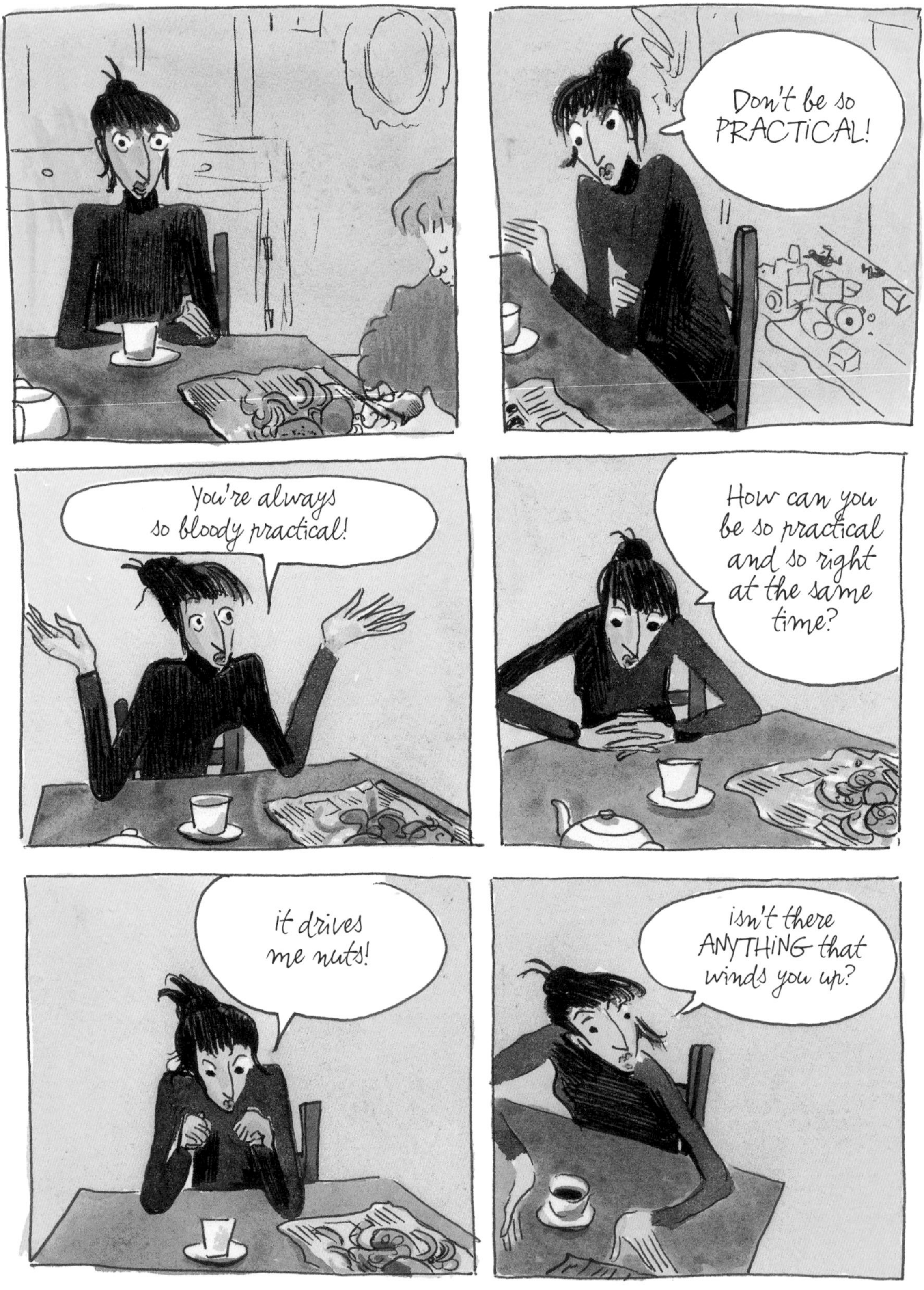
Don't be so PRACTICAL!
You're always so bloody practical!
How can you be so practical and so right at the same time?
it drives me nuts!
isn't there ANYTHING that winds you up?

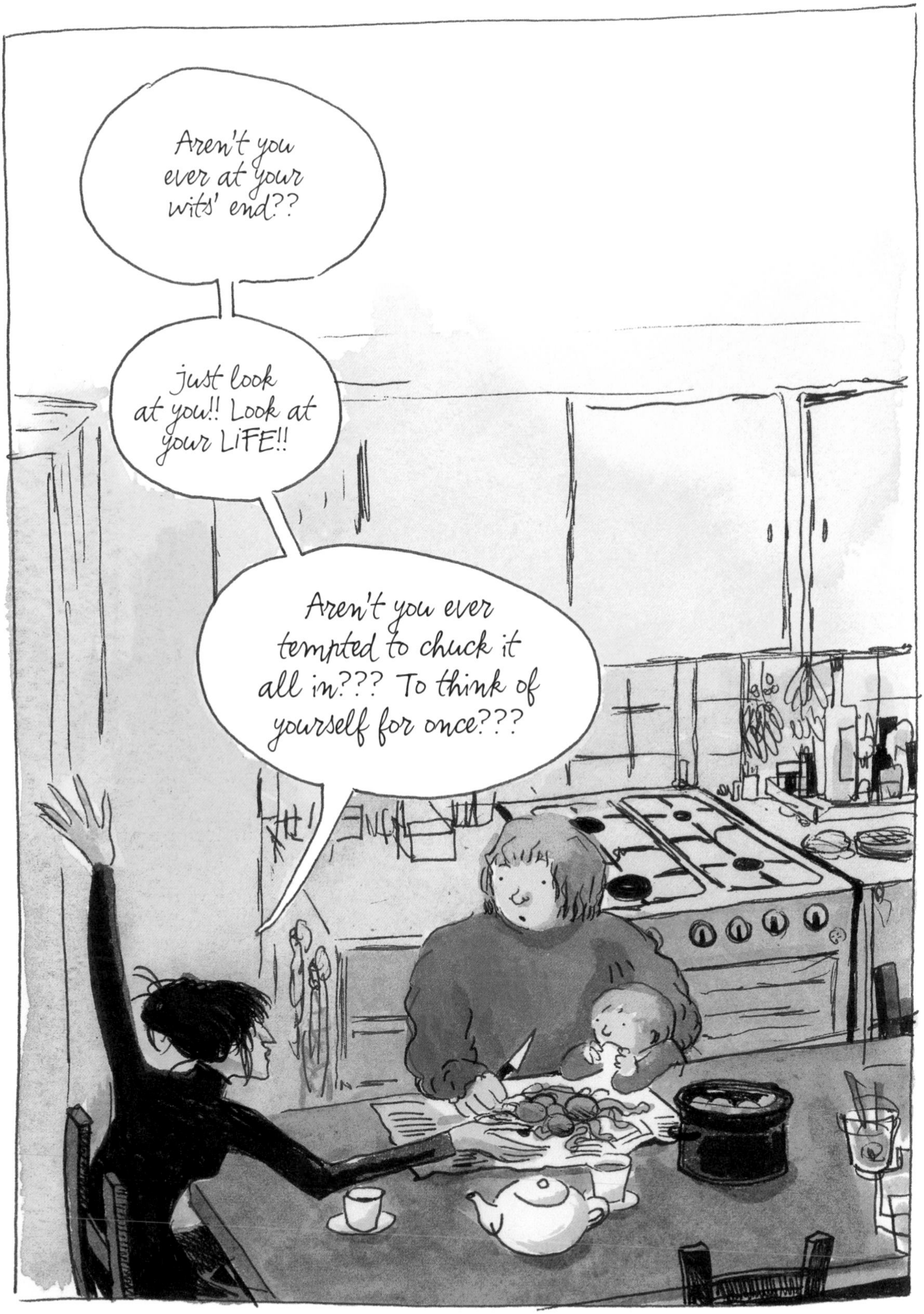
Aren't you ever at your wits' end??
Just look at you!! Look at your LIFE!!
Aren't you ever tempted to chuck it all in??? To think of yourself for once???

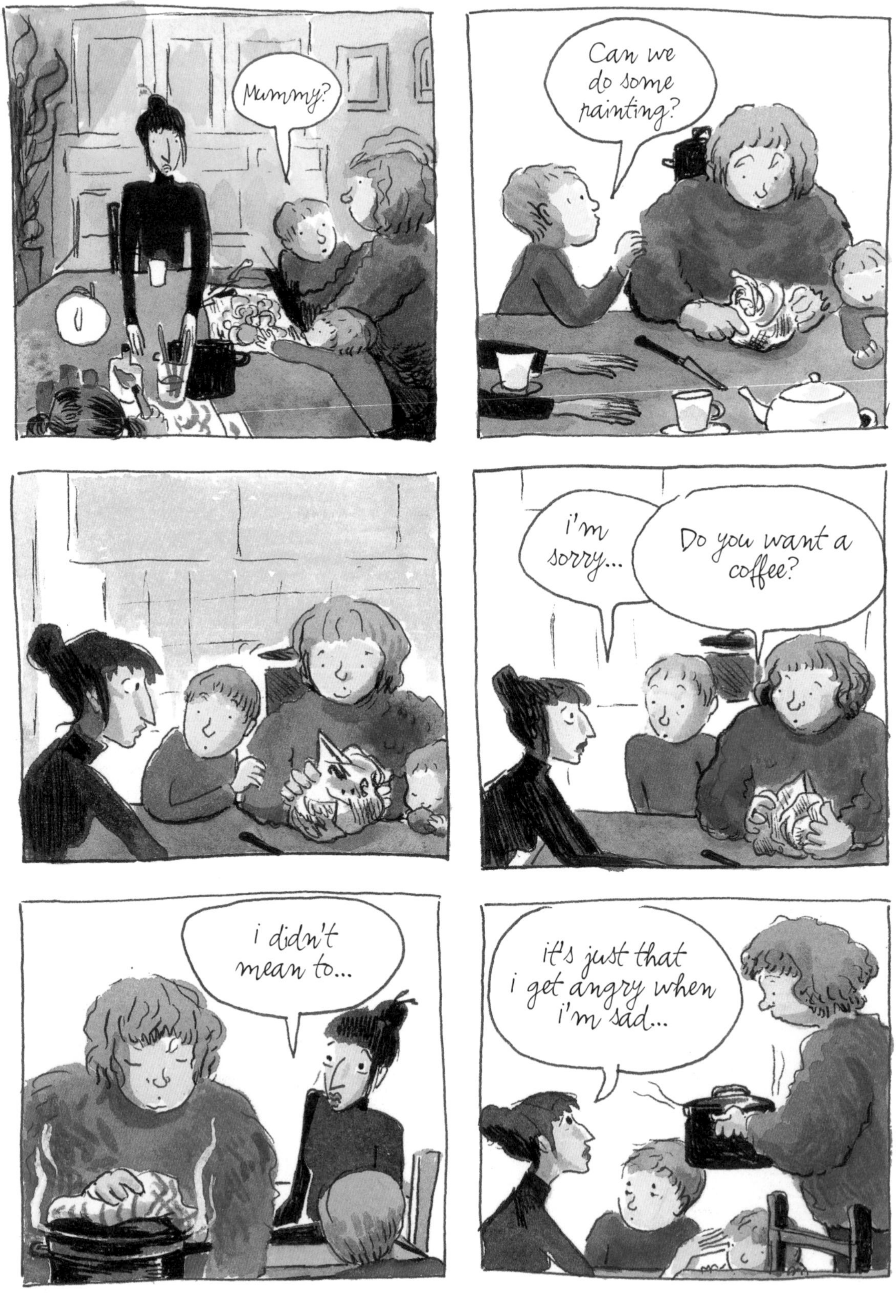
Mummy?
Can we do some painting?
i'm sorry...
Do you want a coffee?
i didn't mean to...
it's just that i get angry when i'm sad...

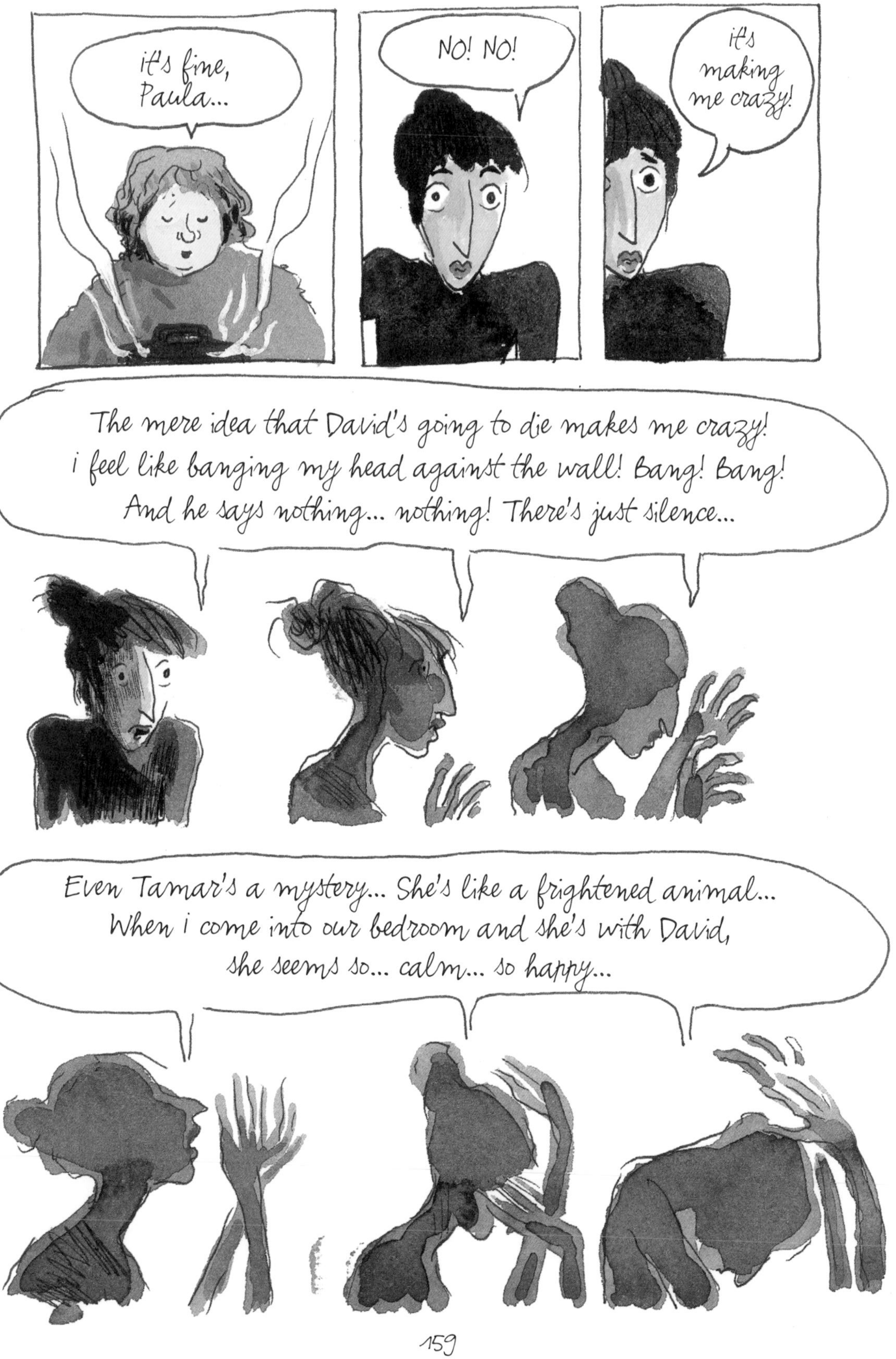
it's fine, Paula...
NO! NO!
it's making me crazy!
The mere idea that David's going to die makes me crazy! i feel like banging my head against the wall! Bang! Bang! And he says nothing... nothing! There's just silence...
Even Tamar's a mystery... She's like a frightened animal... When i come into our bedroom and she's with David, she seems so... calm... so happy...

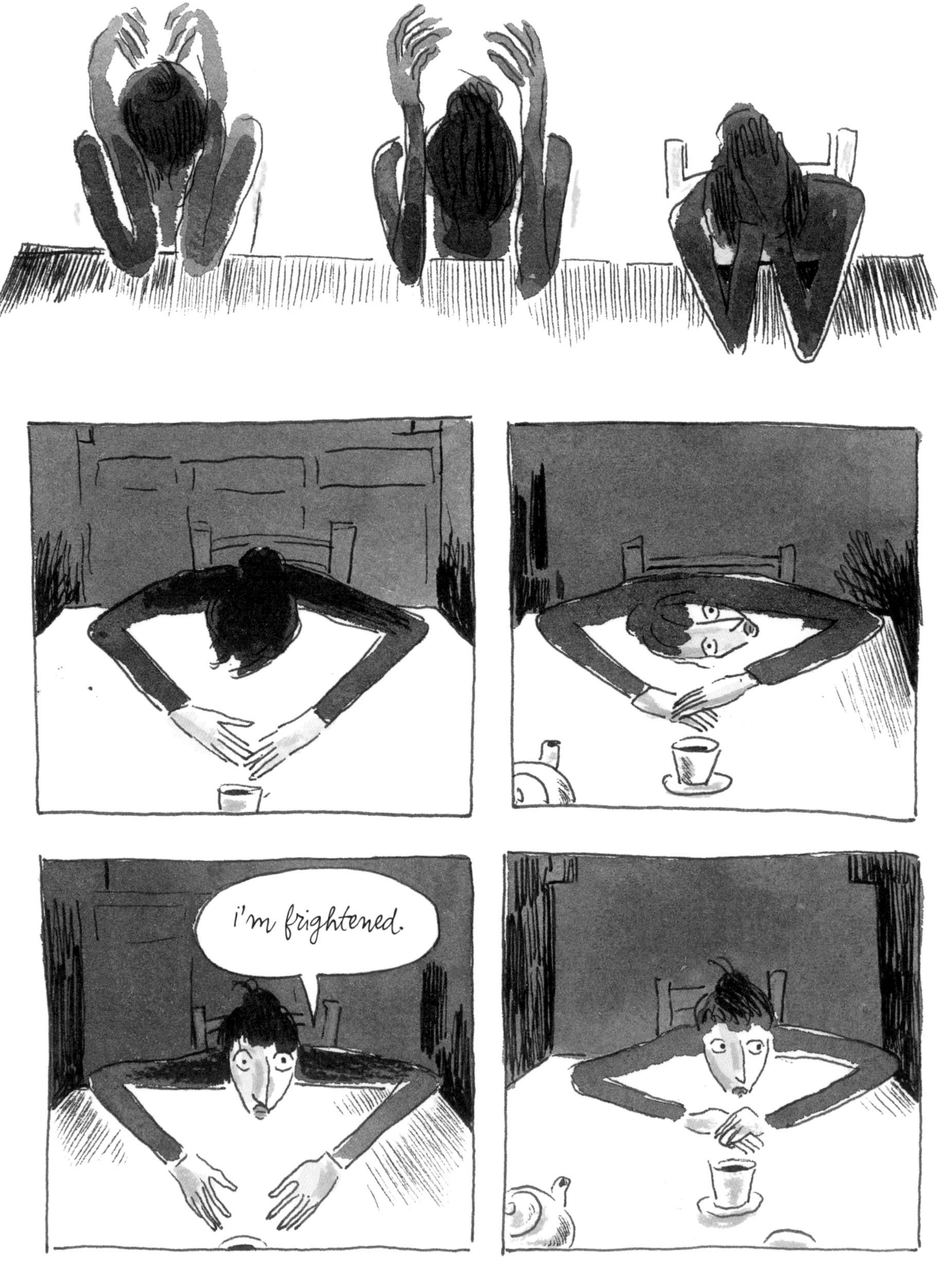
i'm frightened.

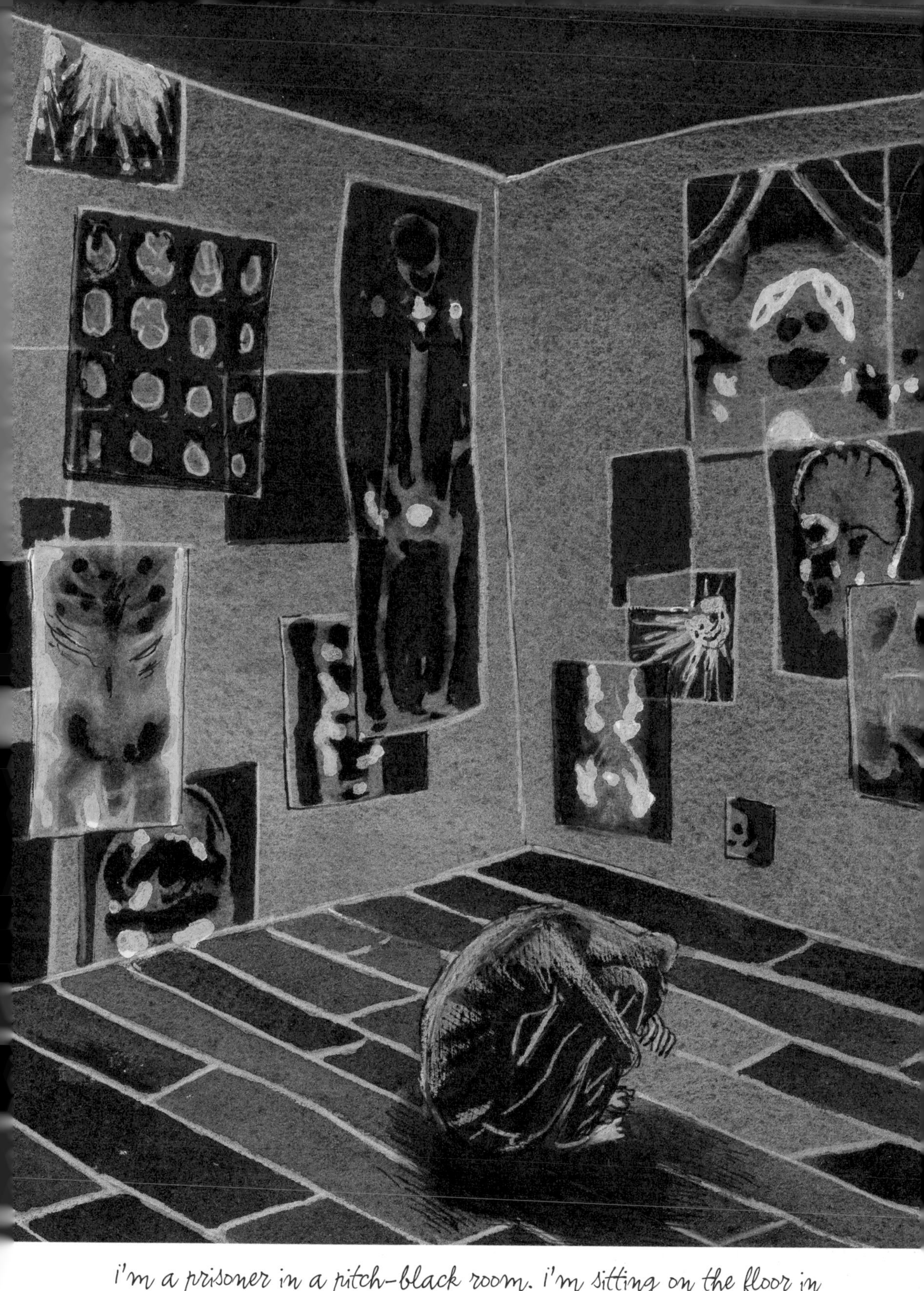

i'm a prisoner in a pitch-black room. i'm sitting on the floor in a darkened room, the walls covered in X-rays of David... The only thing i can see is the pale-green glow of his metastases...

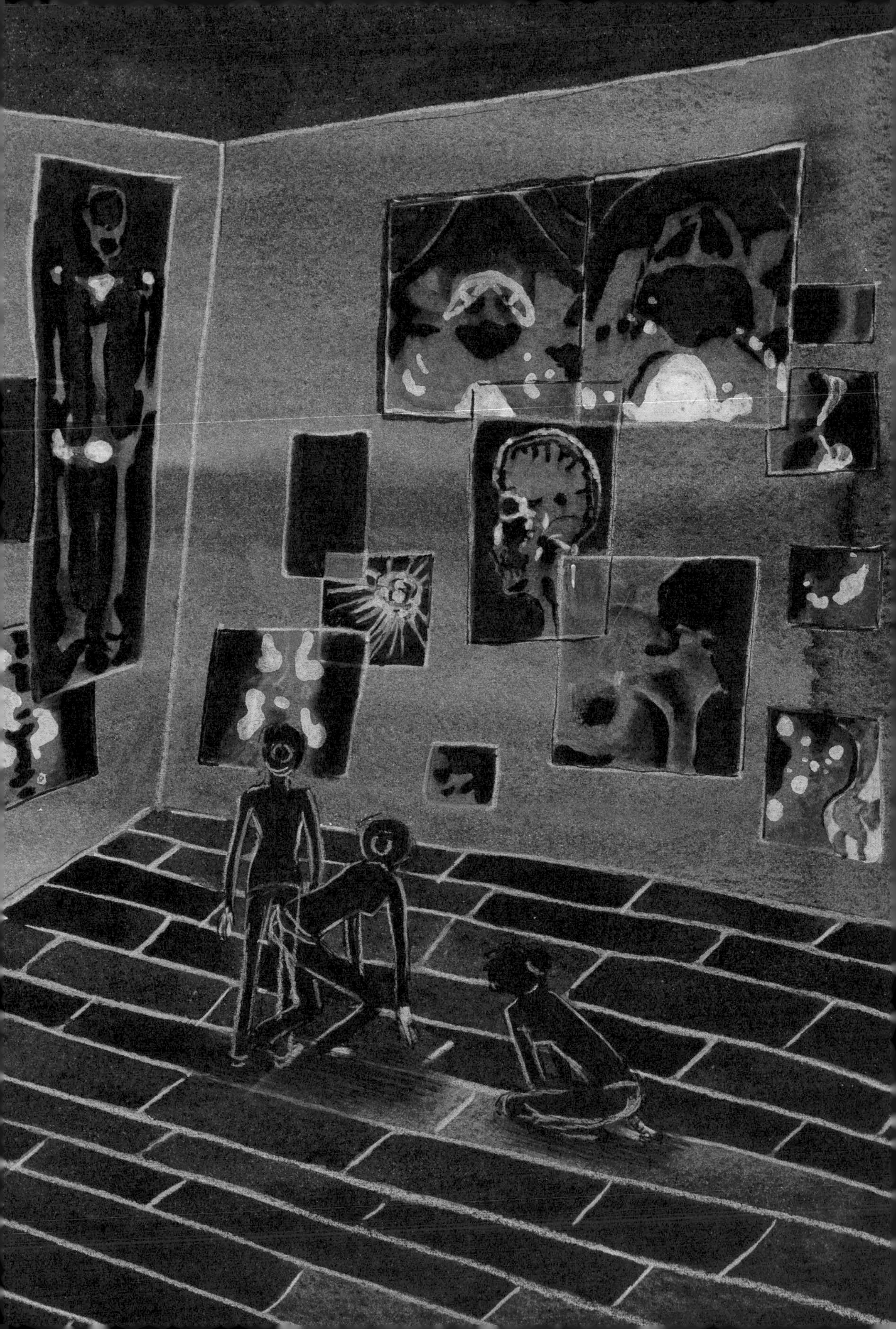

There aren't any doors, any windows, and i can't see anything but the metastases. i see only death and the green light. i'm alone, alone with her... David is in another room. He doesn't say anything. i call to him, i cry out "Where are you?? Are you afraid? Are you in pain??", but i don't get any answer... i'm alone.

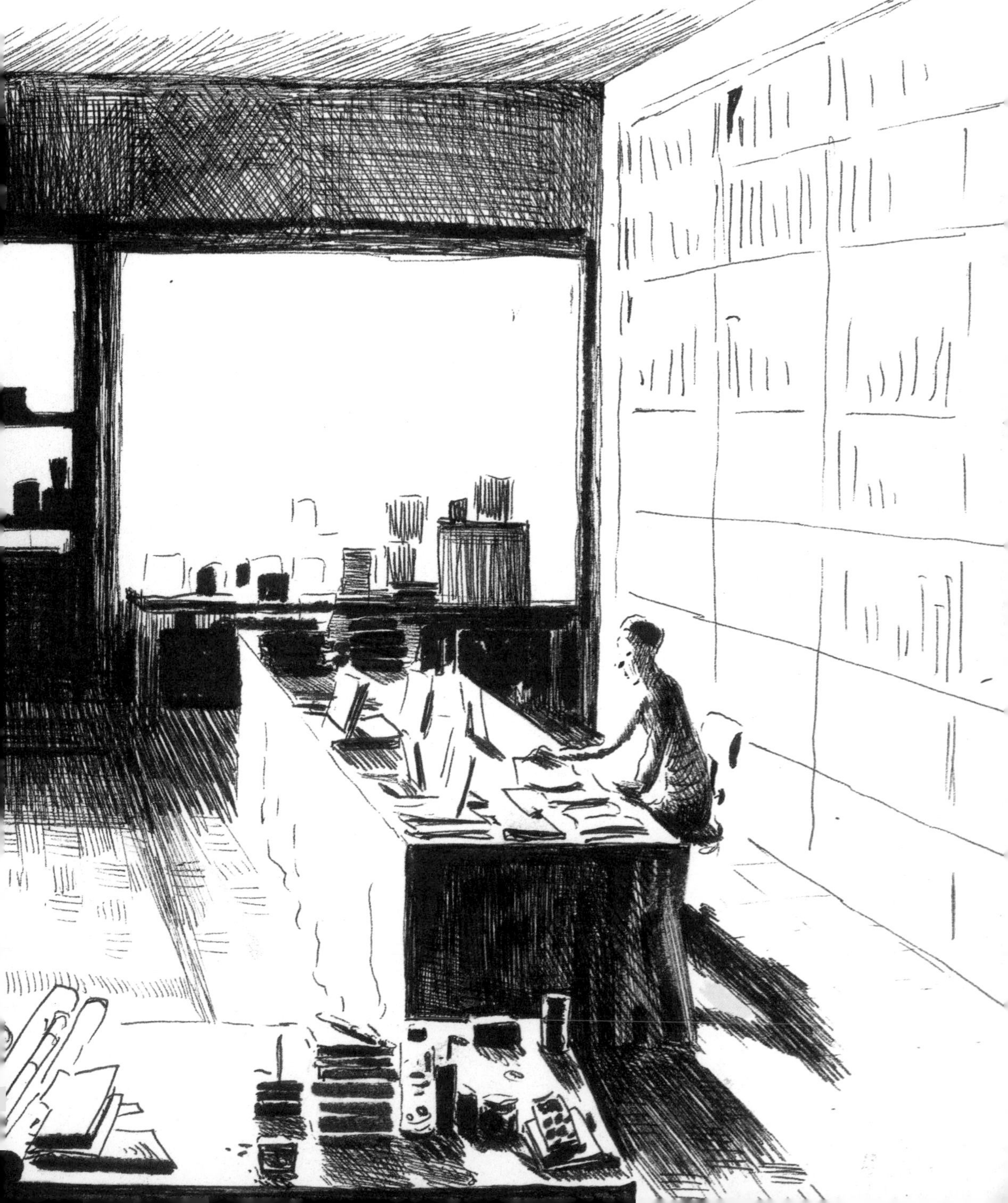

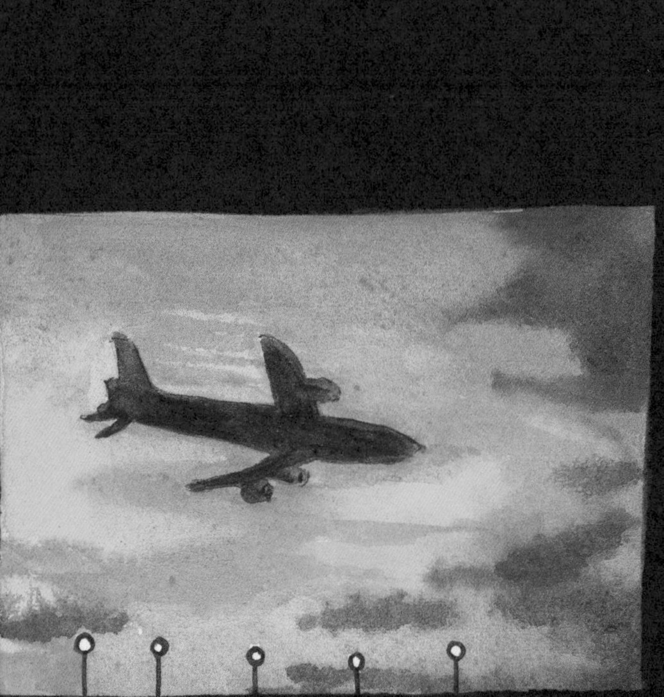

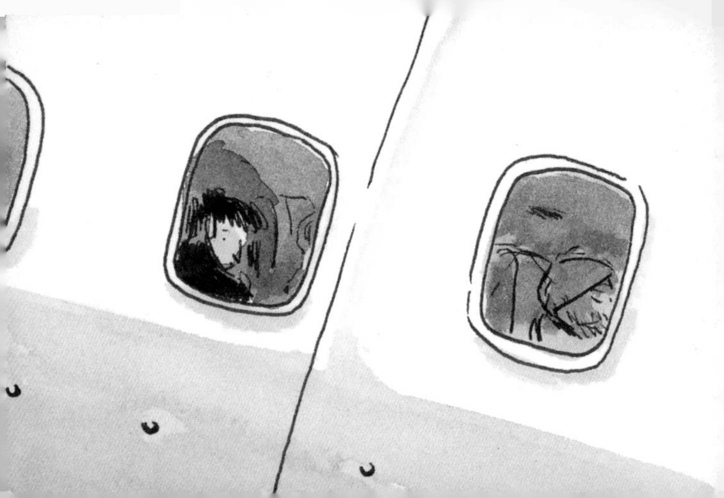

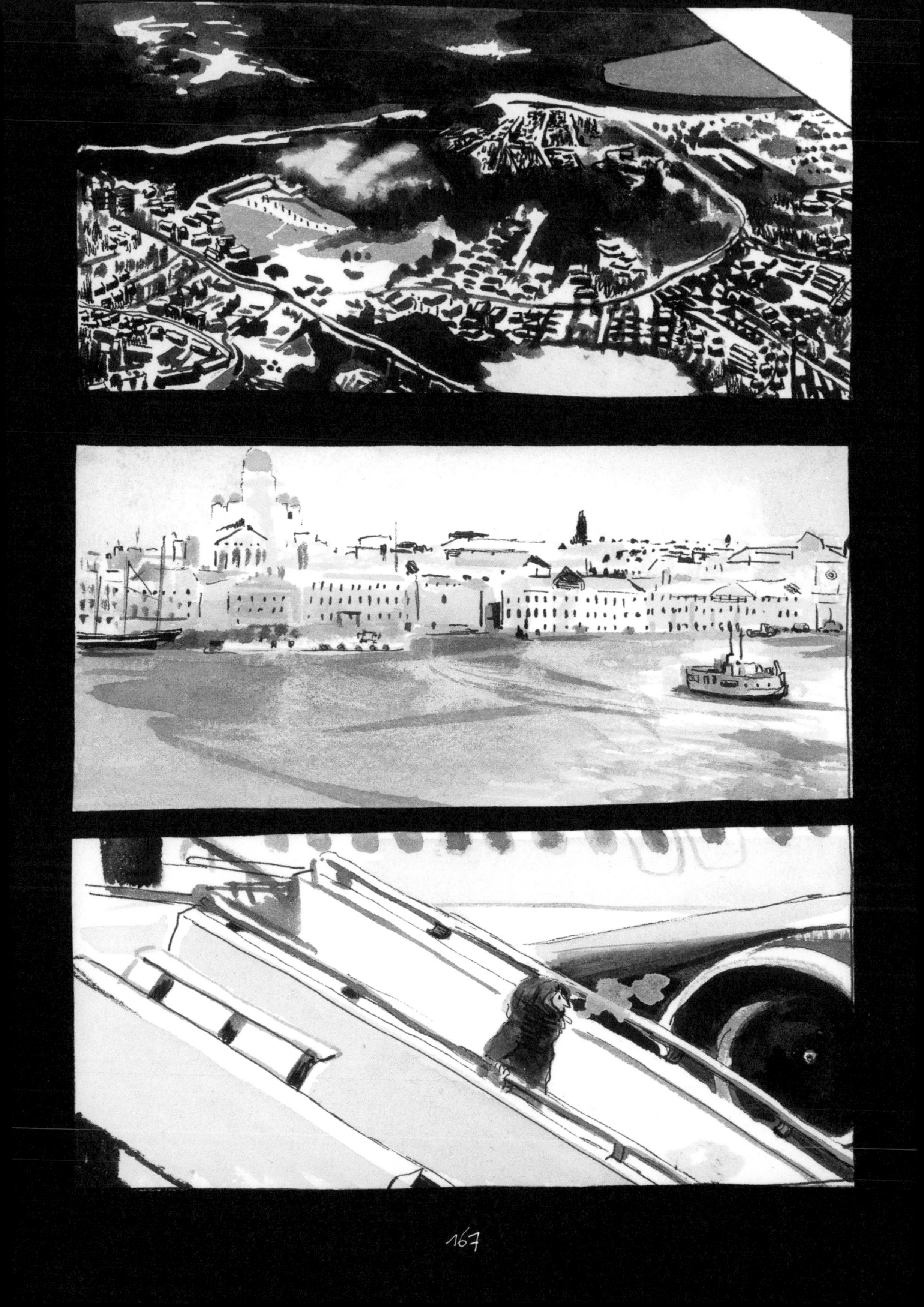

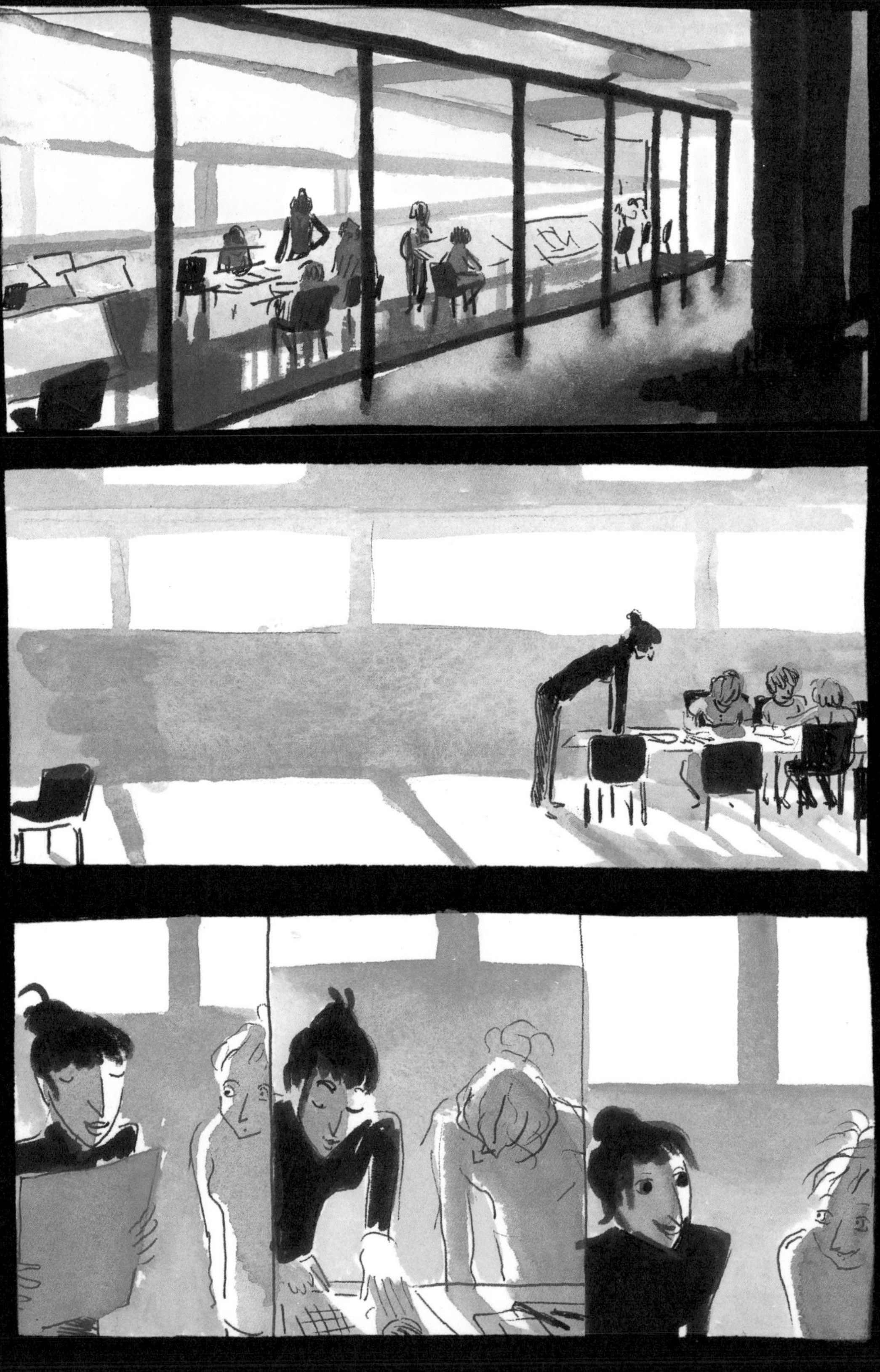

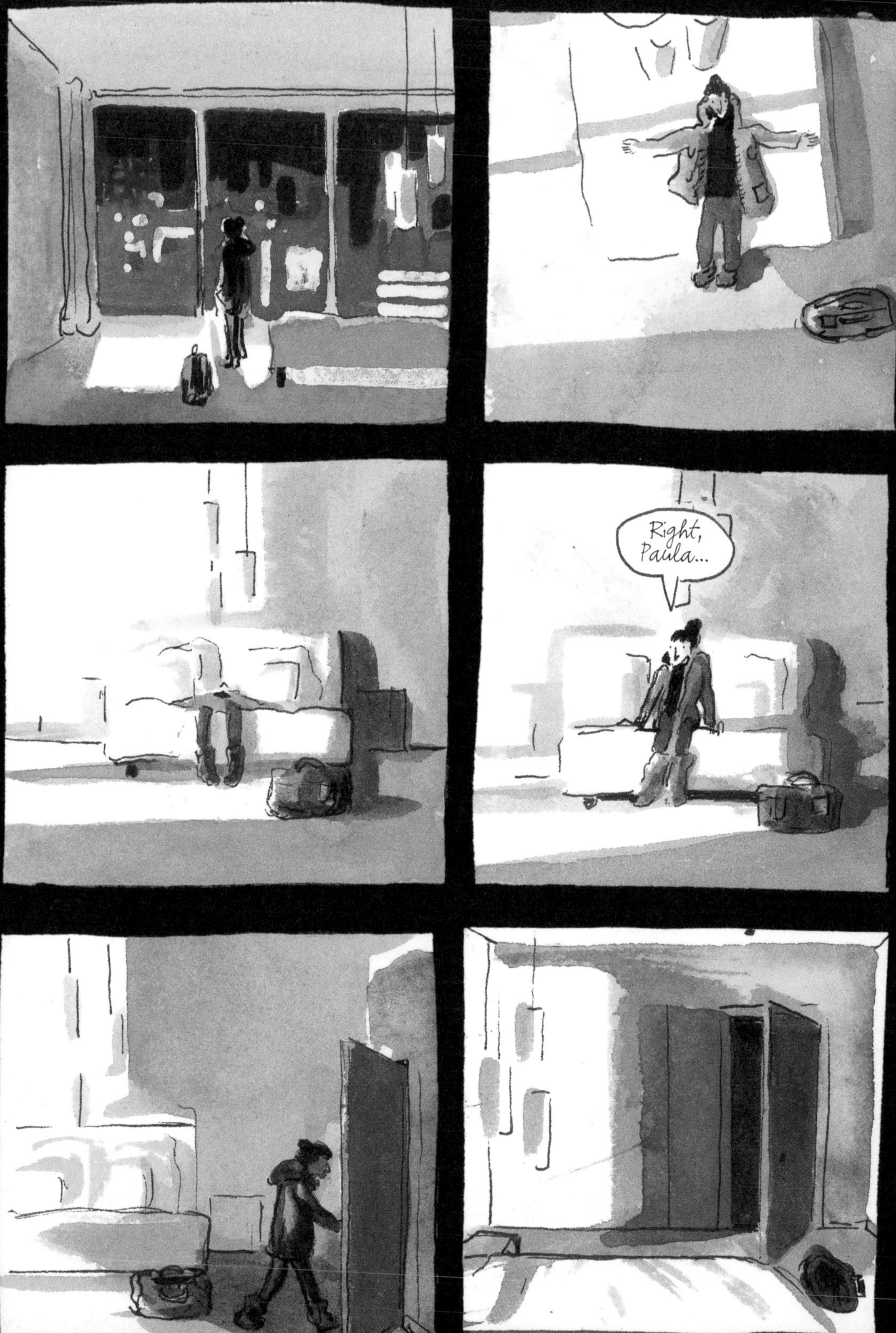
Right, Paula...

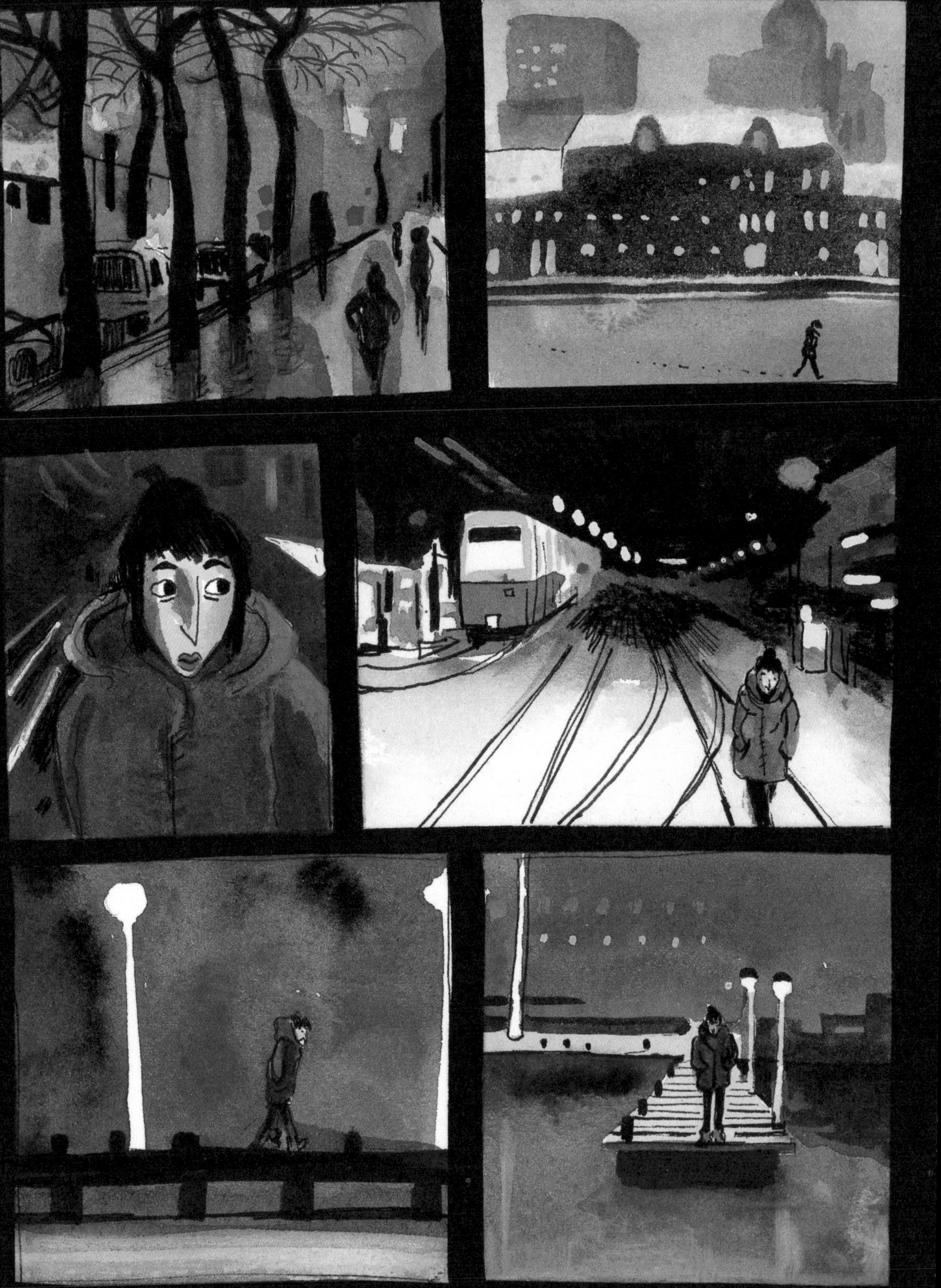

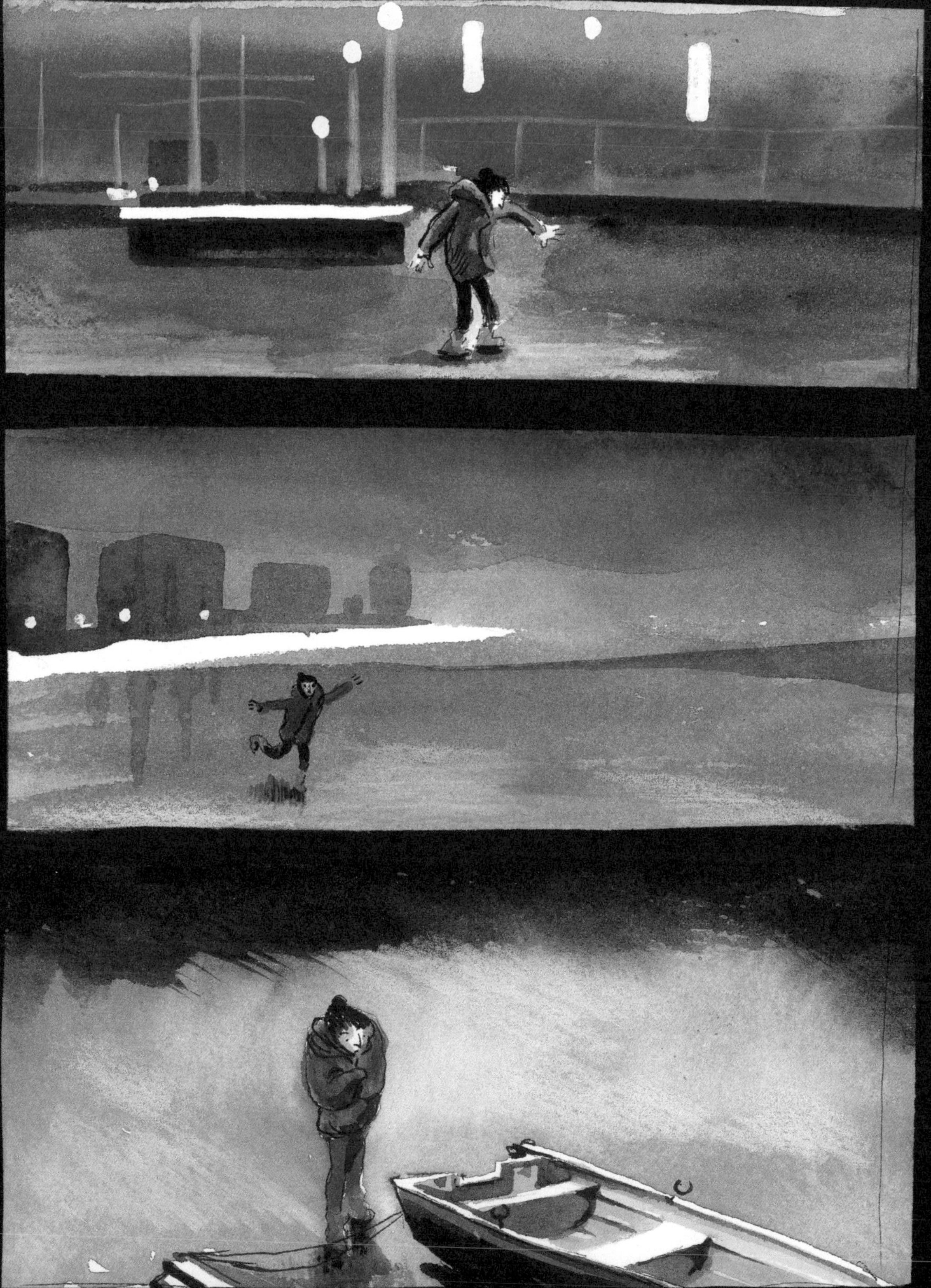

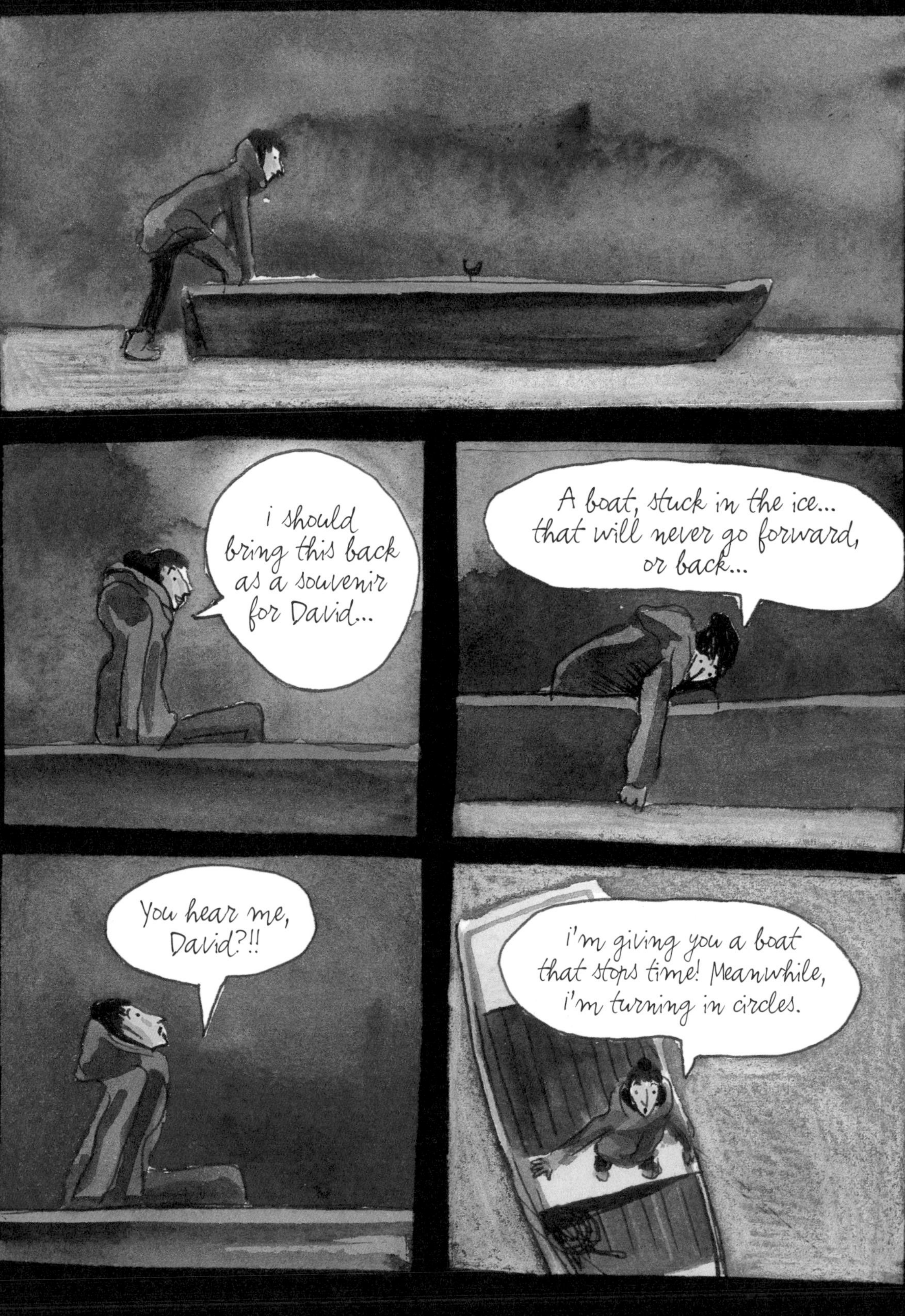
i should bring this back as a souvenir for David...
A boat, stuck in the ice... that will never go forward, or back...
You hear me, David?!!
i'm giving you a boat that stops time! Meanwhile, i'm turning in circles.

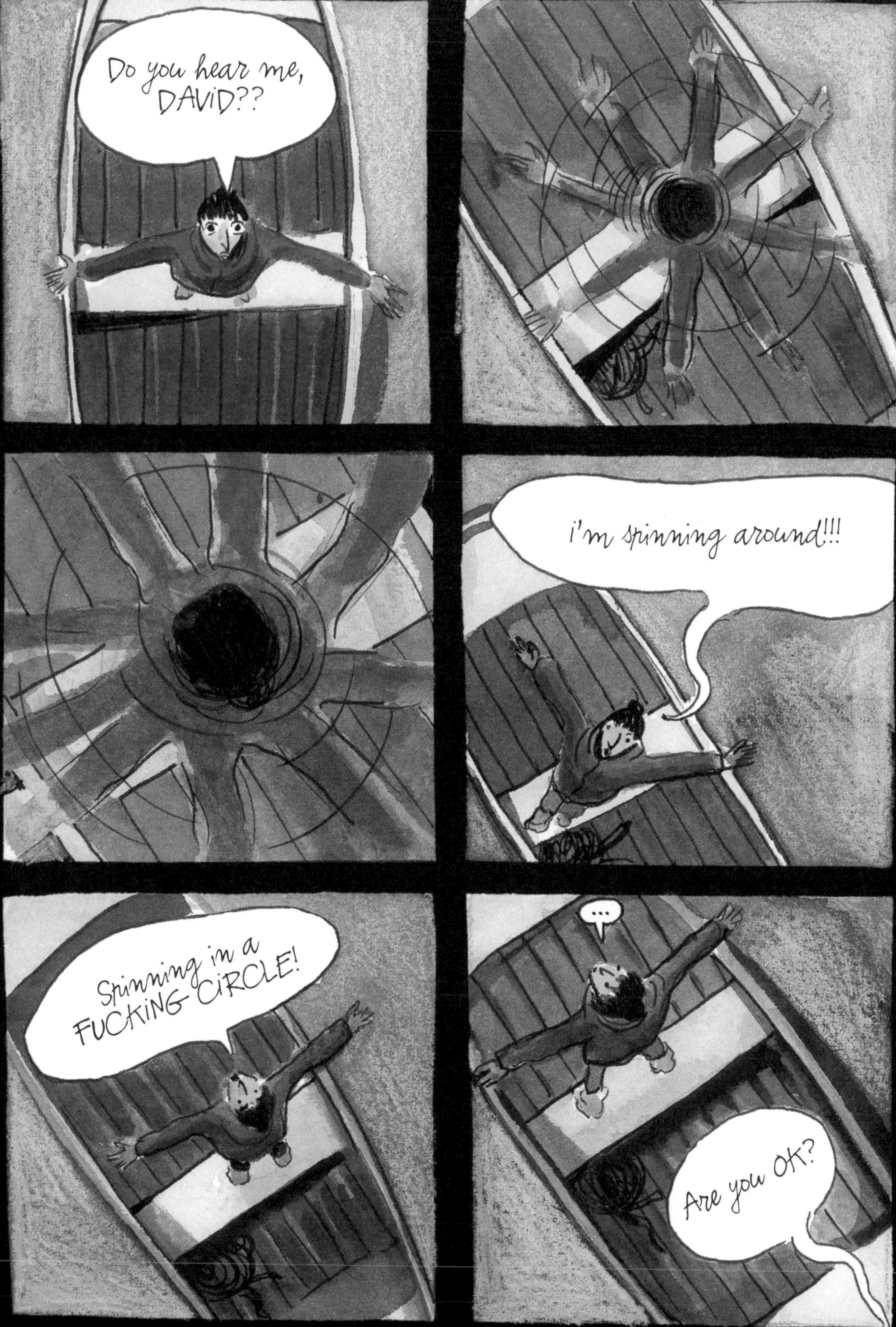
Do you hear me, DAVID??
i'm spinning around!!!
Spinning in a FUCKING CIRCLE!
...
Are you OK?

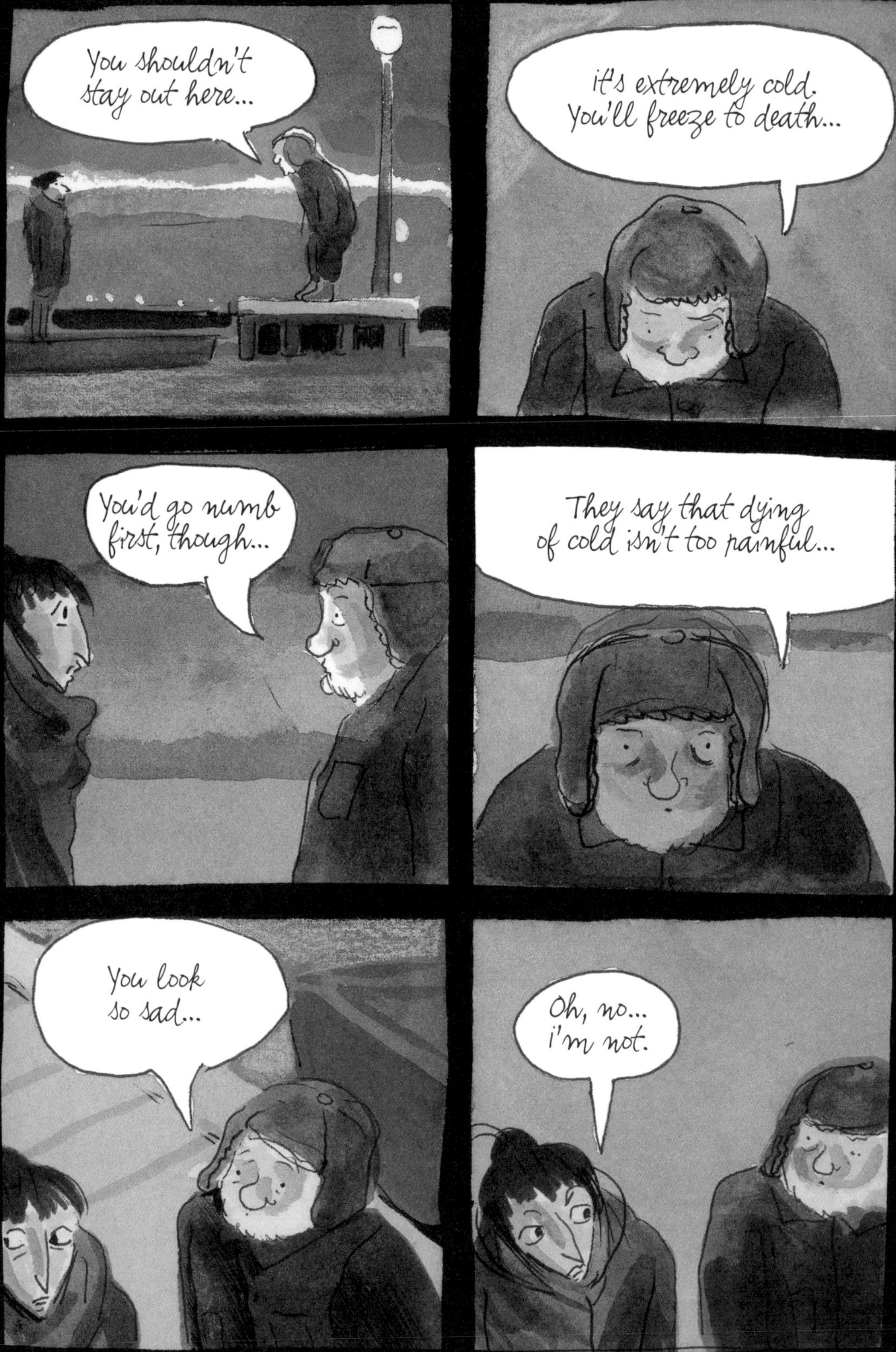
You shouldn't stay out here...
it's extremely cold. You'll freeze to death...
You'd go numb first, though...
They say that dying of cold isn't too painful...
You look so sad...
Oh, no... i'm not.

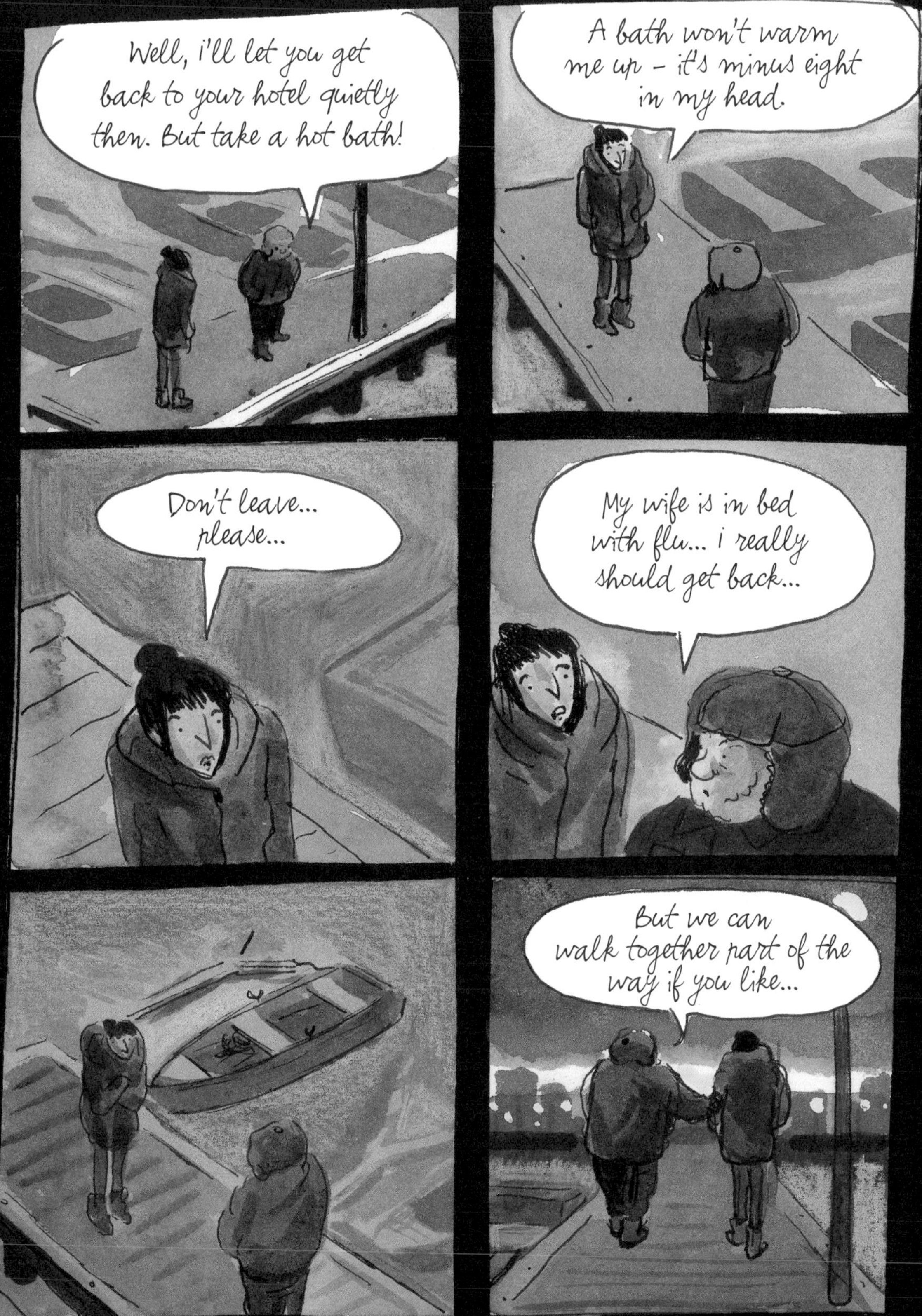
Well, i'll let you get back to your hotel quietly then. But take a hot bath!
A bath won't warm me up – it's minus eight in my head.
Don't leave... please...
My wife is in bed with flu... i really should get back...
But we can walk together part of the way if you like...

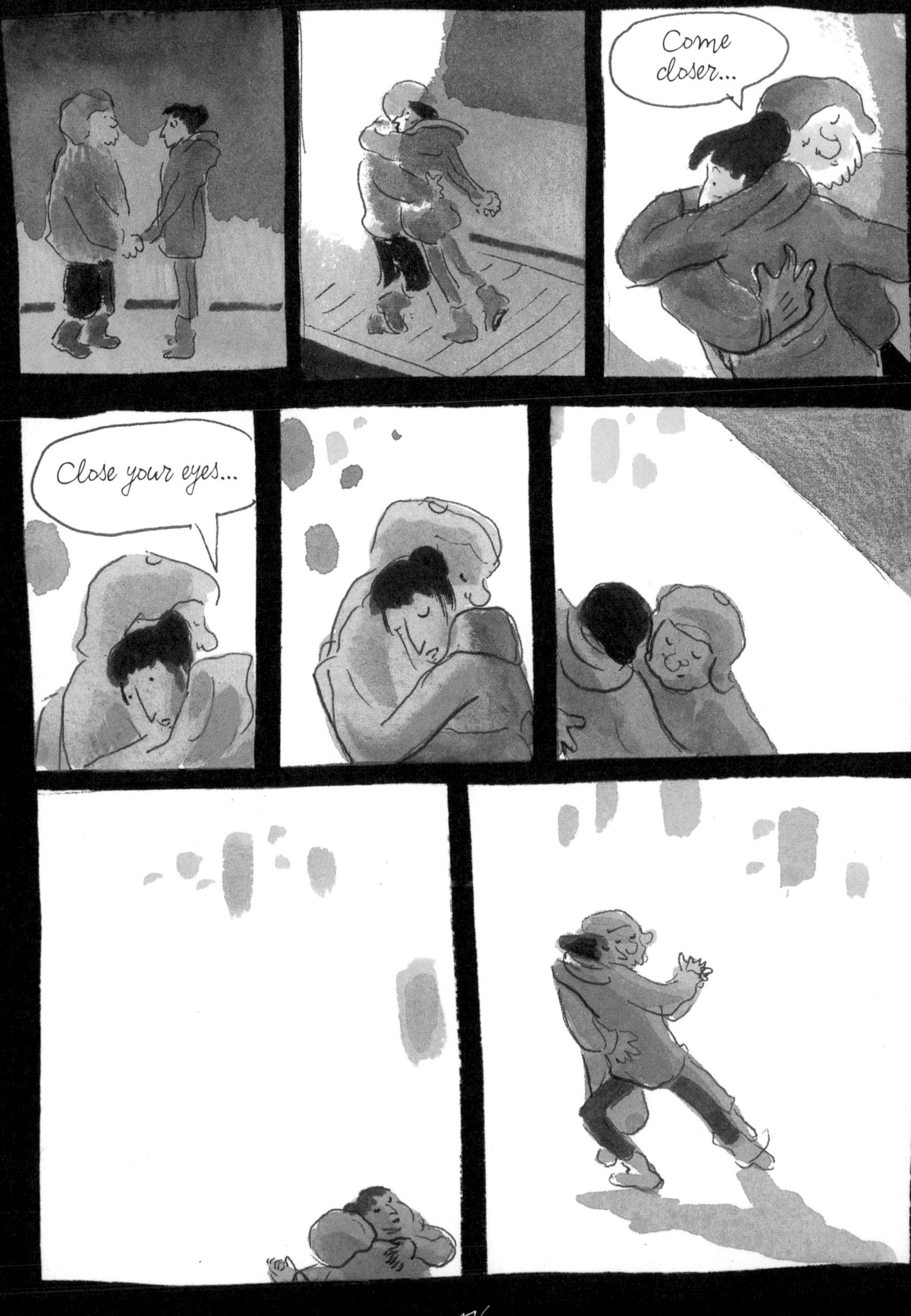
Come closer...
Close your eyes...

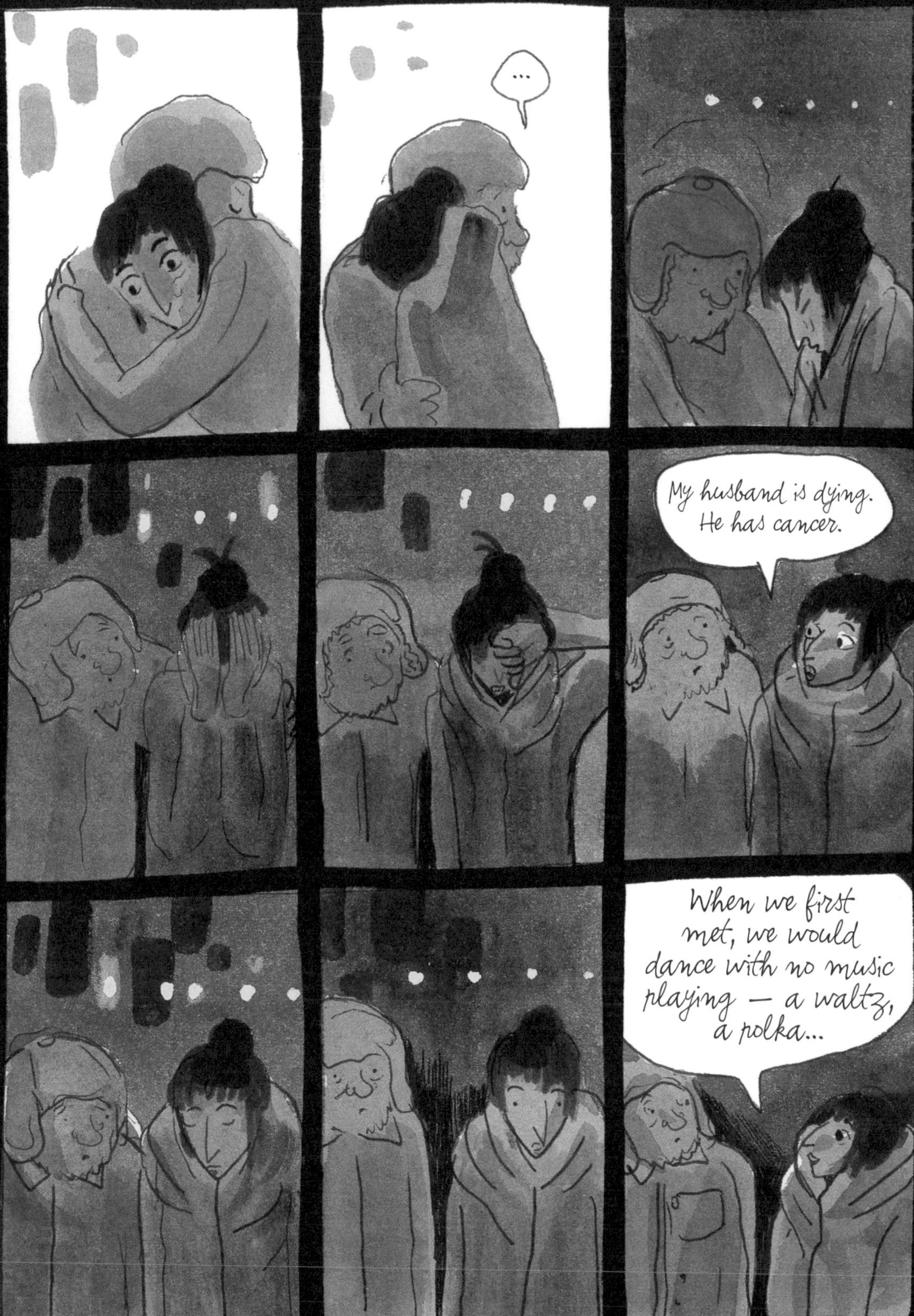
...
My husband is dying. He has cancer.
When we first met, we would dance with no music playing — a waltz, a polka...

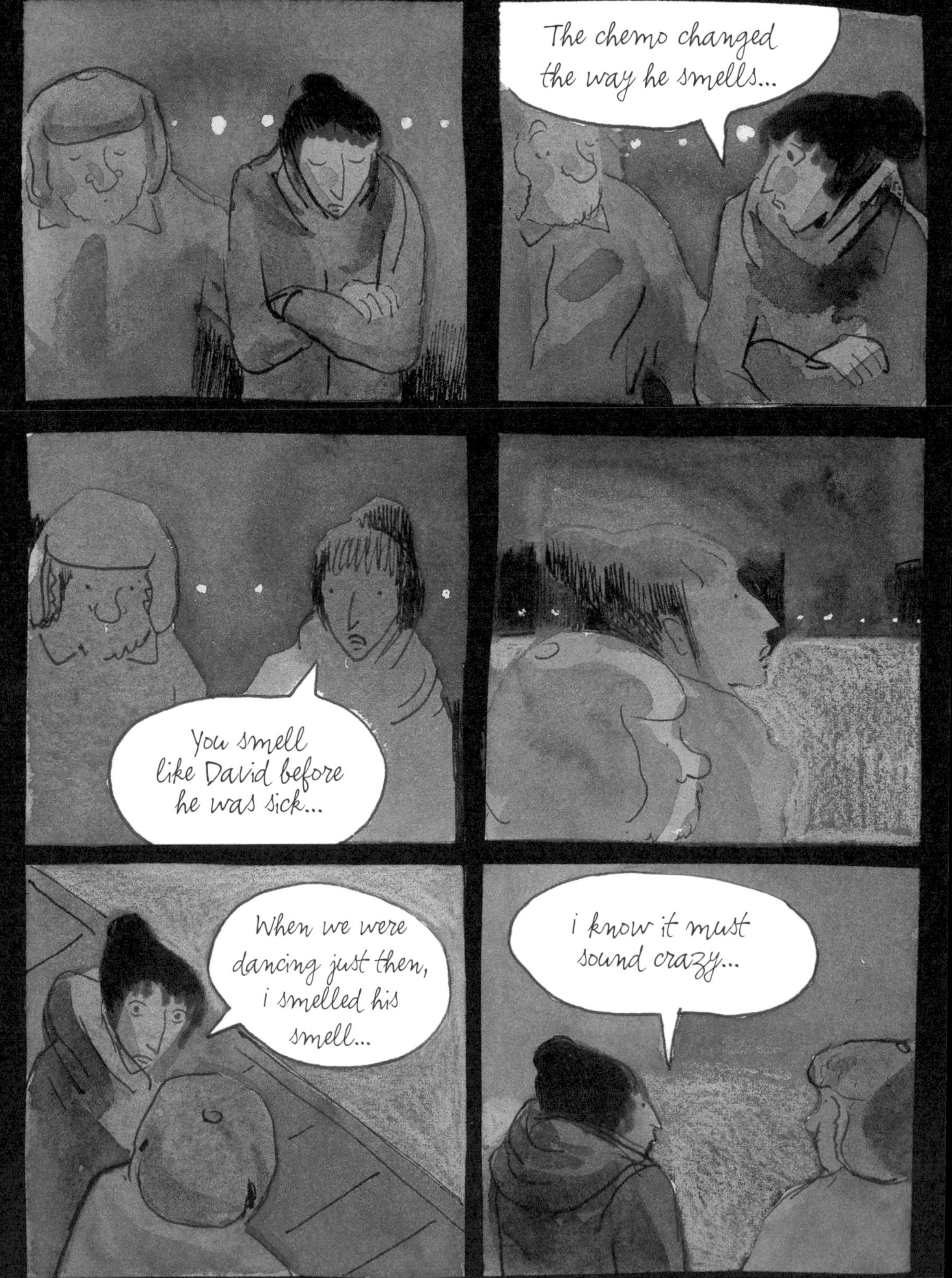
The chemo changed the way he smells...
You smell like David before he was sick...
When we were dancing just then, i smelled his smell...
i know it must sound crazy...

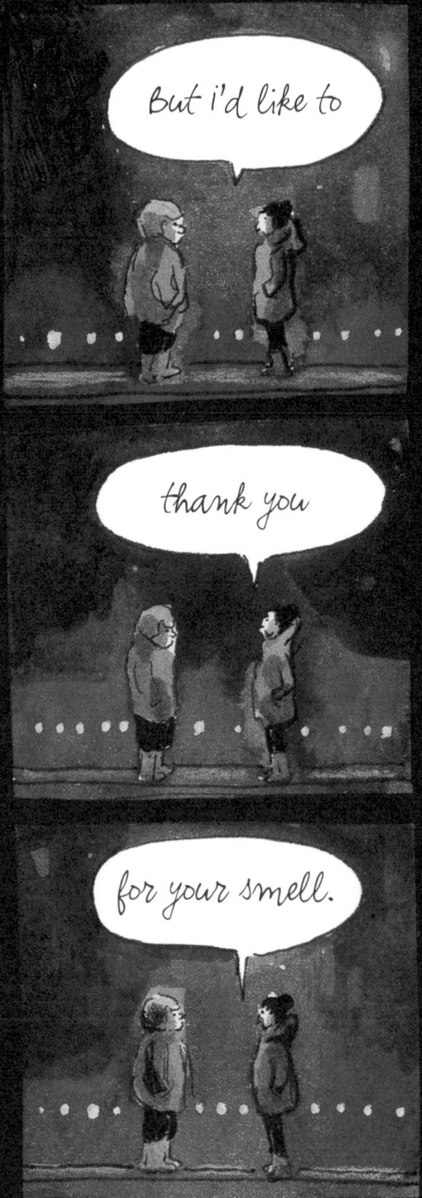
But i'd like to
thank you
for your smell.

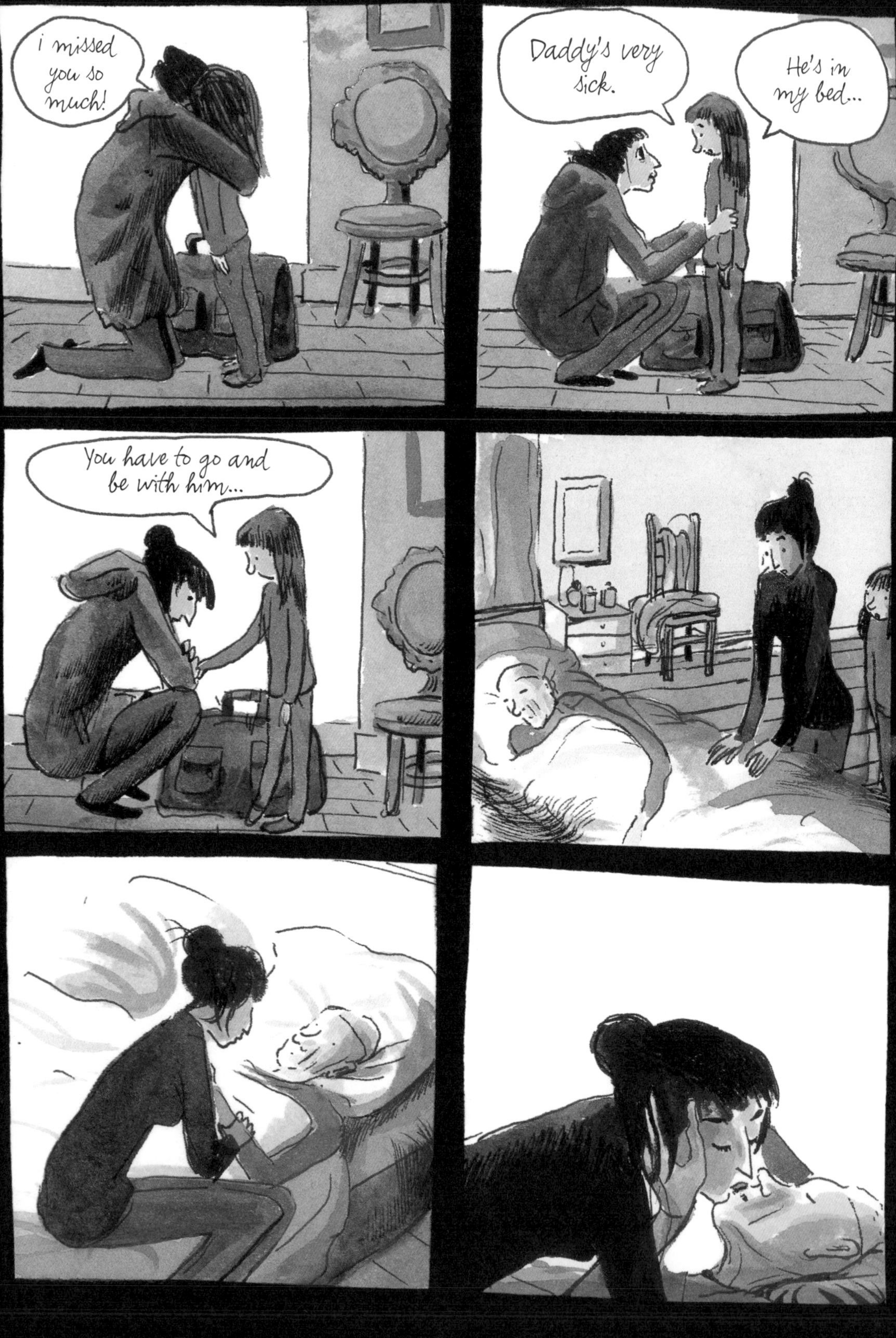
i missed you so much!
Daddy's very sick.
He's in my bed...
You have to go and be with him...

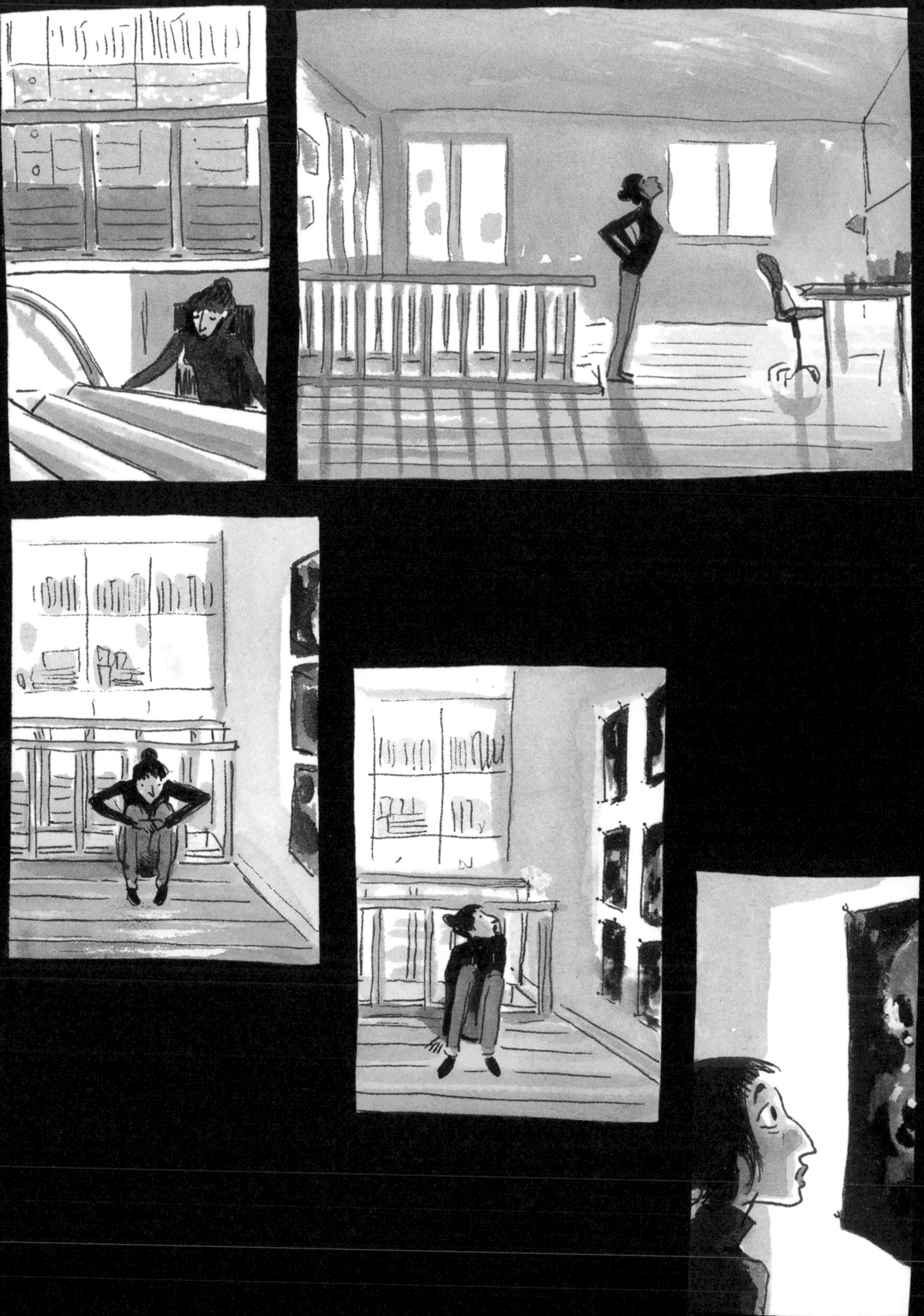

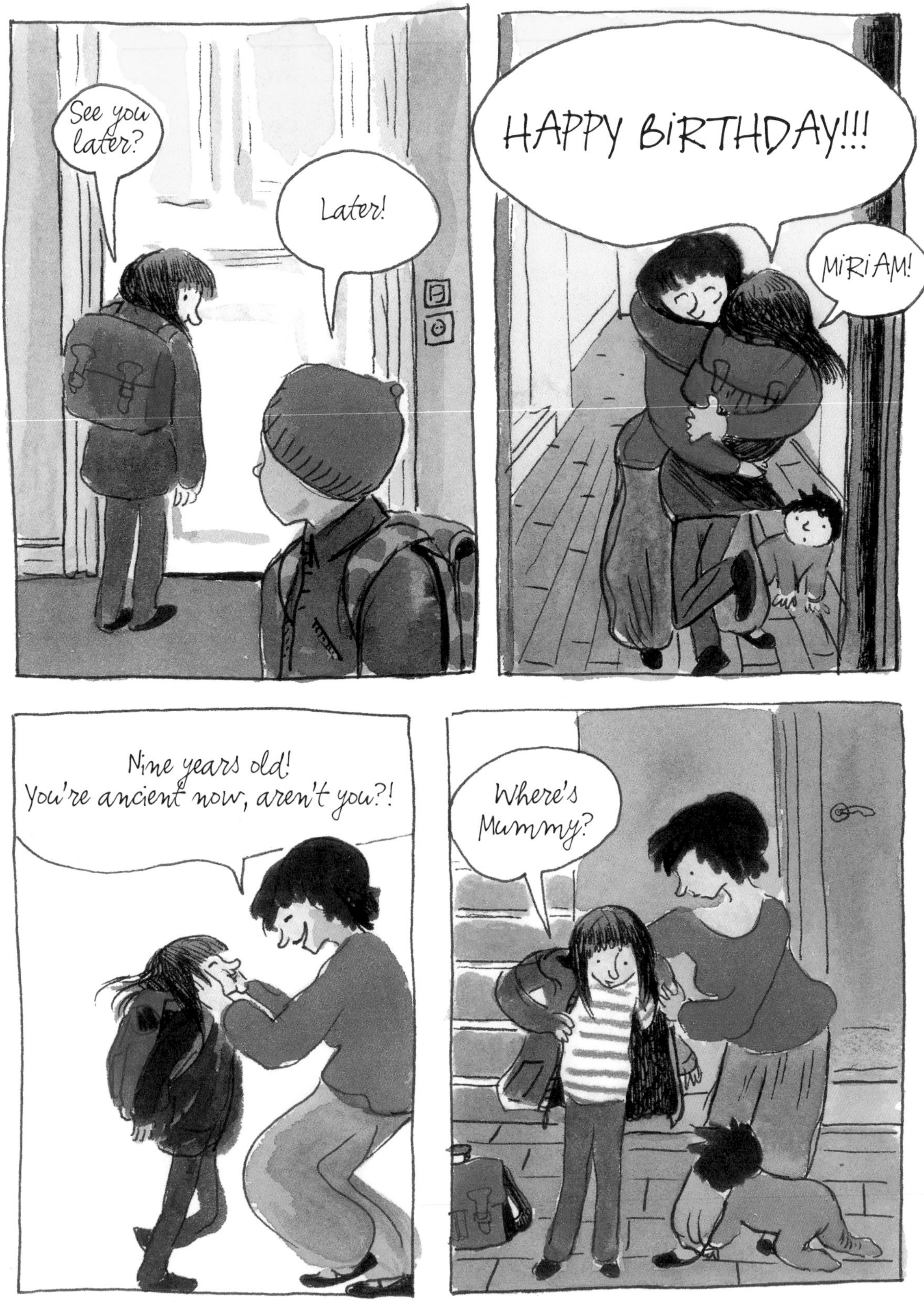
See you later?
Later!
HAPPY BIRTHDAY!!!
MIRIAM!
Nine years old! You're ancient now, aren't you?!
Where's Mummy?

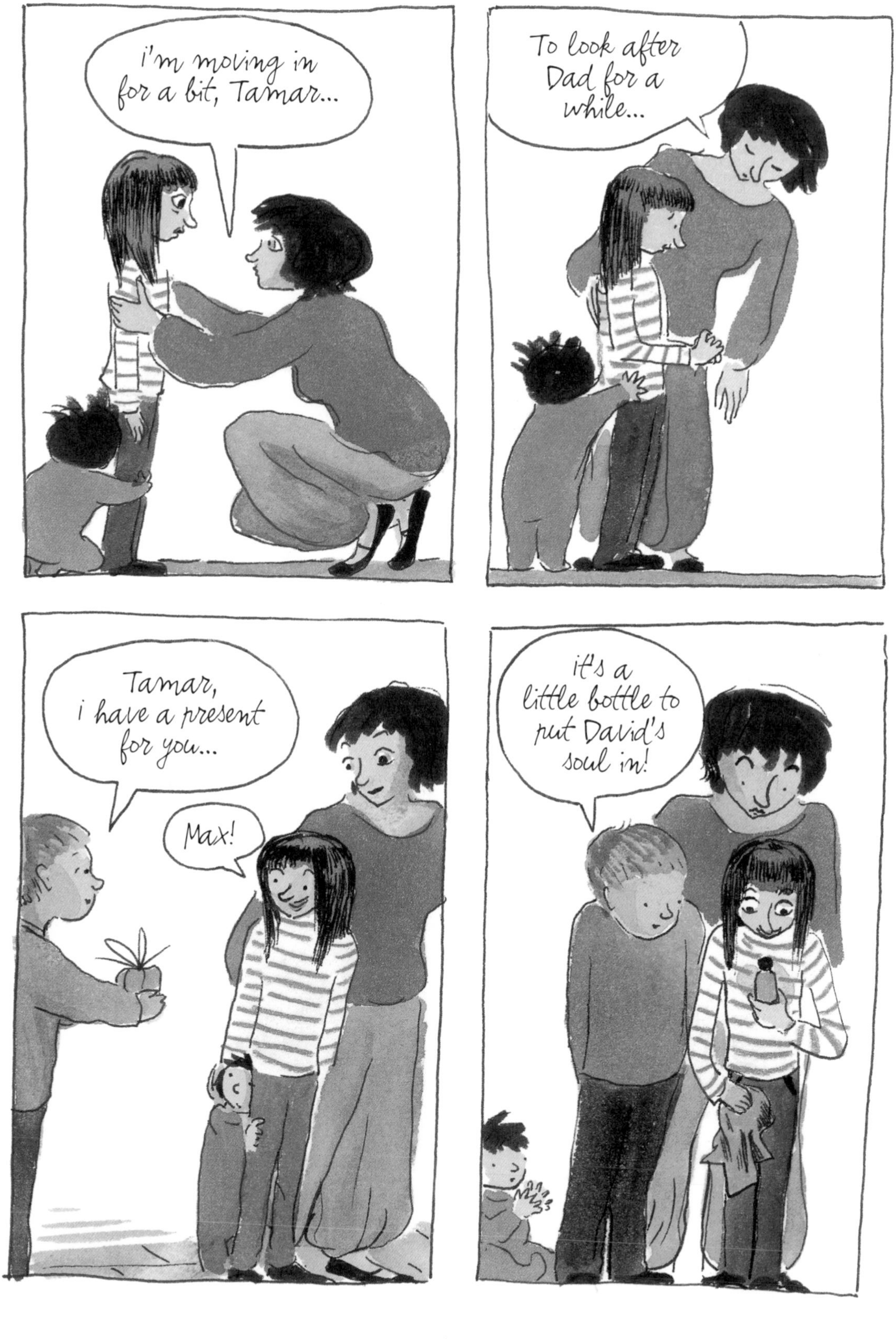
i'm moving in for a bit, Tamar...
To look after Dad for a while...
Tamar, i have a present for you...
Max!
it's a little bottle to put David's soul in!

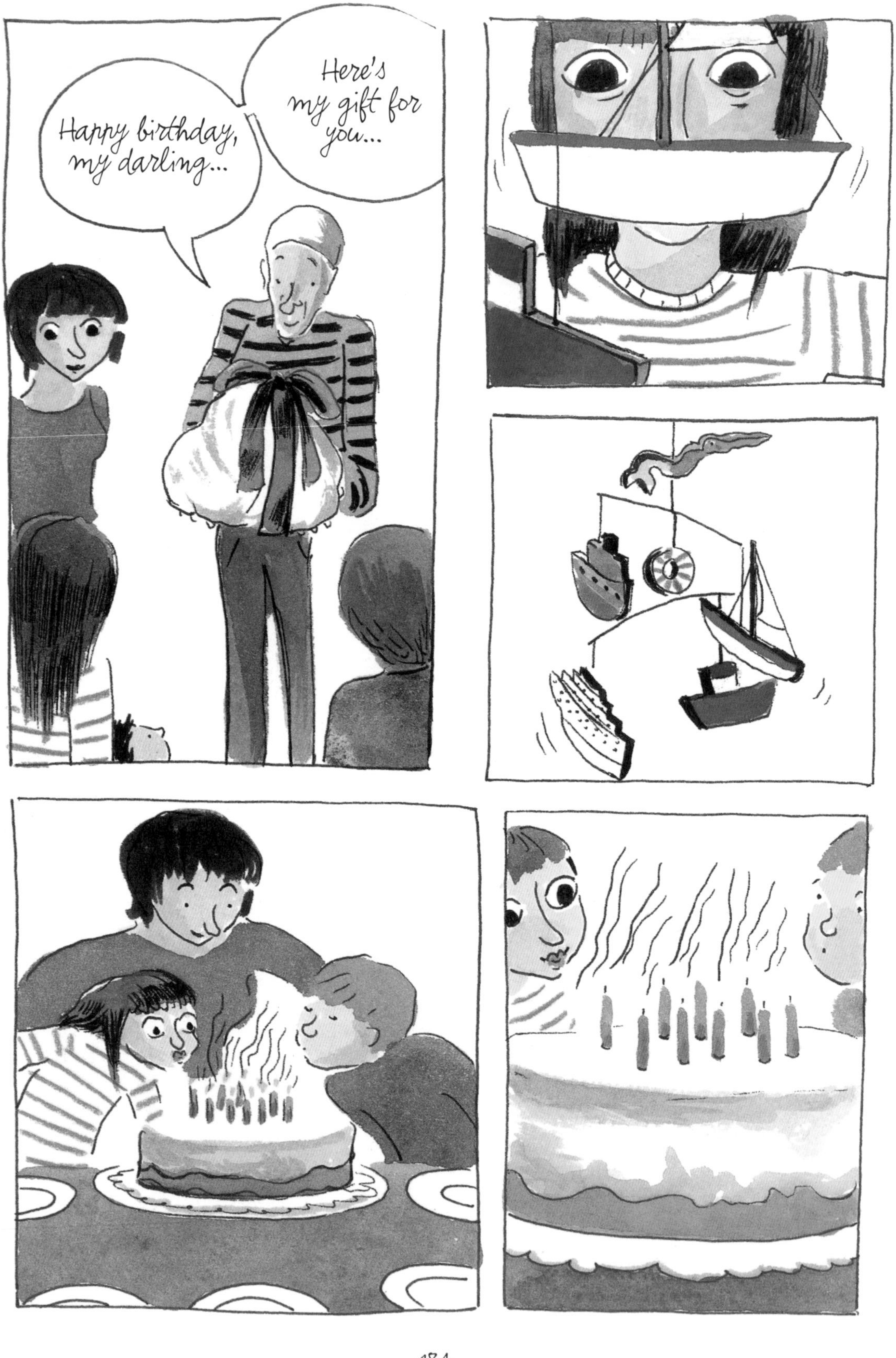
Happy birthday, my darling...
Here's my gift for you...

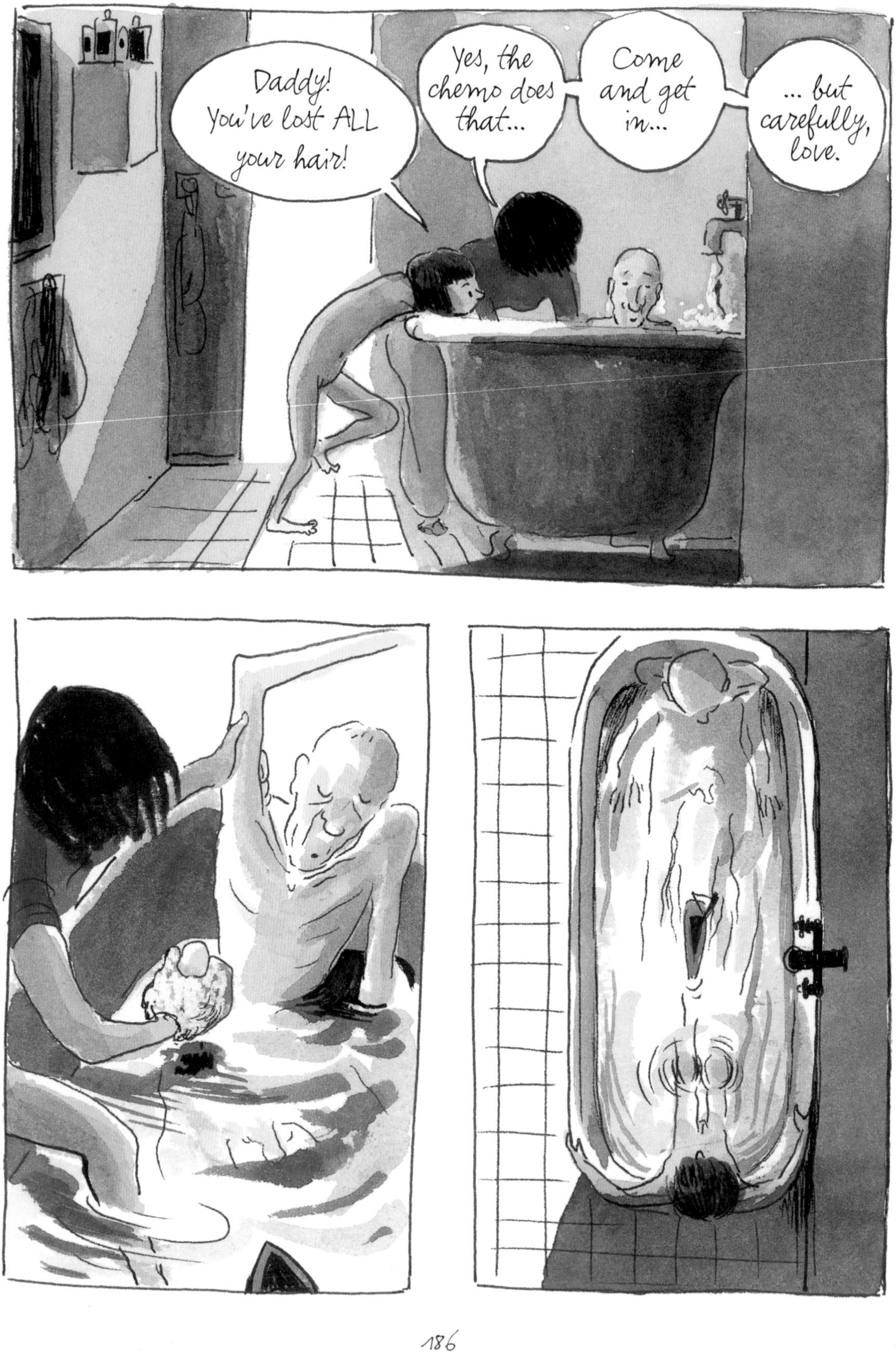
Daddy! You've lost ALL your hair!
Yes, the chemo does that...
Come and get in...
... but carefully, love.

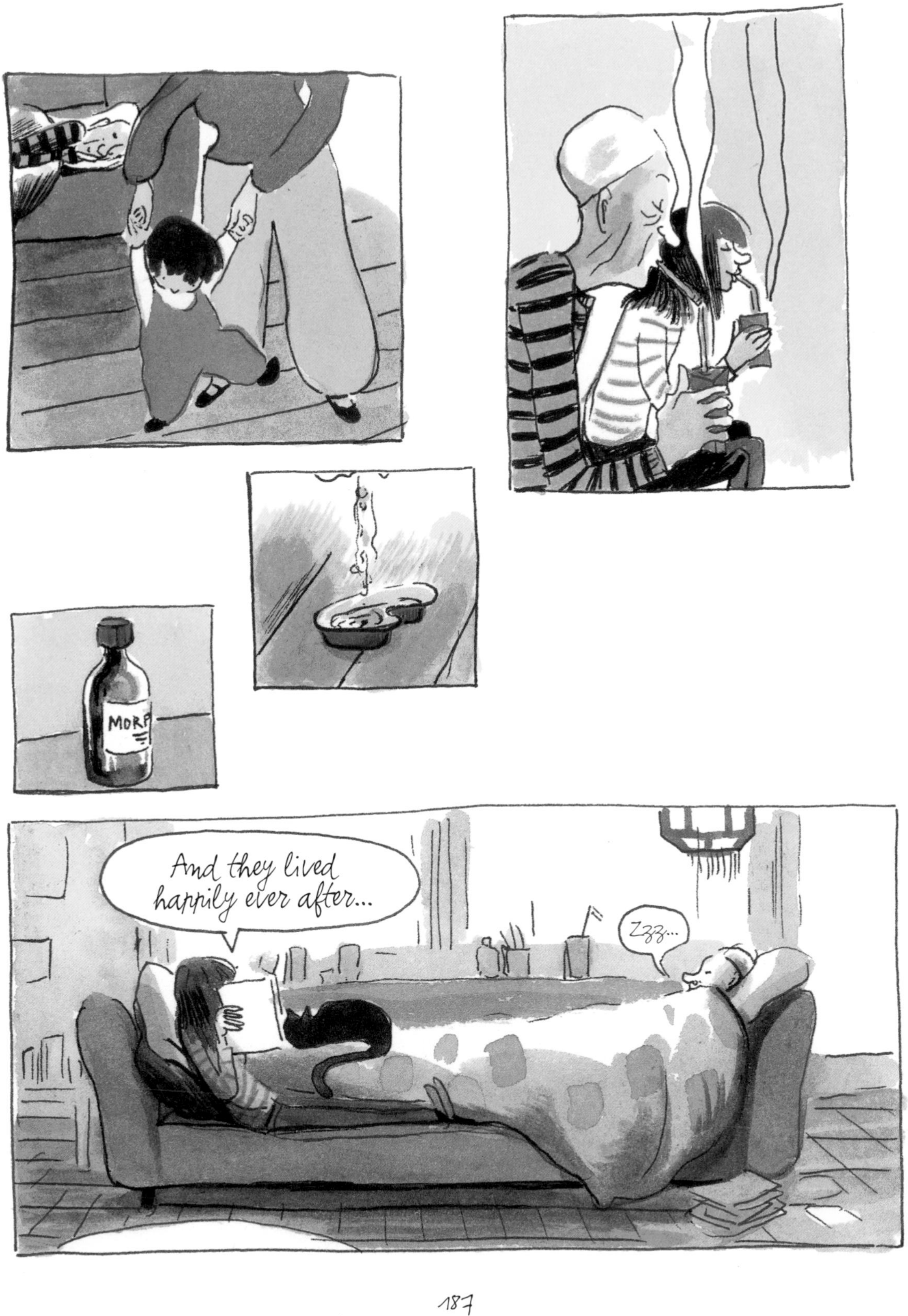
MORF
And they lived happily ever after...
Zzz...

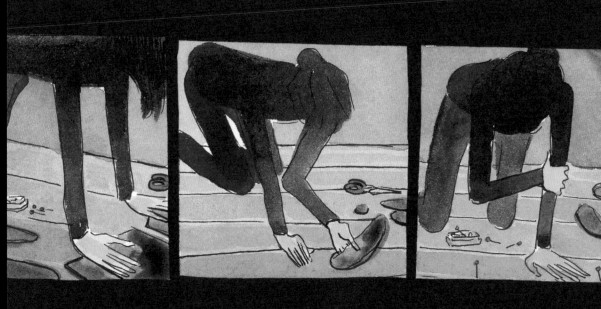

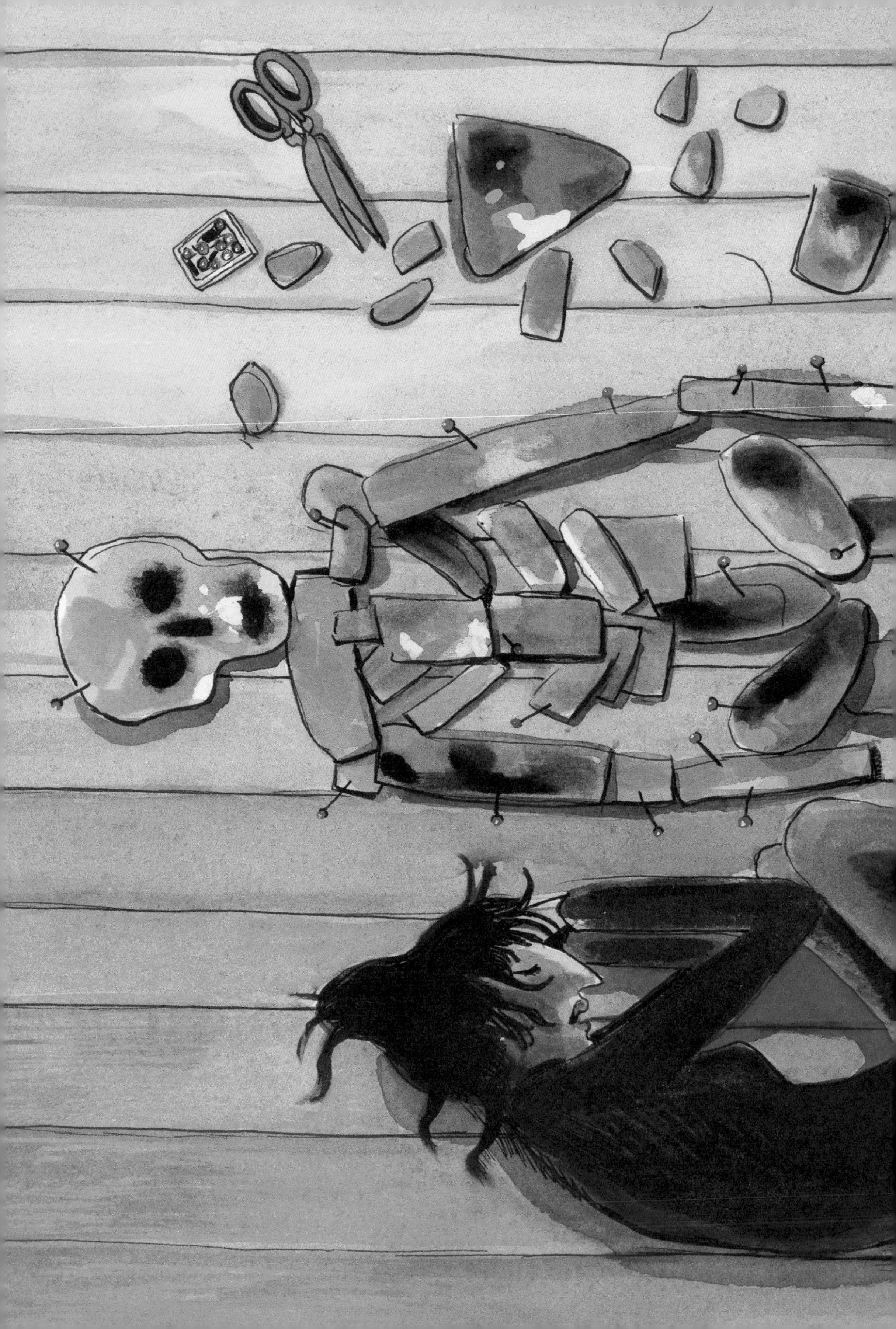

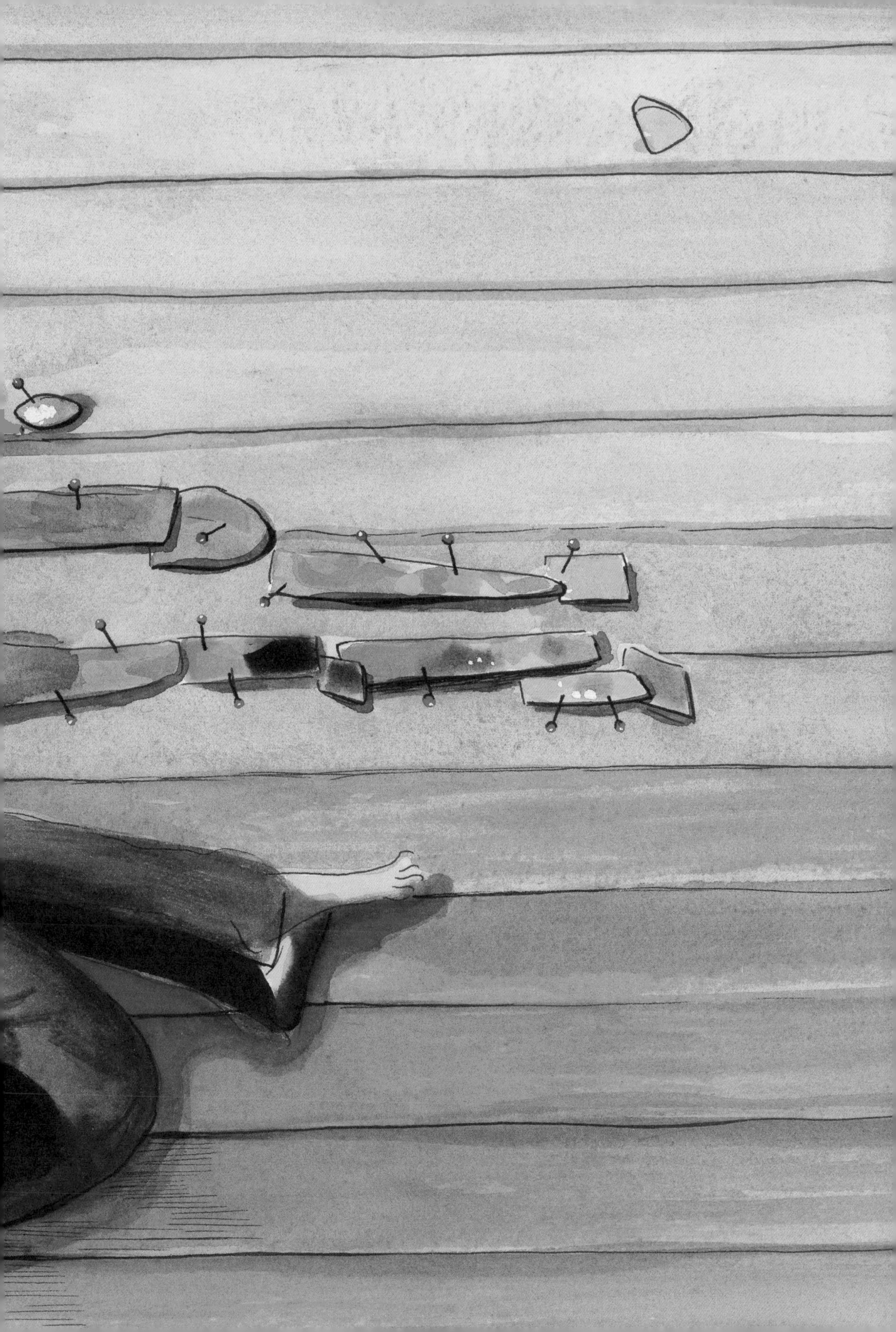

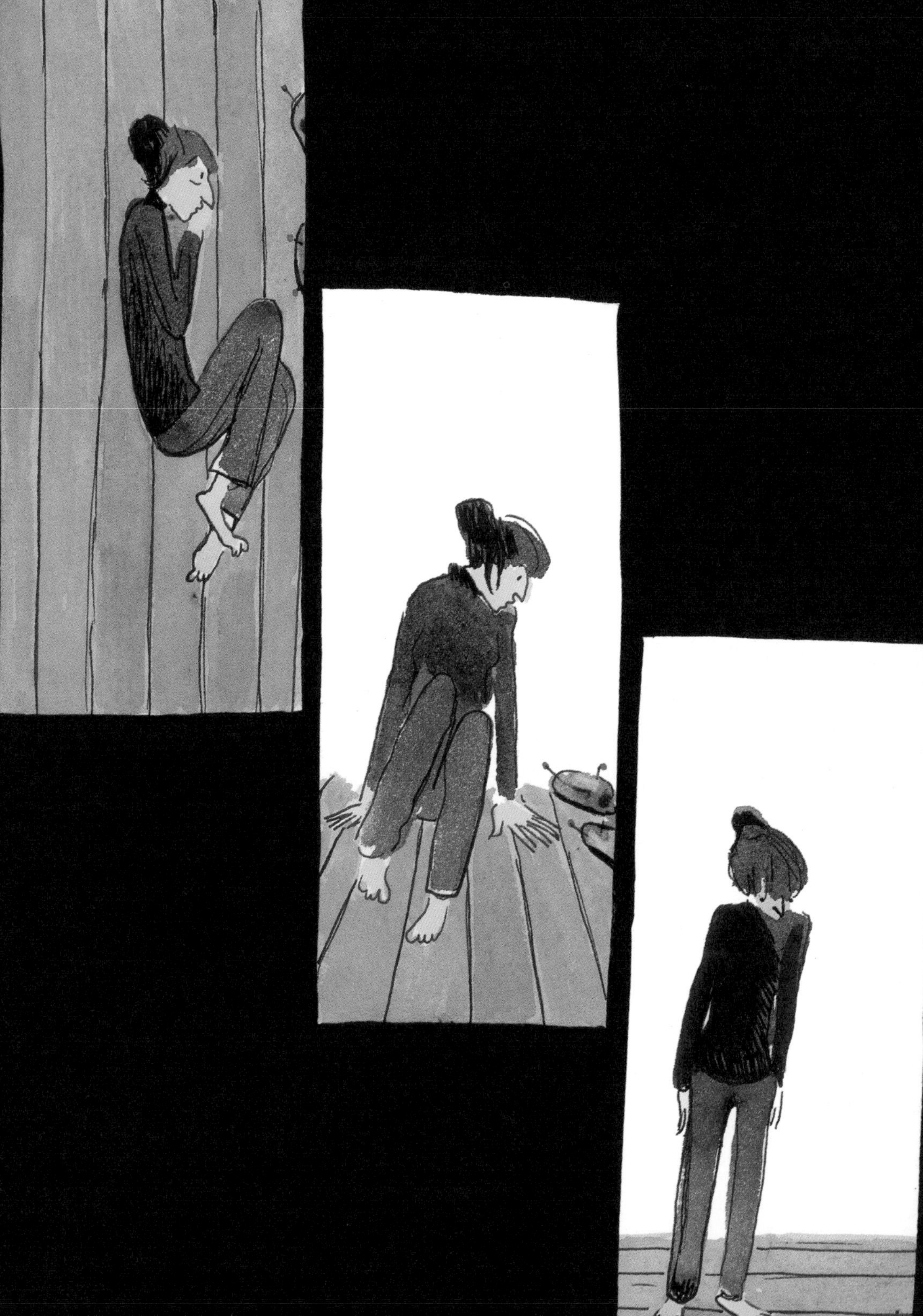

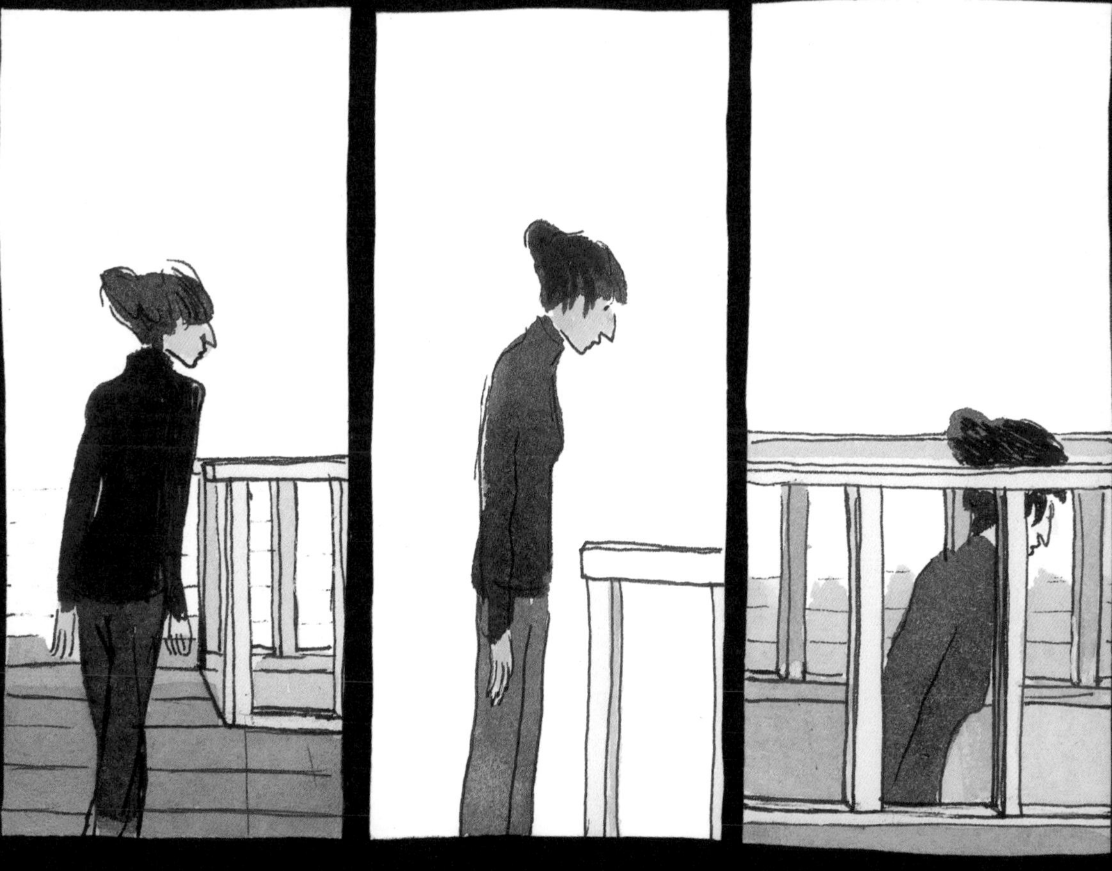

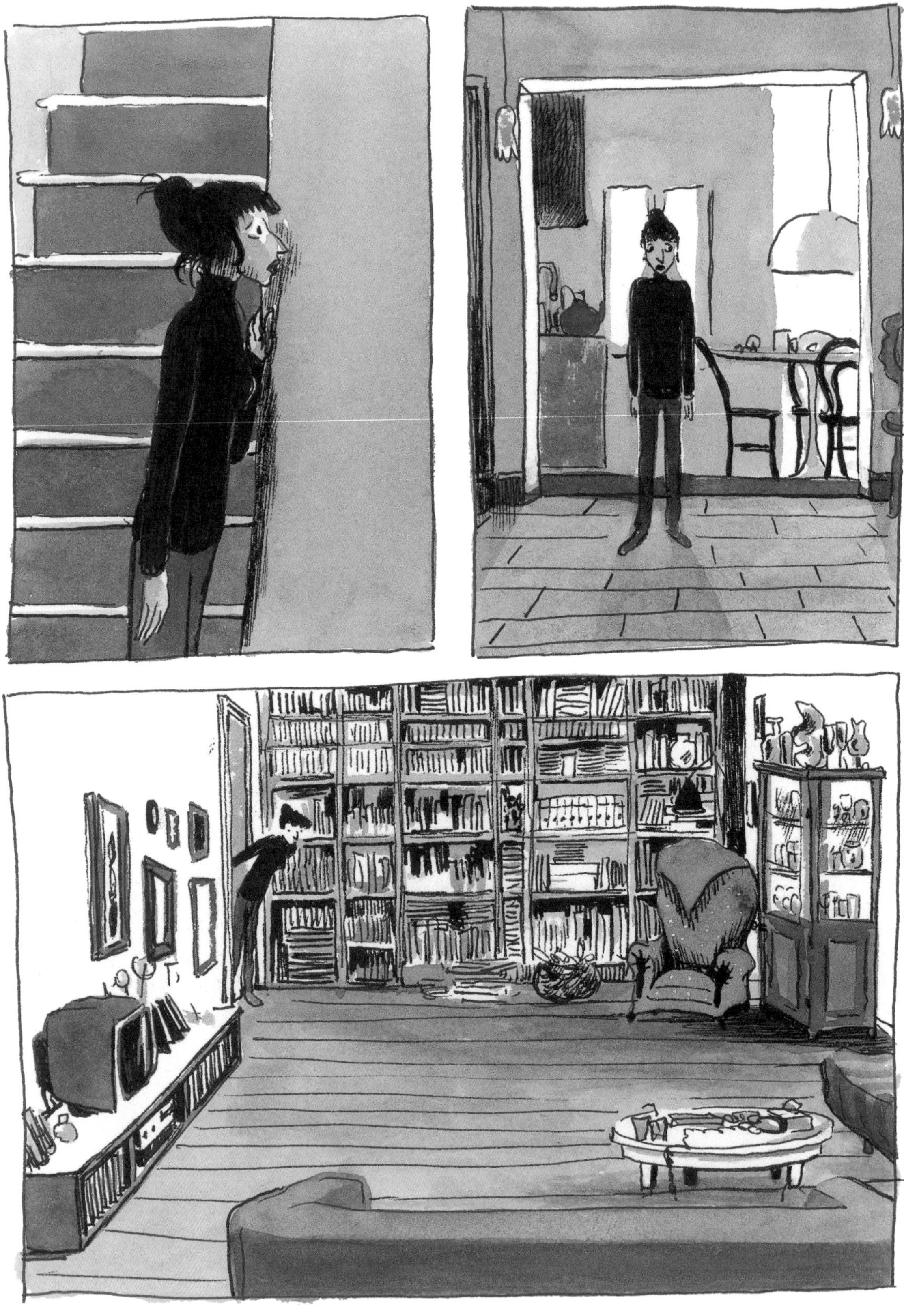

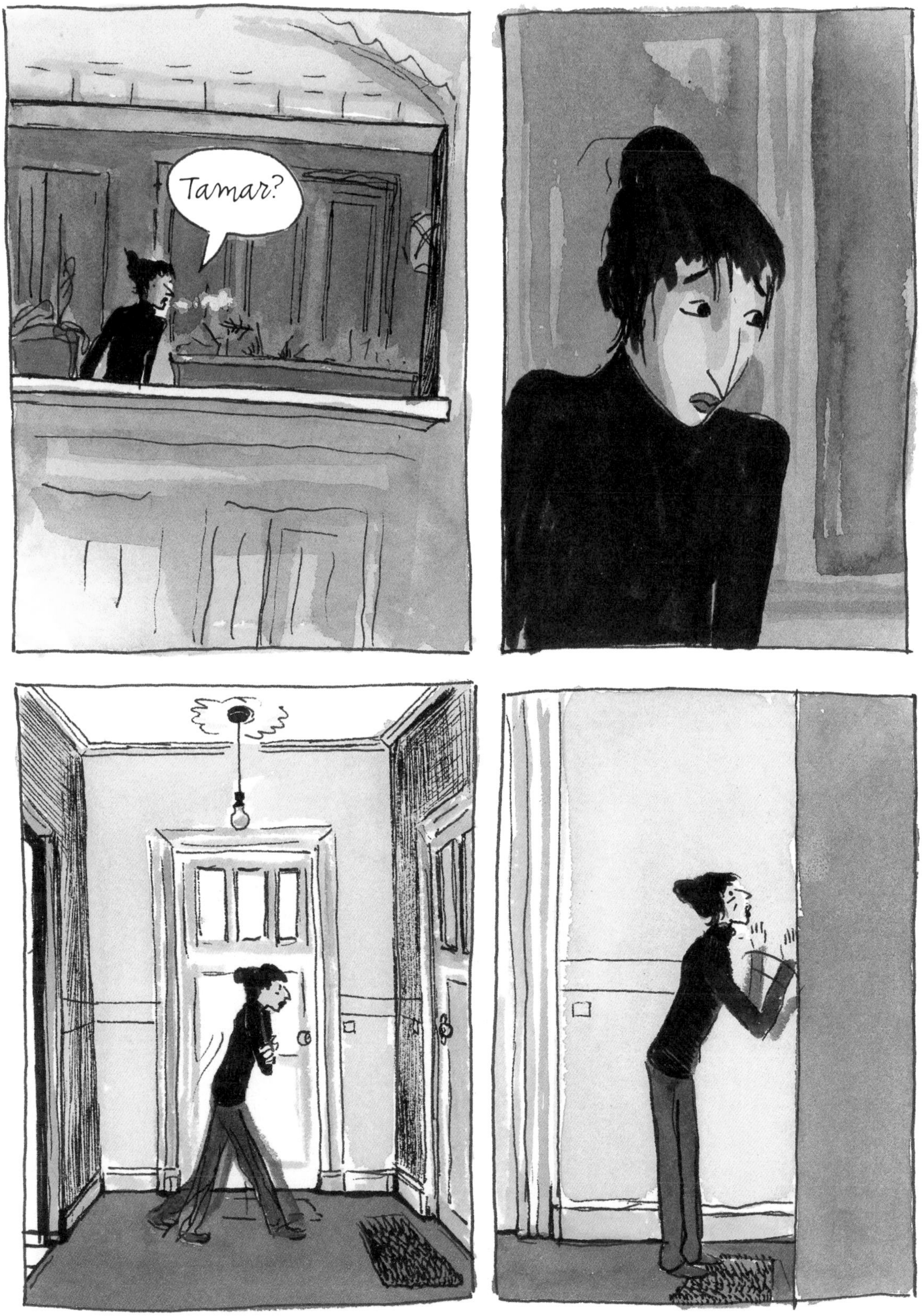
Tamar?

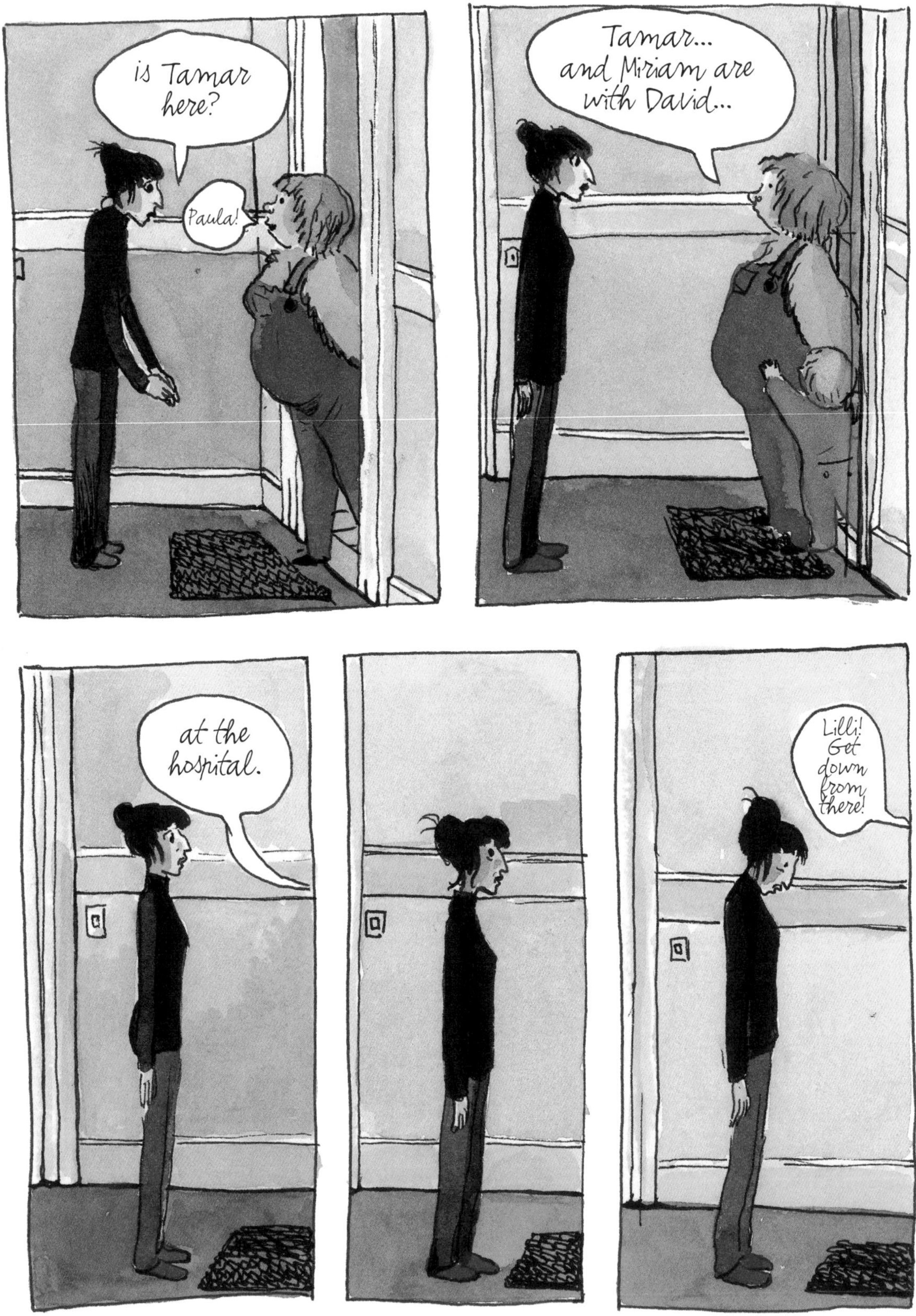
is Tamar here?
Paula!
Tamar... and Miriam are with David...
at the hospital.
Lilli! Get down from there!

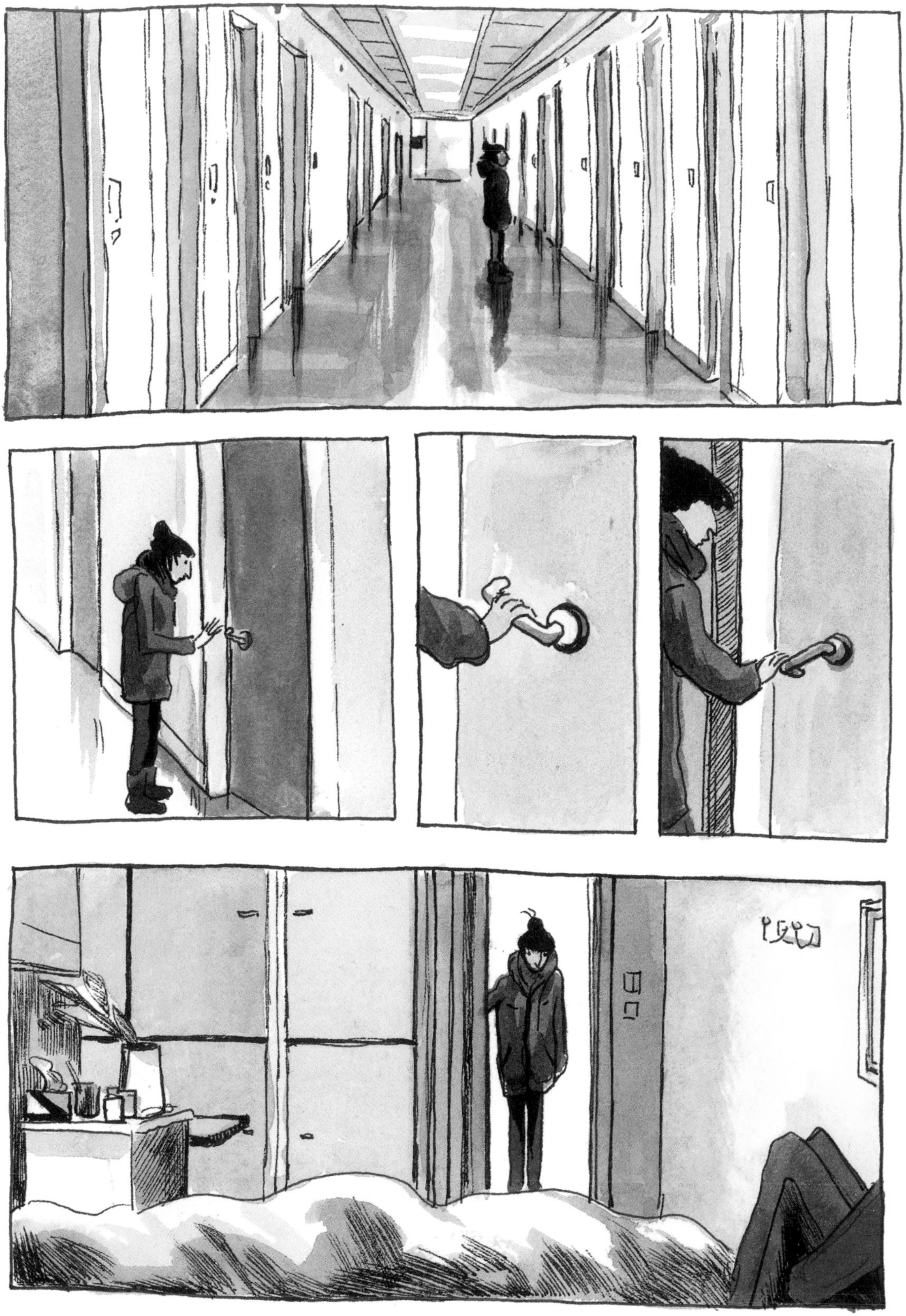

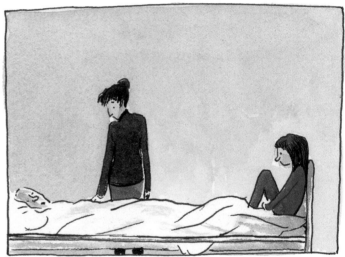

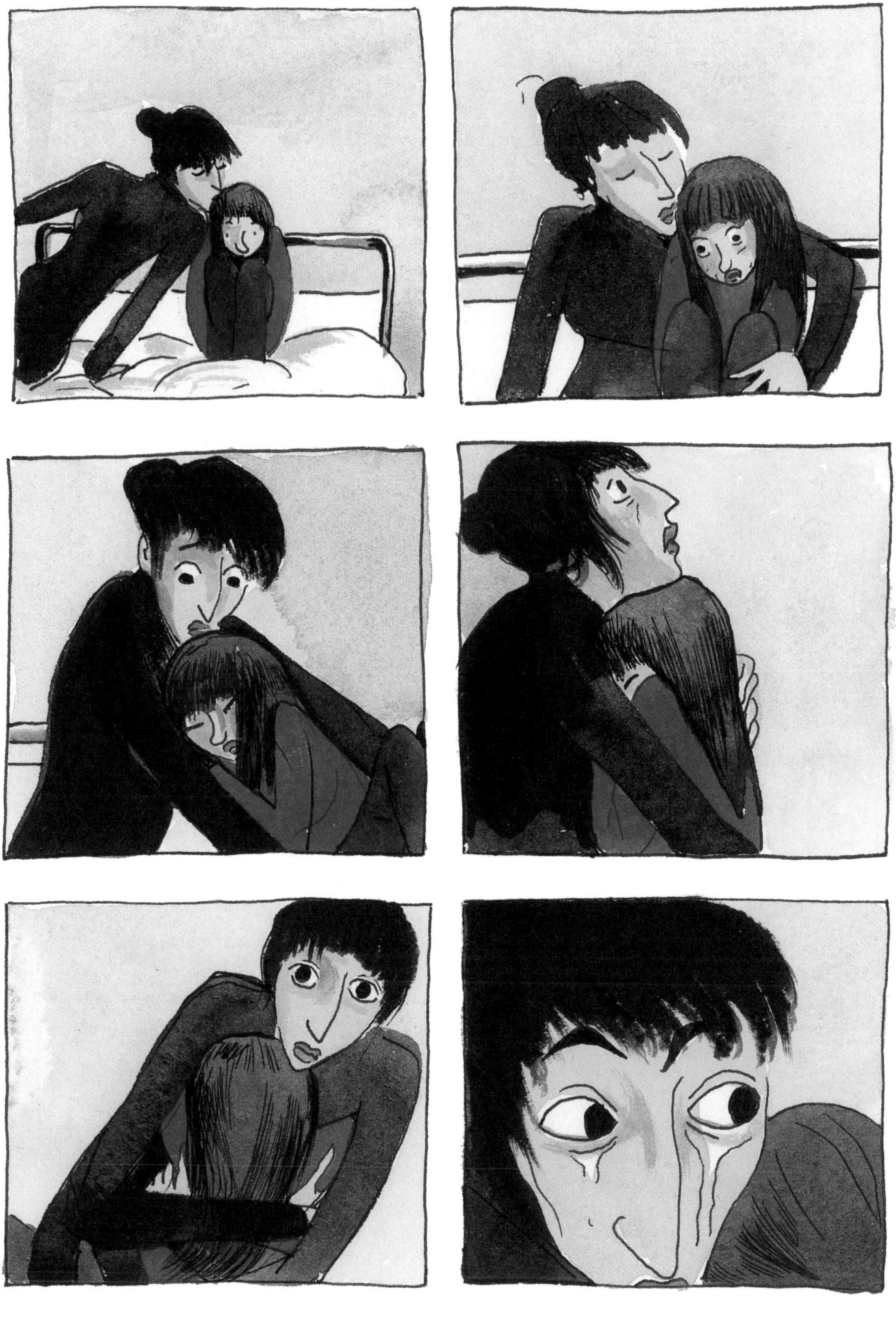

EXTRACT FROM "829" BY EMILY DICKINSON, IN
THE COMPLETE POEMS OF EMILY DICKINSON,
ED. THOMAS H. JOHNSON.
LONDON: FABER AND FABER, 1977.

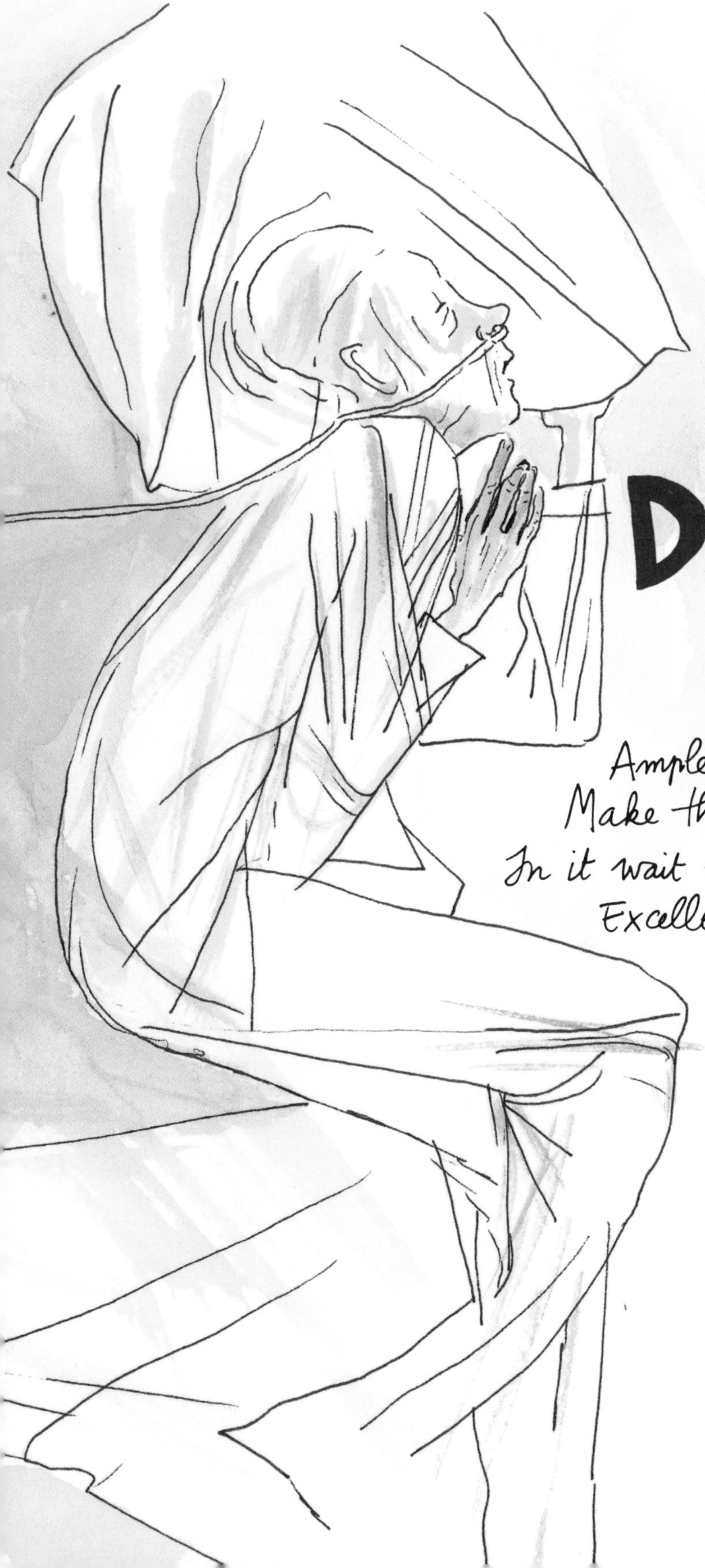

DAVID

Ample make this Bed–
Make this Bed with Awe–
In it wait till Judgment break
Excellent and Fair.

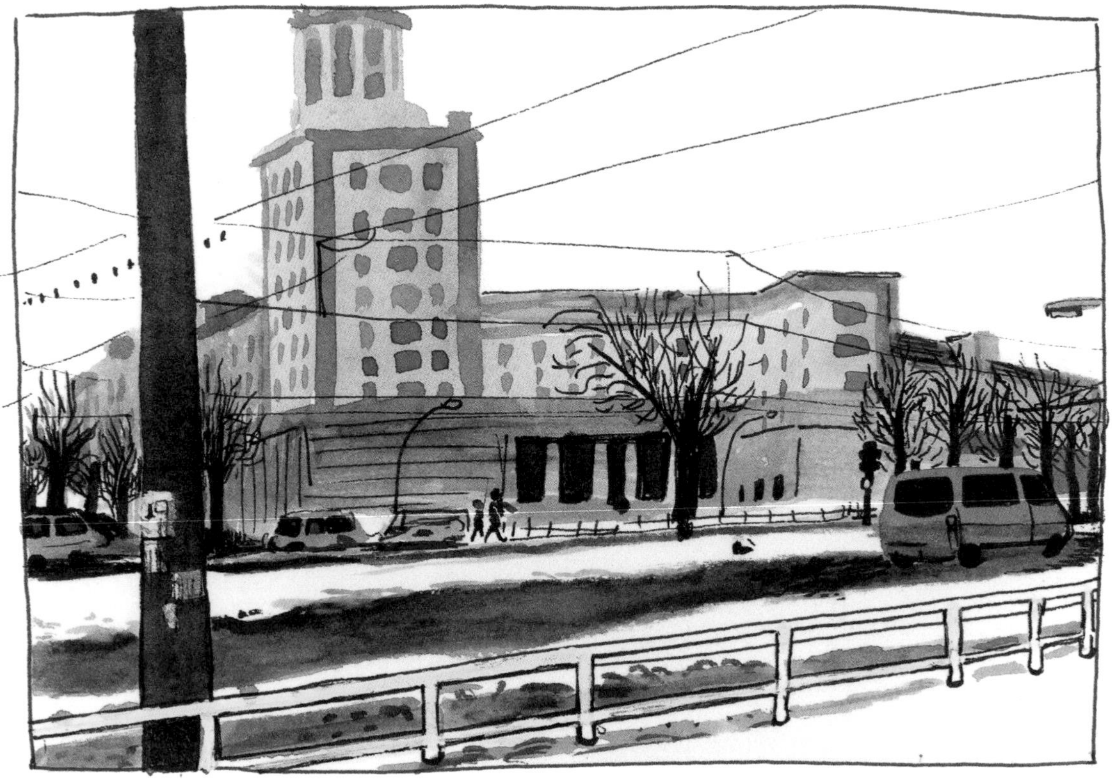

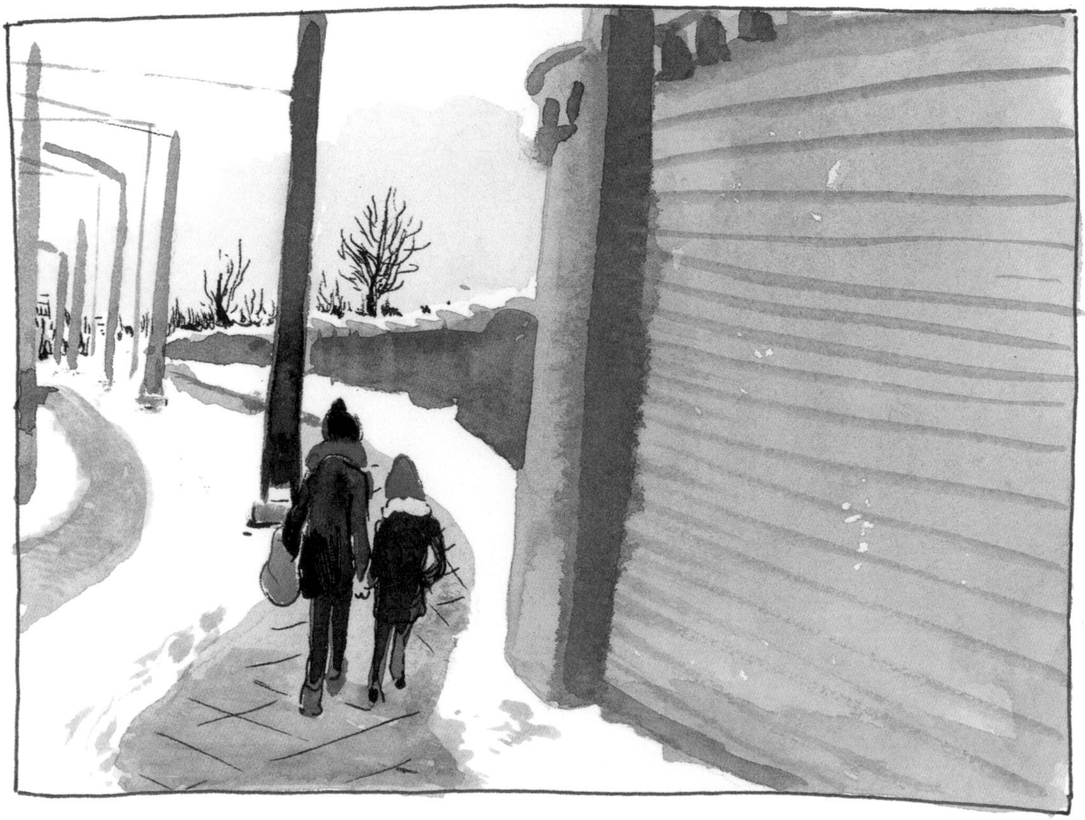

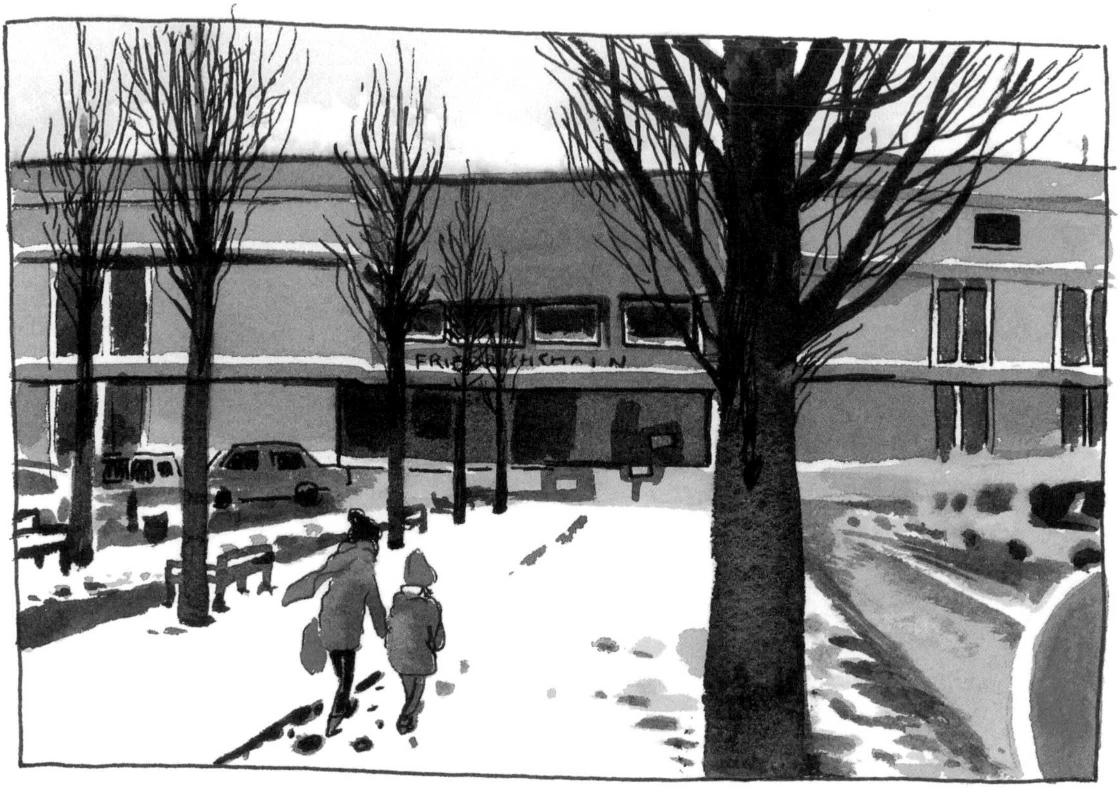

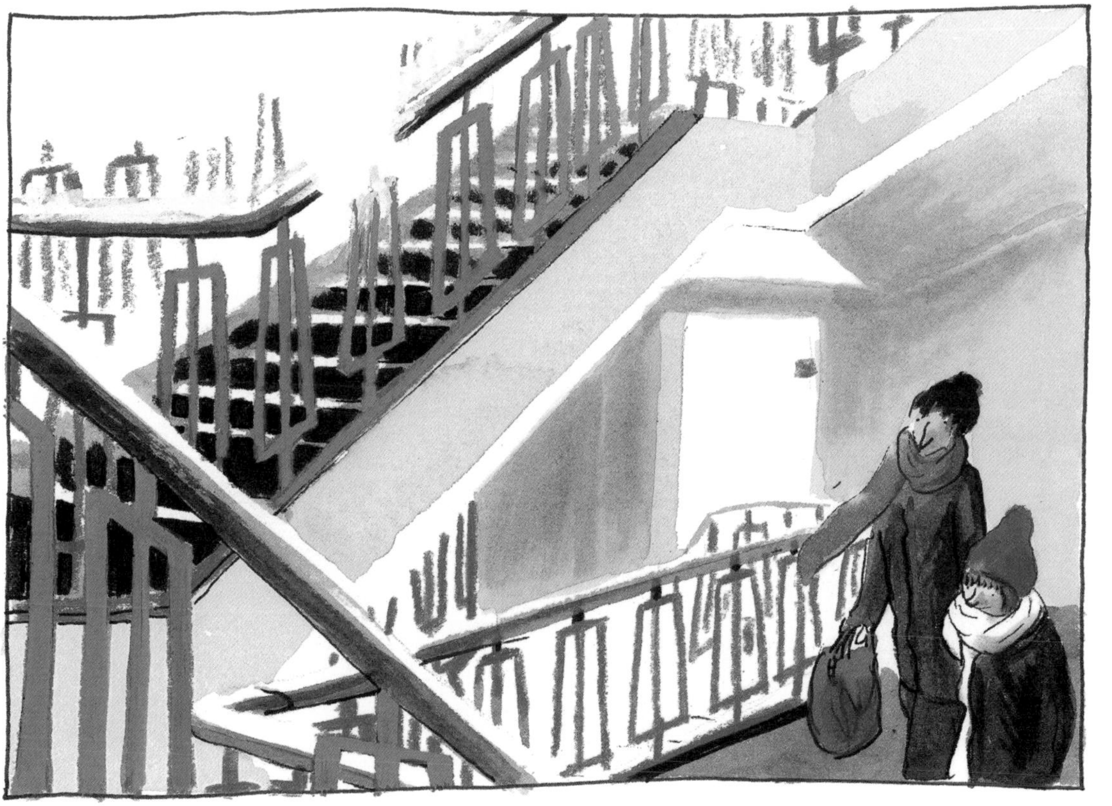

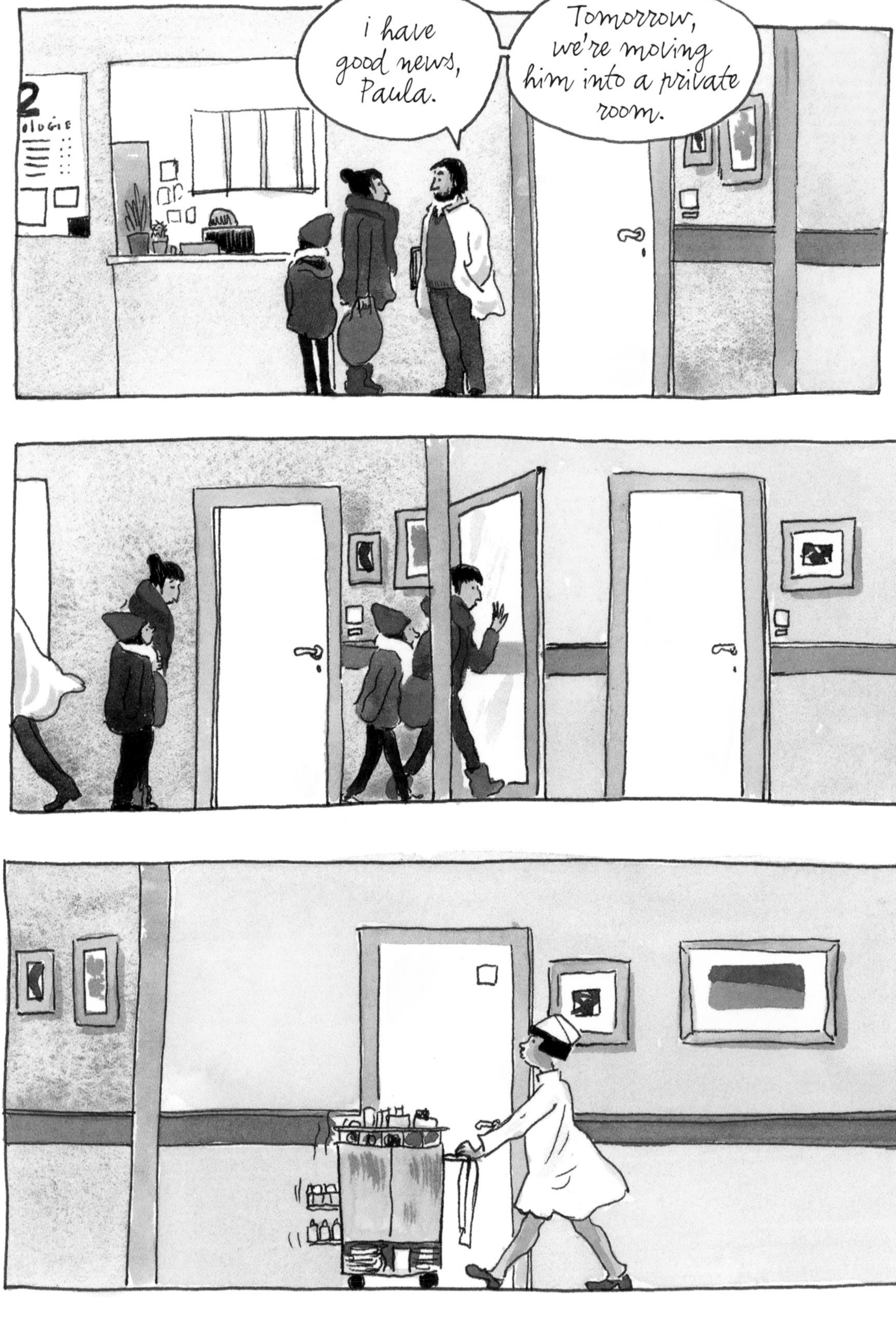
i have good news, Paula.
Tomorrow, we're moving him into a private room.

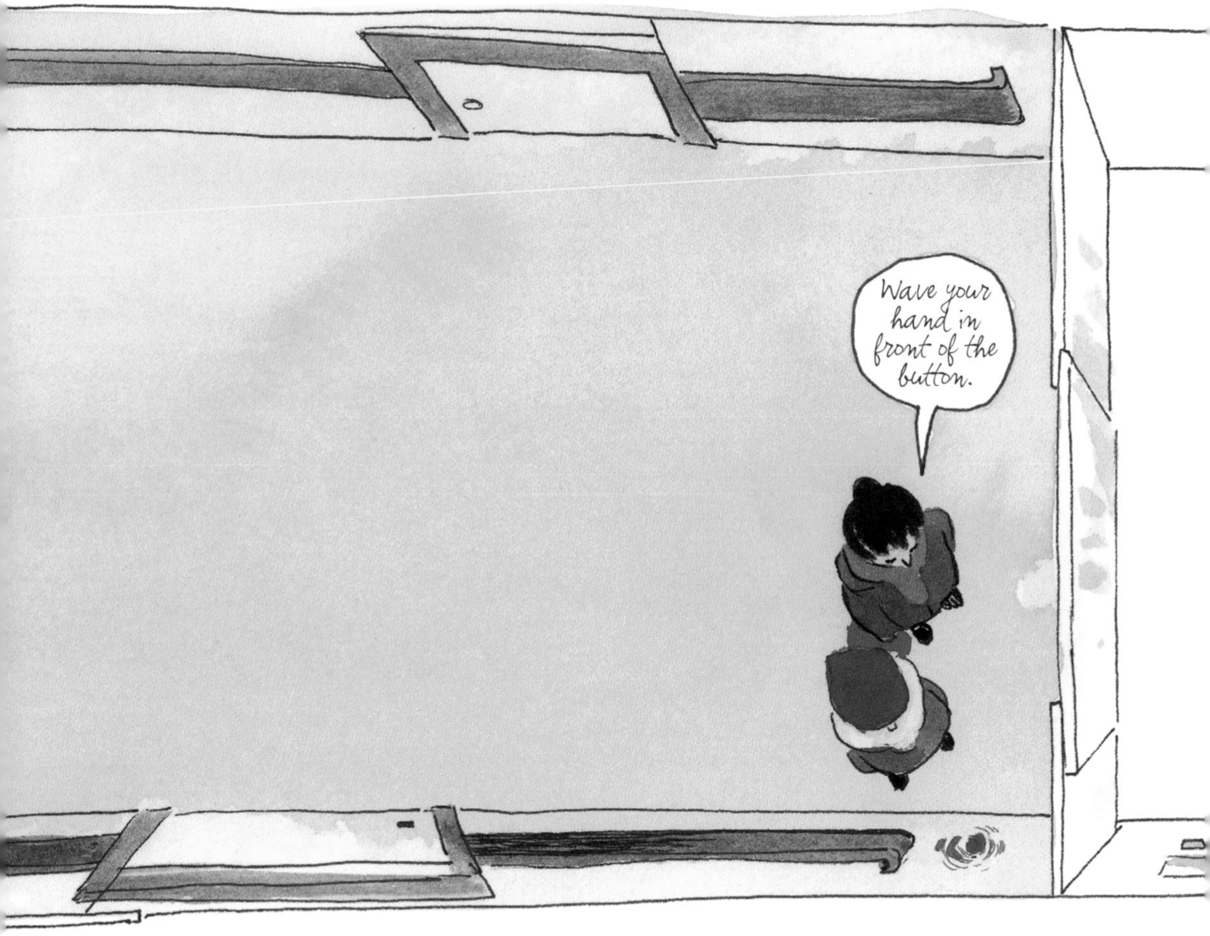
Wave your hand in front of the button.

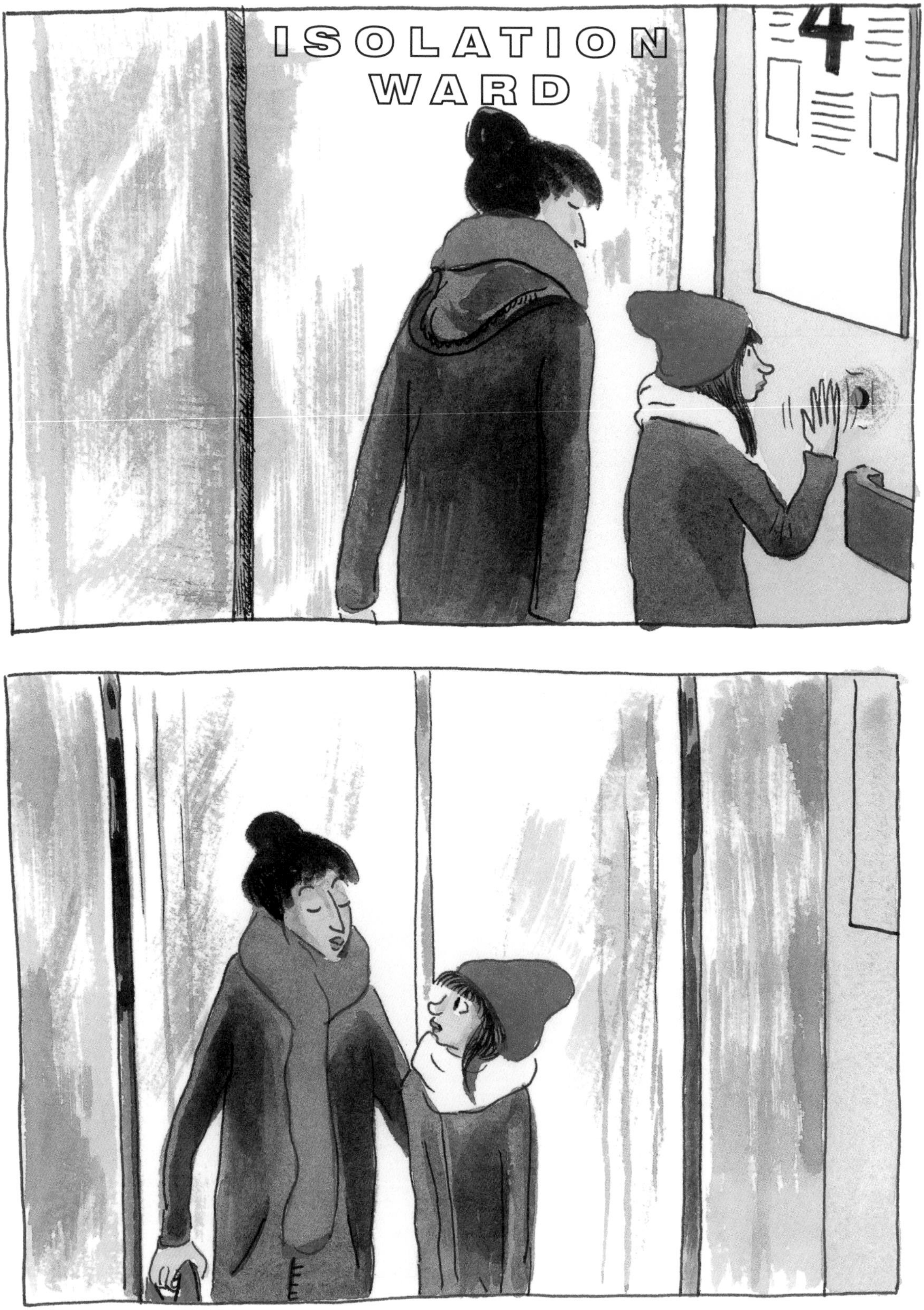
ISOLATION WARD
4

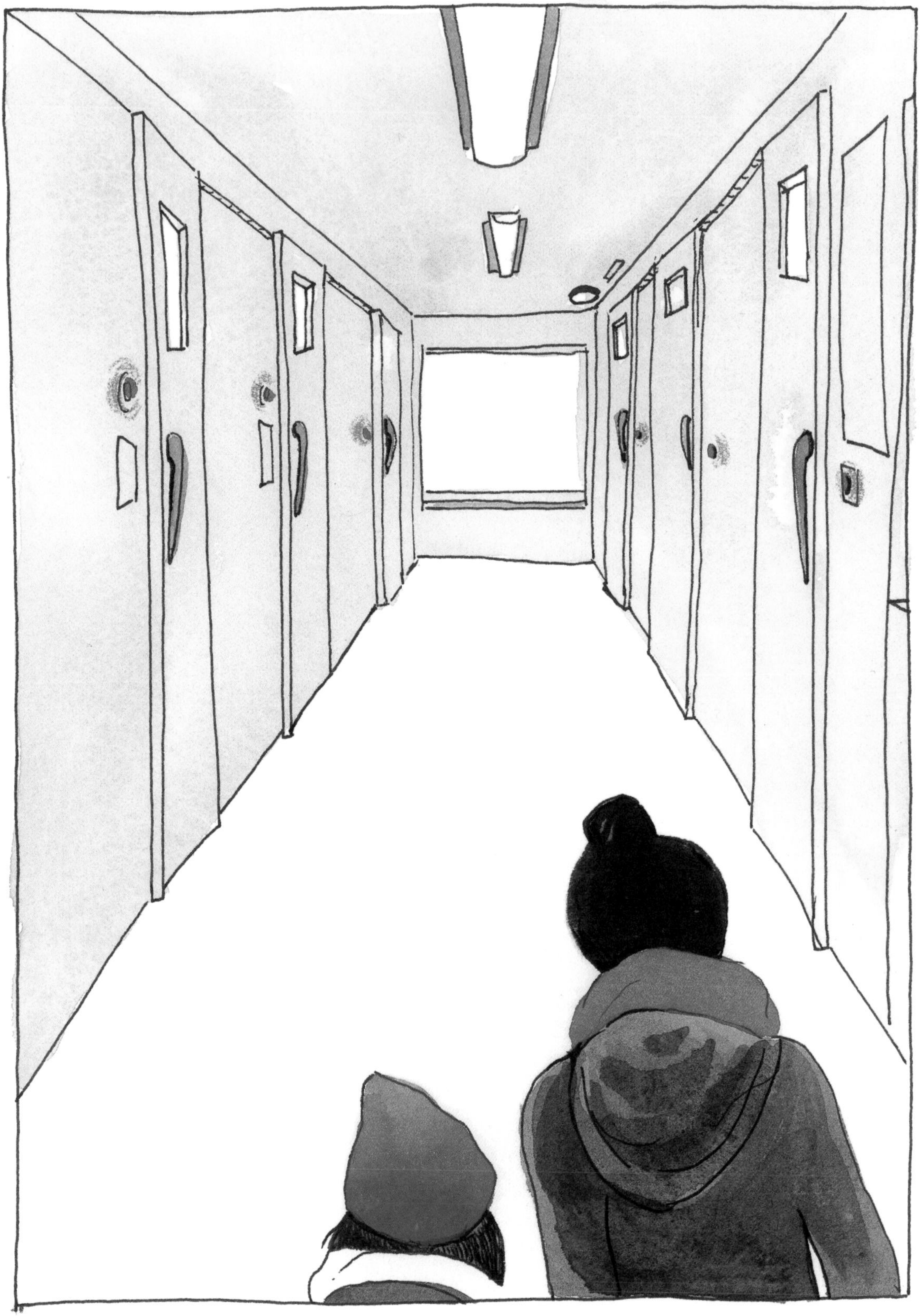

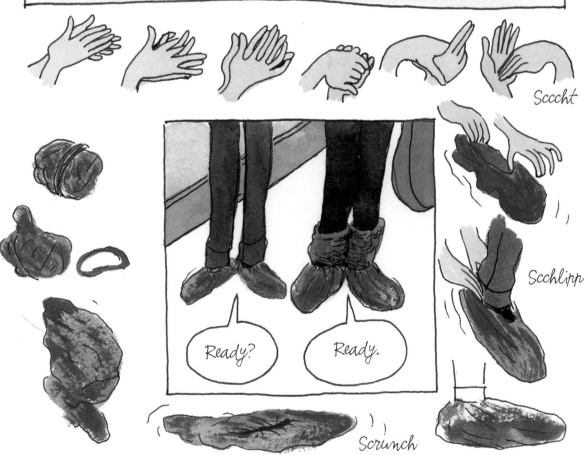

Scccht

Scchlipp

Scrunch

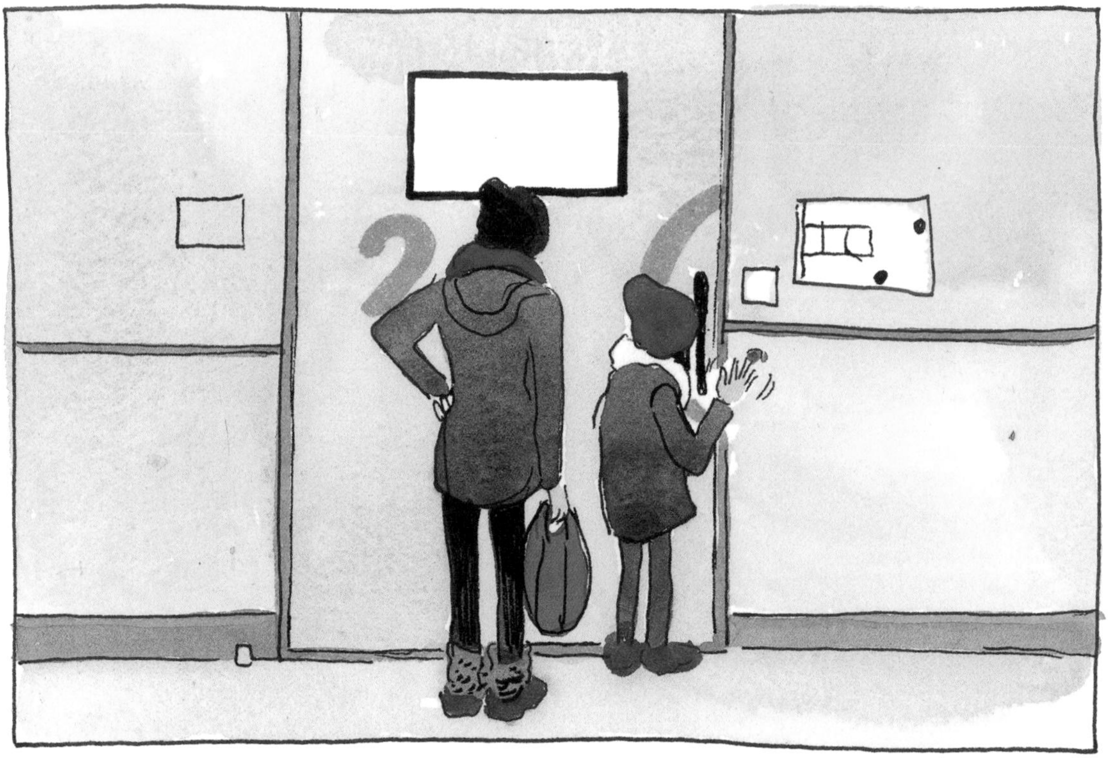

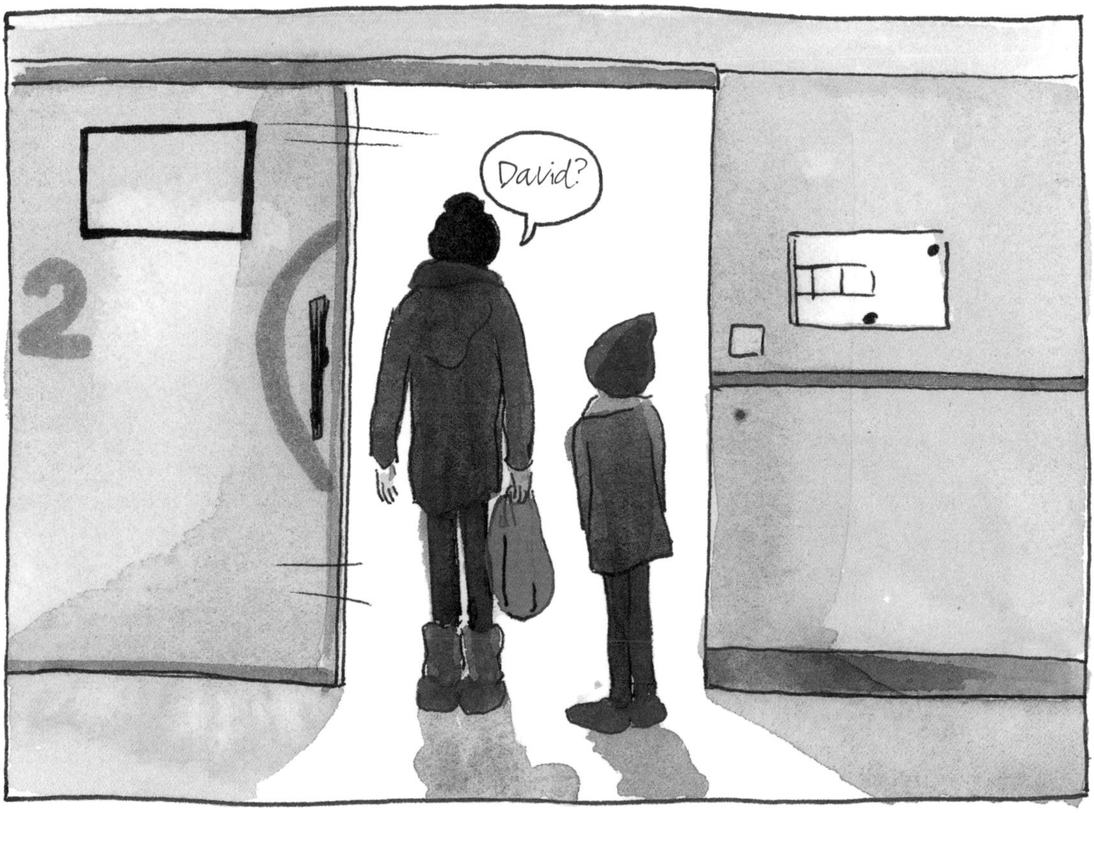
David?

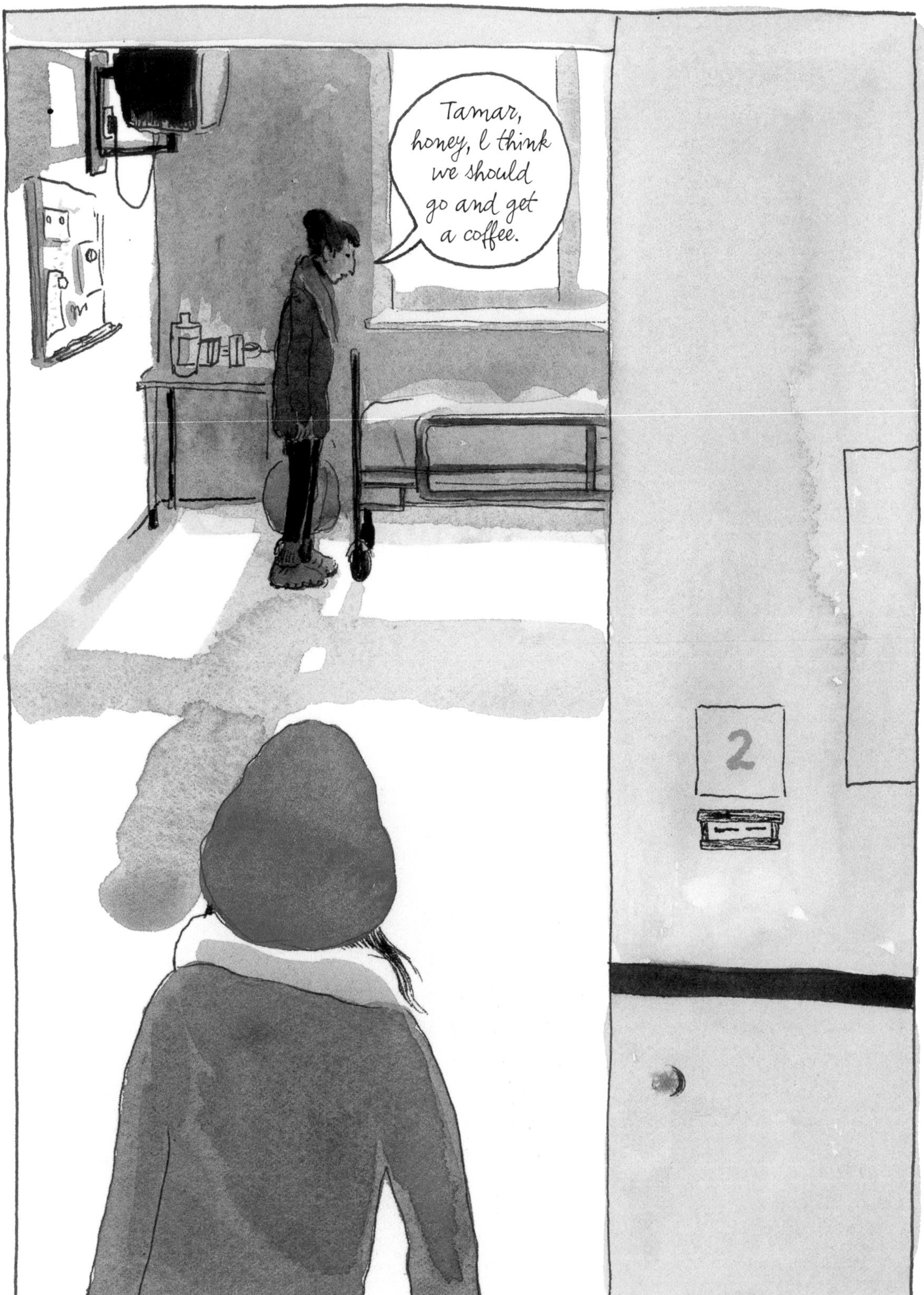
Tamar, honey, I think we should go and get a coffee.
2

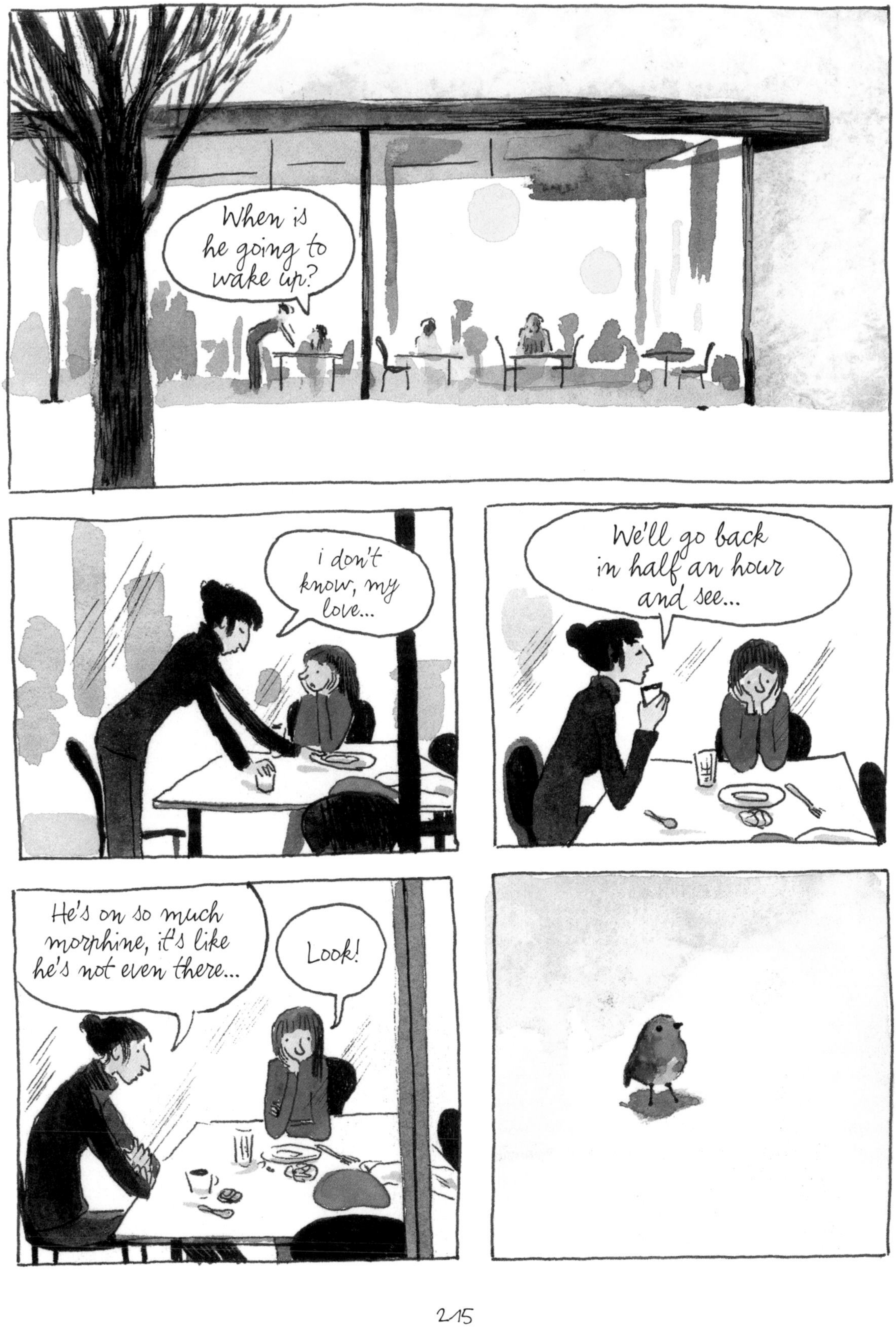
When is he going to wake up?
i don't know, my love...
We'll go back in half an hour and see...
He's on so much morphine, it's like he's not even there...
Look!

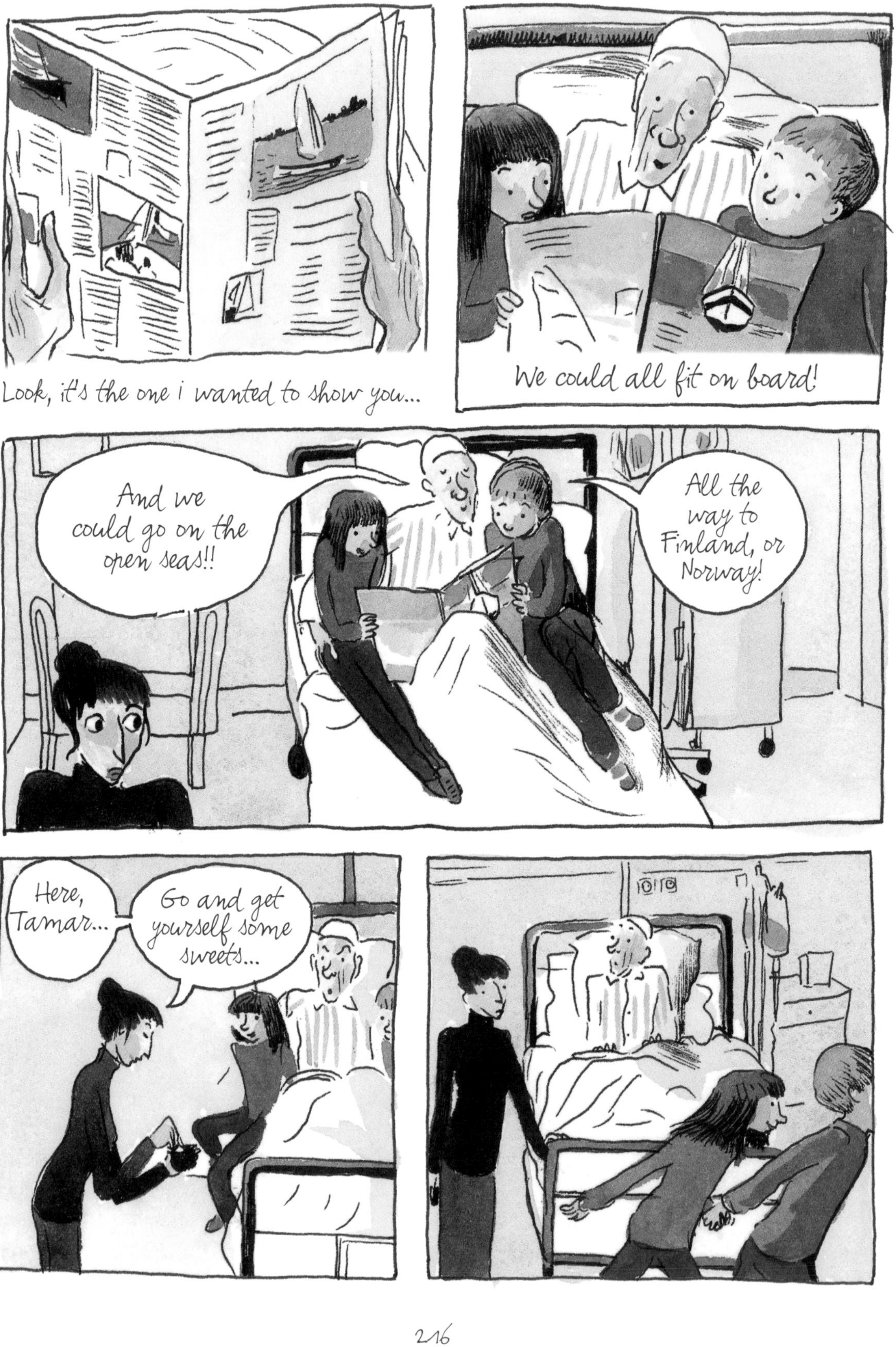

Look, it's the one i wanted to show you...
We could all fit on board!
And we could go on the open seas!!
All the way to Finland, or Norway!
Here, Tamar...
Go and get yourself some sweets...

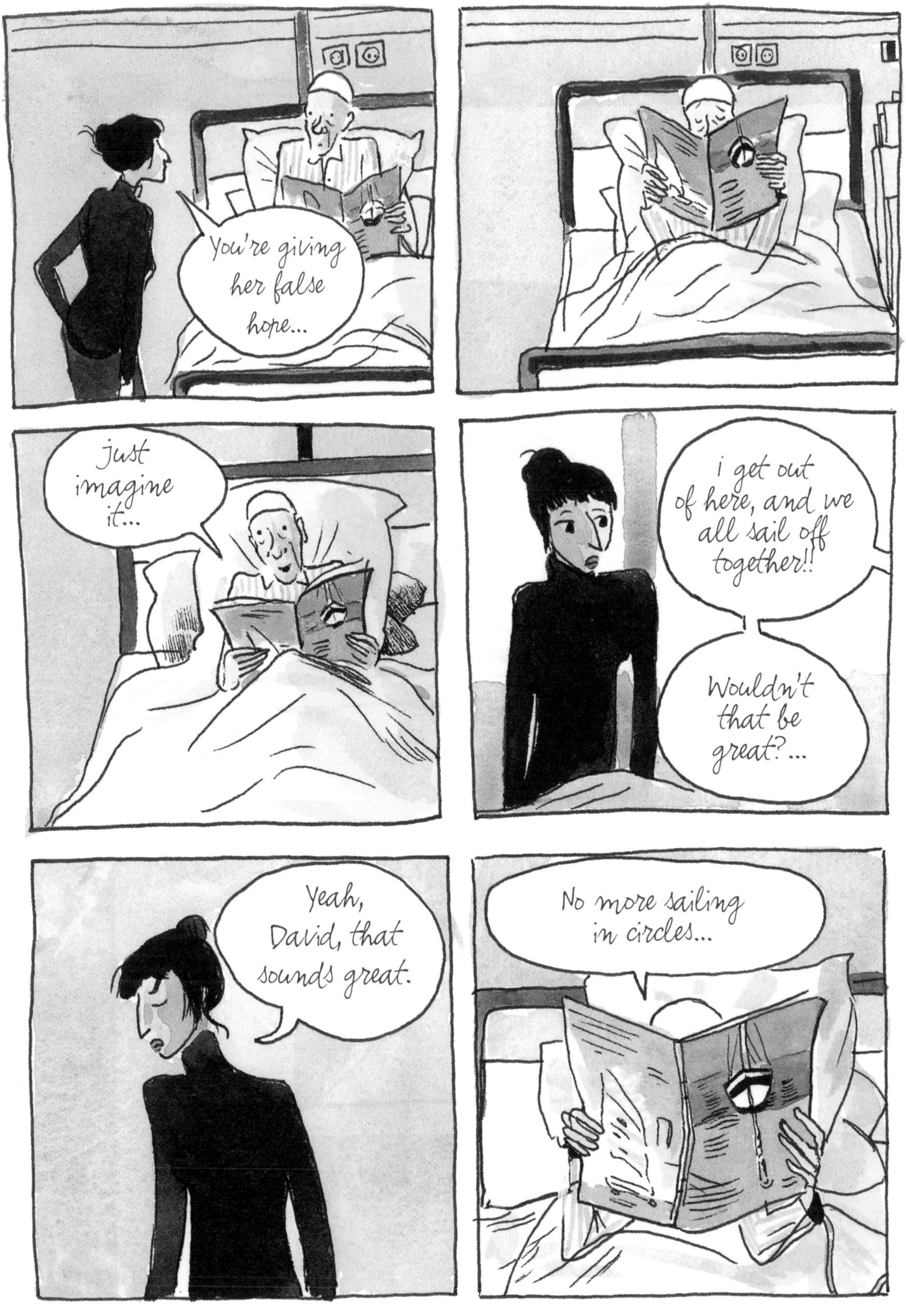
You're giving her false hope...
Just imagine it...
i get out of here, and we all sail off together!!
Wouldn't that be great?...
Yeah, David, that sounds great.
No more sailing in circles...

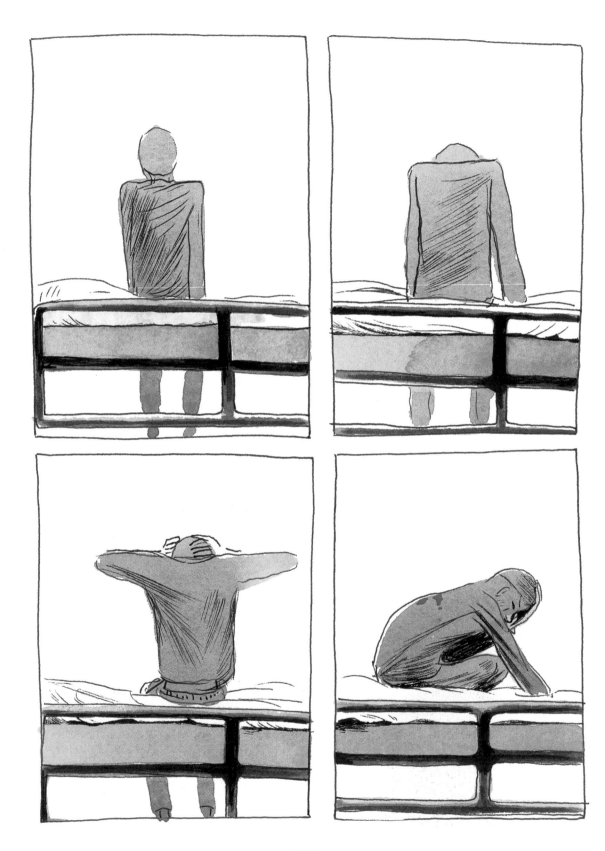

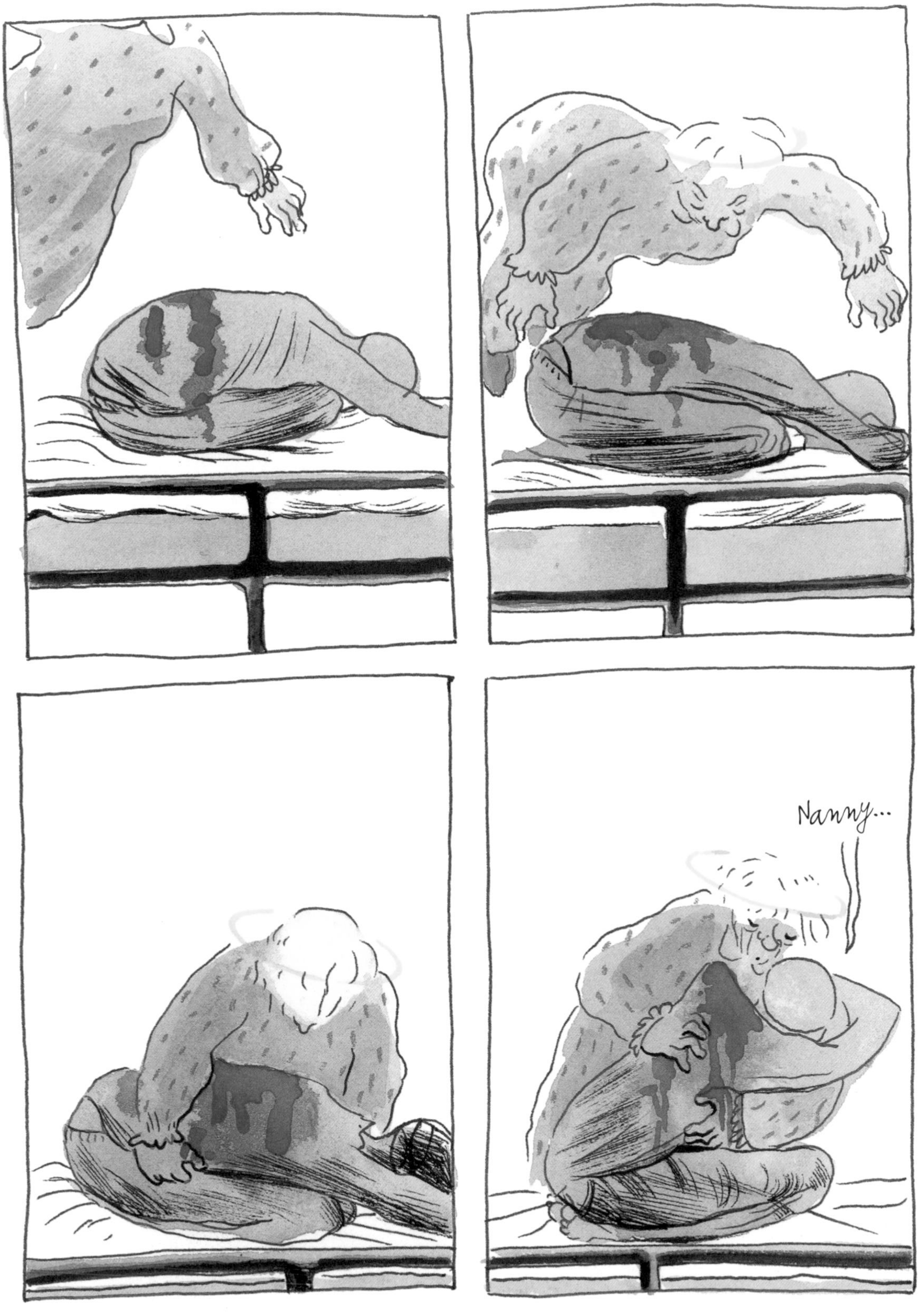
Nanny...

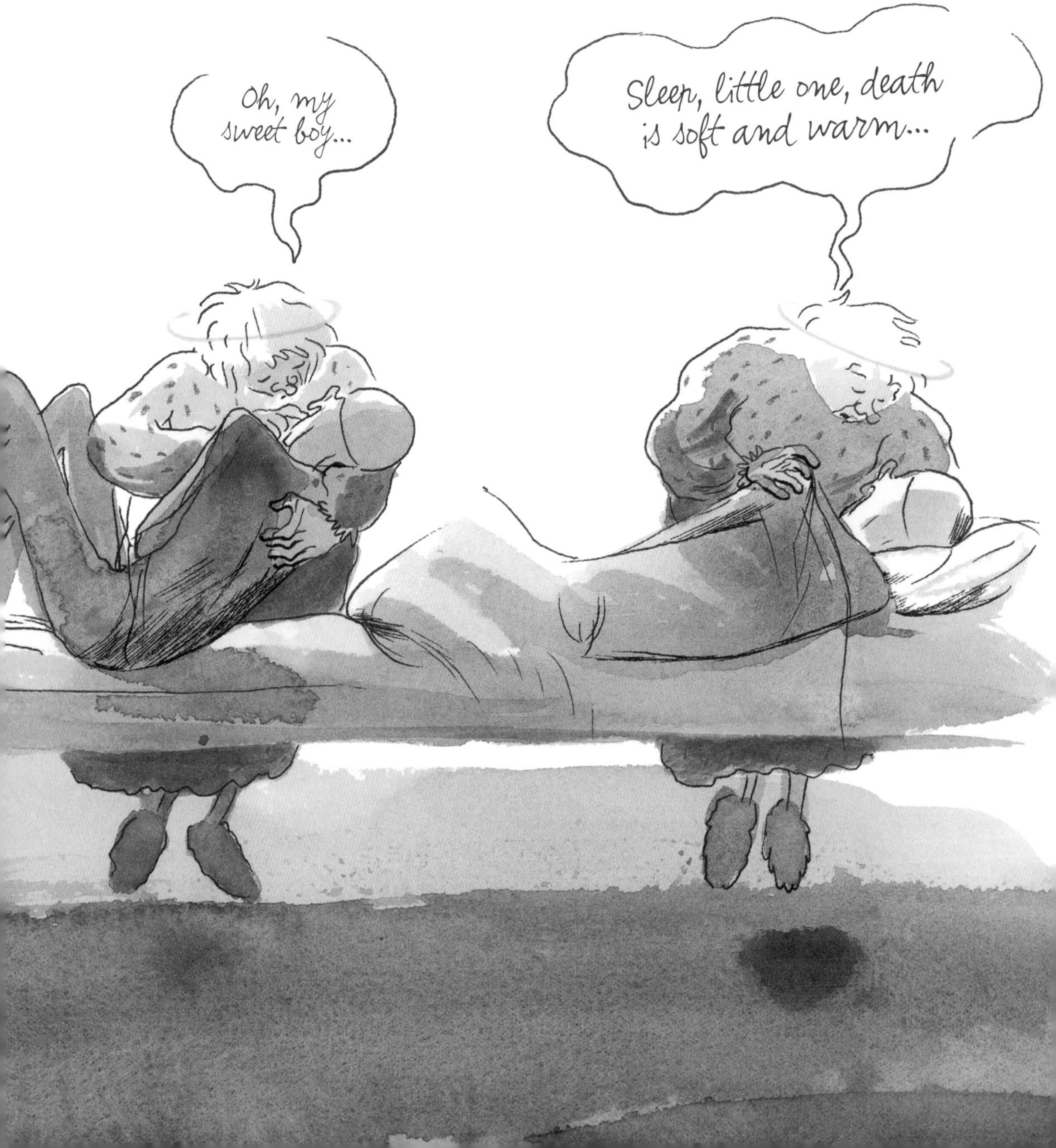
Oh, my sweet boy...
Sleep, little one, death is soft and warm...

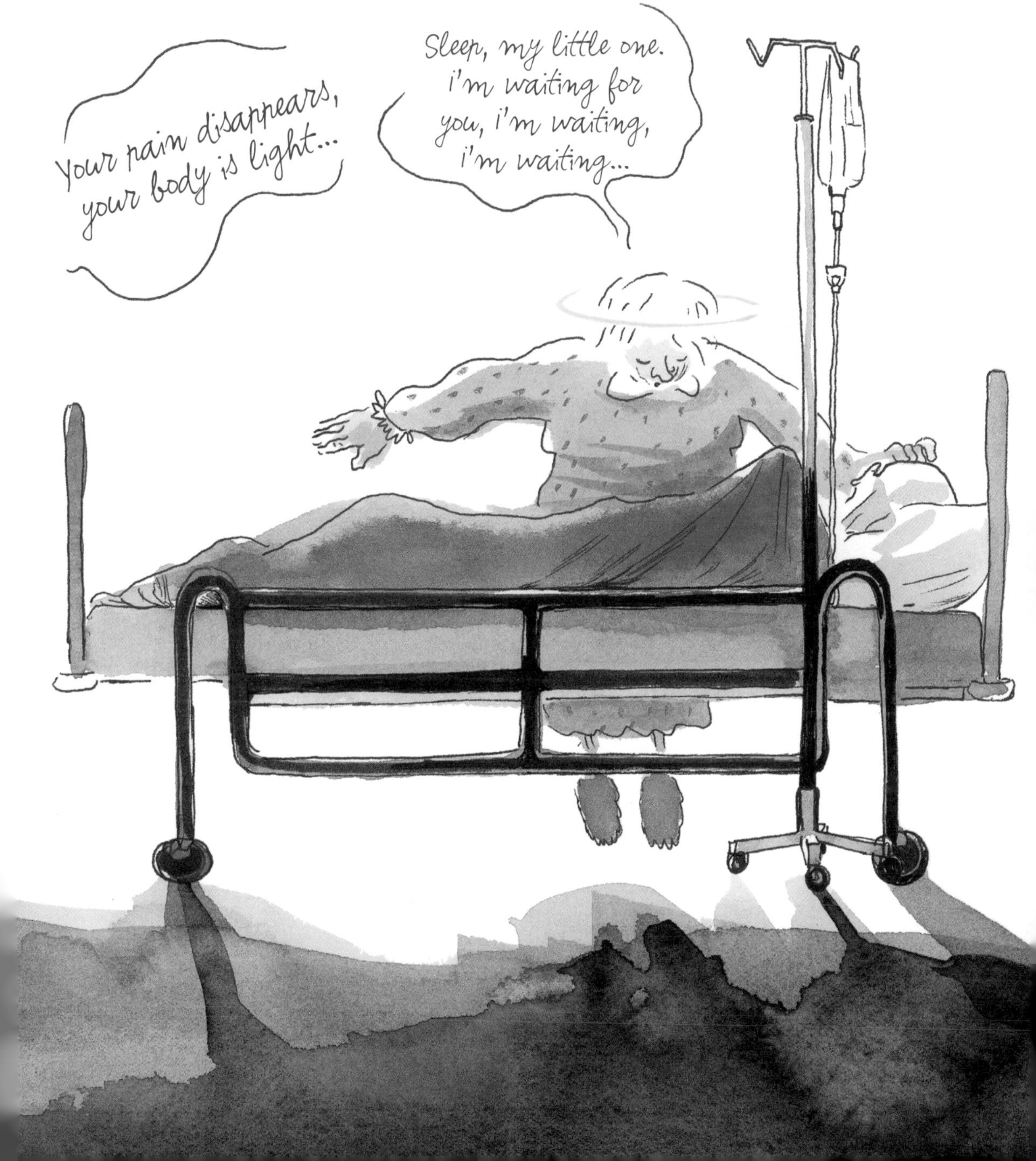
Your pain disappears, your body is light...
Sleep, my little one. i'm waiting for you, i'm waiting, i'm waiting...

julia?

Dad?

Where were you, Julia?

i'm Miriam, Dad...

... your daughter...

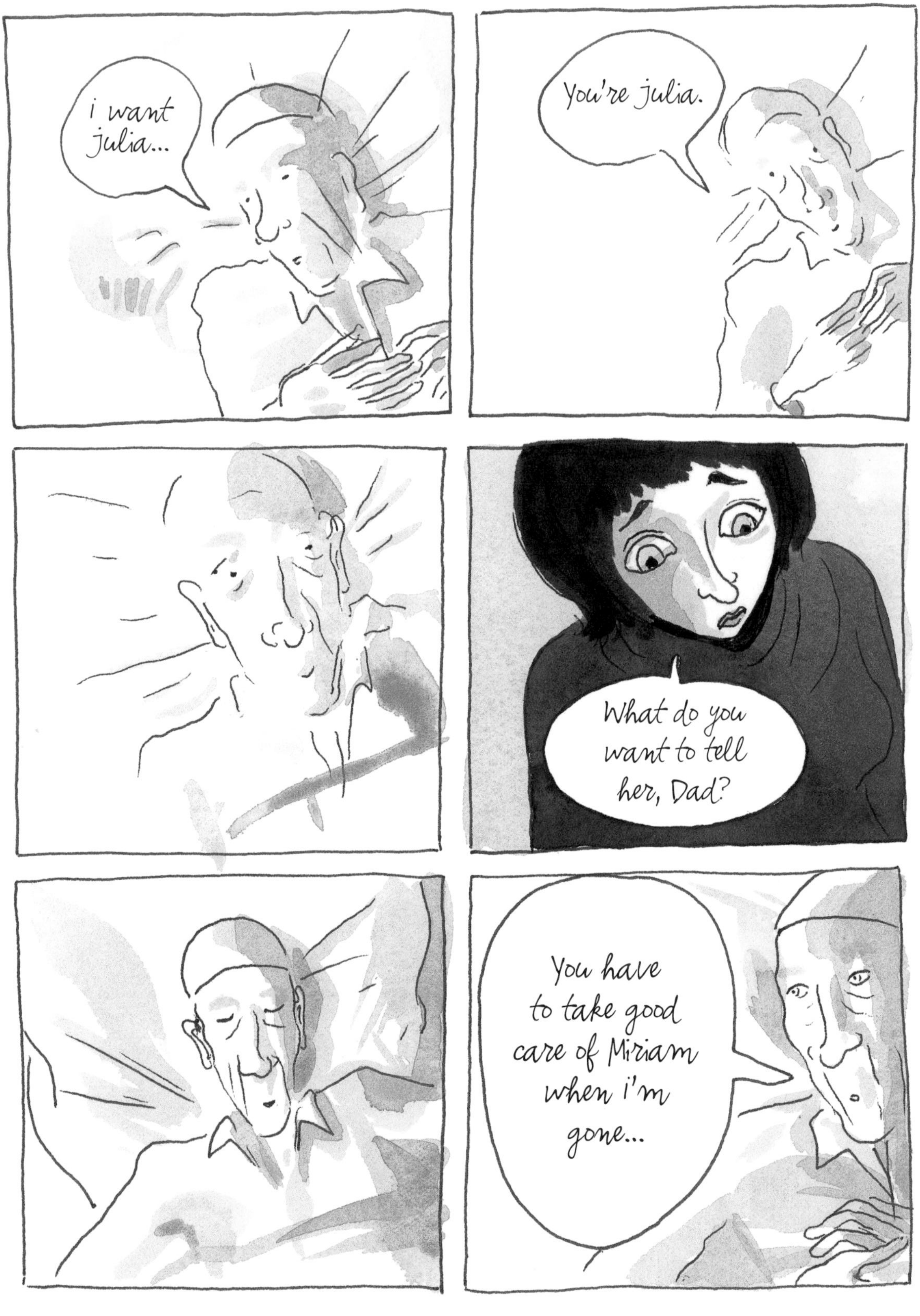
i want julia...
You're julia.
What do you want to tell her, Dad?
You have to take good care of Miriam when i'm gone...

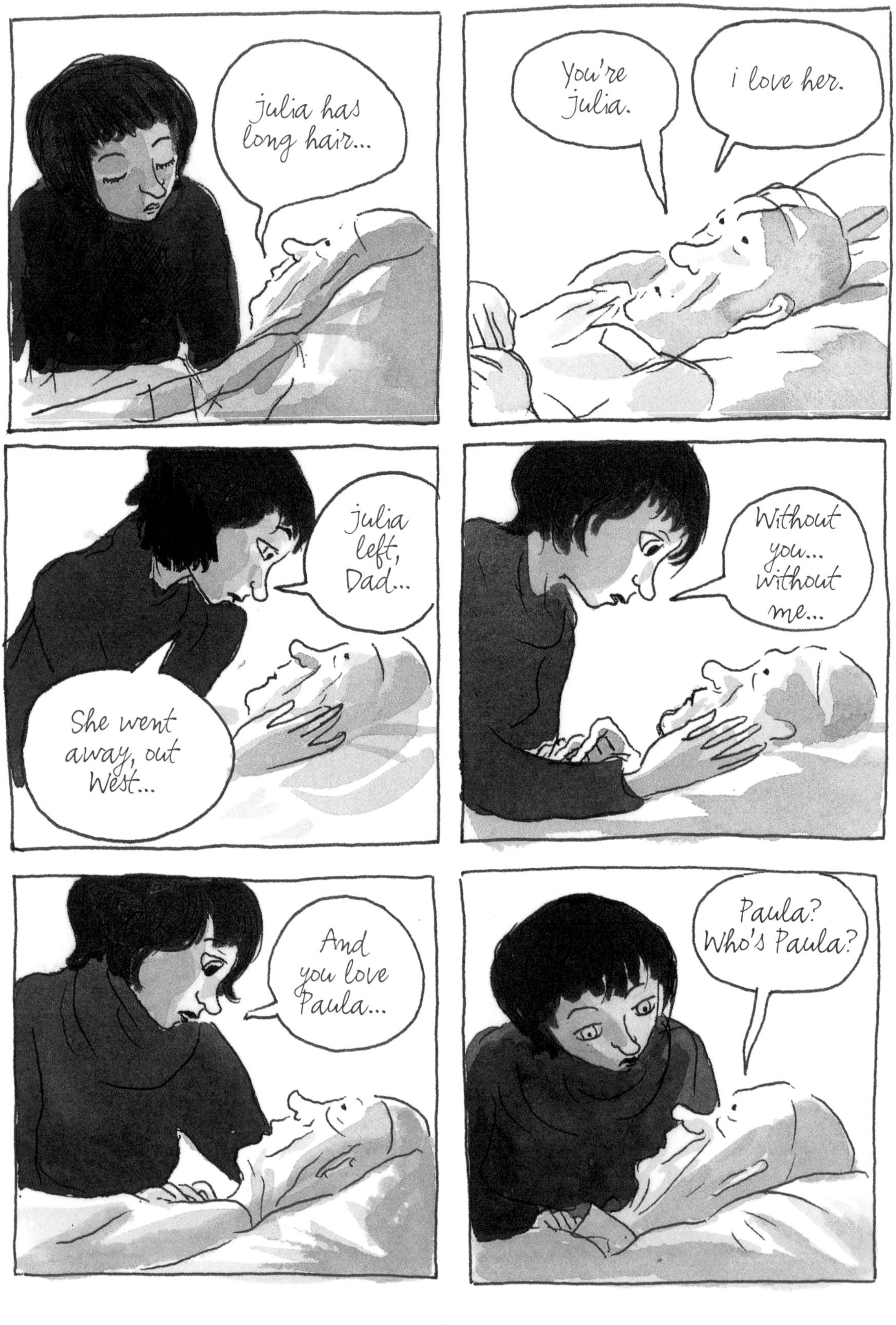
julia has long hair...
You're julia.
i love her.
julia left, Dad...
She went away, out West...
Without you... without me...
And you love Paula...
Paula? Who's Paula?

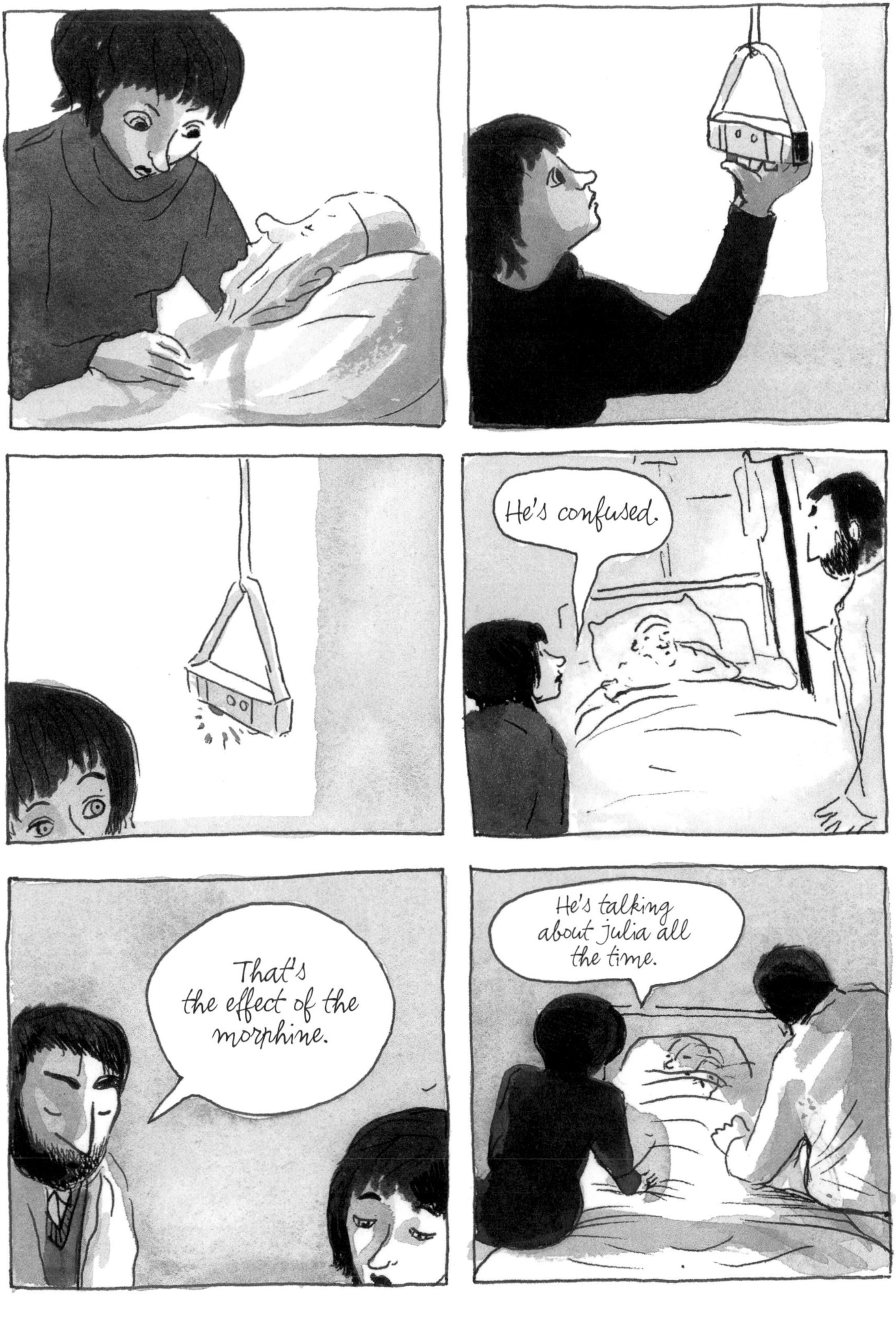
He's confused.
That's the effect of the morphine.
He's talking about Julia all the time.

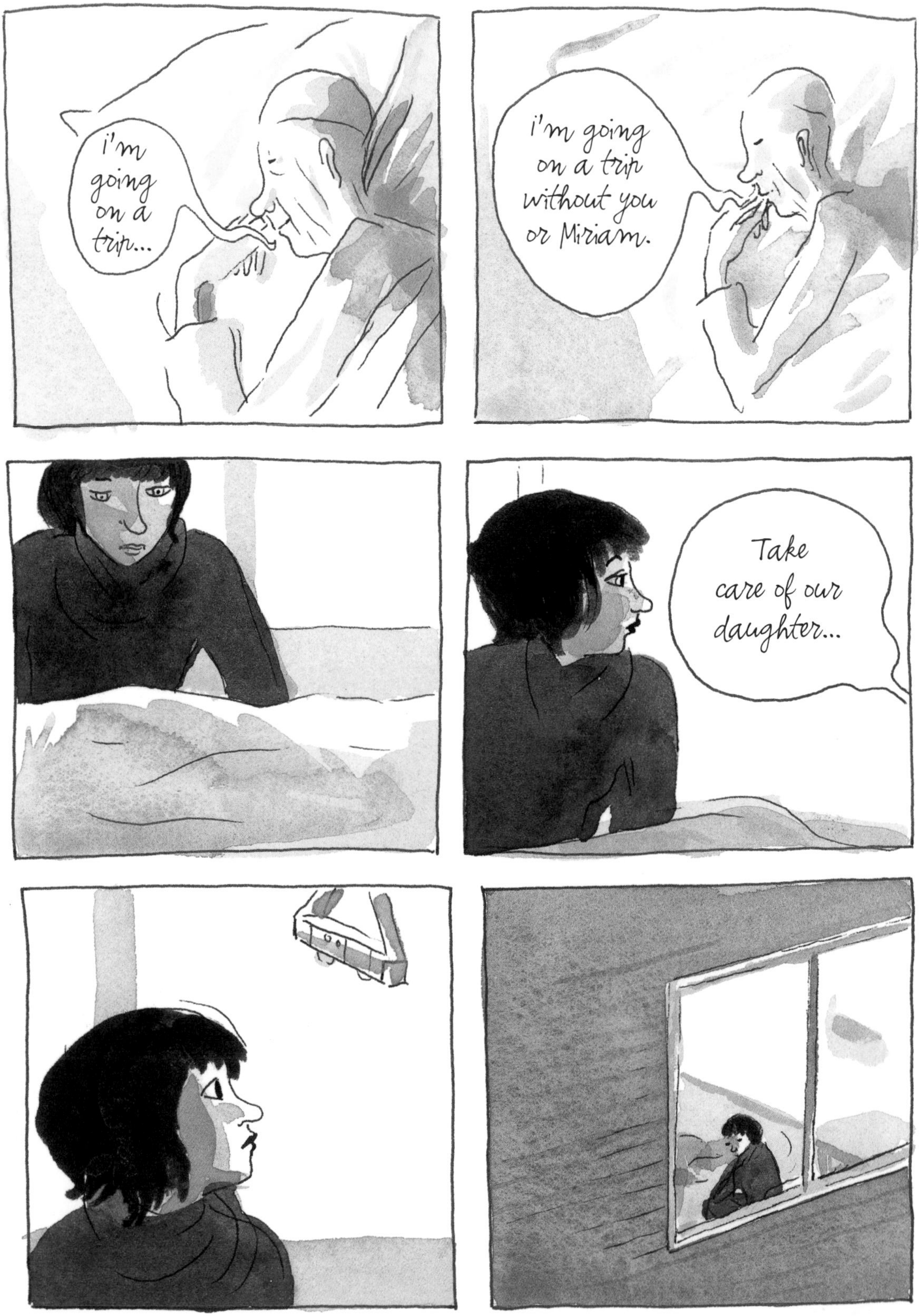
i'm going on a trip...
i'm going on a trip without you or Miriam.
Take care of our daughter...

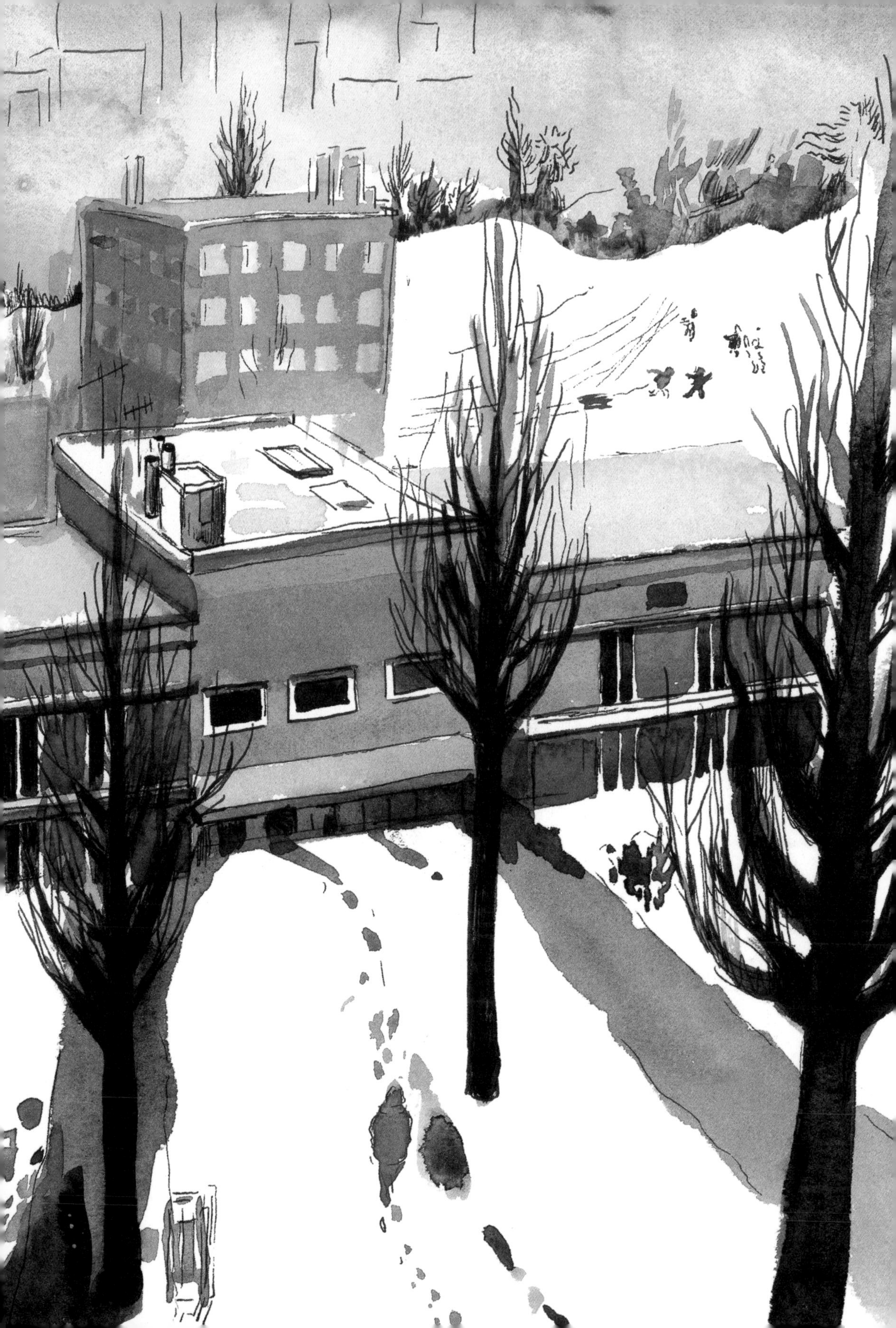

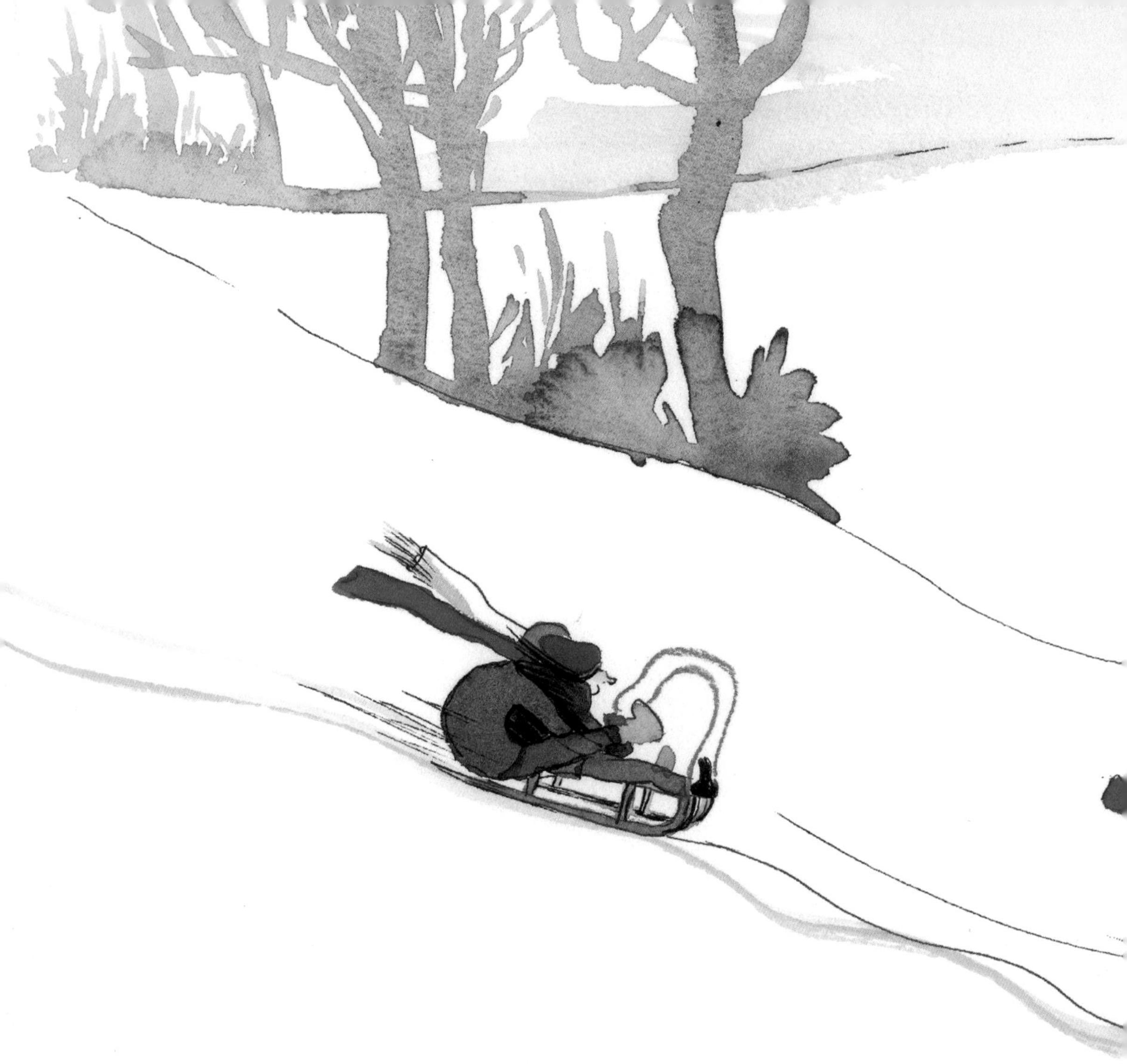

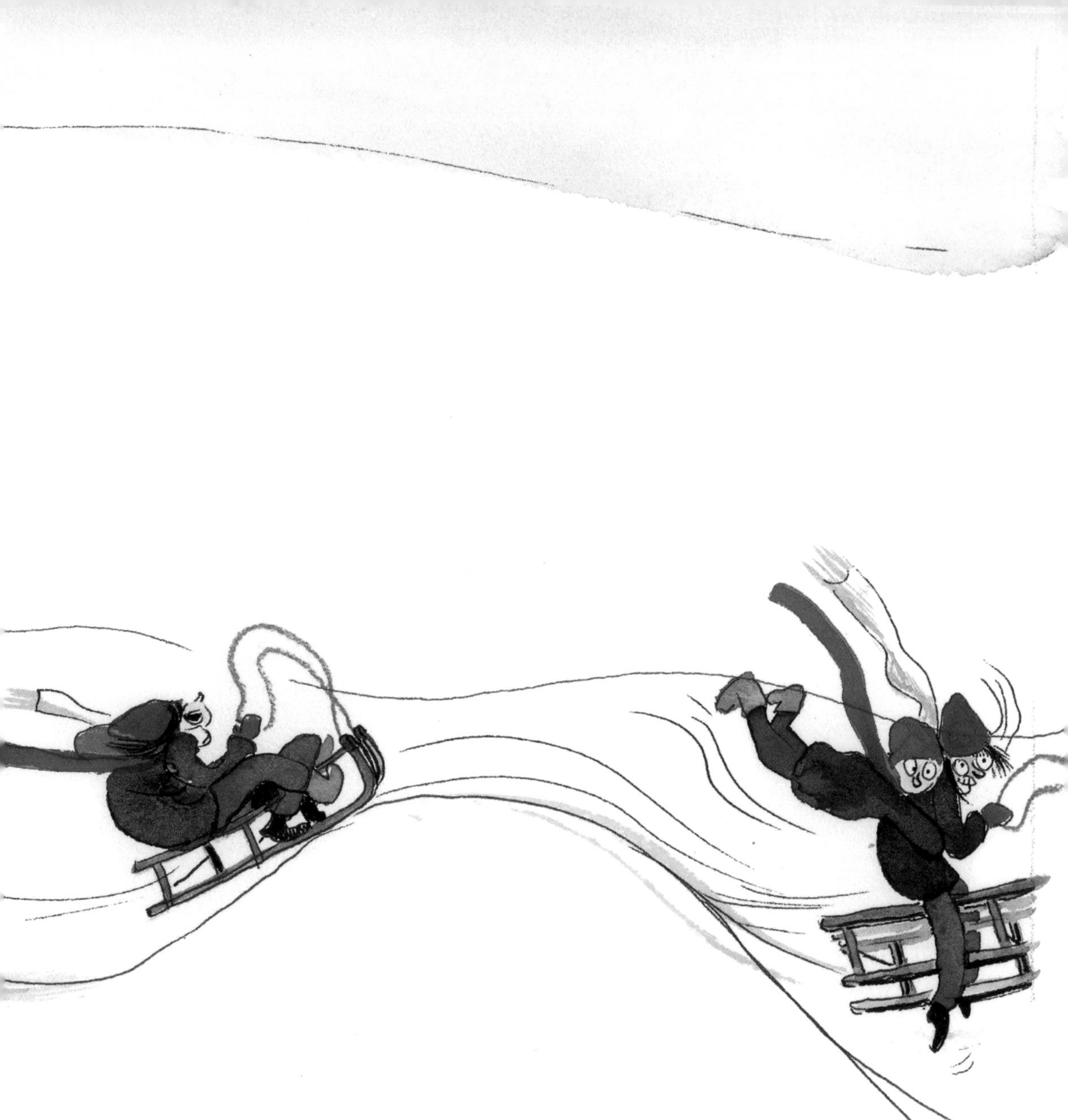

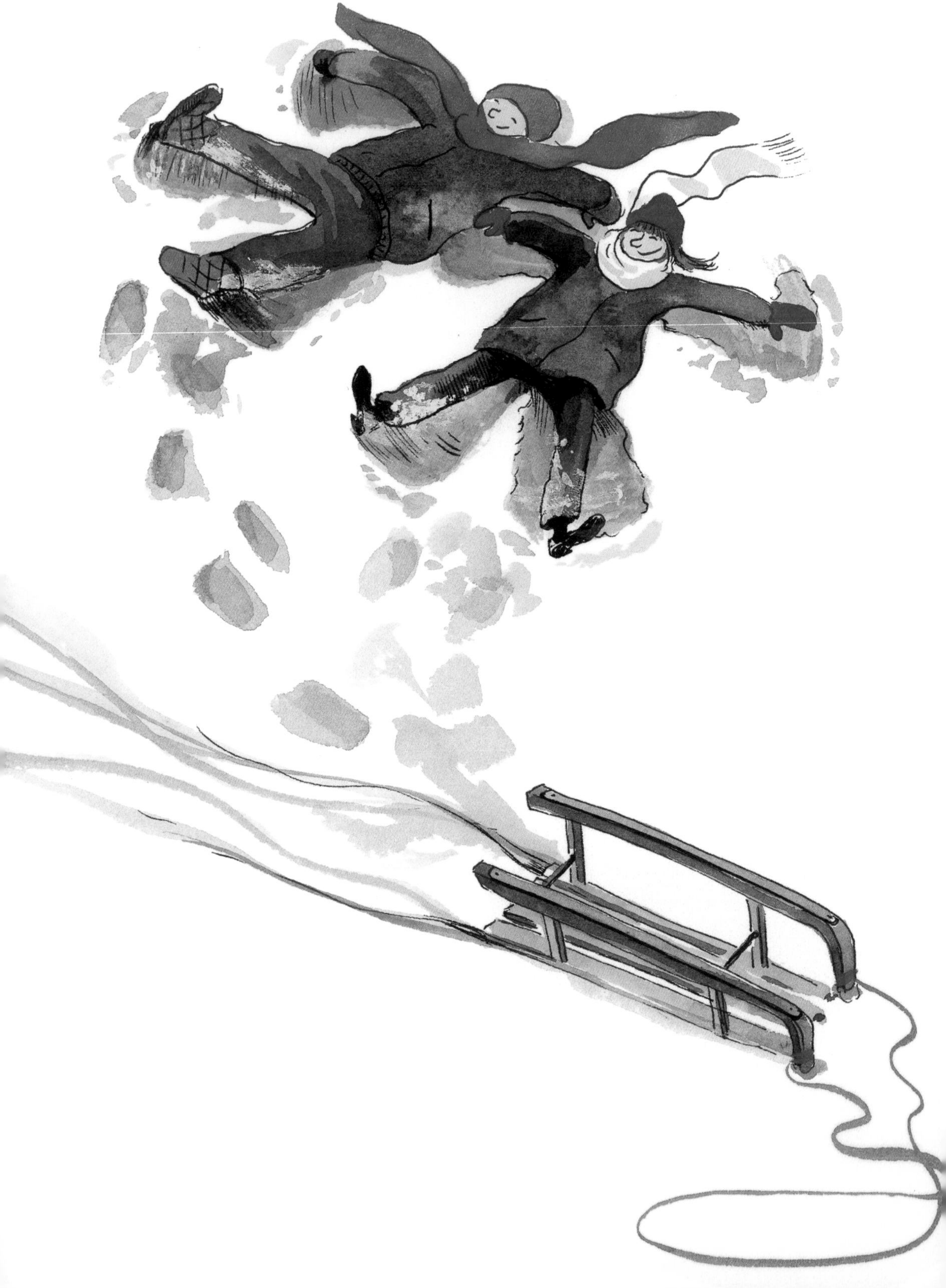

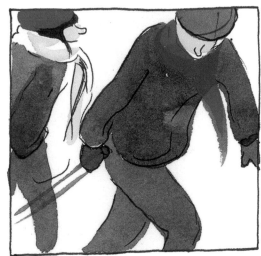

231

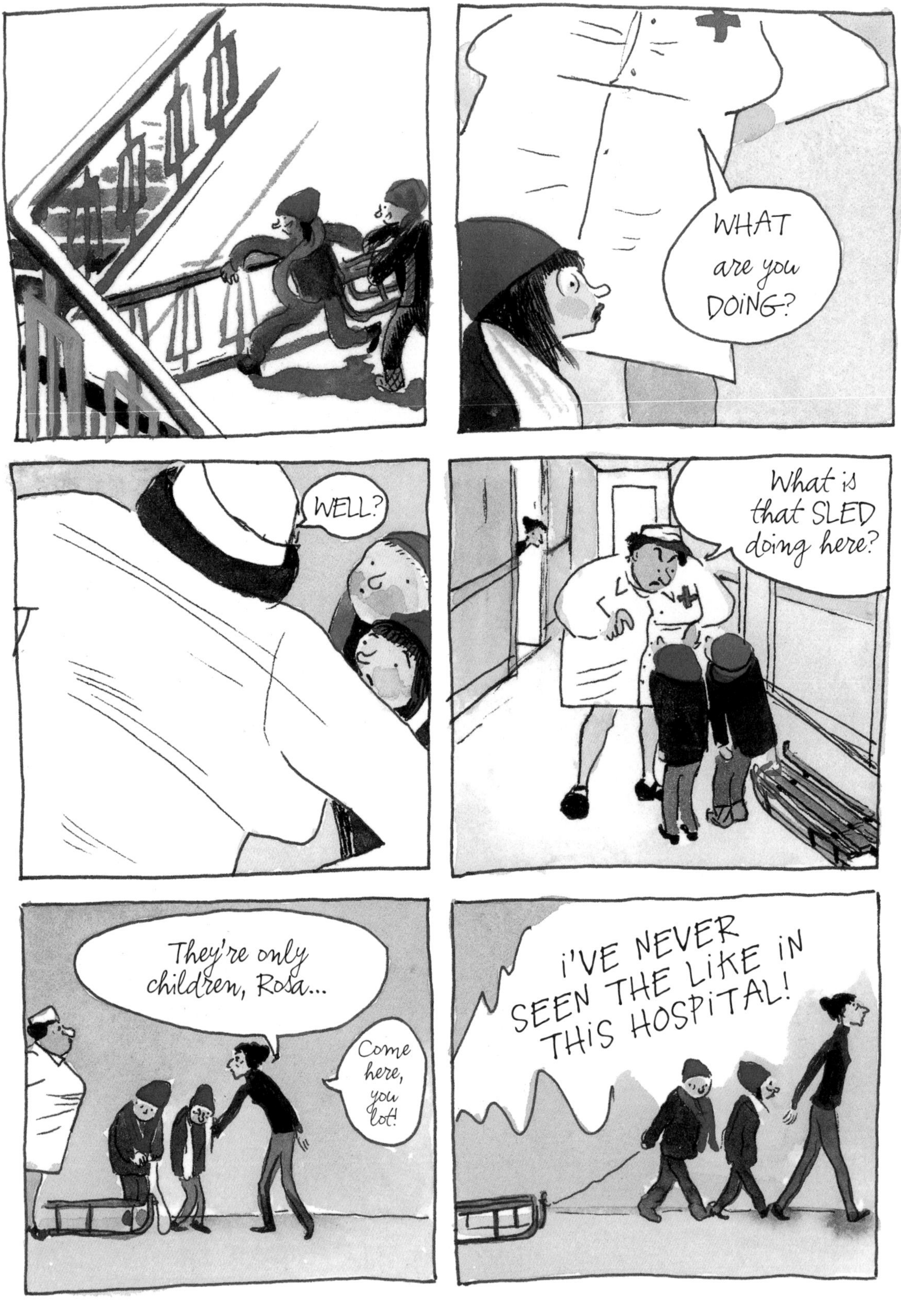
WHAT are you DOING?
WELL?
What is that SLED doing here?
They're only children, Rosa...
Come here, you lot!
I'VE NEVER SEEN THE LIKE IN THIS HOSPITAL!

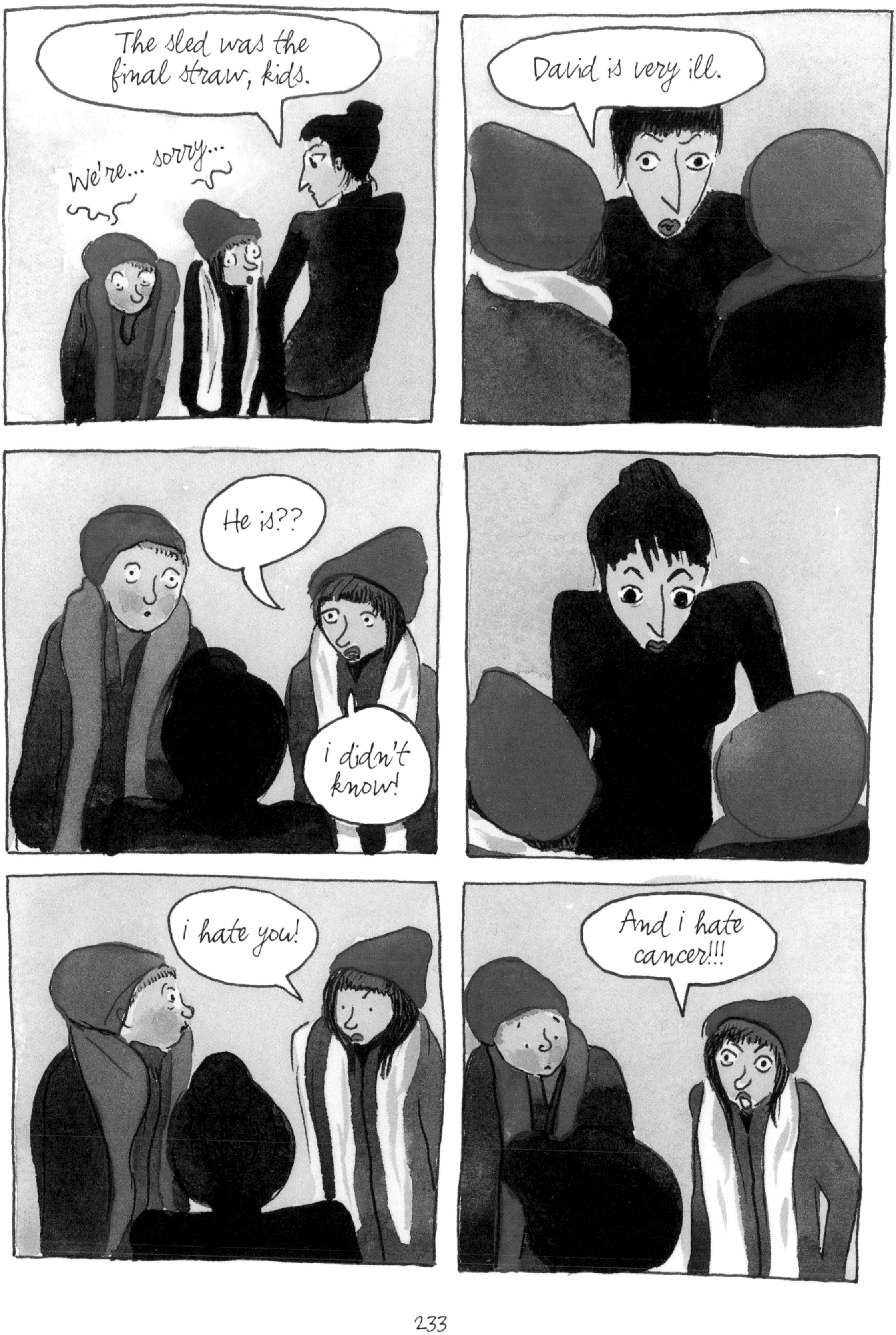
The sled was the final straw, kids.
We're... sorry...
David is very ill.
He is??
i didn't know!
i hate you!
And i hate cancer!!!

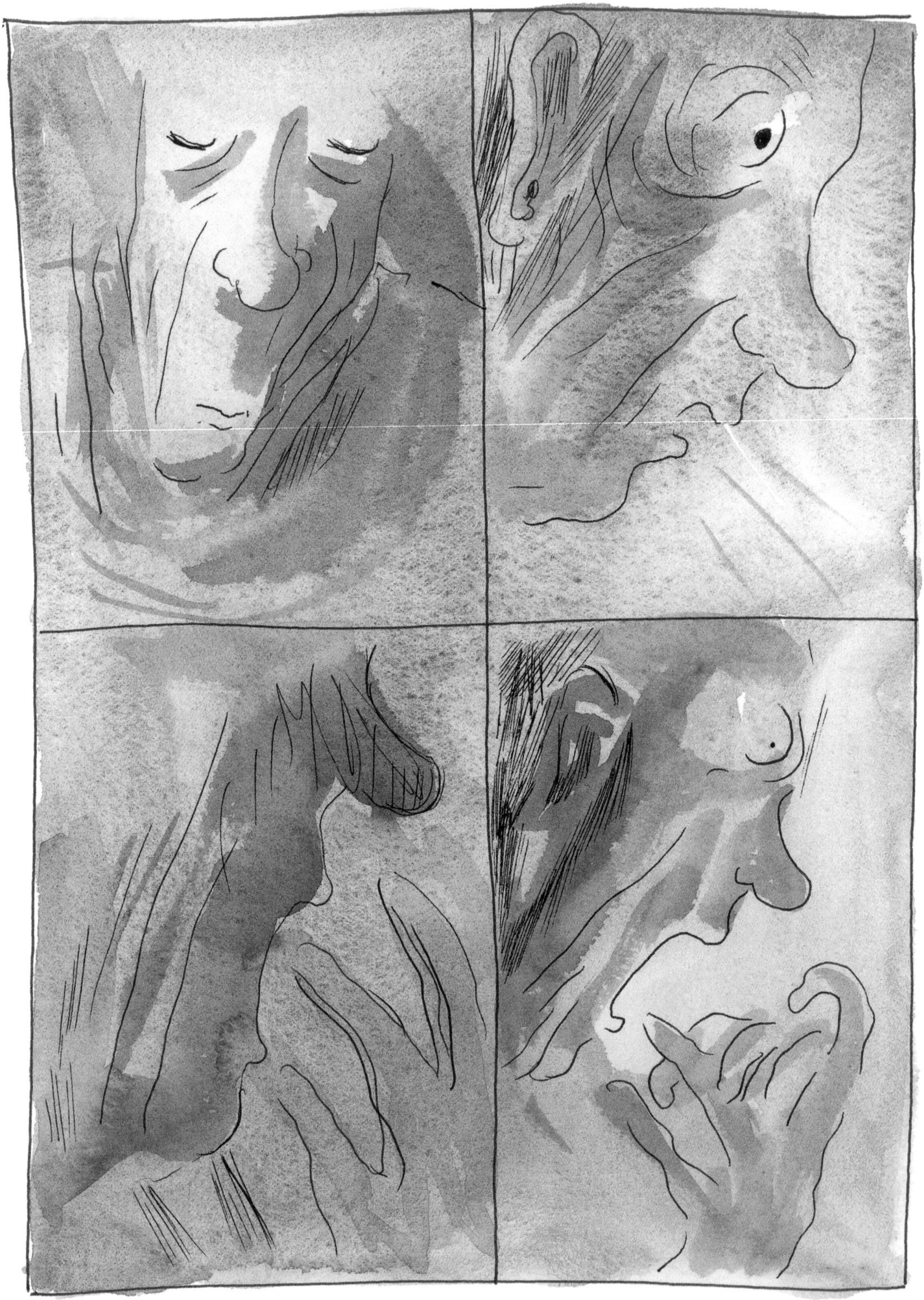

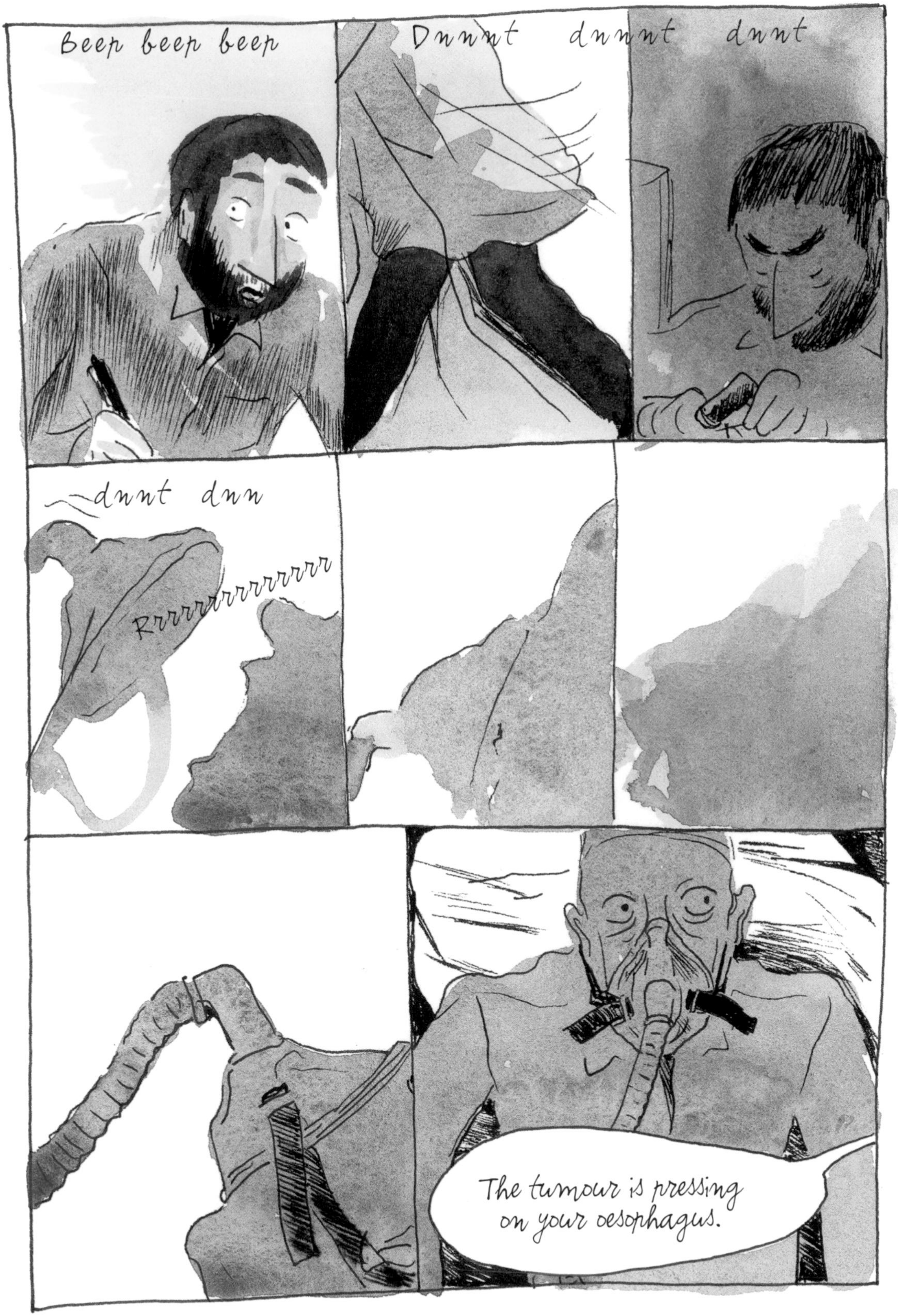
Beep beep beep
Dnnnt dnnnt dnnt
dnnt dnn
Rrrrrrrrrrrrrr
The tumour is pressing on your oesophagus.

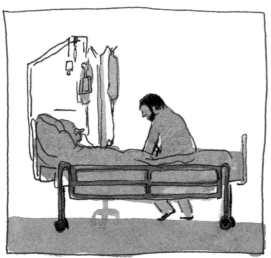

We're going to have to remove your larynx, David.

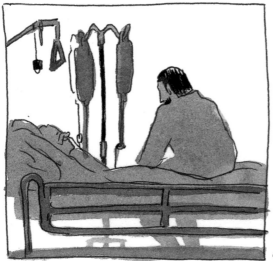

i wouldn't be able to talk any more... i read about that...

That's true, but you'll breathe more easily...

i don't want to breathe any more, Georg.

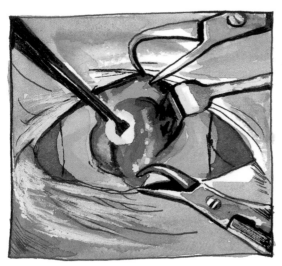

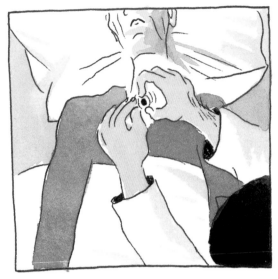

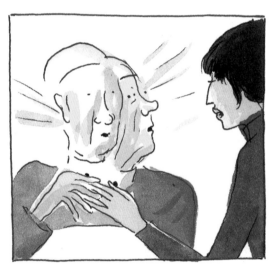

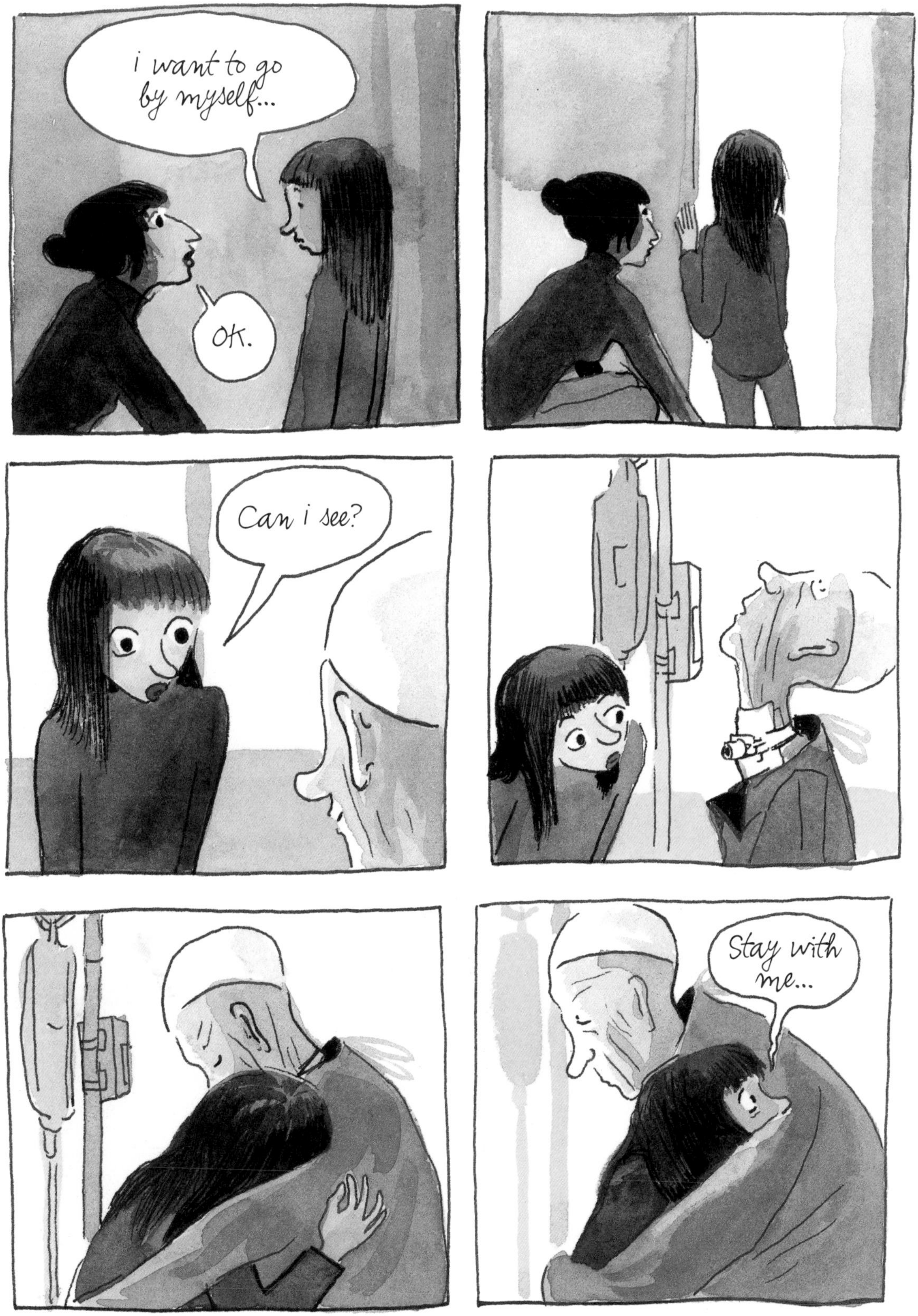
i want to go by myself...
OK.
Can i see?
Stay with me...

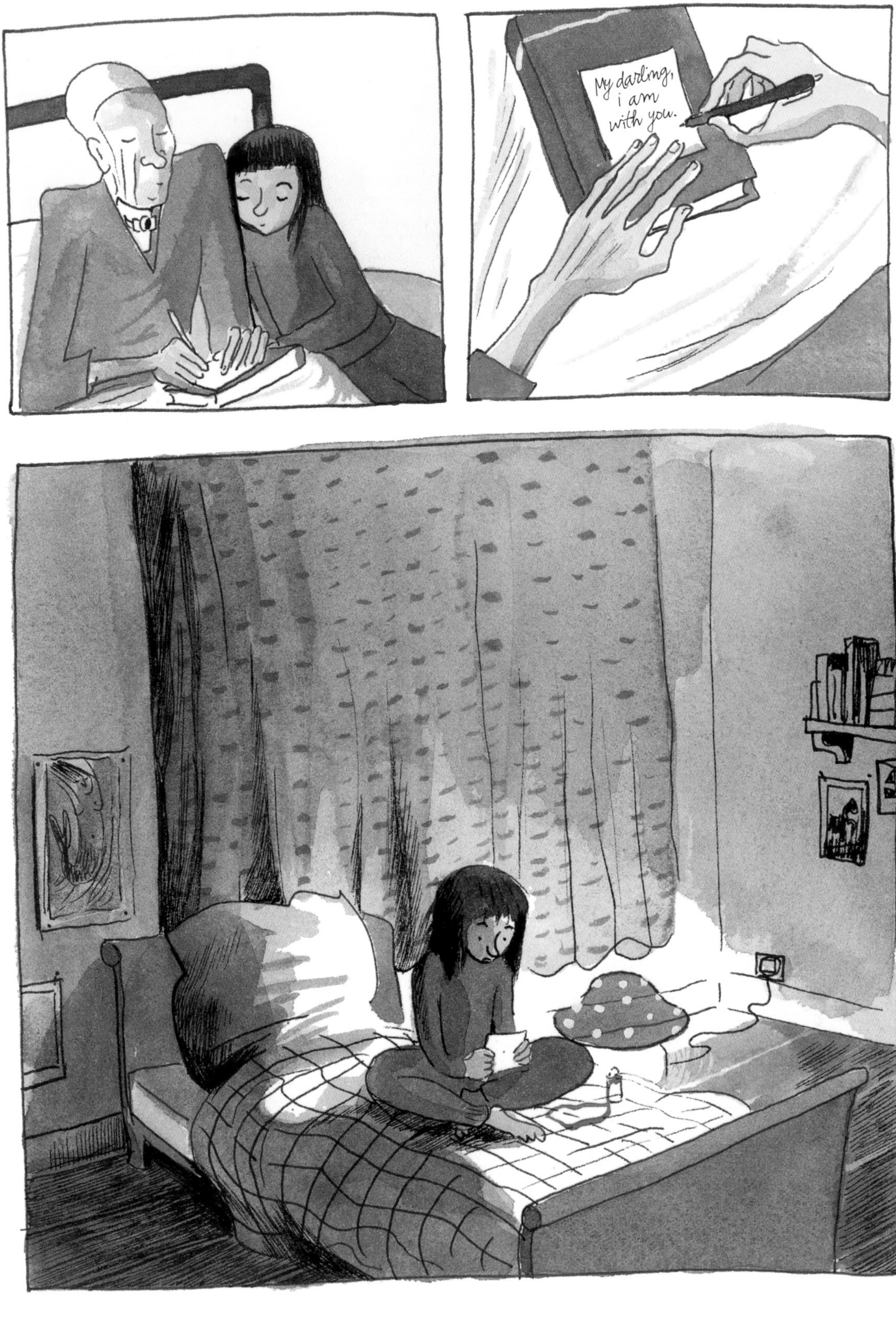
My darling,
i am
with you.

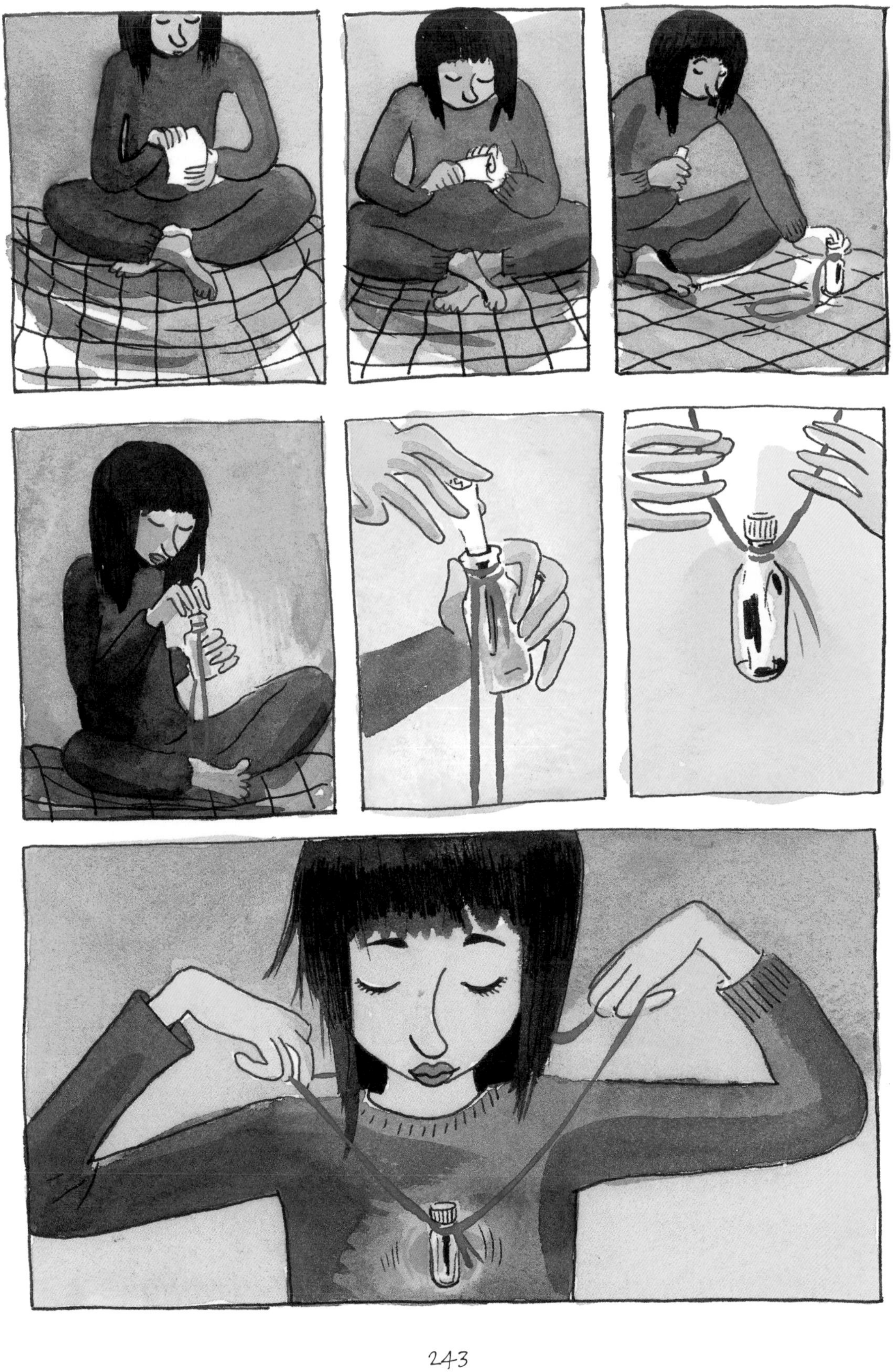

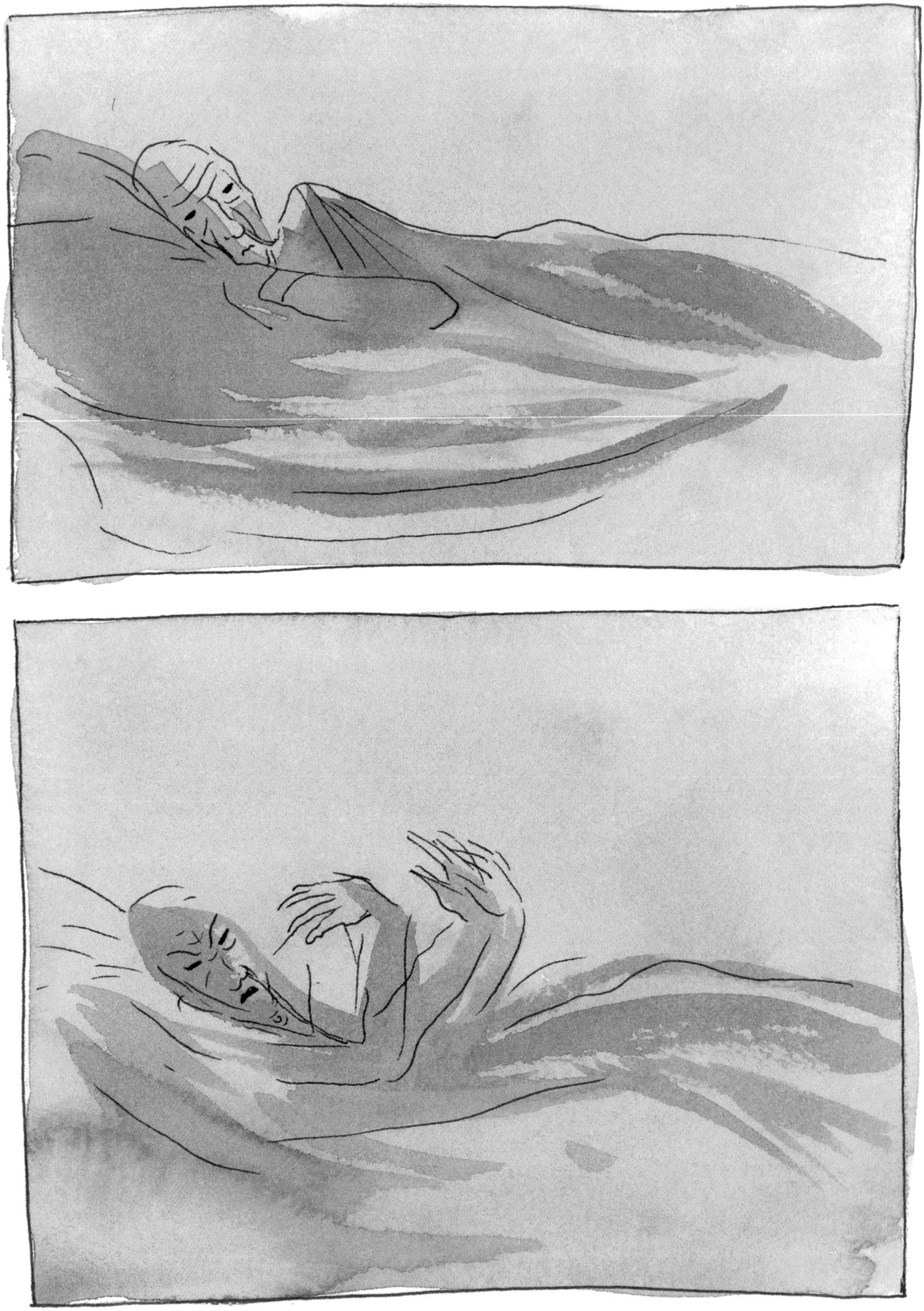

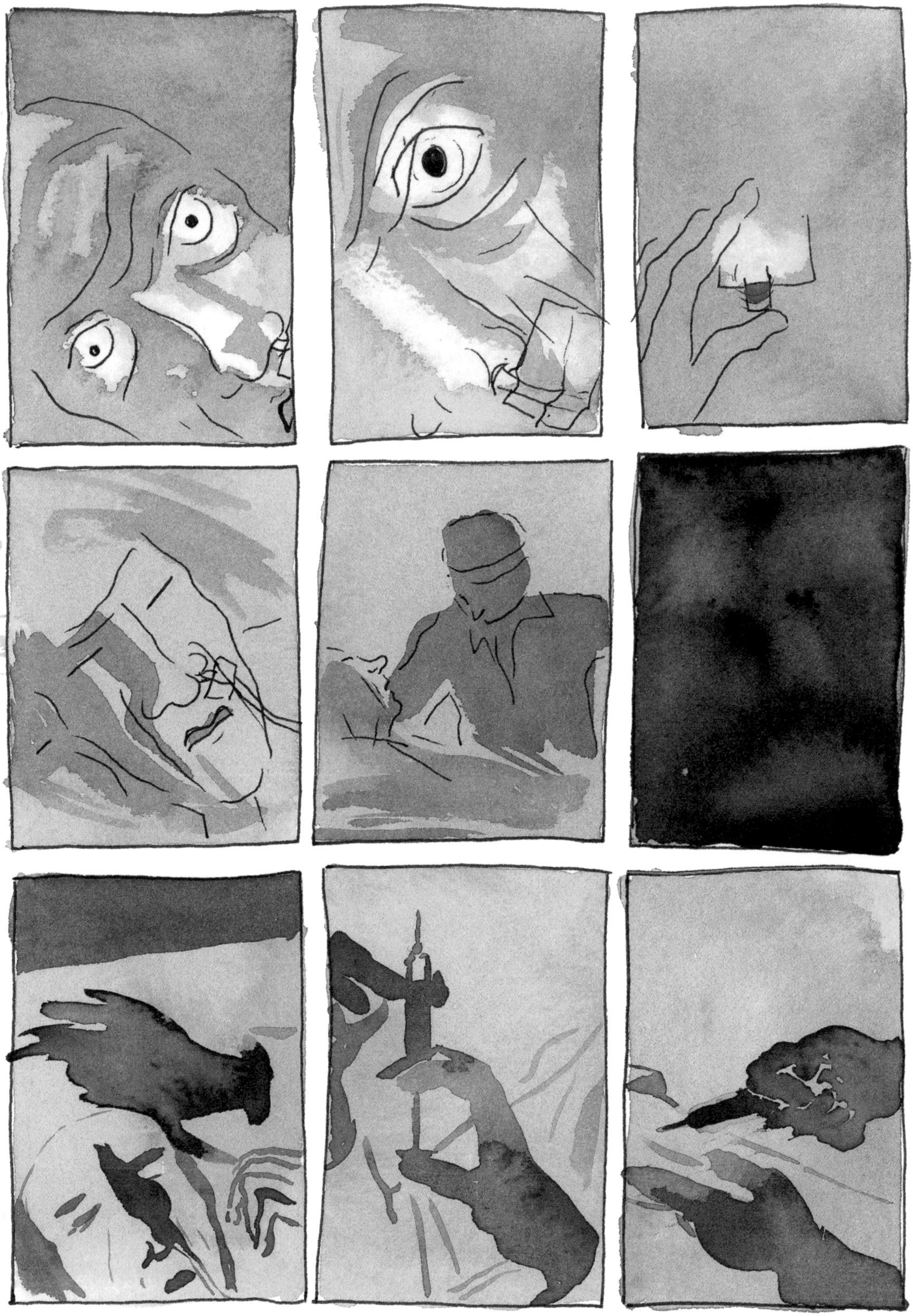

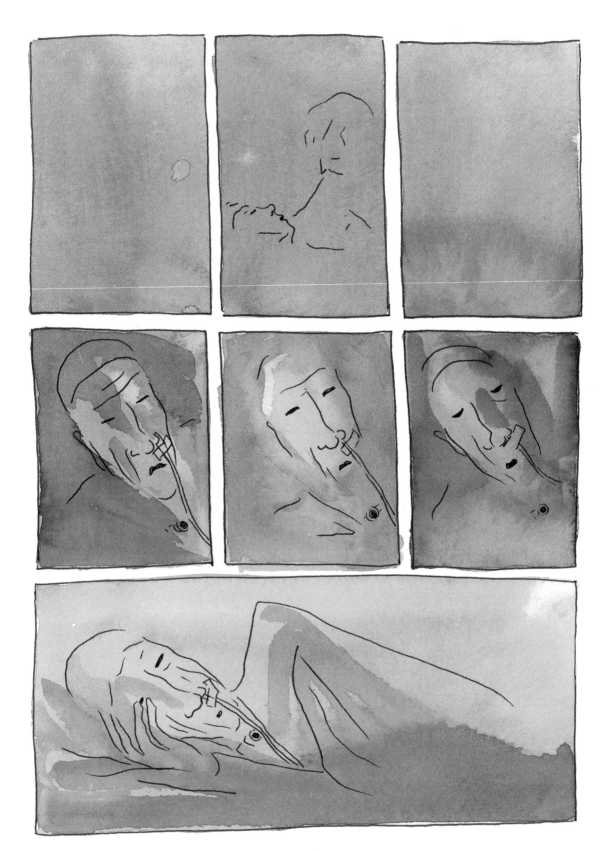

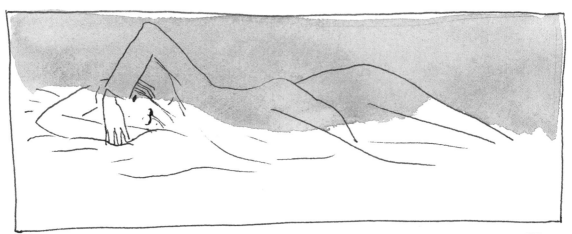

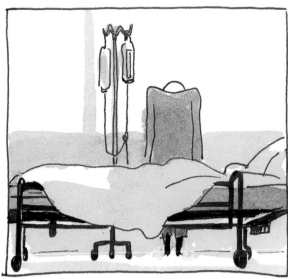

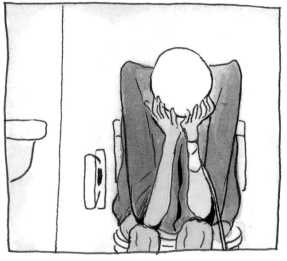

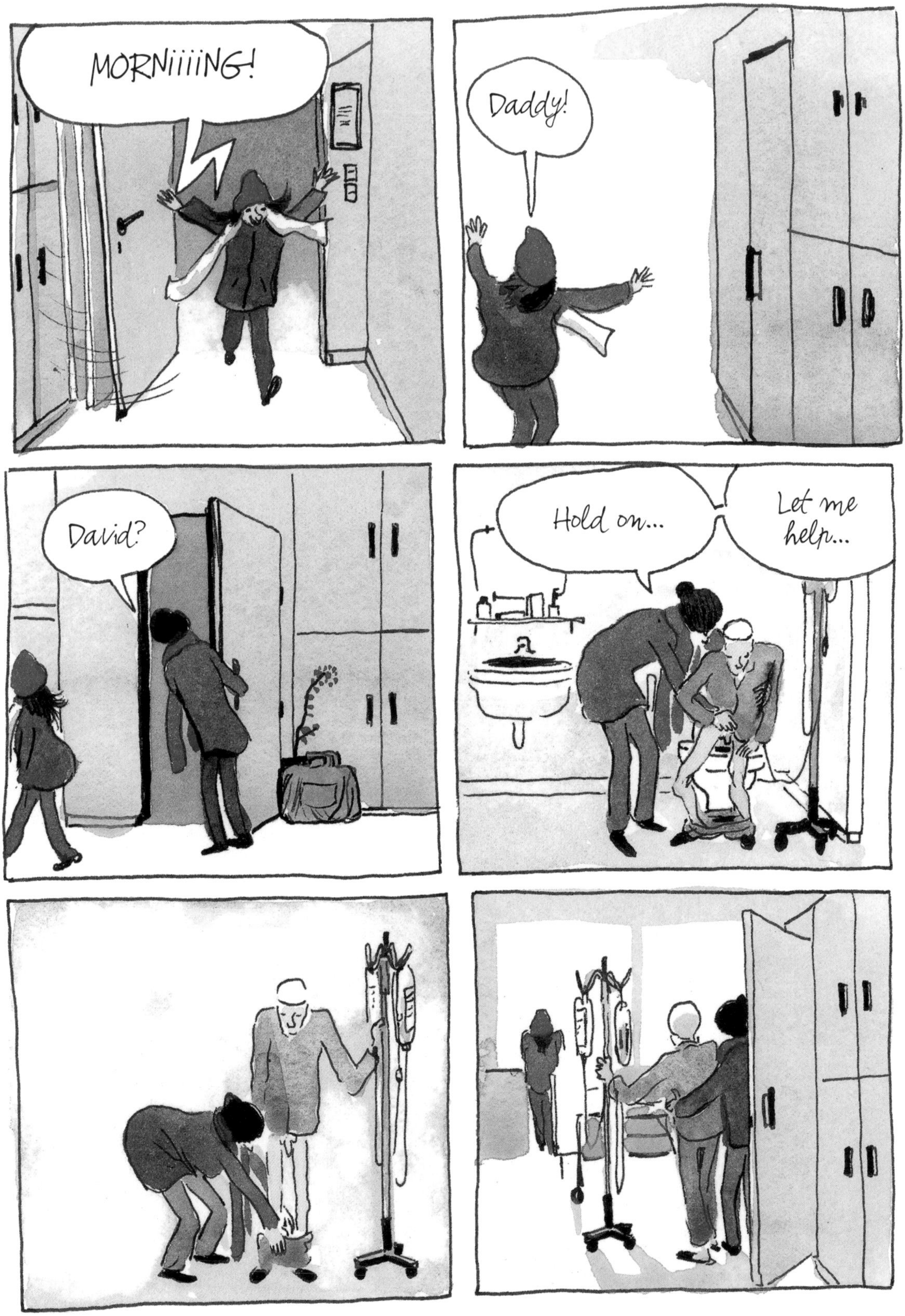
MORNiiiiiNG!
Daddy!
David?
Hold on...
Let me help...

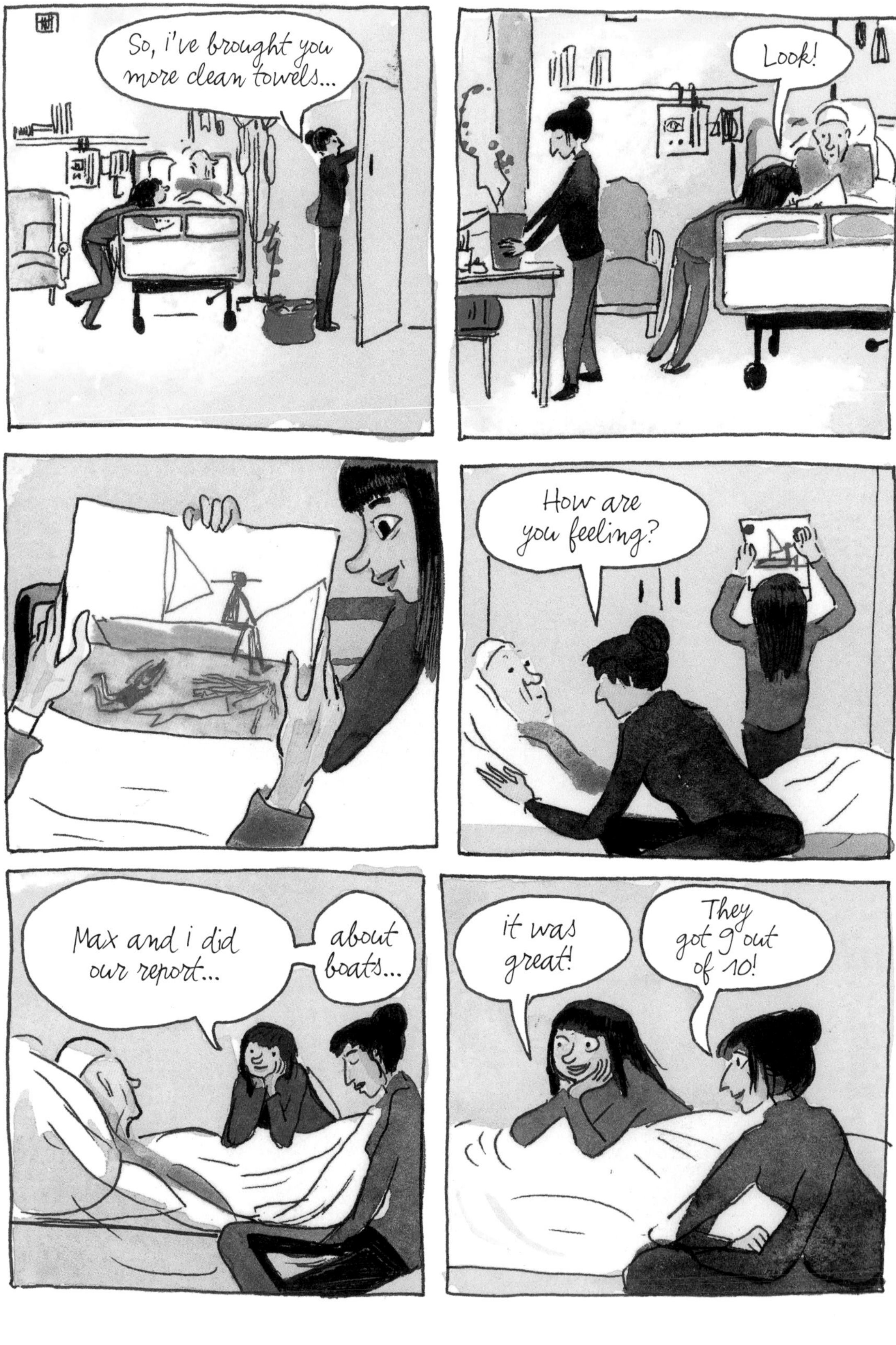

So, i've brought you more clean towels...
Look!
How are you feeling?
Max and i did our report...
about boats...
it was great!
They got 9 out of 10!

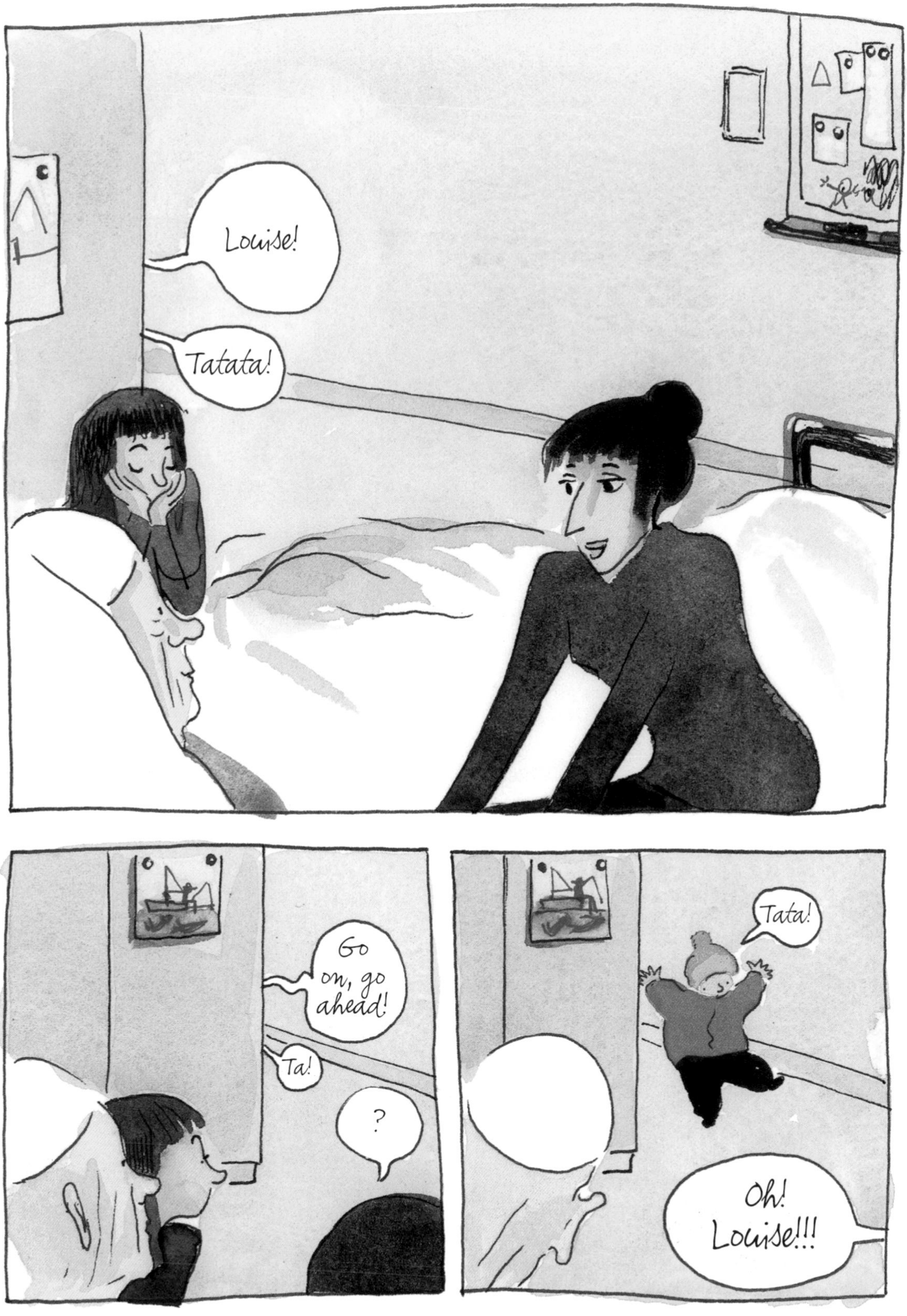
Louise!
Tatata!
Go on, go ahead!
Ta!
?
Tata!
Oh! Louise!!!

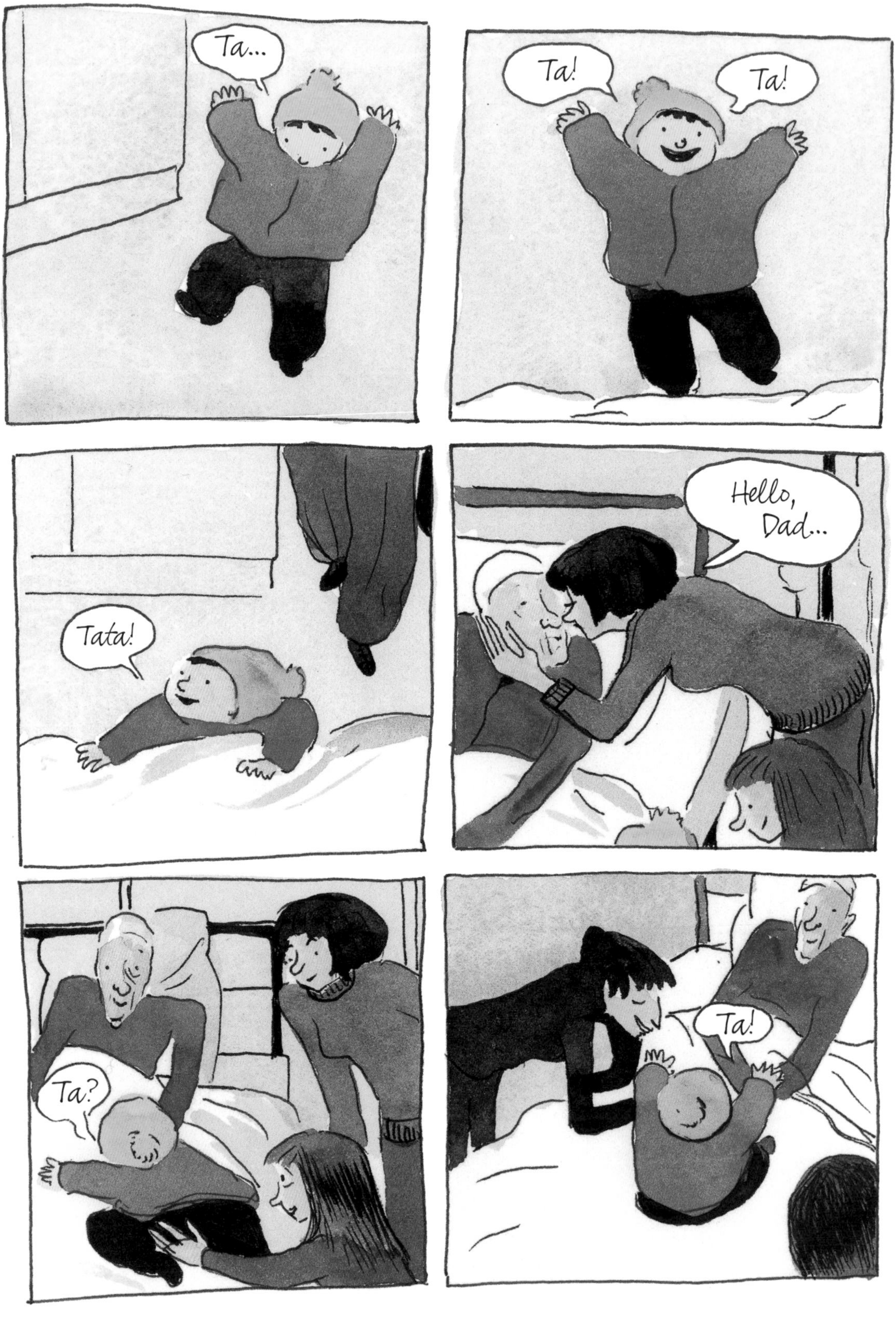
Ta...
Ta!
Ta!
Tata!
Hello, Dad...
Ta?
Ta!

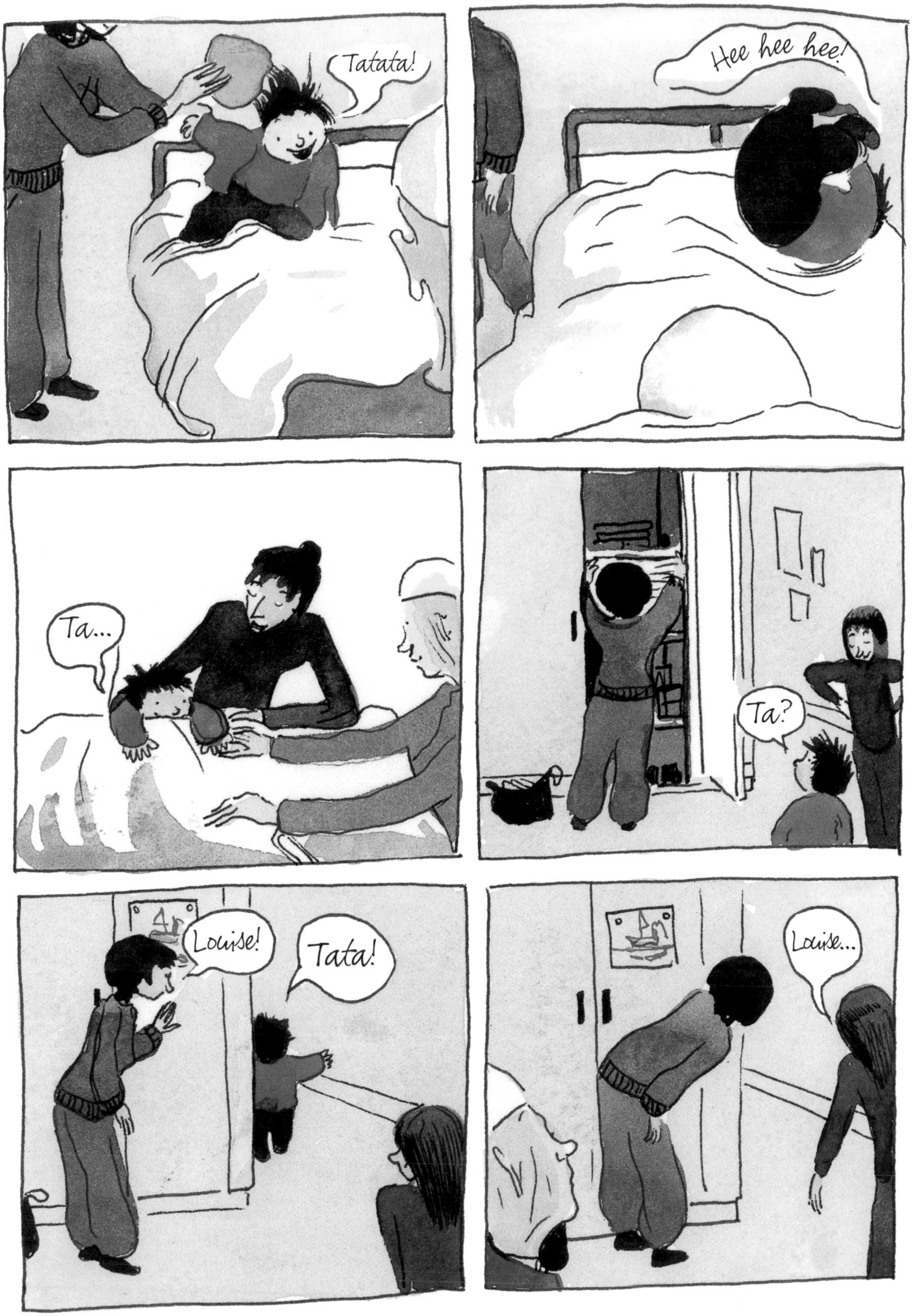
Tatata!
Hee hee hee!
Ta...
Ta?
Louise!
Tata!
Louise...

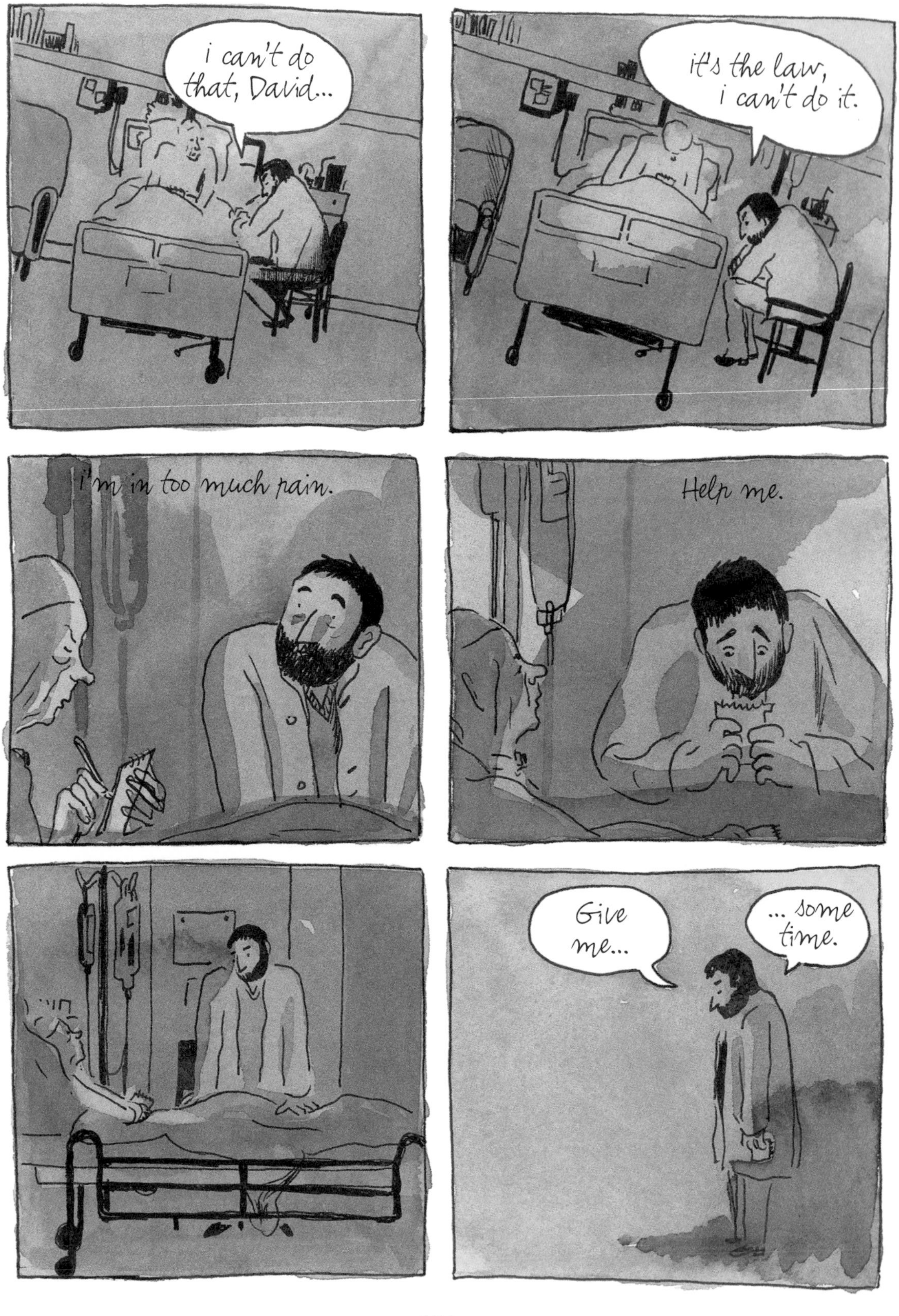
i can't do that, David...
it's the law, i can't do it.
i'm in too much pain.
Help me.
Give me...
... some time.

Georg...

Don't walk away, Georg...

After thirty years... Help me...

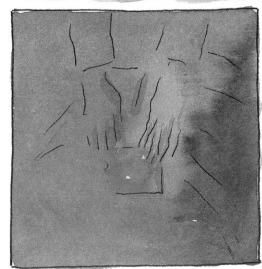

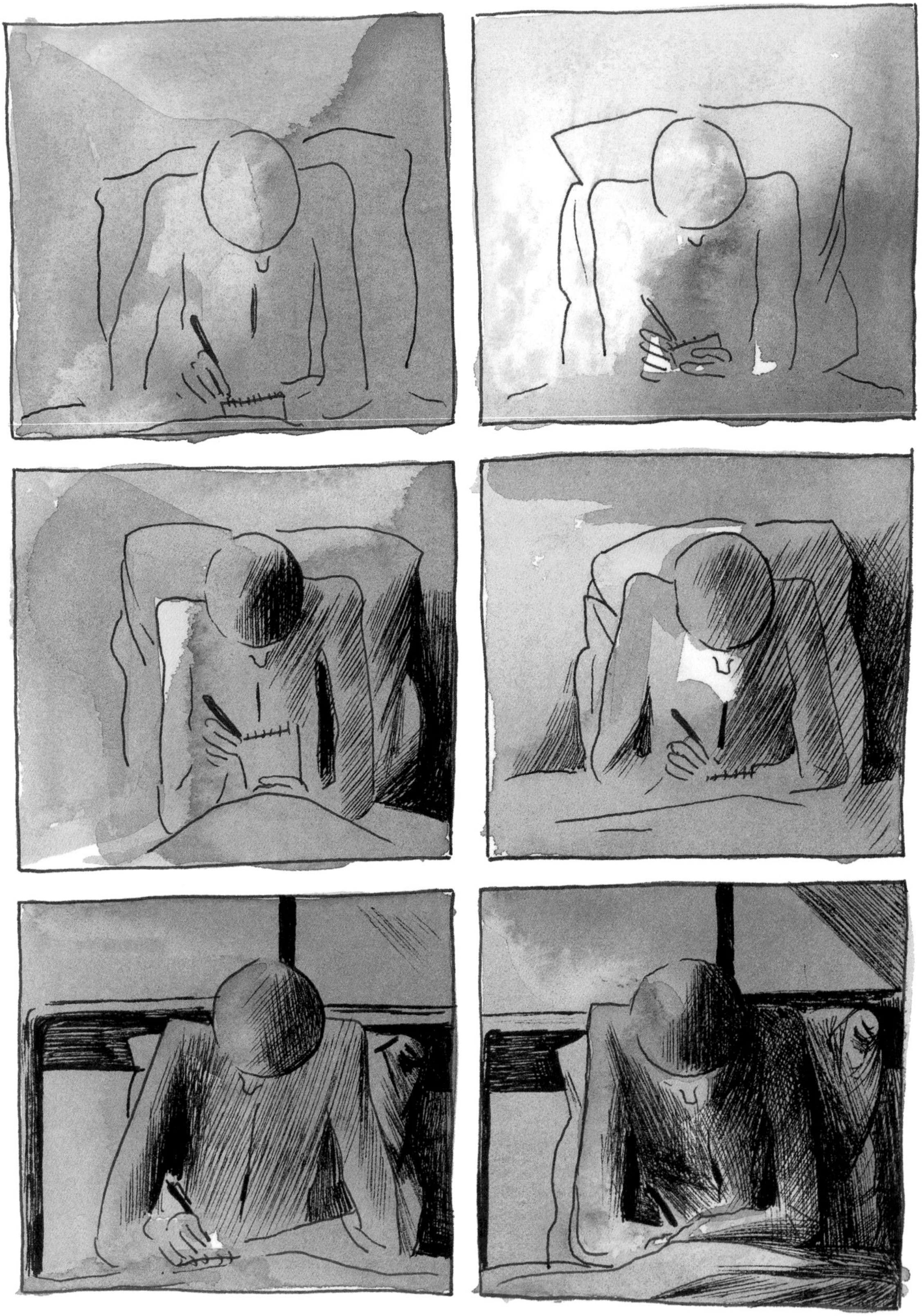

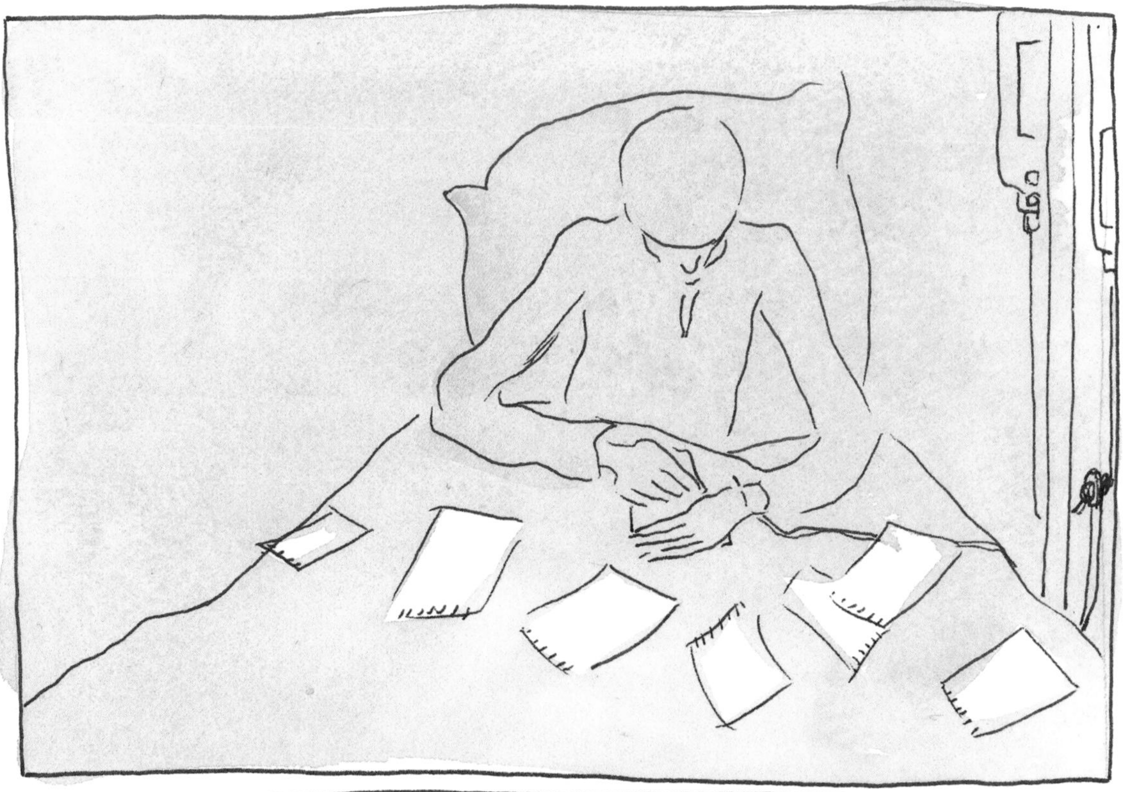

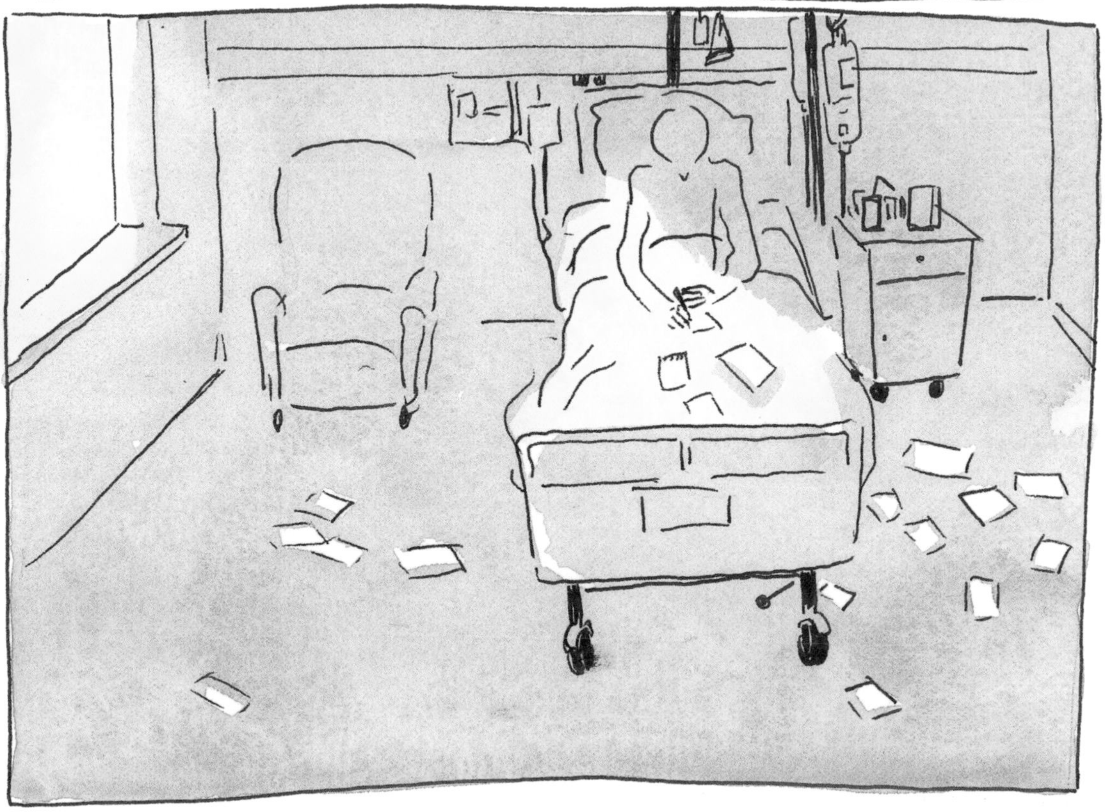

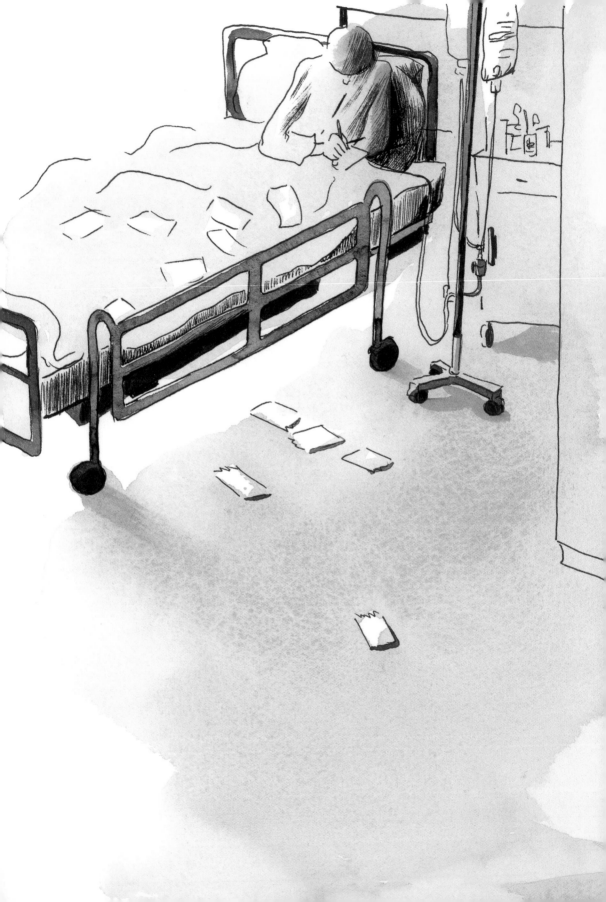

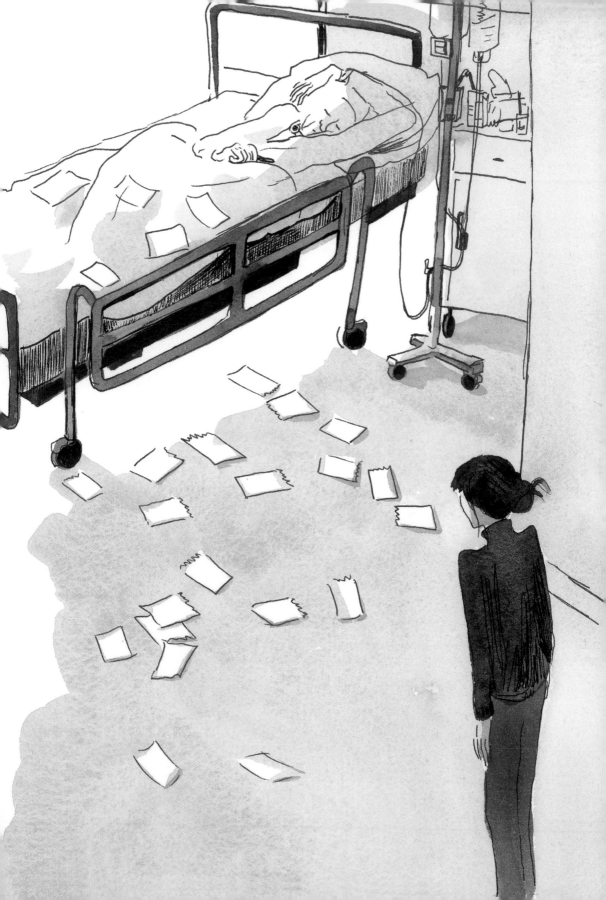

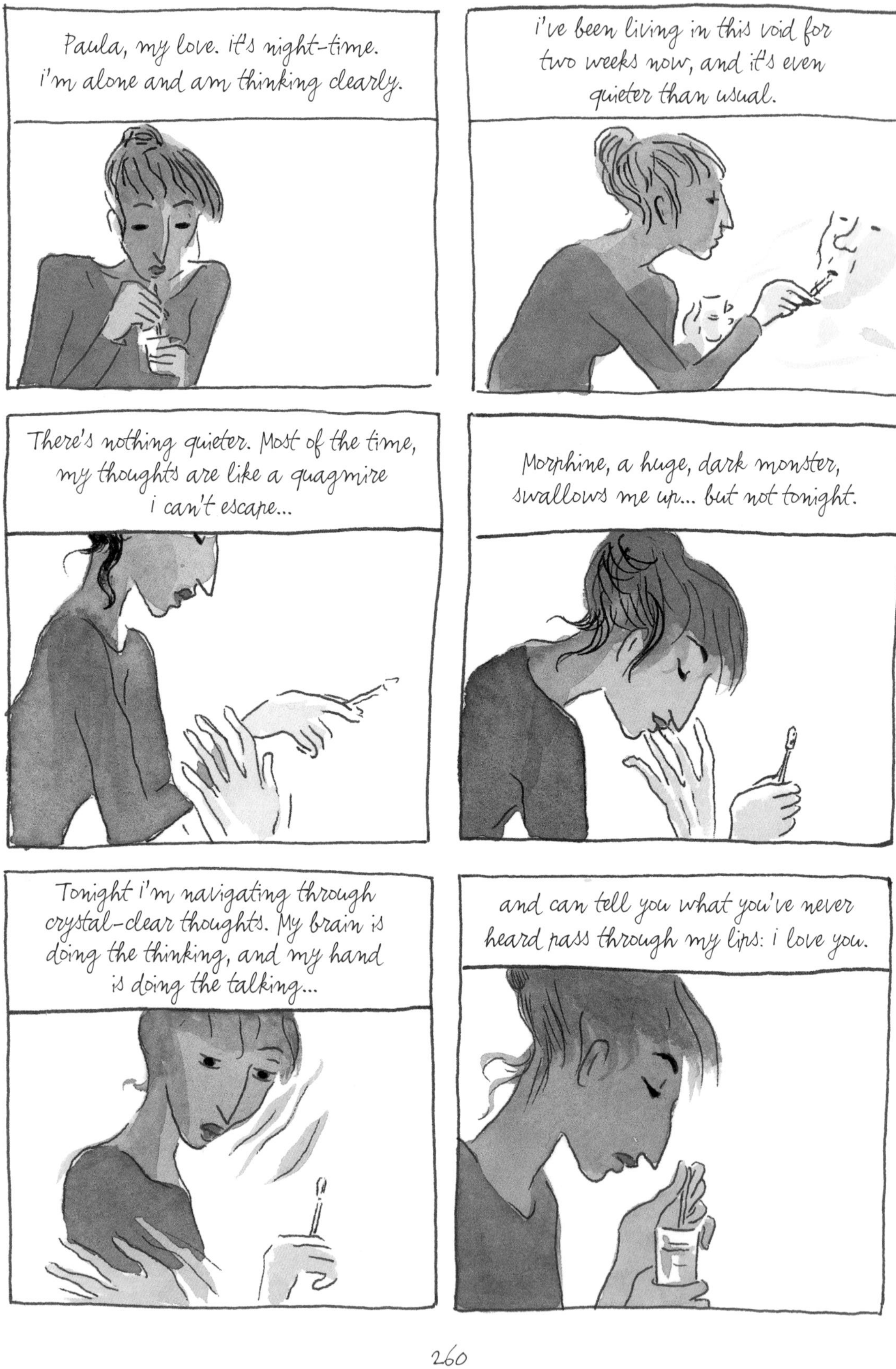
Paula, my love. it's night-time. i'm alone and am thinking clearly.
i've been living in this void for two weeks now, and it's even quieter than usual.
There's nothing quieter. Most of the time, my thoughts are like a quagmire i can't escape...
Morphine, a huge, dark monster, swallows me up... but not tonight.
Tonight i'm navigating through crystal-clear thoughts. My brain is doing the thinking, and my hand is doing the talking...
and can tell you what you've never heard pass through my lips: i love you.

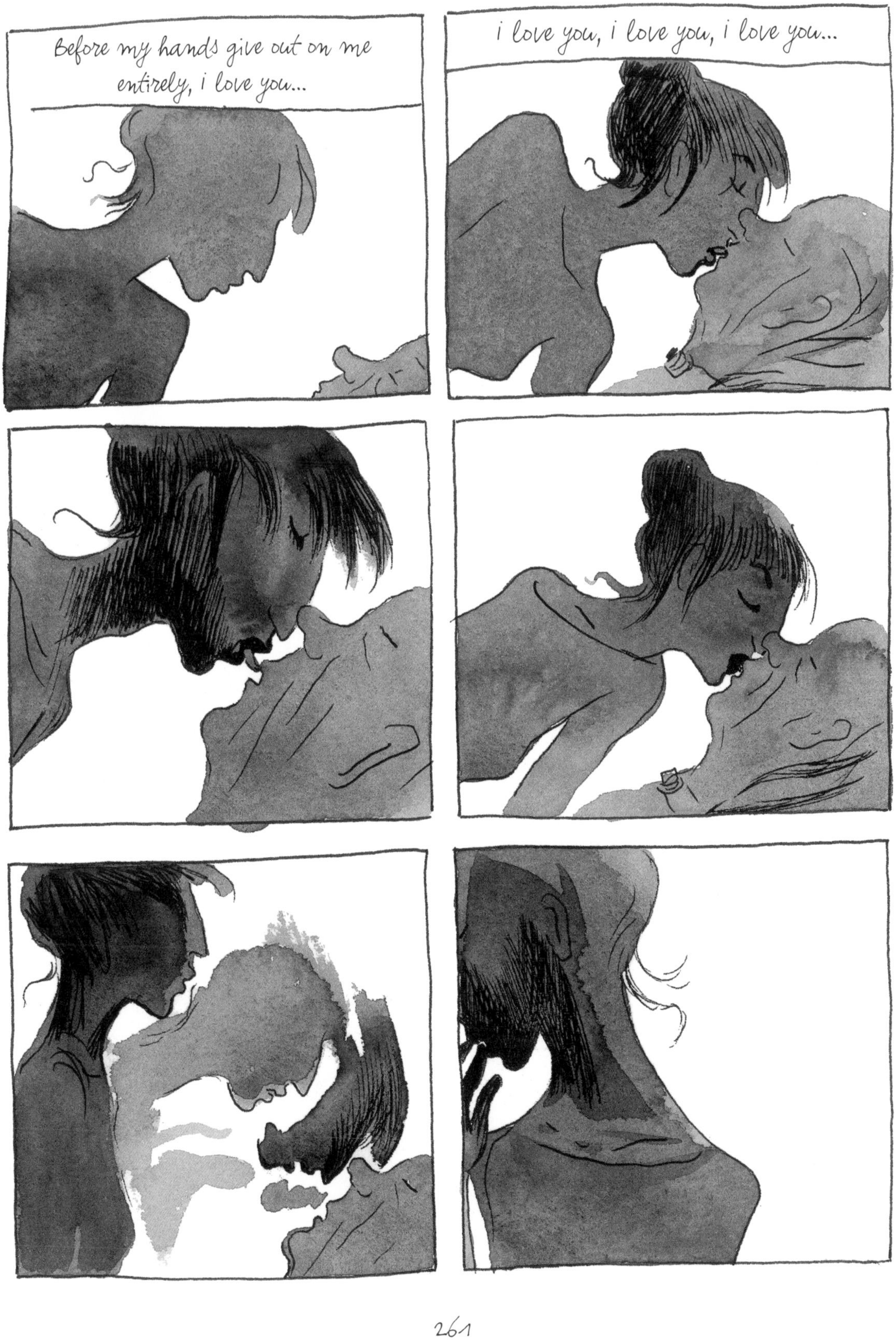
Before my hands give out on me entirely, i love you...
i love you, i love you, i love you...

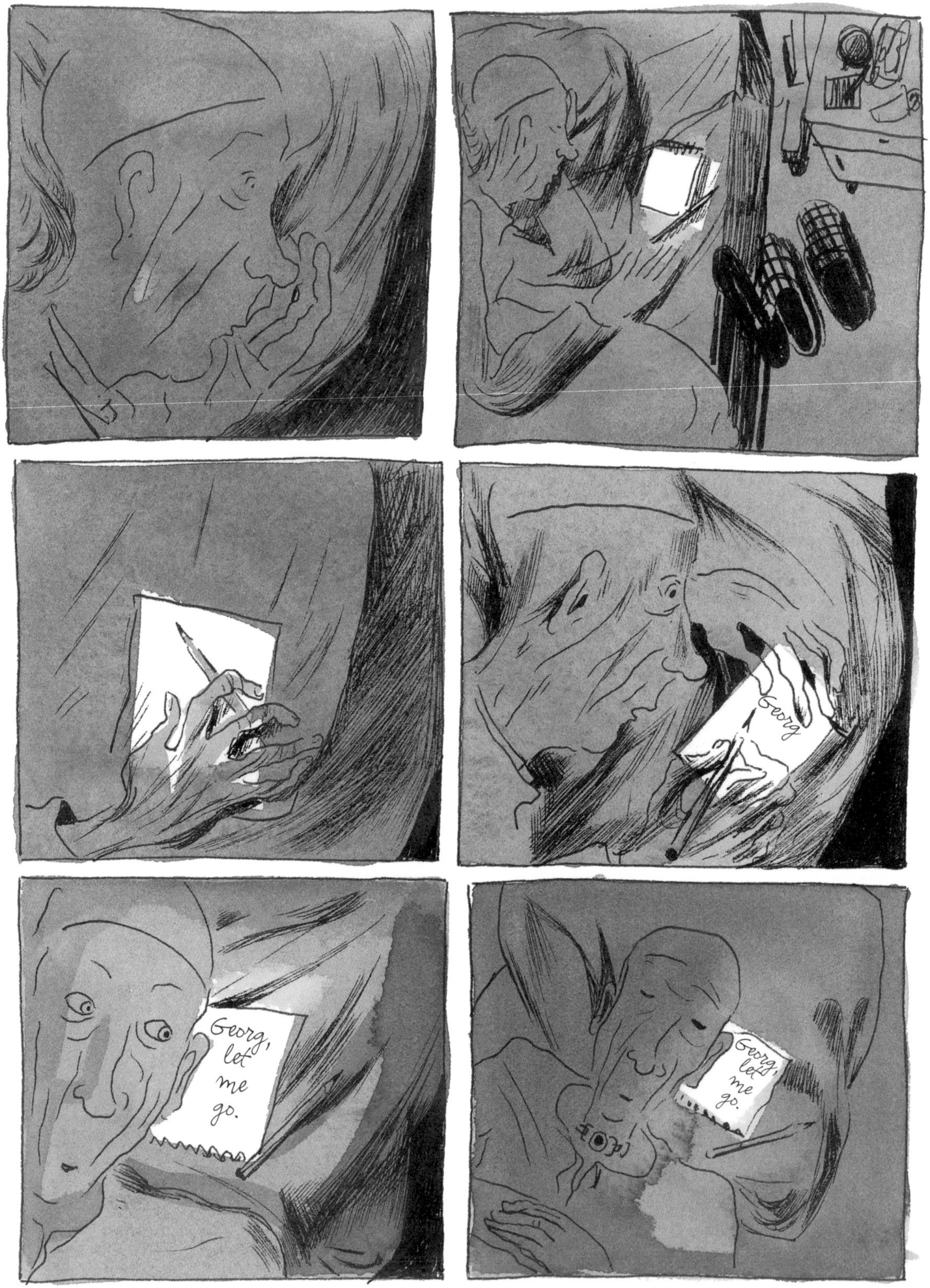
Georg
Georg, let me go.
Georg, let me go.

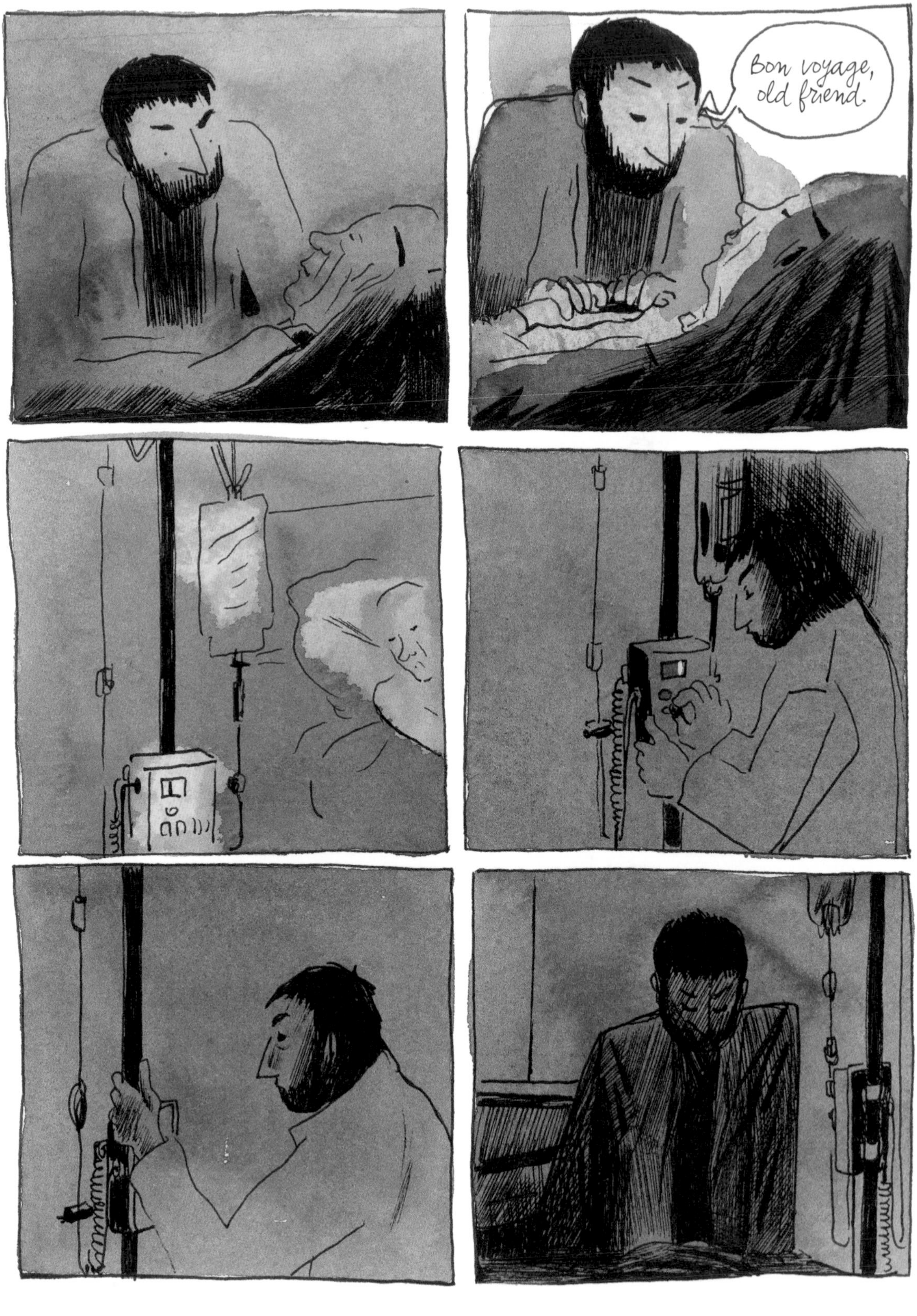
Bon voyage, old friend.

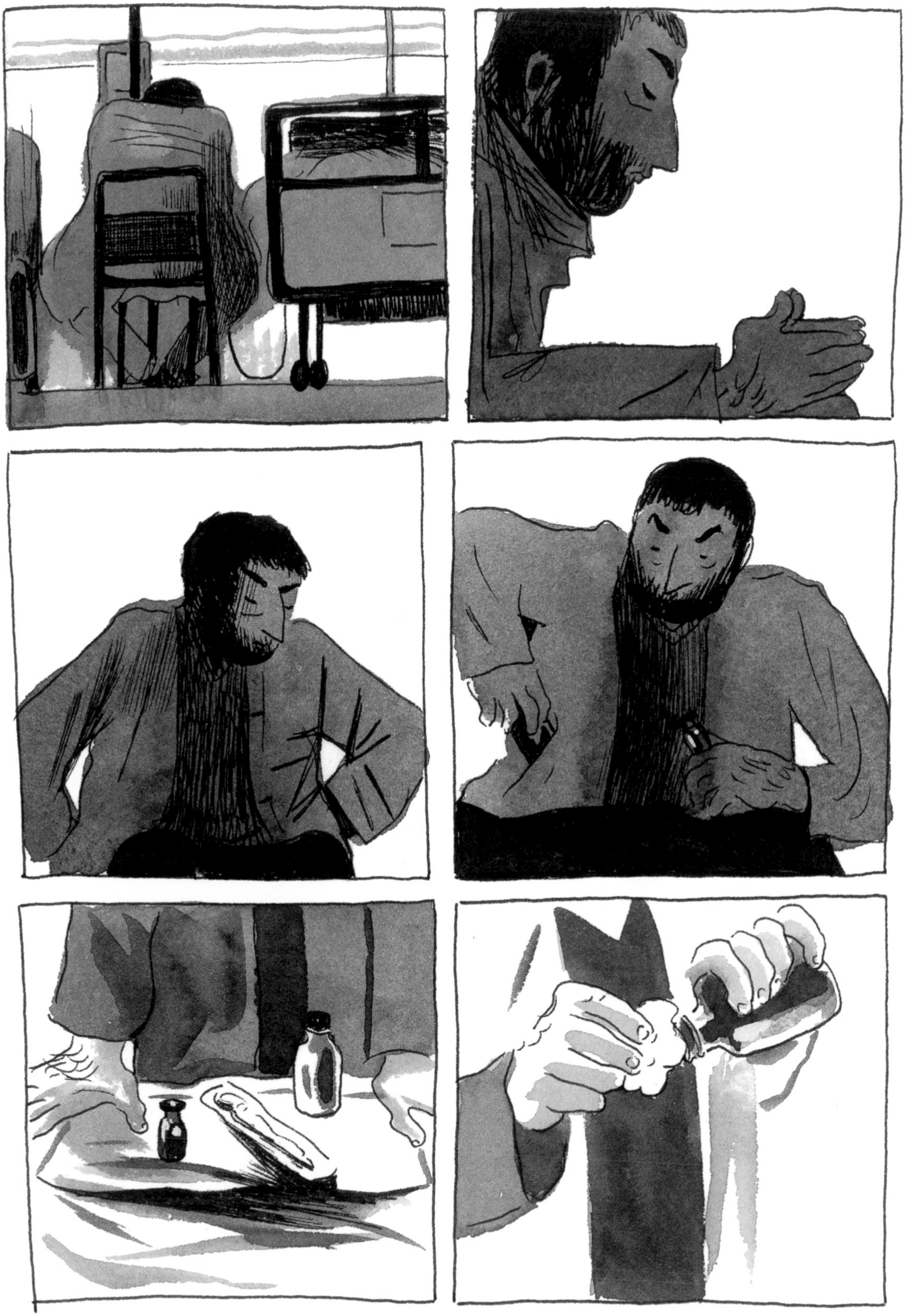

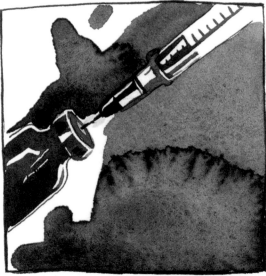
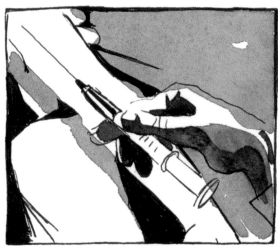

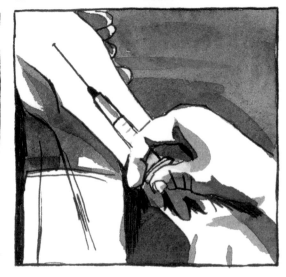

266

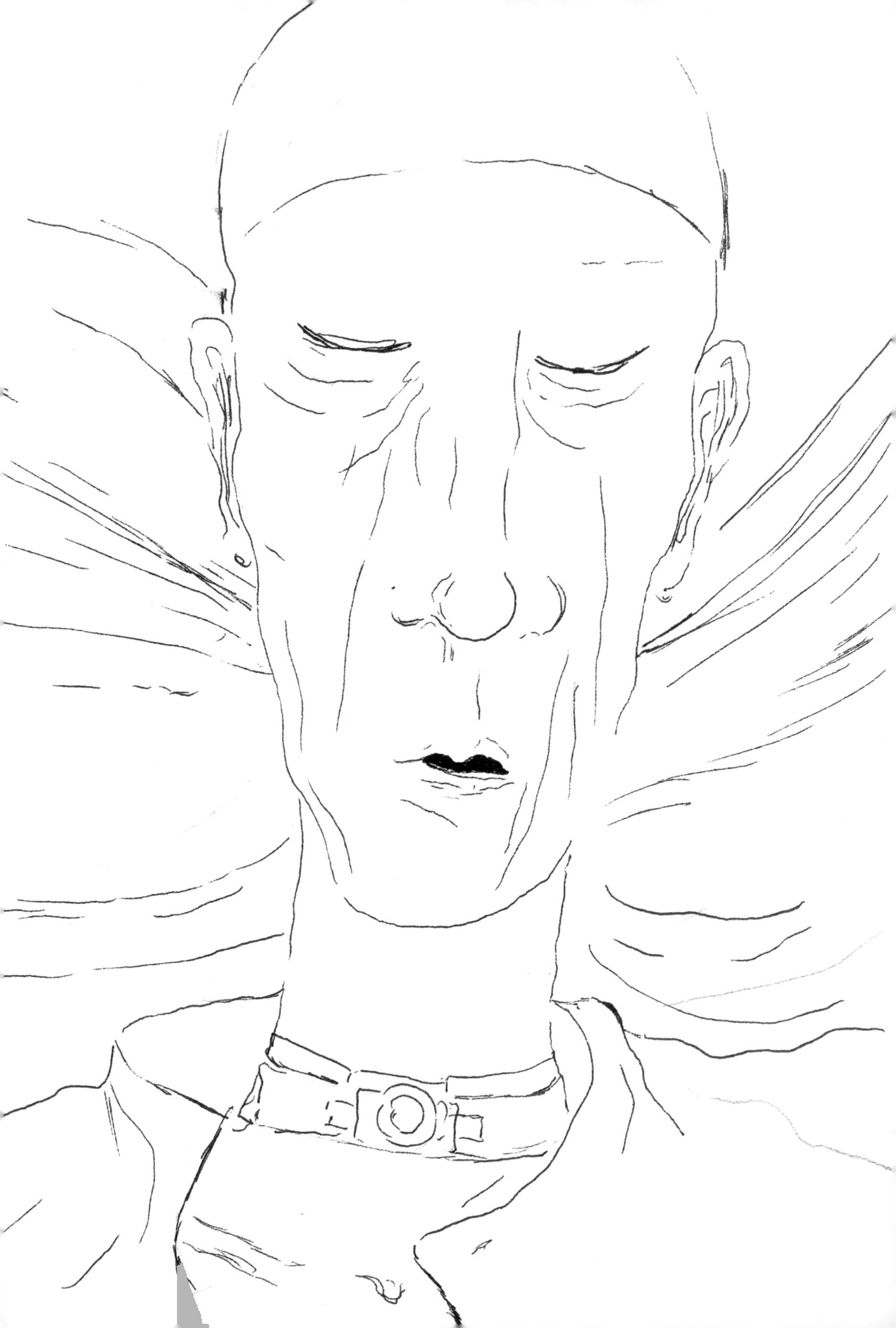

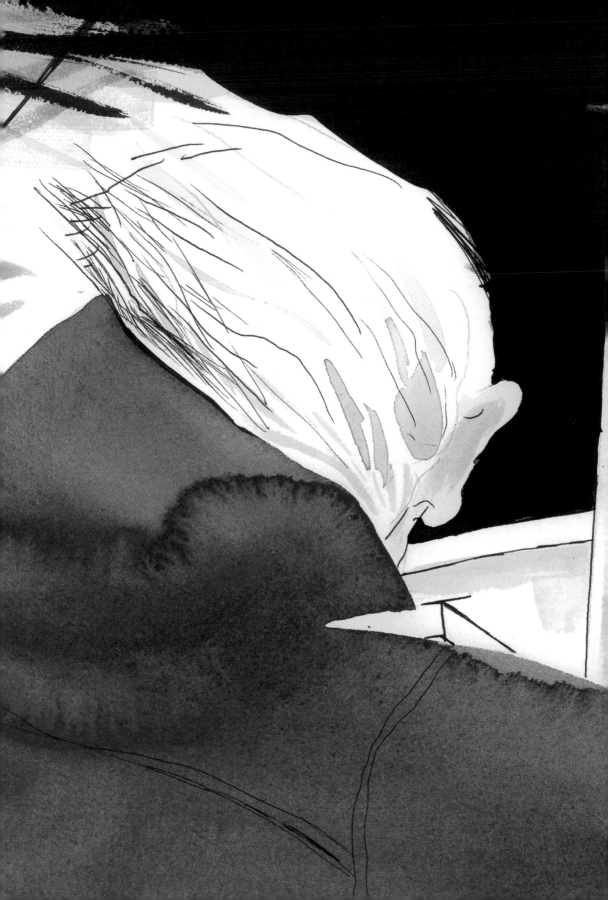

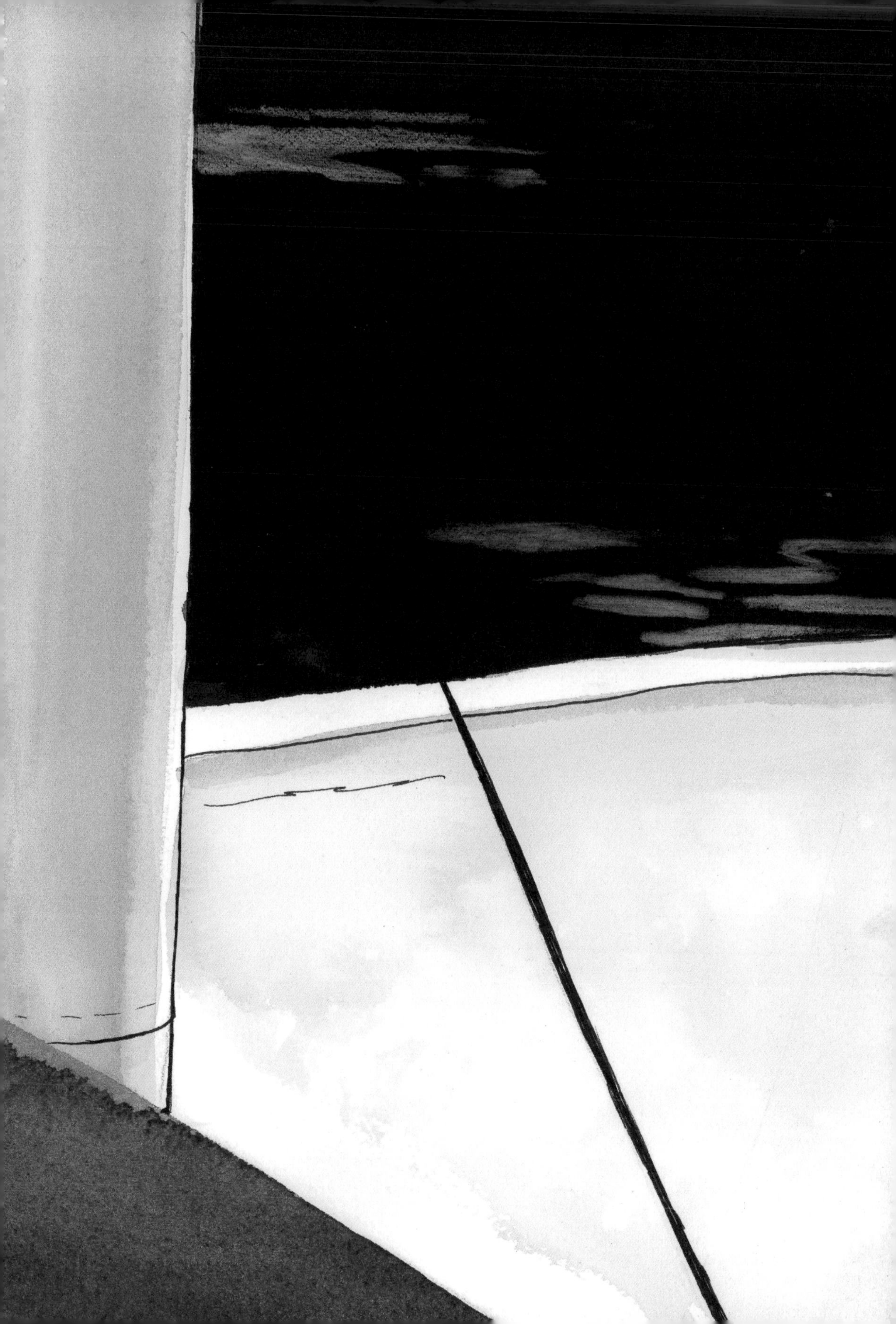

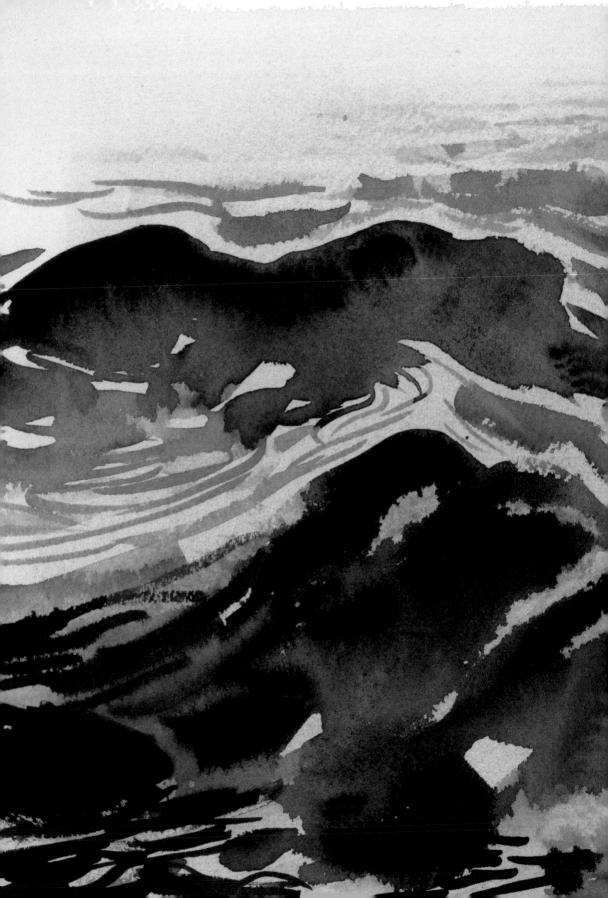

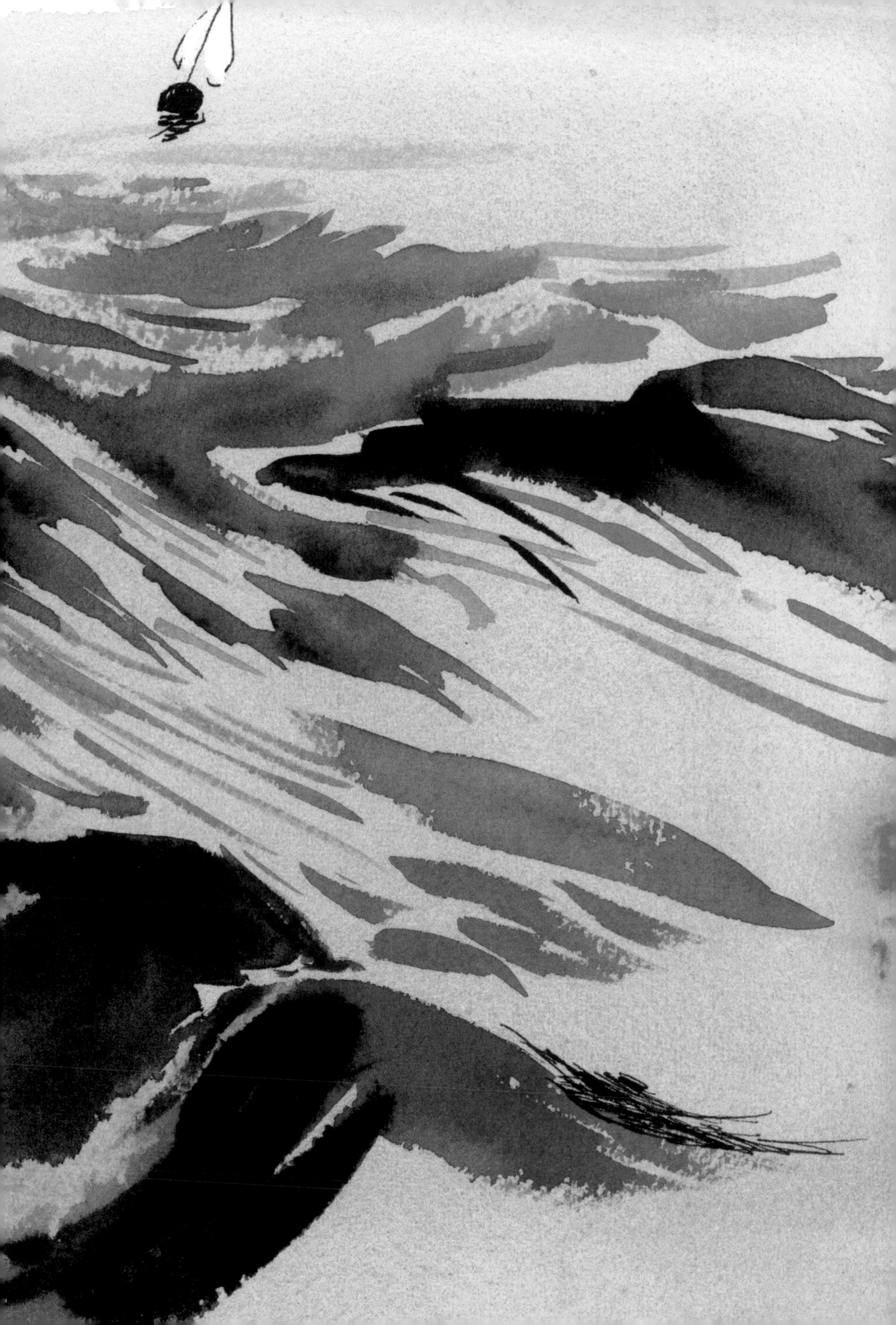

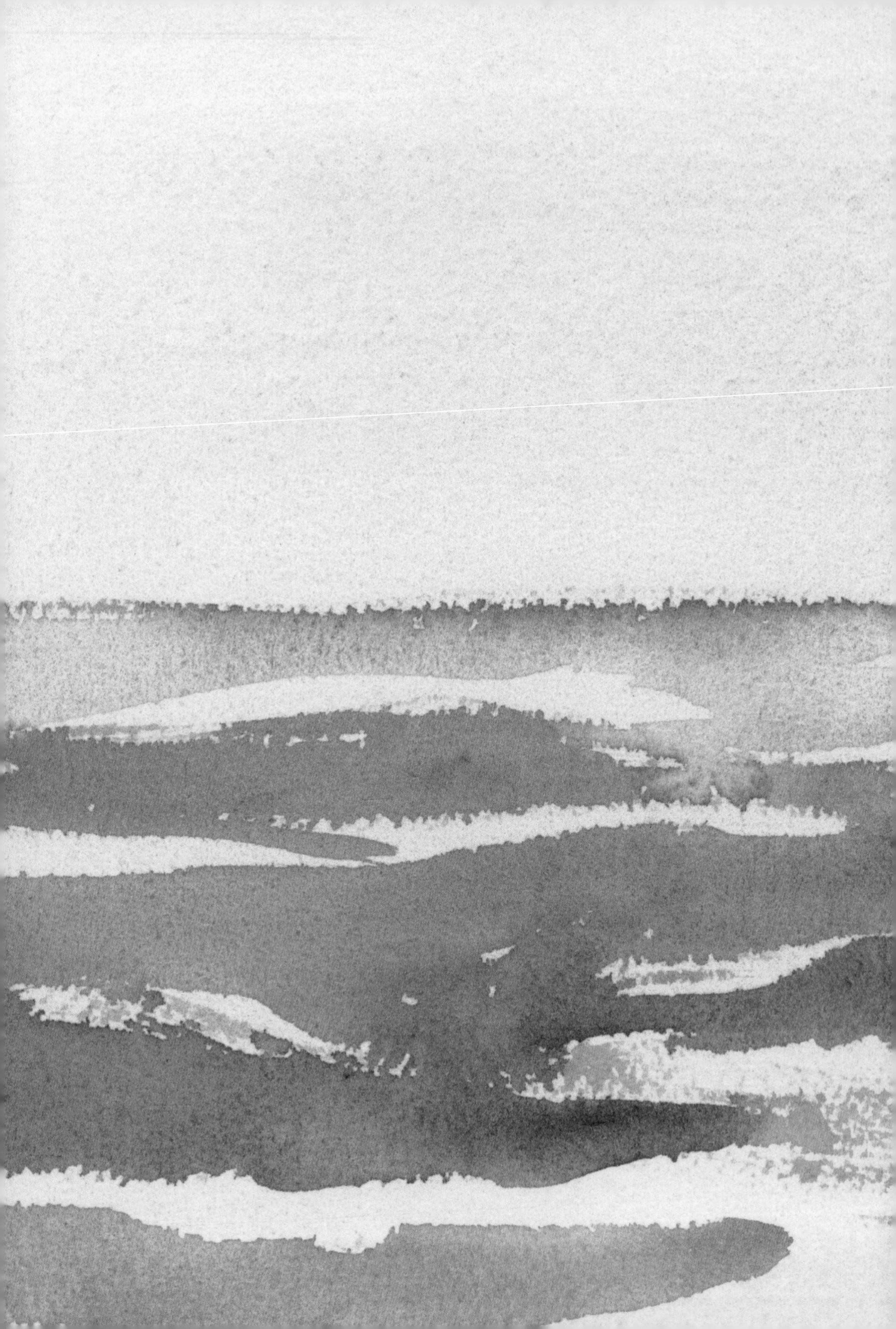

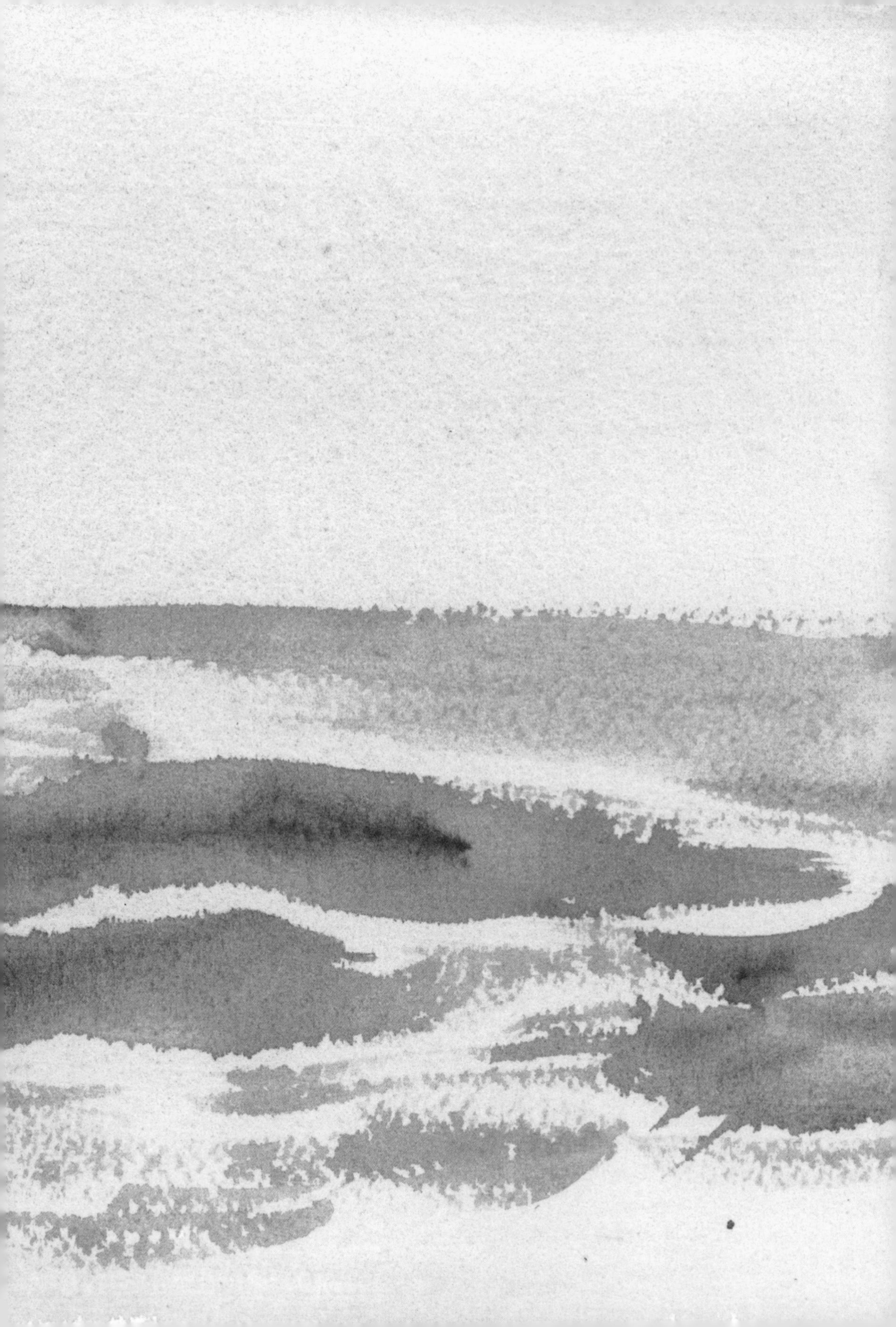

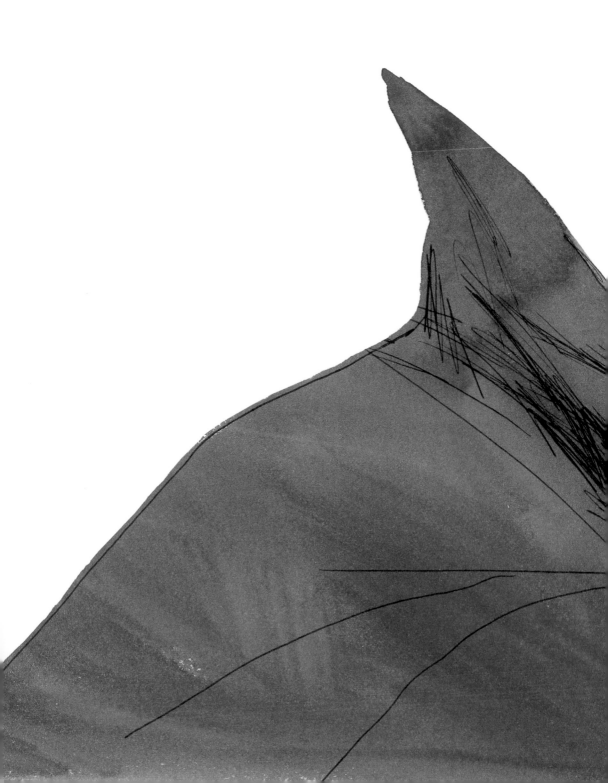

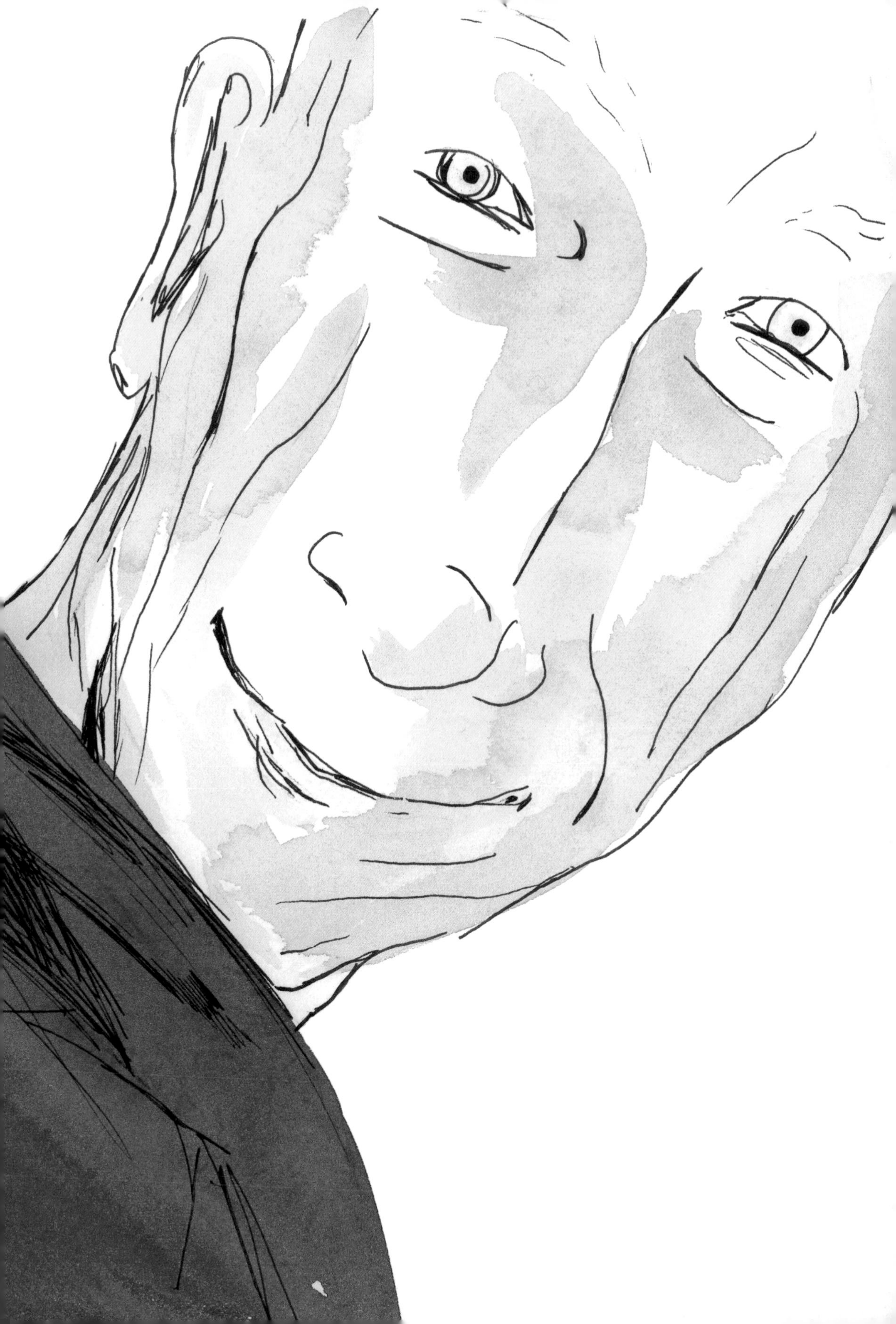

Acknowledgements

A book is never made alone, and so i'd like to thank a few people.

My children, Hanna and Simon, who would make sure day in, day out, that i kept my feet on the ground and got to my studio on time, and who would fill the house with sunshine.

My family, and especially my brother, simply because he's still there and because he brought Tjorven into our lives.

Mara, because she is my lucky star, without whom none of this would have happened. Gauthier and Julie, for their invaluable collaboration and for the golden opportunity they gave me.

Hélène, Bjoke, Sara, Christine, Elise, Laure, Nathalie, Ann, Steven, Stephan, Klaas, Lidia, Marco, Ruth, Armin – you fielded all my questions, fears and frustrations about this book without a second thought, and pushed me, like the wind, ever forward.

i must thank Gilbert Chantrain in particular, the head of the ENT department at the Saint-Pierre Hospital, Brussels, without whom i would not have been able to incorporate the medical aspects into the narrative.

Thank you, Marnix, for the translations of poems by Benno Barnard and Vasalis. And to Nora Mahony, Wouter Mulders and Jethro Soutar.

Thank you, Benno, for the poem "Het meer in mij".

i thank Lutz for his boat and the itinerary, and particularly for the photo of Berlin ("Die Sonne über Berlin") on which i based the drawing of the Fernsehturm.

i thank Ruth for her help, and for her warmth.

Judith

Judith Vanistendael (b. 1974) is a Belgian author of graphic novels and an illustrator. She became an instant hit with her first graphic novel, published in English by SelfMadeHero as Dance by the Light of the Moon, in which she tells a love story between a Togolese political refugee and a young Belgian girl. This work, originally in two volumes, was nominated twice at Angoulême, and has been translated into many languages. Judith also illustrates children's books.